COUP DE COEUR

HALLI STARLING

Illustration © Željka Dobras, Design by Zeljka Debeljak
https://www.artstation.com/dzeljka

Edited by Quinton Li
https://www.quintonli.com/

CONTENTS

AUTHOR'S NOTE

New York City at the turn of the 20th century was a fascinating place. In order to evoke some of the proper atmosphere and ensure I was portraying the city *somewhat* historically accurately (this is a fantasy novel, after all), I did a lot of research and took a notebook's worth of notes to use while writing. At the back of this novel is a list of sources I consulted, should any reader be curious. Writing a fantasy romance novel based on real events, places, people, and culture is a strange miasma that allows room for plenty of authorial judgment, even if the main track on which you write stays fairly on the straight and narrow. But if you read any one thing off of my sources list, I cannot recommend more highly *Gay New York: Gender, Urban Culture, and the Making of the Gay Male World, 1890-1940* by George Chauncey. Chauncey does note he focuses on the gay male world in this book, as the lesbian world was its own culture and he didn't want to portray that history unjustly by adding it in like some kind of remainder. But Chauncey's scholarly work is broad in its scope and yet, narrow enough to understand that time and place - as much as we can understand it 130+ years later.

One of my biggest curiosities was how gay and queer people were viewed at the time. We tend to think that history always had a poor or low consideration for anyone different, but strangely enough, New York City was considered the gay capital of America even then. As I read further, I came across certain facts that were startling to a "modern" mentality, but I wanted to incorporate in this novel. The biggest one – and perhaps the most shocking – for me was that the end of the 19th century and the beginning of the 20th saw neutrality, if not genuine acceptance, for gay men and their culture, including drag, in many parts of the city. This is an extremely general brush I'm using here, but it was fascinating to read about the prominence of gay culture in a time of great upheaval, change, and industrialization. I wanted to include some of this in my novel, instead of relying on the idea that gay people would have been hidden and persecuted without me rcy.

Readers will see references to "fairies", "inverts", "perverts" and more terms, both with very positive and negative connotations, for the setting of the novel. When these words are used, they are applied as historically accurately as possible. I wished to give some of that historical accuracy while writing a world that felt more even, and yet more real, than many fantasy novels of a similar vein do. The next page has a list of words and their historical uses, so that readers can be forewarned and understand the context in which these words appear. I was not, however, interested in using the colloquial speech of the time period, or dress (again, fantasy novel), since that can provide yet another barrier of entry for reading. I was thinking of that kind of historical accuracy in the vein of Baz Lurman or David Jenkins - mostly not, but with certain nods to the time and p lace.

As far as historical and occult/magical context goes, many of the locations and objects mentioned in this book are inspired by real counterparts. The Minotaur Bathhouse, for example, was loosely based on real bathhouses from that time and place, though of course magic allows for much more leeway as far as the construction and services. Bathhouses played a key role in gay and queer culture around this time, as they were often one of the few secure locations queer people could meet without interference from religious folk or the law. They were sometimes raided by law enforcement officers looking for people to charge with "sodomy" (not surprising, I'm sure). And the queer community would band together to protect their sacred places. It was an interesting note in several of the books and articles I read, and was one I didn't want to miss out on including. The bathhouse is not included for the sake of titillation; they were an integral part of queer life at the time (and in some places, continue to be, though that may seem strange to certain modern sensibilities).

There are other nods to real history - the carnation brooch Calix wears is an iteration of the symbols gay men at the time used to signal to one another; the palm reader Lawton mentions was a real person and quite popular at the time; museums were all the rage, as were the city's parks (which were also popular meeting spots for those in the queer community). There's so much I wanted to fold in without being horribly blatant about it, and I hope these small details add to the color and vibrancy of the time.

Considering race and history: I want my books to represent a variety of experiences and backgrounds. One of the reasons I set the book in New York City, and not somewhere like London, was because the city has always been a melting pot of cultures, languages, beliefs, and people. Queer communities at the turn of the 20th century were much more welcoming to all, and even with the persecution and bigotry one could experience in the larger city, the small enclaves were typically safe. Places like Harlem, where mostly people of color lived, helped give birth to the idea of safe queer spaces for everyone and anyone. It must be noted that drag culture was brought to the forefront by those very places; something we should be eternally thankful for, given its modern breadth and depth. My cast of characters had to represent a larger group of experiences and backgrounds, and you will find under the Representation section a breakdown of this. The city suffered less racism and bigotry at the time of the novel, and Aubrey and Ethaniel do provide some insight into their lives as queer men of color, which is based in as much history as I could make it without making their stories only about their identities. It is a fragile web to weave, and I hope it meets with expectations.

A note on Cunning Folk and Aubrey: Aubrey Lavigne, one of the main characters and the love interests, comes from a line of Cunning Folk who trace their roots to France. The history of Cunning Folk is wide and varied and very much reliant on the part of the world from which they came. If you are not familiar with the term, Cunning Folk were the local healers, midwives, and apothecaries. Many times, one person in a village filled all of these roles and more. Their history can be accurately traced to the 16th century, though some scholars have found evidence of them even further back. Cunning Folk were also often advisors to village elders or leaders, bringing with them a sense of humanity and knowledge considered to be magical. And yes, many times it was believed by all that Cunning Folk used magic to help heal the sick and wounded. Their history starts to fold into the history of the persecution of witches around the 17th century (again, this is reliant on the culture and part of the world we're talking about), and soon Cunning Folk were sometimes deemed as witches and punished without mercy. It is a fascinating, oft bloody, history, and I encourage anyone interested in this to consult the research sources at the back of the novel.

Aubrey's family history, which we get glimpses of in the novel, is murky on purpose, for both the sake of plot and for character development. Aubrey himself struggles with this history and knowledge, as his own abilities run a different course than the rest of his relations. I hope the notes here provide an extra layer of meaning to Aubrey's backstory.

And finally, on John Dee and Edward Kelley/Talbot: Dee and Talbot were both real people, and Dee's work was a big influence on notable figures like Aleister Crowley (who in turn influenced people like Jack Parsons...it's a conspiracy board full of red string, but it's all true). While the sequel to this book, DEMIMONDE, will go into much greater detail on their work, it is worth mentioning their historical significance, and their importance to this story.

Word Use Guide

- **Fairies**: Typically used to refer to an effeminate man, regardless of sexuality (it was largely assumed most fairies were gay, but this varied by neighborhood and population). Most fairies didn't go out in what we would now consider full drag, but often wore rouge, lipstick, dangling jewelry, bright colors, etc. In modern terms, these people might have been trans, or genderfluid or genderqueer. The concepts of sex and gender during this time period are not ours.

- **Inverts/perverts**: Largely used by doctors, psychiatrists, and law enforcement when documenting gay and queer people

- **Bisexual**: the connotation at the time was not someone attracted to two genders, but a person who seemed to have half a man's soul, and half a woman's (this was a time where other genders were not largely considered or had names for them, as we do now)

- **Slummers**: The connotation then is not far off from today's, though slummers in NYC in the late 1800s were sometimes seen as easy money as well. Typically these were middle class people who didn't go to the saloons that catered to the manual laborers, but also wouldn't be able to get into the upper class salons. They would go to Brooklyn or Harlem to gawk at the fairies and pretend to be scandalized.

Content Warnings

Content Warnings for anything not addressed in the Author's Note

- Alcohol use/consumption (not to excess)

- Drug use/consumption (not to excess)

- Discussions of sex and gender

- Discussions of magic and the occult

- Religious musings and considerations

- Discussions of homophobia and bigotry

- Discussions of mental health and the impact of magic upon it

- On-page sexual content

- Foul language

Representation

- Calix (he/him) is gay and cisgender. He is white and comes from wealth, but also hails from a mother plagued by visions.

- Lawton (he/him) is queer and genderfluid. He is white and comes from a noble, but destitute, family.

- Ethaniel (he/they) is pansexual and cisgender. He is Spanish-American and comes from a long line of dark magic users. Ethaniel was raised by a single father and left home as a teenager to care for his ailing uncle and learn magical patterning.

- Aubrey (he/they) is demisexual and genderqueer. He is Black, hailing from a line of Cunning Folk from France. He is a first-generation American and the head of a magical museum collection.

FOLIO ONE:

What Twisted Paths

"I want to make Romeo jealous. I want the dead lovers of the world to hear our laughter and grow sad. I want a breath of our passion to stir their dust into consciousness, to wake their ashes into pain."

– 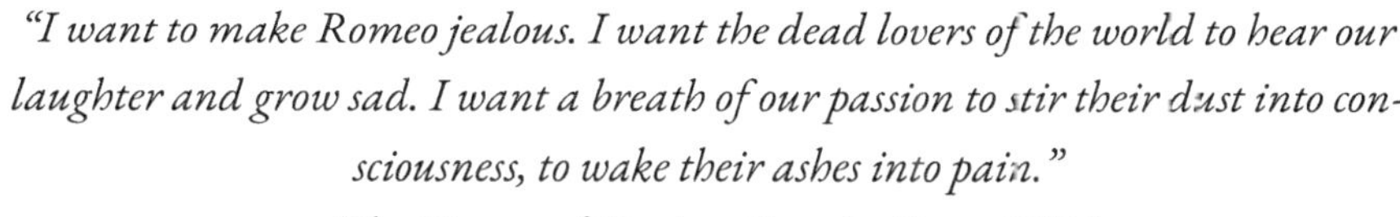 *The Picture of Dorian Gray by Oscar Wilde*

One

New York City, 1899

Acadia Gardens, Brooklyn

CALIX

The man standing guard outside the townhouse's bright blue door had the crooked nose and sunken eyes of a bare-knuckle brawler who had taken one too many hits to the face. And the broken teeth revealed when he pulled back his lips to snarl, "Fuck off, twats," only reasserted Calix's supposition.

Those tangible bits of evidence gave him the confidence to repeat his earlier words to Lawton. "I told you he was going to deny us entry."

Lawton waved a hand in the air. "Well, pardon me if I pooh-poohed your *hunch*, my dear one, but you know I'm never one to take a backseat to my own fortunes."

Every emerald and ruby in Lawton's rings glittered under the soft pulses of light from the gold and silver enchanted lanterns that hung overhead. The gems were as beautiful, as lustrous, and as sharp as his friend's *pointed* words. Lawton was a lot of things, but the man understood what airing Calix's little proclivity toward prognostication could do to them both, even in New York City, a place more accepting of magic in general. Calix had always counted himself fortunate that the man's sharp tongue was rarely aimed in his direction.

This guard, however, was not to be so lucky.

As Lawton puffed out his chest and pushed his orange-red curls off his forehead, Calix let his gaze travel down the corridor north, where more lanterns tracked the boundaries of Acadia Gardens. Brooklyn wasn't Manhattan, but it had a sense of charm and style that the magicked, moneyed, and powerful of Times Square couldn't locate if it had been...well, this guard's horrifically crooked nose.

"Now sir...what is your name? Ah, charming, I do love a good classic like *John*." Lawton leaned into the man, not touching, but definitely edging toward familiarity. John's eyes narrowed into thin black lines, making him now look more cartoonish than frightening. "You see, we are here to see Madame Twilight and partake in her salon. I know we're not late, as the drapes haven't been pulled. So if you would just turn that little handle and open the door—"

"No." The word was more grunt than anything else, but it got John's point across. As did the shift and bunch of his rather impressive muscles.

Calix bit down on the lung-deep desire to say *I told you so*. It would make Lawton grouchy and he'd probably spend half the night sulking. Calix was usually quick to assuage his friend's sour moods, but tonight the magic of Acadia Gardens was thick, almost choking.

Friday nights were for carousing in the city, and places like Acadia Gardens were practically overflowing with magical energies in an attempt to entice both locals and tourists. "Slumming", as the moneyed of the city put it, drew over-dressed people in throngs and tonight was no different. As Calix looked around, he saw the jewels and furs, the glittering embroidery that twisted and turned due to simple, but expensive, patterning work. This world should have been one he reveled in. Money afforded him all kinds of privileges, but so often it was Lawton who helped him to take advantage of them. Madam Twilight's salon was just one of many frivolous things Lawton loved, and Calix knew he had a very hard time saying no to his only close friend. Usually. But tonight he found himself growing impatient.

Lawton was still arguing with the doorman, and it looked as though this John would hurl them both down the street by their coats. "Listen, any amount. Just name it," Lawton was saying, his gaze firm on the doorman but his hand straying into Calix's pocket.

"Why are you pushing this?" Calix hissed between his teeth, feeling a hot flash of indignation rise up. He swatted Lawton's hand away, not caring about the doorman seeing. "We'll find somewhere else to go."

Lawton's pout deepened, and with it, Calix's irritation grew again. It was like a mold spore blooming and Calix wished to be anywhere but here right now. "Because the Madam is the *best*, and that's what I want." Lawton's fine brow furrowed, his thin lips all but disappearing into his sharp-angled face. "And it's what you should want, too, Calix. Look around at who is out and about, all these gallivanting lovelies dressed to the nines. We are them, they are us. You should –"

"I've looked around. I'm not impressed." Calix pressed a twenty-dollar bill into the doorman's hand as he brushed by. Righting the collar of his dark green wool coat gave Calix an excuse to square his shoulders as he walked away, and the miniscule motion made him feel a tad better. Lawton would notice the movement more than mourn his absence, but for once, Calix didn't care.

The throbbing in his temples, coupled with the heaviness of magic from all the shop lights and enchanted clothing worn by almost all he passed, made Calix long for home. There, it was quiet, still, and he could close his eyes and not worry about what he might see in the hazy horizon of lucidity. His mother had warded her estate when he'd first presented *signs of prediction*, as she so often put it. The wards would hold for a few more years before he'd need to renew them, but finding someone to copy his mother's strange, esoteric energy work would be a high bar. Her powers had been barely on the edge of acceptable in civilized society, and she'd wanted Calix safe more than anything, so the mistress of Earl Batherton stuck to high society and let go of all of the Earl's more interesting friends. Even if they could have provided her with some assistance where Calix had been involved. The downside of that had been he'd never been fully warned about his own abilities, but that wasn't a path of thought he wished to trod down right this moment. All he knew was that home was safe, and safe was a valuable commodity in a time and place like New York at the turn of the century.

Hurried footsteps sounded behind him, as quick as Lawton's slipping against the wet cobblestones allowed. Calix braced himself for either anger or disappointment. What he got, instead, left him baffled. Lawton looped his arm through the bend in Calix's elbow, created by how his left hand was stuffed into his pocket.

"Well, I'd say I almost had the man convinced and then they pulled the drapes inside and just left me standing out there!" Lawton shivered dramatically, as if it were some great social faux paus he'd just survived. "But then I remembered we haven't been to the cabaret in ages. And I do want to show off this new cloak."

Lawton shifted closer as they turned the corner and dove straight into the packed main walkways of Acadia Gardens. Supposedly the builder wanted to model London's infamous Covent Gardens, but the structures lacked all of the original's seedy charm. Acadia was all clean lines and glistening cobblestones, and given the rigorous rules for both occupants and businesses (and the hefty "maintenance fee" every building owner had to pay), it was meant for society's top echelons.

People like him and Lawton. Or, the roles they played out in public.

"I've no interest in the cabaret," Calix said calmly, even as the press of Lawton's hand to the inside of his elbow made him ache. Moments like this made him wonder if he'd be so attached to Lawton's attention, as fleeting and fickle as it could be, if he had anyone else close to him. If anyone else had been there when Mother had died and Edna Monroe, her longtime companion, had taken over the estate. To be fair, Edna had been a fine manager of his inheritance and of Calix himself. But Lawton had been a presence in his life for nearly a decade and a half now, and such a thing was impossible to simply shake off. They were too enmeshed at this point, and he was far too needful of Lawton's glinting amber eyes and the way his red lips parted when Calix was his target.

When Lawton looked at him with such desire, Calix found it echoed within his own chest. A cavity waiting to be filled. Even now, as frustrated as he was with his friend and as much as he longed for home, Calix needed Lawton's windswept curls tangled around his fingers, the salt-sweet taste of skin on his tongue and flooding his sinuses.

"I should have asked you how you wished to spend the night, Calix. I'm sorry." Lawton steered them around a group of slummers gawping at the fairies in dresses walking arm in arm with stout dockworkers. "Let's find out what you wish to do, hmm? And while we do that, we can watch these pariahs and see if anyone interesting goes into The Delphine."

Calix shook his head. Slummers would never step foot inside most places here, whether they'd heard the tales or not. Frequent visitors to this area knew places like The Delphine Hotel across the street were popular drinking spots for those firmly in the "middle class" — too full of polished crystal for the workers who gathered at saloons near the docks, and too bawdy for...

Calix looked down at his custom-made coat, then over at Lawton's flowing navy cape and its enchanted embroidery. The flowers that blossomed, bloomed, then died, over and over again, seemed to wink at him as if to say, "You know we don't belong in a place like The Delphine." And he felt all manner of conflicted because he *did* want to go in.

"Let's go," he said, tugging on Lawton's hand to drag him across the street. Lawton went along gamely, chuckling as if he didn't believe Calix was serious. "We're going to The Delphine. Now."

They reached the other side of the street, narrowly avoiding the near-constant mud and ankle-deep puddles — heralds of spring in New York City — before coming to a stop just before the wide double doors. When he turned at Lawton's insistent tug on his arm, Calix found himself staring at Lawton's arched eyebrows. The damn things were plucked to within an inch of their lives, but they were the same fire red-orange as the man's hair.

"Not going to ask me if I'm serious, then?" Calix asked, unable to keep the challenge out of his voice.

"You could stand to lean back and relax every now and then, so if you want to spend our evening at Cock Suckers Hall, dear one, I'm all for it." Lawton's voice echoed across the space and next to them, the group of slummers voiced shock and outrage in equal measure. They began to leave and Lawton sneered at them. "Go on, shoo. Take your modesty and your church-led morals elsewhere. No one here is catering to your ilk."

"Lawton..." Calix warned softly, trying to pull him to the door. "I don't want the attention."

"Neither do they, apparently." One man in the group was edging toward them, fists balled at his sides, but was quickly tugged out of reach by a woman clad in ill-advised petal pink. "Ah look, the bit of reason amongst the teeming masses. How wonderful."

And with a last disdainful sniff in the group's direction, Lawton flung open the door and gestured Calix forward with an elegant sweep of his arm. "My dear. After you."

It was always like this with Lawton. Many years of experience had taught Calix temperance in all forms when it came to his fiery, brash, unquestionably charming and handsome friend. What else could he do but accept?

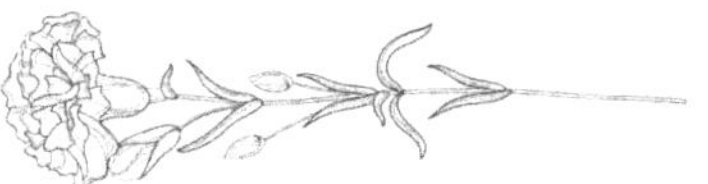

The Delphine Hotel had opened several years ago, one of the flagships for Acadia Gardens and a mainstay for anyone looking for good entertainment. Converted from tenements as this part of the city rose to a certain kind of prominence (and notoriety), The Delphine now housed several bars and small dance halls, along with more private accommodations in which dancers entertained groups for a fee. If anyone sought anything beyond a bit of flirtatious wiggling for bills stuck into boots and bustiers, one would have to seek it out. The "Cock Suckers Hall" part of the place's notoriety was also well-earned, but it wasn't on the official menu.

While Lawton checked their outerwear, Calix craned his head to stare up at the frescoes painted along the arching ceilings. The Delphine had undergone massive renovations a few years back, taking advantage of the lust for all things classically Italian that had swept through the city. Even now, the tiny cherubs and flowing togas didn't seem out of place in such a building; they added a strange kind of gravitas amongst the swinging horns and rich vocals echoing down to them from the dance halls. When Calix blinked, he swore the cherub wings were *moving* — beating in tune to the music. He shouldn't have been surprised.

As Calix looked around, he was able to take in the full breadth of The Delphine's patronage. There were formal suits and tuxedos, sparkling gowns and elaborate hairstyles. But unlike the opera houses in Manhattan, clothing here didn't conform to gender. *Everyone* stood out. Lawton looked right at home, almost underdressed, though Calix would never say that to his face. For Calix, standing out meant eschewing his everyday clothes and adopting pieces he'd picked up over his years of living in the Village — a bit more bohemian, with flowing fabrics and playful patterns.

Calix had adorned himself in scarves and silver jewelry, the blues and greens of his clothes nicely contrasted with his brown eyes and hair. He preferred to keep his own sense of modesty, especially when Lawton was his company for the evening, so he bared no skin below the neck. His friend was often eager to lose certain items of clothing over the course of long evenings, usually winding up in shirtsleeves or even shirtless and sprawled in the lap of someone enamored with his hair. Lawton's elegantly cut shirt in carnelian silk, open at the throat even with the chill outside, and ocean blue waistcoat were likely not going to last until midnight.

Lawton gave Calix's ensemble a once over before reaching out to flick a finger against the oil-slick hued scarf at Calix's shoulder. "Pretty. Is it new?"

Calix nodded. "Little Evie at the haberdashery is learning a few new patterns. She might not be able to make hats, but her enchanting work is impeccable. Even if this peters out over the night, it'll still have her embroidery."

"Hmmm." Lawton's gaze traveled over Calix again. Sweeping in its assessment, Lawton apparently found his outfit at least passable. Calix was far too used to Lawton's scrutiny at this point to squirm in its grasp, but he was also quite attuned to the flash of *interest* in those amber-brown eyes.

Our eyes are so similar, and yet, we're not related in the slightest, dear one. All the better for us, since I've so wanted to stare into yours and see myself. Would you let me stare at you, Calix? Would you let me admire how I appear in your eyes, the ones so like my own?

"Sweet of you to let that girl dress you up. She has good taste." Lawton dropped his hand and that gaze left him.

Calix let the compliment warm him, smiling over at Lawton and getting a twitch of painted red lips in response. After a moment, Calix sensed a presence at his right and found several feet behind them a tall, well-built man in a forest green tuxedo and swept back blonde hair giving them a look of interest. He had intense green eyes a few shades lighter than his clothing, and Calix found himself staring.

"We should have come here to begin with," Lawton purred.

The man in the tuxedo righted his lapels before saying, "Many things are on the menu, good sirs, but I am not one of them."

While Calix snorted into his hand, Lawton replied, "Ah, a pity. But a menu? I thought this place was all dance halls and drunkards."

This didn't faze the man in the least. "The Delphine recently passed into new ownership. We're more interested in patron comfort over drunken antics. We do have bar counters with live music, one on each floor, and many rooms for conversation and parlor games. But we also provide proper hotel services."

Calix lifted an eyebrow at that but Lawton barreled forward. "Charged by the hour, I'm sure."

"No, by the night. Like any good hotel." The man plucked up a piece of paper from a nearby counter and handed it over. "The menu."

The man wasn't lying. There were different rooms, including suites and penthouses, along with room services including food and drink, barber services, masseuses, and tailors. "I haven't had a proper massage in ages," Lawton murmured while they stared down at the gold-foiled menu. The gold filigree around the paper's edge shimmered, the line moving in a constant clockwise motion. Expensive patterning; perhaps a sign The Delphine was coming up in the world. "And that beautiful hair of yours needs a trim, Calix. You have such gorgeous copper streaks. You really should show it off."

Calix flushed. Lawton meant well, even if his comments had drawn the cutting edge of this tuxedoed man's attention. He felt like a bug under a microscope, so Calix brushed his hair off his collar and said, "I suppose a night couldn't hurt."

"*Excellent.*" Lawton was grinning ear to ear, the kind of grin that made fine lines form at the corners of his eyes and curve around his mouth. He was so much prettier like this, slightly unmasked from all the moorings of whatever company they were in. Calix liked Lawton the most when he smiled. "My good man, we'll need your biggest room, the most ridiculous baths, and then a barber, and a masseuse. Food and drink too, naturally."

"Of course." The tuxedoed man bowed elegantly, then motioned them forward to the golden-door elevators down the right hall. The marble floors were shot through with veins of the same gold, and Calix idly wondered if the gold had all been enchanted to match exactly. Even the small tray the attendant pulled out from a cabinet nearby was that same shade.

"Open an account, please," Calix said quietly as he and the attendant followed behind Lawton. "All on mine."

"You are a generous friend," the man observed. "But of course."

They piled into the elevator and Lawton gave the attendant another grin. "My understanding is that fine hotels like The Delphine have gorgeously, grotesquely large beds." In a move Calix had seen a thousand times, Lawton lowered his gaze, then flicked it back up so the attendant caught sight of his long, brown-red lashes and the dimples in his cheeks. "Are you certain you're not on the menu?"

Their room attendant was a beautiful man with thick gray hair and a square jaw that could break concrete. His name was Jacob and he had been so kind and warm that Calix could almost fool himself into thinking he wasn't paying for the best service. The man's authenticity rattled something deep and needy in Calix's belly. And those same square-fingered hands he'd been watching all night now sat down a tray on the small table between his and Lawton's baths. On it were two crystal tumblers and a slim glass and pewter absinthe fountain. Jacob bowed his head at Lawton before looking at both of them. "As you requested, Mr. Adler. We only serve Louchambouque absinthe here, as it is unrivaled in both color and taste. May I serve you both?"

"Him first, Jacob," Lawton drawled as he flicked a wet hand in Calix's direction. His eyes were closed, his angular face lax but slightly pink from the water's heat. "My friend is in a bathtub full of scalding water and flowers fit for a king, and he still has that little crease between his eyebrows. So pour, my good man, pour!"

Calix huffed but obliged Lawton by rubbing his thumb over…yes, there was a small furrow between his eyebrows. Why it was there, Calix wasn't sure; he was quite relaxed, sunk neck-deep in water thickly blanketed with rosebuds and cornflowers and violets. And this was in the echoes of a wonderful meal buoyed by the promise of soft linens on the — as Lawton had properly put it — gorgeously, grotesquely large bed. He hadn't felt quite so light in a long time. It wasn't as though his life was difficult, not by halves. But being allowed to unclutter his mind was a certain kind of relief, one that melted into Calix's very marrow.

"Thank you," Calix said as he took the proffered glass from Jacob. Those thick fingers taunted him, beckoning him to come closer and cozy up to a man at least two decades, if not more, older than Calix's near-thirty.

Would that be so bad, their age difference? He'd tried finding someone — a partner — but gay men his age were typically bargained off into loveless marriages in order to appear "decent". Youth was for being pushed onto one's knees in a dirty alley, taking pleasures where they were offered. Go to the right part of the city and you'd find someone willing. But anyone with social clout was expected to, at some point, extend the family line. And once one got to a certain age, well...it was all but demanded. Even in a place like New York.

"Enjoy, gentlemen," Jacob said before backing out of the lavish dark wood and white marble bathroom. The thing was big enough to host a small salon in, but was easily dwarfed by the size of the attached bedroom and sitting room. From his tub, Calix could barely see the remains of their food cart; the green bottles of wine empty, the water by half, and the gold serving trays winking just beyond.

"You haven't touched your absinthe."

Lawton wasn't pouting but the effect was similar inside Calix's gut. A twisting of guilt, molasses-thick and churning, made him hold up his tumbler to the golden sconces enchanted to glow warmly. "It's a darker green than I'm used to. I'm letting it breathe," Calix replied.

"It's not a cabernet, dear one. But I understand." Lawton held up his own glass to the light, then extended that pale arm so it stretched across the space between them and pushed into Calix's. If Lawton extended a little more, his knuckles would brush the bone-white porcelain tub. "We should toast."

"To?"

"How about....to new opportunities?" Lawton now leaned over the edge of his tub and Calix watched as water droplets played tag with the petals stuck to Lawton's supple muscles.

He couldn't take his eyes away from Lawton's chest, even as the other man smirked. Calix held up his glass, then leaned over to clink it against Lawton's. "To new opportunities."

Silence between them often sat with a heavy air, but tonight Calix could tell Lawton was more relaxed than normal. Perhaps "relaxed" wasn't the right word; "content" was more like it. And for a man who was always strolling from one moment to the next, hoping for the grass to be greener elsewhere, it left Calix feeling a tad odd. As if he were missing something.

"So besides spending my money," Calix said as he gingerly took a sip of absinthe, "why were we out tonight? I get the feeling you didn't think you'd actually get into the salon."

Lawton's smile was hazy and he didn't bother to open his eyes as he turned his head to Calix. "Of course I thought we'd get into the salon. Granted, I figured you'd pay that brute of a doorman to let us slip by, but it all worked out." He cracked one eye open now, a smirk growing on his feline features. "Oh, you're not...surely you're not *bitter*, are you?"

A trio of answers rose up in him: *yes*, *no*, and *it's complicated*, but none of them could convey the sense Calix so often had when in Lawton's company. He'd known from the beginning that they had an uneven relationship; Calix had the money and influence Lawton, as the son of an asset-poor shipping merchant, craved so badly, and Lawton had the charm and guile that could open any door money couldn't. Calix had often ruminated on how easy his life would be if he had an ounce of Lawton's personality, just as he was sure Lawton coveted what had been passed down to him through his mother. But Lawton fed some needy, grasping thing in him, and he had been a good friend when he'd needed one. But there were also times, between the easy moments where a hug and a few whispered words healed a wound, that Calix knew he was being used.

He simply couldn't let Lawton go. And he was quite sure Lawton was stuck similarly.

Calix flicked water at Lawton's face, making the other man smile wide. "I'm not bitter," he finally said, his words ringing with truth, "but in the future, maybe we can plan together? You know I'm not one for spontaneity."

"Oh, I know, darling," Lawton drawled, now pinning Calix with a heated look. "Lucky you, I have a very well thought-out plan for once we're out of the bath."

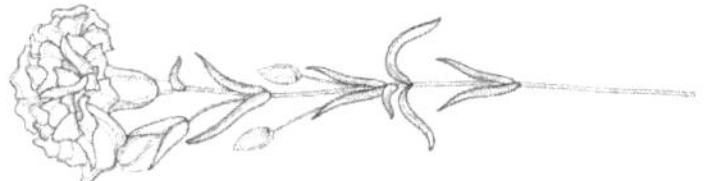

Calix awoke to a cold, empty spot beside him in bed. His fingers met cool linens, then paper crinkled at his touch. He fumbled for the tiny set of buttons on the bedside table until one lamp over his head flickered to life. Magical lights were much better than gas, but sometimes the enchantments didn't hold up after sustained use. Or, so magical theorists said.

The paper was creamy and thick, a single sheet folded in half. Calix read over Lawton's note quickly once, then again more slowly as his brain shook itself awake.

You were out cold and I was restless, so I wandered down to the bar. If I'm not back by dawn, assume I found company for the night. And don't forget, I'm going out of town for a bit of business over the next few days. Got a lead on a large estate sale going up soon, and if I'm lucky, I can get the auctioneer to let me take an early peek. They're supposed to have an original John Milton and that kind of jewel would help get my antiques business on the map.

Ta, dear one

—Lawton

Two

E THANIEL

"Easy, easy," Ethaniel said softly as he helped his uncle to sit up in bed. "When you're ready, uncle. There's no need to rush."

The older man who clung to Ethaniel shook his head. "You brought me tea and I can see it steaming. I'd rather drink it hot. Push that pillow behind me and I'll be fine."

Ethaniel tried not to frown. His Uncle Jeremiah had good and bad days, with no way to predict what each morning would bring, but even the exhaustion that carved deep circles under his uncle's eyes wouldn't stop his morning tea. "All right," Ethaniel replied, arranging the pillows until his uncle nodded.

"You're such a sweet boy," Uncle Jeremiah murmured as Ethaniel handed him the tea and put the small tray with oatmeal and apple slices on his lap. The warmest blankets were piled high on Jeremiah's bed, enough to keep the chill away. Morning had come a few hours earlier, but the fat gray clouds dropping early spring rain erased any sunlight they might have had. The shadows were deep across part of his uncle's room and Ethaniel found himself wishing they could afford a place without the stairs that made Jeremiah wheeze for breath as he climbed to his room. Using the stairs was difficult now, with the way his lungs were growing weaker. Jeremiah insisted almost daily he could do it, and Ethaniel replied every day that they'd try but not to expect much.

They never tried. Jeremiah had only the strength to make it to the small bathroom a few yards away and back. If Ethaniel found his uncle managing to sit in the armchair near the window, he counted that as a very good day.

He wanted, desperately, to be able to take care of Jeremiah in these long hours, listening to the man's rattly breathing, handing him clean handkerchiefs when he soiled his sole enchanted one, the one that used to clean itself. That had been Ethaniel's first major success as an enchanted tailor, and his uncle had kept it all these years, even renewing the pattern when it slowly faded. But keeping them warm and fed was priority, which meant Jeremiah's shop was priority.

In those first few months, Ethaniel had lost more customers than gained. Jeremiah had a reputation as long as his arm and everyone from railroad magnates to minor nobility came to see him. But he wasn't Jeremiah — no, he'd been sixteen and run ragged trying to eke out a living going to patterning classes while working two jobs. He'd been too proud to ask his uncle for work, and Ethaniel had known the patterning classes would pay off. Enchantment work in tailoring was run by the Patterning Union, named after the first magical tailors who had called themselves "patterners" for copying designs from nature into their clothing. It was a history that went even further back, to the days of Cunning Folk and their hedgewitch magics.

Those with a Patterning certificate attracted higher-paying customers and got a vote in union matters. A civilized affair for what was considered civilized work. Ethaniel was reliant on this system, just like Jeremiah had been. The unions did well protecting workers, but like any organization, they had their issues. He'd rather stay part of the union — and under its umbrella of protection — than be an unlicensed patterner. It wasn't illegal, but it was no way to make a living. The cruelty of the system was that you needed money to afford anything in this damnable world, and he had made the choice, as had his uncle, to stay on one side of the line.

Good patterners could not only sell their work at a premium, but also sell copies of old designs. Each design came with an inherent copyright, but any copyright holder could let others copy it to use on their own work for pay. Buy a copy of the pattern from someone with a reputation for craftsmanship, learn it, use it and charge others for it. Buying an "aged pattern" wasn't cheap; most patterners couldn't afford it, or saved for years for one choice. And that was if it wasn't sold during those years.

Ethaniel clenched his jaw as he watched Jeremiah slowly spoon oatmeal into his mouth. Magic had done much for society, and yet the money was a continual barrier. Wasn't that always the case?

With a sigh, Ethaniel got to his feet. "Do you need anything else, Uncle? There's water by your bed and oh, wait, your books—"

"I'm fine, boy," Jeremiah rasped, waving his empty spoon at Ethaniel. "You worry too much. I'm not dying today."

"Uncle."

"Go on. I know you've got someone coming in this afternoon." Jeremiah's eyes, as rheumy as they were in the weak afternoon sunlight, seemed to glitter a little. "Tall, likes dark colors. Works at the museum, right?"

Anticipation and dread rose up in Ethaniel, mirroring each other, twining together until all he could feel was a flutter of nerves in his belly. "He's a friend." *Sort of.* "And I'm only fixing a ripped hem. Nothing drastic."

Jeremiah only chuckled in response and after a few moments, Ethaniel took the creaky stairs down to the shop's backroom, where bolts of fabric in every color sat waiting to be molded into something new. He liked it back here — it was quiet and had a low, humming energy that didn't bother his innate magic. The spools of enchanted thread would lay dormant until Ethaniel activated them with his patterning, but sometimes he swore the very promise of magic lay like a thin haze over the room.

The jacket he'd promised to mend was ready to go, but its owner would come by in person to pick it up. Aubrey wasn't the type to send an errand boy to handle much, especially not his clothing. The man was rather particular, and Ethaniel found what most would call *fussiness* rather attractive.

What he wouldn't tell Jeremiah was that he and Aubrey were a tad uneasy with each other of late. What had once flourished between them had gone sour over an argument about Ethaniel's magic and a difference in what they each believed to be his potential — Ethaniel liked patterning, liked running the shop, and Aubrey firmly believed Ethaniel's talents would be in high demand at the museum. Aubrey was in charge of the Magnificus Collectio, a secret curation project attached to the tourist trap museum Darwin's Attic. And Aubrey insisted the Collectio needed Ethaniel's keen eye and knack for patterns, both magical and mundane. But it hadn't been until Aubrey expressed a belief that they could find a caretaker for Jeremiah that their conversation had broken down. Ethaniel wouldn't give Jeremiah up for anything — or anyone.

Over my dead body, Ethaniel remembered saying, watching with a sour taste building in the back of his throat as Aubrey registered the venom, the defensiveness. They hadn't seen much of each other since, and apologies had been exchanged in terse handwriting. The very air between them felt unresolved. They didn't own each other, of course, and neither he nor Aubrey had ever made mention to be more than quiet moments exchanged in the dark of the shop's backroom or Aubrey's office. Ethaniel didn't have proper privacy with his bedroom next to Jeremiah's, and Aubrey was particular about who he let into his home.

But what Ethaniel feared out of all the possibilities that came with the jangle of the shop bell was how his heart would feel upon seeing Aubrey again. Delight? Remorse? Wariness? A combination of all three, perhaps?

With a shake of his head, Ethaniel plucked up a neatly folded bundle of white cloth and went to the front of the shop. He had work to do, and worrying about Aubrey's appearance in the very near future wouldn't finish the patterns he'd yet to enchant.

Over the years, Ethaniel had found that doing more of the "showy" work in the front of the store tended to draw in the observers — and the tourists. Jeremiah had never been one to turn away tourists and their questions; many smaller towns didn't have many magic users (if any), and if they did, it was one poor sod stuck fixing bent horseshoes or mending sunken roofs. It wasn't that geography played a role in those born with magic versus those without…but it did factor into decisions made later in life. Cities had more opportunities for magic users, more chances to use their talents for money or fame. Or, in the case of some, a chance to flee the harsh whispers and dirty looks aimed at them from a very young age.

Despite all the advances of society, religious animosity and superstition still reigned in many places where small minds tended to rise to power. There were dabblings of it even in metropolitan areas like New York, but mostly through the signs of street preachers yelling hoarsely about the ills of "magic and sodomy". But those sentiments weren't kept to ragged men and women standing on banana boxes with handwritten signs. It chilled him to think of the larger implications, especially considering anyone dressed like a normal person could be so bigoted.

Ethaniel picked a spot where the spring sun shone through the front windows of the shop; a cure-all, hopefully, for the way his thoughts rambled about. And he needed a clear head to finish the delicate patterning on a lawn shirt for his newest customer. Mr. Addington had wanted Ethaniel's best quality lawn — not cheap by any means, but not the finest of fabrics — and had given Ethaniel a beautifully drawn diagram to follow for the pattern.

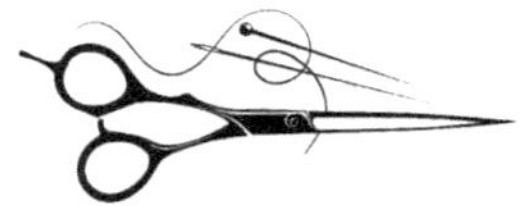

"I want it to shine, but only in lower light," Mr. Addington said the other day when he'd stopped by. The man instantly caught Ethaniel's attention, and not only from a prospective customer's standing. He clearly was moneyed, that posh London accent ringing home in Ethaniel's ears, so he let his gaze lock on the newcomer. The man's garments flowed with bohemian influence but also with the sensibility of someone used to much more rain. And even from the shop counter, Ethaniel saw the fine embroidery work, the perfect fit.

The man's focus was keen as he eyed fabric books, and when he leaned in over a swatch of dark blue silk, Ethaniel smelled neroli and beeswax. It instantly went to his head. Mr. Addington was a complex knot of contradictions, from the accent to the dress to the way his hair was a bit too long to be fashionable, but shone all colors of copper and chestnut in the thin sunlight streaming through the shop windows.

And the man caught him staring. Oh no.

But instead of castigating Ethaniel, Mr. Addington cast his own gaze away, as if embarrassed. "I'm desperate for spring weather, so I might have dressed the part," Mr. Addington said, running a hand down his overcoat. It rippled like water, the blues and silvers glistening. It was very good enchantment work and likely a custom pattern.

Ethaniel heard a vague apology in the man's words and instantly felt badly for him. "It's beautiful," he said, motioning to the man's coat. "I've seen work like it before but if you want something similar, I'm afraid my patterning isn't up to the task." A small lie, but a necessary one.

"Oh, no, it's not that at all." Now the man smiled, shoulders pulling back. It was like that with some folks — a bit of kindness and they found themselves once more. "Please call me Calix. I've heard wonderful things about your embroidery work and was hoping to get a spot on your calendar."

Ethaniel shook Calix's hand with an even, professional smile as warmth flared in his chest. It was nice to hear a London accent again, and Ethaniel couldn't help but feel a sense of kinship. That was far easier to focus on than the way this man appealed. "Ethaniel. Welcome to Twisted Silver Tailors." He pulled out his patterning catalogs along with a menu of garments, from popular to unique, all with prices and fabric availability. He'd never go back to paper now that enchanted slabs were available. "What did you have in mind, Calix?"

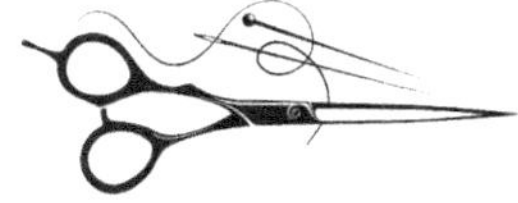

Calix — Mr. Addington's — design wasn't the difficult part of the patterning. Ethaniel could do this part with his eyes closed, if need be. He let his gaze flicker up to the windows, catching sight of a few passersby leaning in. Waiting.

With a smile meant for himself as much as the strangers outside, Ethaniel made a bit of a show of laying the shirt and Calix's artwork flat on the counter. He smoothed his left hand over the bright white shirt while placing his right on the parchment. Parchment made transference a bit easier, for reasons still not fully unraveled by magical theorists. Warmth instantly cascaded up his right arm, and Ethaniel let his eyes drift shut as that sensation rushed up through him, elation and pain at the same time blending into a mindless haze of power.

That feeling bolted up and over — over his shoulder, into his neck, across his face like a whip crack, and just as he could feel his energy begin to wane, it all at once shot down his left arm. It was lightning in his skin, leaving behind ozone and lingering warmth and a numbness in his fingertips that would last only a few minutes. And even with his eyes closed, Ethaniel could see the haze of blue and gold light dimming as the pattern settled into the shirt, then disappeared.

Ethaniel cracked one eye open to check the parchment. Blank, as it should be. He didn't need to look at the shirt to know the pattern was there, waiting for his enchanted thread to finish the job. The power sang to him, a low thrumming of energy under his palm. Beckoning. Uncle Jeremiah called it their family's siren song, and continually reminded a younger Ethaniel to be thankful their calling was in threadwork and fabrics, and not in something more flashy but far more dangerous. That was the other side of his family's specialty.

Ethaniel slowly, carefully sat down on the stool behind him and chanced a glance at the windows. Those same tourists were still staring at him, except one now was reaching for the door. Ethaniel motioned the woman inside, and it looked like she would, but another figure rushed inside.

"You!" A gnarled finger pointed in Ethaniel's direction. "Magic! You were doing magic!"

Ethaniel froze, giving him time to swiftly take in the older man's appearance. His clothes were ragged but clean, and his silver hair and beard were neatly combed. But there was a wild look in the man's eyes that had Ethaniel reaching for the knife concealed under the counter. "Can I help you?" he asked, concern growing.

"Magic," the man whispered. "The air reeks of it. Do you know what you're doing with your magic? Are you using it to help humanity, or are you one of those frivolous types who flaunt it?" The man slid closer and Ethaniel's grip on the knife handle tightened as the man pulled out a thin book. "Do you know that man is not meant to use magic this way? Do you know that every time you enchant a shirt or handkerchief, you're committing a grievous sin?"

Ethaniel let out a breath but didn't relinquish the knife. "And who are you preaching for, grandfather?" he asked, voice as calm as he could make it. If he showed relief, the man might take it as an opening to continue preaching, and he did not need that driving away customers, not with spring retinue and wedding season fast approaching.

The man's hand shook, but his voice was steady as he answered. "I preach for the truth," he declared, "and the righteous! Those who need to know the dangers of magic, and understand that our world is poisoned! We need order in chaos! We need magic in the proper hands!" The man flapped the little book in Ethaniel's face, suddenly aggressive. "We need *order*, my boy! Take this, read it, learn it, and come to us when you understand your sins and the error of your hedonistic ways!"

The pamphlet was dropped on Ethaniel's counter and the man turned to leave, but then spun around and said, "Are you one of those perverts? You shouldn't be doing magic if so! You're denigrating magic for your own disgusting purposes!" He spat on the floor and yelled, "Perverts!" before dashing out the door, leaving Ethaniel with that word echoing in his ears.

"Of all the fucking days," he muttered as he finally let go of the knife and glanced down at the pamphlet. It was a neatly printed thing, bright gold lettering on a navy background, proudly proclaiming that "The Golden Order is the only path forward! Repent, rejoice, and learn the ways magic is harming our world!"

Ethaniel fought back an eye roll. On any given day, those walking the streets would be shouted at by street preachers standing on boxes and accosted by highly intrusive questions about their lives, their beliefs, and their *proclivities*. For all the parts of New York that welcomed those typically living on the fringes, there were just as many individuals and organizations fighting against what they saw as vice and sin. What the vice was, what the sin was, depended on the literature. The Golden Order was something he'd heard a bit about, but they'd never made their beliefs rather clear...until now.

Curiosity got the better of him, so Ethaniel flipped open the little book to see a handwritten message in the front.

To those reading this little book of miracles:

Know that the Golden Order is for honesty and fairness, order in chaos, and the proper containing of the magic that suffuses our world. We may never know the source of this magic, or why some can wield it and others can't, but we at the Golden Order know it, like any power, needs to be regulated. It shouldn't be in the hands of everyone; only those with proper training and soundness of mind should practice such a dangerous, yet beautiful, art form.

If you seek advice or counsel, our doors are open to you. Order in chaos, my friends, and soundness of mind and body!

Below that was an address off the newly built Riverside Drive in Manhattan. A very expensive bit of property for sure, since the Riverside was being touted as the new playground for the moneyed and powerful. Ethaniel drummed his fingers on the countertop, thinking. The particular slant of the handwriting pulled at him, as if he'd seen it before, but after a moment he scoffed, flipped the pamphlet shut, and promptly dropped it in the bin. He had no interest in any of these organizations. He'd seen it all before – religious or charity organizations promising to help those in need, only to have them turn away anyone who wasn't light-skinned or didn't dress "properly". The Golden Order was one of these, using thinly-veiled language to proclaim their real values.

Ethaniel took a few more deep breaths to focus and shake off the encounter before putting his hands back on the shirt to check the enchantment's stability, when a familiar head of copper and chestnut hair popped up between the sudden gap of the door and the rush of sunlight. "I'm so sorry," Calix said as he shot Ethaniel a hesitant smile. "Did I interrupt? Are you open?"

"Do come in, Mr. Addington," Ethaniel said, trying to cover his surprise at the man's appearance. "Apologies. I was just transferring your pattern over and that bit of the process always leaves me a tad discombobulated."

Calix's smile grew sympathetic. "I'm so sorry. I...I had no idea."

Ethaniel waved him away. "No worries. It's different for every patterner, even if the general theory behind the magic is the same. Miescher's work with nuclein a few decades ago made other scientists curious about the nature of magic work and..." He stopped, bit his lip. "Well, like I said, it's a bit different for every patterner. Now, what can I do for you?"

Calix was staring at the counter, eyes drifting between the shirt and the now blank parchment. "Fascinating," he said softly as he moved closer. "I'm guessing I just missed you transferring the pattern?"

Ethaniel shrugged. His muscles ached with fatigue after the transference, but it would fade within the hour. "Only just, I'm afraid."

"Blast." Calix gifted Ethaniel a dazzling smile. The man surely knew how pretty he was? He had to, dressed in all gold and green today, the colors muted but shimmering softly in the afternoon light, making his hair look like fire in comparison. "Well, I certainly don't want to disrupt your work anymore. But I wanted to bring this by..." and from somewhere in the depths of his voluminous cape, Calix pulled out a sky blue envelope. "The additional pattern we discussed."

Ethaniel was intrigued. They *had* discussed another patterning job, for a proper evening jacket, but only in vague terms of interest. And he would never assume a customer would want more work before the initial job was finished. It was an insane amount of trust to put into a patterner — anyone, really. Calix Addington was either naive or completely trusting of strangers. Either way, it was a very expensive custom order and Ethaniel would be a fool to turn it away.

Calix seemed to sense his hesitation. "It's more detailed than the one you just placed. I thought the extra time might be useful. There's no rush on my end, of course, but..." Calix gestured around to the shop front. "You are obviously quite busy. I didn't want to get in your way."

The apology under his words was evident and it made Ethaniel briefly wonder if Calix was always apologizing where it wasn't required. He'd been like this man once, young and eager and happy to oblige for others. Years of working in the city, with the milieu of customers with which it came, had worn him down some. Ethaniel couldn't get a bead on Calix's age, though he wagered the man was at least half a decade younger. He looked, however, no more than early twenties. A safe, moneyed, cushioned life would do that.

"I'm happy to take on the job," Ethaniel said, reaching for the envelope. The *snap* of subtle magic made his fingertips tingle. His gaze shot up to Calix. "Did you pattern this yourself?"

Calix shook his head. "No. It's...let's say a family heirloom. I've always meant to get it laid down on a garment, and I got tired of looking at it and wishing I had some special occasion to foster its creation. So I decided to change my thinking."

"Hoping the right event will come along." Ethaniel chuckled at that before flipping open the envelope. "Sometimes it does take a switch in one's thinking to make the possible present itself."

As Calix lingered over a fabric sample book, Ethaniel took the time to closely inspect this new pattern. It was not just good work — it was some of the most complex patterning he'd ever seen. And even stranger, the pattern bore no patterner's mark. Worried, he flipped the parchment over to look for any kind of stamp and still found none. Unstamped patterns were dangerous — they could be counterfeit or stolen — and inscribing it on anything would bring the law down on his head. Probably not on Calix's, given the man's status.

He couldn't take the risk. But he *was* curious. "Family heirloom, you said?"

Calix nodded but didn't look up from a square of cashmere so red, it was almost black. A gorgeous choice. "My mother's, actually. Her mother was an incredible patterner, but the laws at the time forbade women in that line of work." Now he did look up at Ethaniel, and they seemed to wear the same expression of suffering, almost a scoff at such backwards thinking. "She'd meant to get it patterned on her wedding dress, but the wedding never happened."

Perhaps Ethaniel should simply ask and not beat around the bush. "So why does it bear no mark?"

"My grandmother couldn't risk attaching her name or the family crest to the work at the time. And my mother never got around to licensing it with the local office." Calix stared hard at the parchment under Ethaniel's fingers. Calculating something, clearly, from the way his fine brow pinched. "I should have realized that would be an issue for you. I have proof of ownership in my mother's letters, if that would suffice."

Relief washed through Ethaniel. "It would, actually. Something we could put on file to ensure the pattern is properly yours." He let his fingers glide over the fine ridges of the pattern, feeling the way the peacock feathers swooped into delicate filigree marks, then back down into floral motifs that could rival any painting in a museum. This pattern was truly a work of art, and he'd be honored to lay it down. But no pattern was worth risking his career, and the roof over their heads.

Calix chose that fine red-black cashmere for his jacket, paid his deposit, and gently put the pattern back in its envelope while Ethaniel wrote him a receipt. The deposit easily paid for another month's rent on the shop, and then some, and Ethaniel felt *good* knowing he was attracting such clients. Knowing he could, for one more month, provide for his uncle and ensure they had a doctor on call and tinctures on hand to ease the coughing and pain.

"Thank you again," Calix said as he straightened his cloak, righting himself to go out onto the busy street once more. "I truly love your work and cannot wait to see my mother's pattern come to life."

The praise was a gentle lantern-glow in Ethaniel's chest. He ought to see this man as any other wealthy customer who came in here — a transaction to be made, money to be put away for his uncle's care. Simple. Clean.

Calix was different somehow. Perhaps it was his understanding of Ethaniel's work, or the awareness of the time Ethaniel put into each order. It helped that all his quick mind came wrapped in a rather beautiful outer package, for certain, but Calix was the kind of person Ethaniel treated as the means to an end. Right?

"You are far too kind," Ethaniel said with a slight smile. "I look forward to making your jacket."

Calix hesitated in turning toward the door, one hand still on the shop counter. Their fingers inches from each other; Calix's hand gloved in soft brown kid leather, Ethaniel's pin-pricked and bare.

"Have a good day, Ethaniel," Calix finally said, leaving Ethaniel with the scent of neroli oil and a head swimming as if he'd been underwater this entire time.

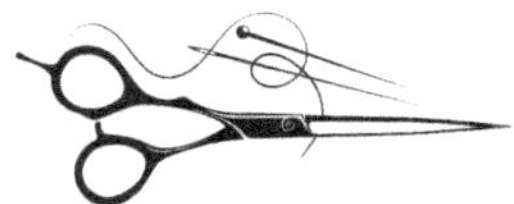

An hour later, Ethaniel paused in the shop's back doorway, peering out of the thin space between worn, molded edges of wood. The bell had rang only moments before, but he knew this customer all too well. His heart thundered in his ears. He could be a professional. He *could*.

Ethaniel pressed his eye to the gap and sighed. Aubrey was turned out beautifully, as always, in a navy so deep it bordered on obsidian. The subtle texture on the coat lapels, at his pant leg cuffs, and even on the ribbon around the man's top hat were all the same crushed velvet of fine taste and understated luxury. So while in hiding, Ethaniel savored the moment to stare.

Aubrey preferred disguising his sinewy, powerful build behind dark, cleverly cut clothes and some *very* minor enchantments. Ethaniel had never questioned it, but sometimes his mind floated back to a memory of wandering hands and silent delight at feeling the strength in Aubrey's arms, his stomach. But it had been the little spark of something darker in the man's light green eyes that had sent shivers through Ethaniel. They hadn't been able to take it any further that night, but the recollection of Aubrey in that moment had left Ethaniel floating for days.

Ethaniel watched Aubrey take off his hat and tuck it under his arm, his gold and teakwood cane curled over the wrist of the same arm. Staring at the architecture of Aubrey's face, Ethaniel felt a pang of longing he'd sworn to shake off. Aubrey was an enticingly beautiful man, all carved slopes for cheekbones and a jawline that made onlookers sigh. But getting to know the man himself had been a challenge Ethaniel willingly stepped up to, from the first time Aubrey had come into Twisted Silver Tailors.

He missed Aubrey.

Ah, that's what that pang in his chest was. Their argument a few months back had somehow left them stranded on either side of a valley neither was willing to trek across, so here they were. But Ethaniel could be professional, and he knew Aubrey undoubtedly would be as well; perhaps too much. So with a deep breath in and a calm smile on his face, Ethaniel let the door creak open and made his way into the shop.

"Wonderful timing. I pressed your jacket this afternoon." Ethaniel motioned to the tiny alcove to his right. "Let me retrieve that for you. I'm sure you've got business elsewhere."

As even as Aubrey's gaze was, Ethaniel could feel himself flush. The visual inspection Aubrey gave him should have been perfunctory. Instead, it lingered on Ethaniel's face. "Are you ill?" Aubrey asked, his deep voice nearly rattling Ethaniel's ribs. He ached to hear more of it, on anything Aubrey wished to speak of. He could read apartment building placards out loud and Ethaniel would weep for more.

Aubrey continued, his expression unmoving as he gestured to Ethaniel. "You're sweating. Just there, along your upper lip." That glass-green gaze flicked up. "Is your uncle well?"

"We're both as well as we can be. The cold nights don't help him, but we manage." *And I'm sweating because you make me terribly nervous.* "Let me fetch your coat."

Ethaniel ducked back into the hallway, then the alcove, where Aubrey couldn't see him lean against the wall and press a hand to his stomach. He *felt* ill, that much was certain. Aubrey made him dizzy — that was how Ethaniel had explained it to Jeremiah once. As if all the air was sucked out of the room and the only light at the end of the tunnel shone like the bottle green of Aubrey's eyes.

He took twenty more seconds, then pulled Aubrey's coat down and slung it over his arm before reappearing behind the shop counter. Aubrey had moved to the other side of the shop, bent at the waist to peer at a display of buttons that had just arrived. They were lovely things, pewter and brass and mother of pearl carved into intricate designs, all based on the Fibonacci sequence. They could hold a standard closure enchantment, certainly, but Ethaniel had hoped someone *appreciative* of his skills would make the buttons do something more interesting. Swirling designs, color changes based on the ambient lighting. *Something more.*

"The ammonites are my favorites, I think," Aubrey said softly upon Ethaniel's return. He didn't look toward the shop counter, simply kept staring down at the buttons. "Reminders of a past that we can never claim, because it existed before we were a thought to the world."

The pithy response he held back nearly choked him. That statement was completely in line with the man Ethaniel knew Aubrey to be, but the wistfulness in Aubrey's tone was new. What could he say to that? Did Aubrey want him to reply? Torn, floundering, Ethaniel simply hummed in noncommittal agreement and waited for Aubrey to turn his attention back to the matter at hand. Business. Only that. No bantering, no bickering. Just two grown men conducting business.

But then Aubrey continued. "I'll need the ammonite ones on another coat. I'll bring it by on Friday, if you've room for a drop-off."

The noise in Ethaniel's ears was a continuation of his earlier hum, but now it was a buzzing, soft and droning. Threatening. "What?"

Aubrey straightened and took with him the strong, proud line of his back. "The ammonite buttons will look very nice on my wool walking coat, I think. Is a Friday drop-off all right?"

Ethaniel nodded, but his head felt too heavy for his neck. It was a disconcerting sensation. "Friday's fine."

"Excellent. I'll put a deposit down now." Aubrey was now before him, pulling out a fine leather wallet and peeling off bills. "Or would you rather I pay for the buttons until you can see the coat, and we'll use that as the deposit?"

"I—" Ethaniel distracted himself by pulling open the coat bag Aubrey had come by for. "I can't ring you up until you check that everything's to your liking." He refused to look up, knowing he'd get caught there, a fish on Aubrey's hook.

"I trust your work, Ethaniel."

It was *nice* to hear Aubrey say his name again. But that buzzing, that low, smooth droning somewhere between his ears and his brain was making it hard to focus. Ethaniel knew Aubrey was only coming around to pick up what he'd paid for. But there were magical tailors with patterning skills a dime a dozen in New York, so why continue to give Ethaniel his business?

It might have been an olive branch, but to Ethaniel, it weighed more than a ship's anchor.

Ethaniel drew his gaze up, hoping he'd dredge up some courage to keep his lips from quivering as he replied, "Check it anyways. Trust is lovely, and I appreciate the generosity of yours, but I can't afford to have a single unhappy customer."

The argument Ethaniel expected never manifested. Aubrey's silent nod came before he began to gently examine the seams and hems while Ethaniel priced the ammonite buttons. The moment of quiet between them helped settle Ethaniel's nerves, enough so that when he handed Aubrey the invoice to be paid, his fingers didn't tremble.

"As I said," Aubrey rumbled softly at him before backing away from the shop counter, "you do beautiful work. The best in the city."

Ethaniel foolishly let him go without another word.

THREE

C*ALIX*

Cambridge University

Twelve years ago

"I have a plan," Lawton whispered as he slipped into bed beside Calix.

Calix groaned into his pillow and blindly fumbled around, not sure if he wanted to pull Lawton closer or slap a hand over his mouth so he'd hush. "It's the dead of night. Why are you in my bed?"

"I can leave," Lawton replied just as softly. "But my bed's cold now and I've been thinking about your little conundrum."

With another groan, Calix acquiesced and turned his head to the right. Lawton was rumpled from sleep and whatever strenuous activities he'd been up to across the hall. Calix had long learned how to ignore the sounds coming almost every night from Lawton's apartment, but he was surprised the man from the pub had left Lawton before dawn. They usually stayed.

"I don't have a conundrum," Calix replied as he let Lawton tug on the thick goose down blanket until it covered them both.

"You do, I'm afraid."

In that sinuous way he had, Lawton snuggled closer, nudging his knee against Calix's thigh. That single spark of contact sent a shiver through Calix and under the pillow, he clenched his left hand into a fist.

He'd known playing ignorant wouldn't hold Lawton back from trying to "fix" his lack of a life in society. Was it so wrong that Calix enjoyed the quiet: his apartment, the University Library, that corner at the Richfield Club none of the other members liked because it was too close to the kitchen (and too close to the servants who were scurrying about to meet their every demand). Calix knew he was incredibly fortunate — wealthy, educated, given everything he could ever want. He was happy in life, too. He had the choice to live quietly even when his means afforded much more. But his head often felt heavy with questions, playing at his sense of morality like a finely tuned instrument. Knowing which keys to play, which strings to pluck. Calix was a lucky, lucky man with too many thoughts about the nature of being and belief.

Having Lawton as a direct source of confoundment made things easier somehow. Like in this moment. Calix could lose himself in the red-orange curls sleek against Lawton's forehead and stare into eyes heavy with sleep. It was the spark in those eyes, an ember of something precious and panting, that beckoned him near. The heaviness in Calix's body was not all due to the time of night, but was tangled up in Lawton, the same way Lawton tangled his fingers in the collar of Calix's silk pajamas.

"Your problem is overthinking," Lawton whispered. "Along with your terribly grounded sense of ethics. And I realize, dear thing, I may not shake loose your foundations. But I would so love to see one pillar tumble. Crack, even."

Calix was hypnotized by him. Lured in, pulled ashore. Because for all Calix's confusion, Lawton could pull apart the knot of it with nimble fingers. One string gently freed, and Calix would bend and his head would feel weightless for a little bit.

Lawton knew. He knew Calix and how to navigate their world of money and parties and comments that complimented and chewed on you at the same time. He had been Calix's guide since they'd met ten years ago, alone at boarding school and wondering what those storied halls had planned for their futures.

"Don't you want to stop, dear one? Catch your breath?" Lawton was so close now and the nearness forced some noise out of Calix's throat. Their dance had gone on for years, but of late, there was an additional urgency. It scared and infuriated and thrilled Calix. As Lawton did.

"You're the only one saying I'm spinning," Calix whispered back, the lie so easy it was done in a single breath. "What if I'm not?"

Lawton chuckled softly as he let his hand drop to rest on Calix's hip. The slide of silk over his skin made Calix want to crawl away and draw closer all at once. "Can I make you spin, then? Wind you up like my own toy?"

"Lawton..."

Calix was pressed into the mattress by two strong hands, Lawton perched above him like a beautiful, strange bird. But the weight, the heat of him, was real. And from this angle Lawton stared down at him as if from on high. Studying his prey. "You think you don't know what you want, dearest one, but I do. You ache to be seen, don't you? Well, I see you."

Lawton leaned down until their faces were even and Calix might only tip his chin up to meet Lawton's lips. Hunger was a second heartbeat in his chest, and its fangs wanted flesh. "Do you?" Calix managed to reply, his voice strained. He was beyond aroused; his vision was only colored with Lawton. "Show me, then."

"I would have thought this to be a bit..." Calix looked around the room. "Stuffy for you, Lawton."

Lawton gasped delightedly. "Are you accusing me of not having taste, my dear?"

"You know I'm not." Calix gestured to the auction catalog over which they both hovered. "But I've never known you to be a fan of auctions."

Lawton gave a noncommittal hum as he turned the page of the catalog. Calix watched his long fingers graze the image of a very old — and very expensive — cabinet from the 1600s. It was a beautiful piece but heavy with carvings and glass and completely not Lawton's taste in home furnishings.

Finally, Lawton replied softly, "I'm here for the books they're auctioning off, and you did agree to accompany me. You know I'm doing some trading on the side, supplemental income and all that. And apparently the poor sod who just passed was quite the collector." Another page was turned. "A few things caught my eye and if I can get them at a reasonable price, they might already have a buyer."

Calix examined his friend for a long moment. Lawton was a constant schemer, always investing in this club opening or that musician who was bound for bigger and better things. He'd dabbled over the years in arts and antiquities, but books were a recent obsession. Calix should have guessed that's why they were here, but most of the books he'd seen in the auction catalog were quite old and being sold in lots — which meant they weren't terribly valuable individually.

Lawton's schemes didn't always pay off. Rare books, however, were a decent bet considering the demand for them had skyrocketed of late. Or so the men at the Richfield Club claimed, from all Calix overheard from his hidden corner at the back. Lawton's finances were constantly in question, so it all made sense.

And yet something prickled at the back of Calix's neck. A sense of…something. Like a shadow looming over him but he couldn't make out any details. His visions were often like this, unhurried and blearily ominous. Calix knew to stay alert, but wasn't going to be too concerned.

Yet.

He left Lawton to the auction catalog, needing the space and air to clear his mind. The Wentworth building housed business offices of all kinds, but its third floor was home to the Sterling Auction Company. Sterling was a fixture in the city for anyone looking to sell or buy antiques and art. Calix had sent some of his mother's things to them after her death, per her instructions. There were more of her things at the family estate in upper New York, but Calix had left them there. Rosehill Manor had belonged to his mother solely, a strange and oft ridiculed maneuver by a woman with property and wealth in the day and age. He could have never bared to part with any of her things from Rosehill, and certainly not at an auction. Looking at the remnants of a life, so casually displayed to be examined and gawked over? It made him feel uneasy.

Was this all a life could be reduced to? Could all the joy and love and moments of anger and wonder and quiet of an entire life be subtracted to mere objects easily passed on to the next person, and not even a lingering wisp of memory clinging to polished wood and colorful enamel? His mother would have said otherwise, that the spirit lives on in those who had loved and lost. Her God was a kind but inefficient one, leaving humanity to deal with death and destruction and questions about the nature of existence with which They never bothered to assist.

It had always felt benignly cruel to Calix, and he felt it again now as he stared at the cabinets and books and jewels on display.

It was a good thing he left Lawton behind to do as he pleased. His friend was never a fan of when Calix got *existential*.

Calix wandered the auction hall, dodging well-dressed men and women as they blithely glided through the different rooms. Upon spotting a door propped open to the outside, he gratefully slipped through the crowd and followed the scent of rain on the wind to a balcony. From here, one could see the Manhattan sprawl, glittering like its own gem in the middle of what had once been farmland and swamp. Built up from nothing, now home to so many. Even the green of Central Park shone, spring-deep and glistening, beckoning. Calix might be homesick for London from time to time, even years after he'd immigrated, but he couldn't deny the beauty of New York.

"I see I'm not the only one who needed an escape from the hall."

It was the clearest voice Calix had ever heard. He looked over to see a tall man in a dove gray suit leaning slightly on a truly beautiful teakwood and gold cane, his ungloved hands dashed with silver rings that glinted in the dull sunlight. The man wore no hat and his black hair was cropped close to his head, leading the eye to a thin scar that cut from his left temple down to disappear behind his ear. He was devastatingly handsome. And then Calix's left hand twitched. Unwillingly, he gasped and the man frowned.

"Are you all right?" the man asked, stepping forward as if to assist.

"Yes, apologies." Calix gripped the twitching hand in his other and pressed his thumb into the palm. "It's just a bit of a twinge and doesn't happen often. It's no worry, I swear." But Calix knew better — the twitches *were* rare and their appearance only precluded something important. His little gift showing itself once again. There were no visions this time, just a twitch in his hand and a sense of *something* looming on the horizon. He could ignore his swooping stomach but the hand twitch was obnoxious.

The good side to all of this was that something else about the man sparked familiarity within Calix, and he remembered the tailor shop earlier in the week. "I'm so sorry, but I think we passed each other before." Calix smiled as the man's frown deepened. He wondered idly if the man could smile at all, so dour was his expression. "At Twisted Silver, that lovely little tailor shop on the edge of the Village. I came in behind you and couldn't help but notice how beautiful your suit was." He gestured at the man, who was so still he might have been a statue. "As yours is today."

Calix might not be one for the social scene of clubs and parlors, but he knew his way around a compliment. The man's eyes, an incredible green like glass, lingered on Calix's red carnation brooch as he answered. "I should be the one apologizing. I interrupted your moment of quiet from the din inside."

Interesting. He seems to either know the symbolism of the brooch...or perhaps doesn't approve? The question made Calix want to know more, even though the stranger was rather aloof, almost standoffish. Calix put out his hand, hoping this mysterious, beautiful man might speak to him some more. He could be politely charming when needed, though Calix knew he lacked any of the pizzazz and sensuality that Lawton wore like a second skin. "Calix Addington. It's a pleasure."

"Aubrey Levine."

And curiously, the man only nodded to him, dropped his hand, and said no more. Aubrey stepped away to lean his elbows on the balcony railing and stare out into the city's mid-afternoon glassy gleam.

Well. I'll just have to try again.

"Are you here as a collector?" Calix asked. "I'm accompanying a friend who has an interest in old books."

Aubrey continued to gaze out over the city as he slowly replied in that sonorous voice. "It's part of my work."

"May I ask what you do?"

"I'm a curator." Aubrey's eyes slid over to him. Calix's hand twitched again, just as he had let it drop to his side. "Rare antiquities and such."

In England, that would have been said as a point of pride. Scholars of all sorts were cherished in his home land, particularly if they were mechanically or magically-minded. Aubrey's American accent, and the dry thump of each word, melded, as the man acted as if his work were tiresome. *What an odd thing to find tiresome*, Calix thought. *Unless that's what I'm supposed to think.* Because no matter the cool depths of Aubrey's words, Calix wasn't one to ignore his sixth sense.

"That must be fascinating," he said. "Is it a private collection, or part of a museum? There are so many beautiful ones in this city."

Calix might have imagined it, but he swore a tiny spark of interest lay behind Aubrey's reply of, "Glad to see they're appreciated. The museums, that is. Sometimes I wonder if we're falling backwards out of our natural instincts toward curiosity. Amongst other things."

Now Calix was paying attention. After so many years around people like Lawton, he'd gotten rather good at hearing buried layers under the mundane. *Works at a museum, appreciates scholarship and scientific curiosity, likely here because the museum has its eye on something.*

Calix started to speak but was cut off by the sharp rap of a gavel. With a nod, Aubrey left the balcony, leaving Calix to navigate the surging crowd that piled into the large room to the right. He caught sight of Lawton near a bank of windows on the left, but immediately paused in step.

"Watch where you're going, young man," an elderly woman grumbled at him as she barely avoided clipping him with her elbow. Calix apologized but kept his eyes on Lawton. His friend was talking to a dark-haired woman, her sharp features intense as she said something. Lawton gave the room a quick glance before taking a thick, pale envelope from the woman's gloved hand, then stuffing it inside his jacket. The red velvet of his jacket bulged and the woman rolled her eyes at Lawton before giving Lawton's lapel a tap, then turning on her heel and walking away. Not to a seat, but out of the room, right past Calix as he locked eyes with his friend. As she passed, he caught a whiff of honeysuckle; on its heels came a deep feeling of dread. Just like the wave he'd been hit with when they'd entered. He was already on alert, but now Calix's stomach churned with anxiety. There was something *here*, deeply magical and strange, but he couldn't pinpoint what or where.

When he turned back to Calix, Lawton was a heartbeat too slow at hiding his expression of wariness and worry, and it brought Calix up short. Worry of his own flared in his chest, making the skin and muscle feel too tight, as if trying to bind his lungs with a band of iron. He went to Lawton's side as the man shook his head, curls bobbing against his forehead as if he could physically rid himself of that which bothered.

"There you are," Lawton said, slapping a smile on his face. It was too big and too bright to be forthright, but Calix appreciated the attempt. "Come, come, the auction's starting and as luck would have it, the knick knacks and books are up first."

The chatter in the room stopped abruptly as the auctioneer raised his gavel, and on cue, liveried attendants turned up the gas lamps on the walls. "All the better for you to see these lovely items," the auctioneer, a stout, middle-aged man said with a chuckle. "Bidders, please have your paddles ready."

The first few items passed in a blur. Calix's mind was too preoccupied with watching Lawton, cataloging his expressions, his movements. His entire world, it seemed sometimes, revolved around this one man.

"Are you all right?" Calix whispered, leaning into Lawton's space. "That woman seemed angry with you."

"It's fine," Lawton replied tightly. "And my lot is coming up, so if you don't mind, dear..." He sat up straighter, his shoulder nudging Calix's. Dismissed, thoroughly; all Lawton's attention rapt on the cart wheeled up on stage by two attendants.

To Calix's eye, the cart full of neatly displayed, leather-bound books was nothing special. And according to the auction catalog, lot 34 was two-dozen books on varying subjects: natural history, the human body, a book Calix knew to be a rather dry study of the Madagascar cave bat. The catalog noted not all books were described therein, only the ones with "educational" value.

"This one?" he asked Lawton, confounded.

The gavel rapped again.

Lawton's hand tightened on his bidder paddle.

And across the room, the tall man in the dove gray suit sat up straighter as well.

Something swirled through Calix's mind with a flash of pain so startling he nearly cried out. Instead, Calix dug his again-twitching hand into his left temple and watched through a squint as Aubrey cast the first bid for lot 34. And he bid twenty dollars higher than the opening ask.

Lawton gasped. "That cad!" The look Calix saw him cast toward Aubrey was full of seething shock. "Sixty dollars!" he called out, and the entire room breathed in at once.

"Seventy," Aubrey said, matching Lawton's volume. But his voice was dry, serious in a professoral kind of way. Calix peered around Lawton's back, trying to catch Aubrey's gaze. But the man was firmly fixed in his seat, all attention on the baffled auctioneer.

"You gentlemen do know these are just books, right?" the auctioneer said. A few grumbles rose up and even one cry of, "Ah, get on with it!".

"Yes, and I will pay handsomely for them," Lawton cried out. Aubrey simply shook his head.

Calix's entire head *burned* with pain now, the fastest it had ever come on. He was waiting for the vision — something, *anything* — to appear. But even as he closed his eyes and tried to ignore the voices calling out in the room around him, he saw nothing.

Wait

Wait

There is something

Something here

Someone?

No. Yes.

Strange, this feeling.

Calix opened his eyes and the world rushed back at him. He felt sick, dizzy and nauseated, his skin clammy to the touch. Beside him, he registered Lawton shouting, "One hundred and twenty!", his hand clutching the bulge in his jacket.

Lawton was desperate. Calix could see it now. And whatever tied that woman, the money, and those blasted books he wanted together was making Lawton come undone. But Calix's vision swam and he was forced to put his head between his knees and breathe. Otherwise he'd vomit all over the place.

The room faded once more, until all Calix could hear was his breathing and the furious beat of his heart; all he could feel was the soft wool of his trousers; and everything else tuned into the strange sensation rippling over his skin. Magic, but different.

Not just an awareness. Something else. Bigger. Deeper. An ocean of magic next to the puddles he was familiar with.

Between those beats of his heart, Calix understood he wasn't alone in the dark.

He was terrified. And so, so thrilled.

Around him, the room erupted into applause and a flushed and sweating Lawton collapsed beside him, his grin a little too big. "My god, what a rush! I mean, that man should be commended for his steely will but he was no match for me!" Lawton paused, then put a hand on Calix's shoulder. "I'm so sorry, darling one. I got carried away and completely ignored your distress. Let's get you outside for some air and...oh, yes, wonderful. Finally some wait staff in this dreadful place. Yes, can we get my friend some water?" Gentle hands cupped Calix's jaw, helping him to sit up. "Water, or do you want something else, Calix?"

Calix murmured that water was fine. He could see Lawton's amber eyes were hazy with victory but Calix would take any attention in the moment, even if distracted. He was completely exhausted. Whatever that thing had been was gone now, dissipated like the way spring fog burned out with a morning sunrise.

Calix let Lawton steer them to the balcony where he'd met Aubrey, then found a glass bottle of water pressed to his lips. "Drink," Lawton said quietly, other hand coming to rest on the back of Calix's head.

"I'm not an invalid," Calix replied.

"You're not, but you look terrible right now and I'm worried." The bottle was pressed against his lips once more and Calix drank. "Good. Ah, that's very good."

Calix spared a stray, panicked thought to how they must look — in Manhattan, during the day, at an auction filled to the brim with upper crust society-types, and the two of them wearing their red carnation brooches and locked together so. But the water was cold along his dusty throat and he caved, to the delight of the water and the pressure on the back of his head.

"Apologies for interrupting. But I'm afraid I need to speak with you, Mr. Adler. It's rather important."

Lawton nearly snarled as he yanked the bottle away from Calix's lips before shoving it at him, not even stopping to ensure Calix had a grip on it as he marched over to Aubrey. The man had appeared in the doorway like a wraith and now stood, half a head taller than either of them and impeccable in that gray suit. Calix thought for sure Lawton would go on the defensive, simpering and somewhat sincere, smoothing over any slight he may have done the man in their...exuberant bidding war.

Instead, Aubrey shocked them both by holding out a cashier's check. "Double what you paid and good at any bank."

Lawton's gaze narrowed and it made Calix shiver. He'd seen that look many, many times. "Just who do you work for, sir? Your desperation speaks volumes, I'm afraid, but provides no specifics."

Aubrey froze in place. Against Lawton's bright red and navy blue outfit, Aubrey's dark gray gave off no light, no color, but reminded Calix of a suit of armor. A knight going to war. And with his ramrod posture and unwavering gaze, Aubrey did look all the more like a storybook knight come to life.

Somehow, it endeared the man to Calix, almost as much as Aubrey saying, "I'm a curator at Darwin's Attic, in special collections. I'm willing to buy the book we're interested in for the amount on the check." Aubrey towered over Lawton and in the moment, Calix swore he saw Aubrey's shadow widen. "A single book for double what you paid for the entire lot. If that's specific enough for you."

Calix stifled his laugh in his fist, pretending to cough, but neither man paid him any mind. "I'm afraid it's an all-or-nothing lot, as I'm a book collector and dealer, good sir, and I won't know the value of any individual book until I inspect all of them. Thoroughly. And even then, I'd not sell to your slummers' paradise and tourist trap for anything. Darwin's Attic is the worst of scholarship, meant to pander to the lowest."

Aubrey was unmoved, and unmoving from the doorway. "One book. For nearly three hundred dollars. Anyone would take it."

Lawton smiled thinly. "I'm not anyone. And the answer is no."

"Lawton," Calix said as his friend made to leave the balcony. "Surely you're being a little unreasonable. What's one book?"

Both men stared at him. Lawton in utter shock, and Aubrey with his cool, even gaze but a head tip of what Calix hoped was agreement. "I won the auction," Lawton explained, his tone whiplash-quick in the jump from angry to patronizing. As if Calix were a child in need of instruction. "Therefore, I get to do with my winnings as I please. And right now, I'd like to *leave the balcony* to go pay for my lovely books."

Lawton squeezed past Aubrey with a huff, leaving Calix clutching his empty bottle and staring after him.

"Your friend does not understand," Aubrey said as he approached Calix.

"He's stubborn, and a bit of an arse on occasion," Calix replied. His words were weaker than he intended, but the twitch in his hand was back; painful now, like a throb buried deep in the muscle. A particularly violent twitch forced Calix's left hand to spasm, and the bottle fell. Glass shards, white-green and glinting, now lay in a circle between he and Aubrey.

A perfect circle of glass. Those appearing where they shouldn't is an omen. You know this. Mother always believed some of the tales of the Cunning Folk, and had proven their instincts to be right more often than not. And their omens were not to be ignored.

"That may be," Aubrey said as he motioned to the glass. He had stopped his progression forward as soon as the glass shattered. "But I believe you may have a better appreciation for the severity of his decision."

"I don't, I'm afraid." Calix couldn't look away from that circle on the ground.

"That twitch in your hand says otherwise." Aubrey knelt and picked up a jagged shard, holding it up to the light. "As does the absolutely perfect circle at your feet."

His breath left him in a gasp, and Aubrey took the opportunity to hold out a black and gold business card. "For when he changes his mind, or you do it for him, Earl Batherton."

Calix took the card and Aubrey turned on his heel, giving no more consideration to Calix or the glass before disappearing inside.

FOUR

C ALIX

The next morning

Calix rubbed his eyes and combed the final shelf in his study, finding nothing. In the hazy light of morning, Calix couldn't find the answers he sought.

His mother's library, vast as it was inside the walls of his apartments, was still only partial. The rest was at Rosehill, and might yet contain the answers his mind sought after the previous day's strangeness. There was no mess to clean up in the study, only the tangle of questions in Calix's mind that needed tidying. And that wasn't going to happen right now.

It was early, he hadn't slept, and he needed to escape. Just for a little while. Calix got dressed and headed downstairs. To his surprise, his valet was at the front door, coat held out. "It's rather early, even for you, Richard."

"I'd promised Marie I'd grab some of those lemon scones she loves so much." Richard gave Calix a smile. "And you know the old biddies at McTavish's aren't afraid to slap hands."

Calix stifled a laugh. "Or cheeks, if memory serves the last time you arrived a tad later to the bakery."

"All too true."

As usual, Richard simply handed Calix his coat. He and Richard never had a traditional employer-valet relationship, not since Richard began working for him once he'd purchased the apartments nearly six years ago. He'd stayed in England long enough to graduate from Cambridge, put his mother's affairs in order, and hop the next steamer to America. They were still employer-employee, but Calix felt an affinity for Richard, balanced precariously on an edge of familiarity and friendship.

"Any instructions for the chef today?" Richard asked as Calix shrugged into his coat. "I can leave a note before making the rounds."

"Not for them, but I do need a pick-up from the tailor. A different one from the usual." Calix handed Richard a few bills and the tailor shop's paper receipt, which the man took with a raised eyebrow. "Twisted Silver Tailors."

"I know the place. Never gone in though." Richard eyed Calix's understated morning outfit of pale greens and browns. "What am I picking up?"

Calix gave him instructions to retrieve the shirt he'd had Ethaniel make. The tailor had lingered in his mind well after their encounter, pulling at him in a strange kind of way that the museum curator, Aubrey, did. It wasn't his foresight, hopefully, only natural human curiosity and, admittedly, a desire to admire both men again. It wasn't as though he were made of stone.

As Richard departed, Calix shook all of that off to head out into the spring air, his feet taking him north and east for several blocks. There was a more direct path to his destination, but after the strange events and lingering confusion of the last few days, Calix felt the need to take in something more than Lawton's haughty glances.

He also needed to forget the taste of his friend's lips. It wasn't fair to either of them, carrying on like that. Calix trusted Lawton with his body, yes, and maybe even a small part of his heart, but the man pushed and pulled him in directions in which he did not want to tread.

The sun had only graced the city skyline with its partial presence when Calix left his building, the Jenora Palms, for his favorite place outside home. It was by far the strangest apartment building he'd ever been in, a garish and sparkling *demimonde* not fit for anyone of his social strata. Calix loved it, just as he adored everything about the Village. Here, he felt freer. Few locals paid any mind to anyone's comings or goings, even if a man walked down the street at some ungodly hour wearing the smeared remnants of his own rouge and lip stain. And here they adored the small magical conveniences and admired the larger feats found in Manhattan. Magic wasn't othered, and neither were men like him. Lawton wouldn't admit it in public, but Calix knew his friend loved this tiny neighborhood, too. Moving in when Calix did wasn't about how Lawton viewed their friendship; it was more about not needing to hide so damned much, and how liberating that was.

So instead Calix spent the morning away from all those reminders. He took in the morning sun, watched small children dart across his path as he walked the streets. There were stalls to browse at the tiny market the Village moved throughout the neighborhood as the seasons changed, going from the newly drawn green space with a burbling fountain to inside warehouses heated by magical, ever-burning fires in the winter. This was the first week the market had moved back outside, and it made Calix feel a little lighter seeing all the people mingling, haggling over bolts of cloth and baked goods and shiny baubles.

There was no line outside the tea house the next street over, so Calix walked right into the crowded shop, hitting a wall of scent that made him close his eyes in pleasure. Lavender and sugar, ceylon tea and cardamom, and the walls teeming with plants from silvery-green spikes of rosemary to long-fingered purple vines dotted with perfect white flowers. Everything about Jewel House shone, and it attracted a crowd of free-thinkers, artists, musicians, and writers.

There was nowhere else like it in the city, and Calix didn't get to revel in it enough for his liking. *Perhaps if he'd stop letting Lawton drag him about, he could be here more.*

Thoughts like that wouldn't do for a day like this one, Calix decided as he took up a table in the corner and watched the little groups of tea drinkers chat. A waitress bustled over to take his order, a cup of jade rose tea and a slice of thick toast with blackberry preservers, and Calix settled in.

Strains of conversation reached him, filtered through clouds of steam from piping hot teacups: talk of the new bookstore around the corner, a dissection of the latest dissertation from Mrs. Athena Marksman, a feminist and outspoken suffragist, and two women musing on a display they saw at Darwin's Attic. The women were dressed in perfect bohemian fashion for the weather, all flowing skirts and sparkling silver pendants and their curls peeking out from beneath velvet scarves topped with buttons and feathers. One of the women, blonde and bright-eyed, wore rings on every finger and Calix swore she *tinkled* as she moved.

But what caught Calix's attention most was their mention of Darwin's Attic. He didn't want to eavesdrop, but the women were seated just a table over and talking as if no one else in the world existed. His tea and toast arrived on a tray sans waitress; a little trick the tea house engaged in with the help of an enchantment. From the way he understood it, the tray was enchanted to take weight on, and when that disappeared, it returned to the kitchens. It always made Calix smile.

"Did you see the Xylothek?"

Calix glanced over at the two women seated nearby, then kept his eyes on his meal as he listened.

"I did! You were absolutely right, Doris. Such a beautiful collection. I'm glad I waited until Darwin's Attic had a full display. I know even one of those wood tablets is impressive, but seeing all those seeds and leaves...well, there's no better place for it."

Doris's companion chuckled. "Indeed! Half of those tree samples were from Darwin's journeys. But I heard...well, you know how there are stories. Except I heard that their special collections curator retrieved the other tree samples for the Xylothek himself. Went all the way around the world for them."

"No! Really?"

"It's just a rumor. But there are always so many rumors about that place." Calix glanced up and saw the blonde woman grinning widely. "And speaking of that curator...my Lord, what a looker."

"Sasha!"

"What? He's so handsome!"

Calix sighed. Even here, he couldn't escape the mysterious Aubrey Levine. Who else could they possibly be talking about? Unless Darwin's Attic was simply packed with good looking men who were also curators.

Perhaps he ought to pay Darwin's Attic a visit.

He'd been intent on ignoring Aubrey's warning about the lot of books Lawton had purchased the day before. Perhaps Aubrey was superstitious, or held onto some beliefs from elder family members. But he'd dreamt of sharp edges and thick shadows and had needed to chase it all away with spring sunshine and a good cup of tea.

It was all inescapable, even here, and it left a sour taste in Calix's mouth.

Calix quickly finished his meal and left Jewel House, back out into the morning as the fog was burned off and the streets were bustling with residents who were tired of being cooped up against winter ice and snow. Calix took a right on East 9th Street, following a crowd of tourists, curious where their bespectacled guide in a tweed jacket would take them. Union Square was a few blocks north, but the guide seemed intent on going eastward.

"And here, as we round onto world-renowned 5th Avenue, you can see the newest construction to push boundaries in Greenwich Village! Much protested by residents, mind you, but those bohemian types don't appreciate the jobs and money the brand new G.B. Baring department store will bring to the area!" The guide grinned as his remark got a few chuckles. "As you can see from here, Baring's is heavily inspired by the classic architecture of the Italians, with touches of Greek and Roman decoration..."

The guide began walking, his group toddling after him, every head craned up at the half-finished department store that would block the views of 5th Avenue from the apartments on East 9th and stand like a gaudy blister on one of the most traveled corners in the Village. Calix had quietly protested the department store, choosing to donate money to a "Save Our Village" campaign that had, sadly, gone nowhere after the money behind the project got the police involved. Since last autumn, when police officers banged on doors and accosted anyone who dared go near the then-empty construction site, Calix had steered away from this part of the neighborhood. He was glad he had — seeing the ground clawed away for mortar and stone wouldn't have been good for his mental state at the time. Or now, even; staring down the street at a part of the city that was changing faster than residents could keep up with.

"There you are! Richard said you might be on walkabout. Something about looking peaky."

Calix wheeled as Lawton threw an arm around his shoulders. His friend looked better — color in his cheeks from the chill and whatever he was excited about now. But also he was back to his perfectly imperfect appearance, with his curls slightly askew, his lips painted a soft mauve, and his ears glinting with pearls and gold. Even Lawton knew wearing certain things outside the accepted bounds of propriety during the day would get the law called down upon one's head. But his clothes carefully eschewed the Village's bohemian flair, between his finely cut walking jacket (slashed daringly above the hips) and smart Hessian boots and the spill of a vibrant yellow and black scarf, an angry bumblebee of color.

"Should I ask why you're carrying a large satchel down 5th Avenue?" Calix asked, throwing his friend an annoyed look.

"Yes, because *we're* going to Babylon Boulevard, my friend. And, ah, ah, no arguing yet, Calix, let me finish." Lawton smiled brightly at him and Calix could feel his desire to pull away melt. "And afterwards, I've got two tickets to see Cheiro on one of his last nights in the city! We will get our palms read by *the* master of palmistry and maybe even get our fortunes told. I heard Walt Whitman's lumbering ghost has been spotted at Cheiro's little salons. Wouldn't that be a kick, dear one?" Lawton nudged Calix with his elbow, his expression going serious. "It's a thank you, for going with me yesterday. I know I've been springing things on you with no warning and I promise to do better in the future."

Questions swirled in Calix's mind, and his stomach hadn't yet recovered from the sour note at the tea house. All he could manage to ask was, "Why the sudden interest in old books? Is it just the money, since they're so en vogue right now?" He trailed his fingers over the edge of the satchel Lawton wore and watched Lawton's gaze linger there. "What's really going on, Lawton?"

"Babylon Boulevard first, then a quick stop over on 3rd. Then onto Bleecker Street. I'll tell you once we've claimed a table at the White Lotus. I promise."

"I'm going to hold you to that," Calix replied softly.

The cold, shadowed recesses of Babylon Boulevard were not Calix's favorite part of the city, by far or wide. Here was a secret place, filled with the fascinating and forbidden, but as Lawton liked to say, "The freaks really only venture out in the safety of the eve, you know." During the day, the grubby alley that served as the Boulevard's entrance was empty save for a few rats. At night, the entire place opened into a strange miasma that could give Acadia Gardens a run for its money.

"Most of these places don't open until sundown," Calix said as Lawton consulted his pocket watch. "Wouldn't you rather wait?"

Lawton shook his head. "I've business that would be better conducted in the light of day, I'm afraid." He shot Calix a smile. "But that's why you're here. My muscle."

That made Calix snort. "We were both rowers at Cambridge, Lawton, not rugby fielders. Strong winds are liable to knock both of us over."

"Ah, you are ever so fair-minded in your insults, my friend," Lawton shot back as he entered the alleyway. "Come on now, don't fall behind. Lest a *strong wind* find you down here."

Down here was the scent of old alcohol, refuse, and stale smoke, all riding on that particular sting of quick-magic. It was ozone and lightning in the air and it made Calix's head swim and his vision bob until he grew used to it. Quick-magic was what the disenfranchised could afford and it was also employed by businesses like the ones down Babylon Boulevard for showy lights and flashing signs to attract customers. Quick-magic was cheaper than repair services or electricity, and you could find charms and baubles for sale on almost every street corner. The sellers of it in Times Square had a particularly profitable hustle going on in quick-magic, according to what he'd heard.

Magic had been a part of human society since the first time some ancient *homosapien* realized they could make fire with a snap of their fingers. It had done truly stupendous things, but magic was simply a tool to most. It didn't haunt one's footsteps the way magic did for Calix.

You stay quiet about your premonitions, Calix. A little foresight isn't a terrible thing, but anything more than that will call down something none of us want to live through. There's a reason witches were burned and magic was buried for so long.

His mother's words always rang in his ears, particularly in situations like now, where Calix wondered if he was sensing every speck of magic in the air. It was another reason he hated coming to Babylon Boulevard: here the very fabric of reality left him choking.

Lawton paused outside a bright green door, the paint chipped and peeling from years of sun exposure, the single window at eye level grimy.

"Where are we?" Calix asked, his voice barely a whisper.

"It's just business, darling. And here." Lawton handed Calix his satchel, a pretty gray leather bag that made Calix sink under its unexpected weight. He hefted it onto his shoulder with a grunt. Lawton gave him a thin smile. "Try to look menacing, Calix. And guard that satchel with your life. It's more valuable than mere money, you know."

In that moment, something gold flashed as Lawton turned; a bit of glimmer under his lapel in the shape of a circle. Without thinking, Calix flipped Lawton's lapel up to get a closer look. He noticed the shaft of an arrow piercing the circle, but couldn't see more as Lawton batted his hand away.

"Maybe I'll tell you about it later," Lawton said, and the fierceness in his tone sent a shiver down Calix's spine.

Whatever that little pin was, Lawton meant to hide it. Anger like Calix had never felt before rose up. His friend was playing games, and it had worn him down so much that Calix saw red.

"Your secrets, whatever they are, don't involve me," he hissed as he pushed the satchel back at Lawton.

"Stay and help, and then you can go back to wallowing or whatever it is you do in that beautiful apartment of yours."

Lawton's grip was like iron as he shoved Calix inside.

"Bout time you showed, Adler. I don't got all day to wait around for whatever nonsense you're selling."

The voice came from a man, tall and broad, his jacket so tight one wrong move would make the seams screech. He stood above them on a landing that led down to a dusty shop counter, now abandoned to the spiders and mice. Two men stood on either side of that very counter, also tall and broad but bearing the wear-and-tear of former boxers.

Calix didn't have the space in his mind to be taken aback by the other men; all of his ire was focused on Lawton.

"Take it," Calix snapped, dropping the bag to the floor and turning on his heel to go.

"Nah, see…" Heavy footfalls stopped Calix in his tracks. "You gotta stay, friend of Mr. Adler. You can bear witness, if you want."

Defiant was more of a sensation and less of a tone that took him over as he replied, "Bear witness to what?"

The man laughed. "Business, of course."

Lawton had immediately grabbed the satchel, then dusted himself off with a huff. "Well, then, Tomas, let's get to business. The quicker we do that, the quicker we're out of your sadly thinning hair."

The insult must have not bothered this Tomas a bit, because he just motioned Lawton over. "You got everything we agreed on."

"I do. Plus a few that might not interest your buyers directly, but might be good to have on hand." Lawton's smile was now razor-sharp. "Just in case."

While Tomas and Lawton talked, Calix realized one of the two other men had shifted until he was nearly out of sight to Calix's left. A prickle of awareness licked up Calix's spine, but the man had made no aggressive move against him. He kept his eyes on Lawton as he handed Tomas two slim volumes and one larger journal-style book from the satchel.

Time seemed to slow as Calix caught sight of silver foil and some kind of glint inside Lawton's open satchel. Lawton was being careful to shield the satchel's contents, but no amount of caution could have shielded Calix from his mind smashing into the dizzying depths of something deeply, terribly magical.

He was a child's toy, a top spinning round and round again until all shape and color had no meaning but everything felt *wrong*. That sense of wrongness seeped beneath his skin, past the muscle, dripping into his bones as if they proved to be no barrier at all to whatever force of will and power sat within Lawton's satchel.

The voice now beckoning inside his mind was the most seductive, powerful thing Calix had ever heard.

Come to me

Come to me

There was no schooling the expression of shock off his face, nor hiding the way he froze in place. The world jittered out of focus once more and Calix flung a hand out to brace himself on the counter.

Thoughts and words not his own barraged his mind, barreling down like a hailstorm. He had no resistance to it.

I know you hear me

You heard me the first time yesterday
I understand you better now

A very firm hand yanked him away and Calix was spun until he was facing Lawton. "I'm afraid my friend is a little under the weather," Lawton said. Calix pulled his head up so he could focus his eyes. Lawton's face had gone perfectly neutral, and even in his state, Calix could feel his gorge rise. Lawton was *never* neutral. "I'll just take him outside for some air and come back –"

"You won't." Tomas's strong American accent made his words boom through the room. "You do business here and now, as we scheduled, or you leave without pay."

"Just finish what you're doing," Calix whispered weakly to Lawton. Lawton simply shook his head and pushed the satchel into Calix's arms once more. He took it, digging his fingernails into the soft leather. Anything to ground him other than Lawton's touch.

"And bring that satchel back over here," Tomas said.

"It's just a satchel, Tomas," Lawton protested. Calix couldn't see the other man's reaction, but whatever it was made Lawton's eyes widen a bit.

He's afraid, Calix thought.

"Over here. Now." A pause, and then, "Boys, bring them back."

Rough hands grabbed him, hauling Calix away from Lawton and both of them were shoved into place before the counter once more. Dust from the floor was kicked up and Calix's eyes watered. While his head no longer spun so much, he still felt queasy and wanted nothing more than to be back at home, where it was safe and quiet.

When one of Tomas's henchmen tried to pry the satchel from Calix, he clung for dear life. Tomas shrugged his mountainous shoulders and the man backed off. "Open it," Tomas said.

"Really, Tomas, it's just my satchel," Lawton replied.

Tomas leaned forward, until he was nose to nose with Lawton. Calix could only watch on as Tomas quietly said, "And I've never seen a satchel make someone look like they're gonna fucking throw up all over the place. I didn't have my boys check you when you came in, seein' as how we're *such* old associates. But I don't trust you, Adler." Tomas flicked a finger at Calix. "Get the satchel from him."

Calix braced himself to be manhandled, but that plan was obliterated by Lawton yelling, "Run, Calix!" while pinning Tomas's hand to the counter with a knife he pulled from his jacket. Tomas bellowed in pain, making Calix's ears ring.

Did Lawton...stab someone?

The air went out of the room long enough for Calix to comprehend what Lawton had said, then he spun and lurched into a sprint. He practically smashed his face into the shop door as the means of opening it, but it got him out into the alley. He feared his feet would fail him, as that sense of sickening power and wrongness still emanated from the satchel, but run he did.

This part of the city was at the edge of the Village — too far from his home to get there without attracting attention, and he couldn't think of any safe place to hide nearby. Getting out of Babylon Boulevard would be key, and then he could...

Fuck. He had no idea where he could go.

But Calix ran.

He pushed past people, jostling into walkers and shoppers, nearly colliding more than once with a street lamp post. He felt as though his eyes would never stop wobbling. Dashing down the streets without a goal was a very good way to get caught, especially since both of Tomas's men were a fair bit taller and larger, and would be able to spot him even in a crowd.

Calix ducked into one alley, then down another, choking on the scent of dirty rain water and refuse. His grip on the satchel made his fingers ache, and his lungs threatened to give out under the stress; every set of footsteps behind him, even unhurried ones, might be after him.

And then he heard it again.

Safety is near

Right

Go right

It was mad to follow the voice.

He did it anyways.

Calix dashed right again, snagging his coat sleeve on a bit of crumbled brick wall, and when he yanked himself away, a sign up ahead caught his eye.

Twisted Silver Tailors

Calix remembered Ethaniel, the patterner, and how kind his eyes were. They'd even had a nice conversation, veering off the road of polite and onto a track of near flirtatious at one point.

It was a huge gamble. But Calix felt he had no other choice.

FIVE

ETHANIEL

It had been a hectic morning and all Ethaniel wanted was a moment of fresh air. Jeremiah had been sick overnight and the scent had lingered in their apartment even well past breakfast. His uncle's apologies, while not falling on deaf ears, certainly weren't warranted. But Jeremiah didn't like to be reminded of his condition, so Ethaniel had grit his teeth and carried on, torn between the urge to fetch the doctor for the second time this week (and thus disobeying his uncle's stringent orders otherwise), or listening to the old man cough all morning. Every cough made Ethaniel's heart ache, and that was nowhere near the pain his uncle was in day after day. With a second, more fortifying cup of tea between customers, Ethaniel had split the difference and sent a runner with a note over to Dr. Iverson, asking if there was anything he could do to help Jeremiah's cough.

He knew what the answer would be. Consumption was fatal, and Jeremiah was likely nearing the end of his life. But surely the doctor would have something to numb the pain. Ethaniel could only hold out hope.

As Ethaniel stepped out the shop's back door, determined to leave the alleyway's deep shadows and scent of something decaying nearby for the small park across the street, he was barreled into by someone. The other person's weight nearly took Ethaniel to the ground, but he managed to catch himself in the door frame. The move wrenched his arm back and Ethaniel hissed in pain. Whatever the man had been carrying landed beside them with a dull thud.

Stunned, Ethaniel looked down to see a familiar face, with chestnut brown eyes and copper hair that hung in loose waves. "Mr. Addington?"

The other man looked panicked, not even bothering to wipe away the sweat on his brow. "Please," he said quickly. "Someone's after me. Could I duck into your shop? A back room?"

Foolish, perhaps, to agree, but Ethaniel wasn't about to turn away someone in need. "Of course." He pulled Calix to his feet and leaned in to brush the other man's jacket off, but Calix jerked away, lunging for the satchel instead.

"Sorry," Calix said. He was twisting this way and that, looking around for any sign of his pursuer, so Ethaniel pulled him inside with a gentle hand on his forearm. Calix went willingly. As soon as the back door was shut, the other man hurriedly glanced around. "Just a back room, for a few minutes? I won't get in the way—"

The back room was no place for a man like Mr. Addington. Ethaniel had suspected the man was gentry from the moment he'd walked into Twisted Silver the previous week, but Calix hadn't presented himself with any title. Even so, Ethaniel wasn't about to make the man hide in the dark in his supply room. He wouldn't do that to his worst enemy, honestly. It was...undignified.

"Upstairs," Ethaniel said, steering Calix down the small hall to the left and then to the staircase. "My apartment's on the right. My uncle lives in the other one. He's ill, so please don't mind anything you hear from his rooms."

Something in Calix seemed to relax at that; his shoulders pulled away from his ears and he let out a long, slow breath. "I don't want to intrude."

"You're not." Ethaniel motioned him up the stairs. "The door's unlocked. Stay there until I come for you." He eyed the satchel, letting the tiniest bit of his own magic drop like a veil over his eyes. Folks absolutely lost their minds over the strangest things, but this level of danger and mystery made him wonder.

As soon as a slight green haze colored his vision, he could see it. Or...*them*. Thousands upon thousands of strings of a pattern his mind couldn't begin to comprehend. That sight alone made him gasp, but the accompanying blast of heat felt like a warning.

Ethaniel shoved away, his sight dropping back until he was once again whole. It was a frightening experience, but one that left him with a strange kind of lightness. As if someone had tied wings to his back and watched him learn to soar moments before he'd turned into Icarus. After a long moment, Ethaniel managed to say, "This person after you...are they dangerous? If they come here, will there be a problem?"

Calix cast his gaze to the ground. "I don't know," he whispered, knuckles going white where he gripped the satchel. "They meant, I think, to take this from me. I don't even know what it is, not really—"

"It'll be fine." Ethaniel's keen ears heard the shop bell ring and he fought back a sudden punch of nerves. It could be anyone coming through his door.

Including the person or people after this man.

He had ways of protecting himself, though.

"Go, go, all the way up and to the back," he said, resisting the urge to shove Calix up the flight of stairs. With a nod, Calix took off, and Ethaniel sucked in a deep breath before leaving the safety of the back rooms. And because he was no fool, he let that veil drop over his vision once more, pale purple now as he reached out to the store's protection patterns. They echoed back a call in kind, like a greeting. His patterning was good, but only two others knew of Ethaniel's uncanny knack for making and seeing patterns that didn't involve stays of closure on coat buttons.

The man standing in the middle of his shop floor was tall and broad, much larger than even most people in this modern age. His back was to Ethaniel as he approached. Ethaniel could see a slight crackling energy of a pattern on the man, but it wavered sickeningly. A cheap pattern, probably a dime a dozen and sold down Babylon Boulevard or in Acadia Gardens.

"Good afternoon," Ethaniel said, forcing joviality into his tone. He wanted to shut the whole place down for the day and figure out what the devil was going on. He wanted this man gone. And he didn't want to press the button under the shop counter and activate the wards.

The man turned and Ethaniel got a good look at a man with no face. A blank mask greeted him. Shocked, he pulled back a little, holding onto the shop counter for support.

"You all right?" the man asked in a rough east coast accent, the words lilted enough to be mocking. New Jersey, maybe, or even further north. It would be the only way Ethaniel would be able to recognize him in the future. And then it clicked — reports of blank-faced robbers had funneled through the city of late, and Ethaniel had known instantly it was a disguise charm.

This man was after Calix. And he would do harm to anyone in his way. Ethaniel was utterly certain of it.

"No, I am not," Ethaniel forced out right before he slammed his palm against the button under the counter.

The wards rejected anyone Ethaniel deemed harmful, so there was no worry they would affect Calix. But the man before him was instantly trapped in a circle of glowing red, the lines of his pattern slowly winding around their prey's large arms as he struggled.

"Hey, fuckwad! Get this shit—"

"Get out of my store," Ethaniel said before flicking his free hand at the door. "Now."

The warding spell did as Ethaniel instructed, lifting the man up with dozens of thick red vines of magic, and tossing him unceremoniously out the front door. They didn't dissipate until Ethaniel had manually and magically locked that same door, and only then did he hear a crash as the spell dropped the man into a trash cart across the street. If the man approached the shop again over the next day, he'd find himself tossed into another cart. It was oddly satisfying to hear the brute's spluttered curses muffled by the building's thick walls. He shouldn't have felt so...victorious. So Ethaniel tamped down on it while checking the windows and back door.

Ethaniel pulled the veil back from his vision before heading upstairs. Hands shaking, he poked his head into Jeremiah's rooms and found his uncle asleep in bed, a book face down beside him. He could breathe a little easier knowing Jeremiah hadn't heard the racket.

"Mr. Addington?" Ethaniel called out as he went into his apartment. "You're safe. He's gone."

He found Calix sitting stiffly in a chair by the fireplace. The other man had coaxed the embers into a warm blaze. Ethaniel saw fear and flame reflected in Calix's big brown eyes and felt a wave of sympathy wash over him. Did a man like this ever have anything to fear before? Ethaniel had spent a lot of time growing up wondering if wealth secured more than just physical safety, but also an unearned peace of mind. As he'd gotten older, Ethaniel had come to pity his wealthy clients. Many of them were empty, lonely shells who would bend their tailor's ear, taking his time up in that small way on top of securing his clothier services.

Calix looked like a man who wouldn't do such a thing. And hadn't, even during their brief interactions a week ago. But he did look like a man who had experienced fear — real, true, and ice cold — for the very first time. In the shadows of the room and the fire, Ethaniel saw Calix's bottom lip tremble. Ethaniel wasn't sure what instinct made him kneel at Calix's feet instead of taking the chair beside him, but when their gazes met, his sympathy deepened. "You're safe here," Ethaniel said. "The wards last for twenty-four hours and no one else can get in without my explicit invitation." When Calix nodded to show he understood, Ethaniel continued. "Why was he after you?"

Calix's fingers shook as he reached for the latches on the satchel. "I think it's a book," he replied quietly. The soft *snick* of the latches felt too loud for the room. "I was with a friend, and he was doing...business down in Babylon Boulevard. But he didn't want to sell this one to that odious man Tomas for some reason and I could...I could..."

As gently as he could, Ethaniel put a hand on Calix's forearm. It was a touch too familiar for strangers; it felt right despite that. "Tell me in your own time."

Calix's gratefulness needed no words, shining through the obvious exhaustion written in his face. As the clock on the mantle ticked and the logs in the fireplace popped, Ethaniel waited. The sudden drought of energy after everything that happened was a blanket over his entire body, trying to lull him into the comfort of the other chair. He stayed on his knees, quiet and patient.

"I see things," Calix finally whispered, his gaze beseeching as he stared down at Ethaniel. "Your magic is sensical, orderly. Mine has never felt that way. I get *visions*. And not the kind the churches think is ordained. Not any kind that's *acceptable* in civilized society." He clenched his fist on his thigh and Ethaniel saw his forearm quiver with unspoken emotion. It was simpler to focus on how Calix was feeling in the moment and let his words slowly sink in.

Oracles had visions. There were different reports over history of Oracles collapsing under the weight of their power, burdened by flashes of the future that overwhelmed the human mind. But Oracles were uniquely powerful and always sought out by those with influence and money. If true, Calix would need help.

Ethaniel shook his head as soon as the thought crossed his mind. A wealthy man like Calix Addington likely had someone in his corner. He wouldn't need the aid of a lowly tailor. But right now, the man before him needed someone to listen. He could do something as simple as that.

"I'm so sorry," Ethaniel replied softly. He put his hand once more on Calix's forearm, trying to lend support through that single touch. "You carry a burden most could never understand. Did you...see something with whatever is in the satchel?"

Calix shook his head. "No." He squeezed his eyes shut and shuddered, but when he opened them again, Ethaniel could see resignation and resolve vying for domination. "The book spoke to me," Calix said, forcing steel into his voice. "In my mind. It spoke to me in my bloody mind and I've never, ever encountered something like that."

But Ethaniel had. Or, he'd heard a tale of something like that from Aubrey.

Immediately, he knew what they had to do.

"I saw it too, Calix," Ethaniel said. "Patterns. Thousands of them. All tied to what you have there."

Calix leaned forward, eager. "Did you hear it?"

Ethaniel shook his head. "No. I can only see patterns in magical objects. Sometimes. It's not an evergreen talent, I'm afraid." He looked away, trying to mash his scattered thoughts together in some semblance of sense. "But this book you carry is thick with magic. Dense with it. If you trust me enough to assist you, I know someone who can help us."

Six

AUBREY

Earlier that morning

The teacup placed at Aubrey's elbow was one of his favorites — a delicate sky blue porcelain with silver filigree patterns scrolling gently across its surface. The scent of lavender and honey wafted toward him and he drew in a long, steadying breath.

"I thought you might need it," Alon said as he shifted to Aubrey's left — out of the overhead light produced by a magically imbued lantern. Gas lights were fine for general lighting, but for his work, Aubrey preferred a single, bright light he could move as needed.

"I do indeed," Aubrey murmured, not taking his eyes off the small book that lay flat on the table before him.

"Tricky bit of business, then?" Alon asked.

"Something like that. Though..." Aubrey paused to lift the next page with a small iron tool that looked better suited for a dentist's tray. "This one's not as finicky as its companion."

"The one that roared at you or the one that let out a miasma of fungal spores?"

Aubrey chuckled. "Both then, I suppose. No, this one is rather bland. Although apparently it caused a bitter fight amongst members of the University of Paris." Now he slid his gaze to Alon, whose sandy blonde hair and dark gray eyes looked pale in the bright light. "My reports say the argument was over the best time to take laxatives in January."

Alon smothered his laugh with his hand. "Oh, I can't wait to see that in the monthly report."

"I refuse to include it. The board doesn't need to know." Aubrey took a sip of his tea with his ungloved left hand. Contamination of any kind between himself and the book wasn't something Aubrey was willing to risk. Every single artifact that came into the Magnificus Collectio was handled with the utmost care and respect; nothing was taken for granted.

This book, while likely harmless and mildly hilarious in some regards, had been brought in as part of a collection, donated by a wealthy widow whose spouse had considered himself a bit of a *curator*. The deceased had done more than most — lead boxes, iron tools, and where needed, glass and velvet cases for displaying his prized tomes. All of those materials diffused magic, but collectors didn't usually have the specific knowledge, or the particular talents, to deal with the bizarrely arcane.

Aubrey and his team did, however. So they'd spent the better part of the last week examining the books. This one, a strange mix of prophecy and advice, wasn't magical. But it was battered. Aubrey intended to repair the broken spine and crinkled pages, then put the book out on display in Darwin's Attic. Tourists loved "prophetic" books. They loved the scandal and the shock, and the possibility. Strange but harmless items kept money flowing through the Attic, and thus funding the Magnificus Collectio's endeavors was the worst part of the work. But his talents were needed, and for the most part, Aubrey felt the work called to him. It wasn't for *forever*, but the here and now worked out perfectly fine.

If only every other part of his life could be neat and orderly.

Aubrey's thoughts had drifted so many times back to Ethaniel, from the moment they'd parted months ago. He'd made an egregious error, thinking his assistance with Jeremiah would be seen as that...and thinking it was wanted. Ethaniel's defiant fury at Aubrey even suggesting getting Jeremiah more help had gotten Aubrey evicted from Ethaniel's presence. It had been a startling, painful lesson.

Aubrey had felt seen by Ethaniel immediately — yielding where he was unbending, sweet like water against Aubrey's sharp edges and cool demeanor. And Ethaniel had been sweet on Aubrey's tongue, too, in those stolen moments that could have lasted forever and still left him desperate for more. He *missed* Ethaniel. Seeing him at Twisted Silver the previous week had been a necessary wound, a reminder that he wasn't as tortoise-shelled as most made him out to be.

Alon was one of the few who knew Aubrey had more to him. He was a good assistant, a good man, and talented with languages and cyphers. They were lucky to have him on staff. Aubrey knew he should say such things more often. But even when he was surly in his concentration, Alon never treated him any differently.

Clinging to people like Alon, like Ethaniel, made Aubrey feel so completely selfish.

"Hmmm. You've got that distant look again," Alon said, shaking Aubrey out of his thoughts. "Which means you should finish your tea, give it a rest."

"I'm all right," Aubrey instantly replied.

Alon simply nodded. "I choose to believe you, Aubrey, but really...you should step away for a moment. Go outside, even."

Aubrey raised a brow, torn between amused and curious. "Why would going outside change anything?"

"For one, it smells like old glue and bad dreams back here. Horribly whiffy. And two, you are only human and deserve a break." Alon nudged him with an affable shoulder. "Go. This poor old book can wait for your magic. He's not running off anywhere." Alon leaned forward and peered down at the pages. "Plus I'm desperately curious to see if these poor sods who didn't take laxatives in January made it to February without perforated bowels. *Horrible.*"

Maybe now was time for a break.

Glass shattered at his feet as soon as Aubrey stepped outside. Tiny flecks of green-silver glinted in the spring sunlight. A few had sprayed up onto his black brogues; there was even the glitter of it in his upturned pant cuffs.

Above him, on the balcony, two afternoon drunks yelled out apologies. They seemed unbothered by anything that *could* have happened. Nor did they seem to notice the perfect circle of glass.

Twice in one week.

Aubrey's father would have been spinning his Cunning webs as soon as the first one appeared at the auction house while he'd been talking to the copper-haired man clinging to the arm of Lawton Adler. His parents did not believe in coincidence, nor did they see every little oddity as a sign from beyond the veil. They taught Aubrey and his sisters to appreciate the strangeness in the world, and to love it. That love turned to revelry, and idolatry.

No, he was not going to fall back into those old ways of thinking. But two circles of glass in less than a week, and even he was suspicious. But it was a mystery for later.

Later never manifested.

In its place was a well-scrubbed young man of fourteen, bearing a light blue envelope in one hand, the other held out in expectation.

"Is this for me?" Aubrey asked, mildly amused by the boy's candor.

"You're Aubrey Lavigne, yeah?"

"And what gave it away?"

The boy shrugged. "Said you'd be a well-dressed, tall man with a monocle on a chain and eyes that looked like glass."

Something prickled at the back of Aubrey's neck. Emotions washed through him — delight, surprise, shock, and a single, crystal-clear icicle of fear. Ethaniel had described him perfectly. *He already knows you so well.*

"Well, then that's me," Aubrey said, laying a half-dollar on the boy's palm and snatching the envelope away.

"Said you'd be quick, too," the boy said before bustling off.

Aubrey forced himself to wait until he was in the back of the building and down two levels. Back into the Magnificus Collectio, and even further back, into The Cabinet. His office was tucked away in the corner, the door half hidden by seemingly endless bookshelves stocked with all the harmless things waiting for repair or inspection.

Aubrey forced open the creaky door, closed it, and then sat down in the leather armchair to read Ethaniel's note.

Aubrey,

I've come into a strange set of circumstances involving an item that may be interesting to you. I'm afraid I can't say much else, but if I know nothing else about you, I know your skills. Your talents. This is a delicate matter, but one of strange magic. I can't trust anyone else with it.

Please meet me at Bryant Park, the benches on the west side of the fountain. Tomorrow or the following day at ten a.m.

Send any reply back with instructions to ring the back door. I've had to ward the shop for the night.

I liked seeing you last week. I'd like to see you again.

Sincerely,

Ethaniel

Elation was a slow burn of champagne fizz in his veins, but it was tampered with caution. The glass. This note. The lack of trademark wordiness in Ethaniel's letter. It was all *wrong*.

When Aubrey came back to Alon and the book he'd been working on, he found Alon and a few other employees chortling.

"You missed it," Alon wheezed, clapping a hand on Aubrey's shoulder. "Way more intrusive than laxatives. Completely dreadful."

Aubrey shuddered. "I don't want to know." But he let Alon tell him anyway.

When Aubrey returned home that evening, he went into the little-used spare bedroom and stood before his sheet-draped altar. Despite the insistence to his parents that he no longer observed their Cunning Folk ways, Aubrey had kept the altar. Some of it was deference to the beliefs with which he'd been raised. And even his learned Hermeticism hadn't driven away every bit of the occult out of Aubrey's life. It was like when one stared up at the stars and realized that yes, those were flaming balls of gas in the vastness of the universe, but those very stars could make the night feel magical.

In essence, there was nothing wrong, in Aubrey's view, with a bit of superstition, or even awe at how magical the natural world seemed to be. After all, philosophers and priests liked to ruminate on where magic came from, but ultimately, the source didn't matter. Society had long ago accepted that some people were granted gifts, but Aubrey strongly believed real consequences came from what was done with those very gifts. So often they were squandered. And if one listened to the philosophers and priests and lawmakers, those very gifts could be dangerous; even evil. He didn't like to insert himself into the arguments that rang off bathhouse and church walls alike, but it was hard to ignore the way they'd changed over the last few years. The looming nearness of the turn of the century concocted a lot of strange fears and anxieties. Another good reason to not advertise his abilities, or his proclivities.

Slowly and with great care, Aubrey drew off the sheet and let his gaze rest on the obsidian plinth leading to a caduceus of veiny white marble. His family took their gifts seriously — it was magic, yes, but according to his mother and father, the Lavigne bloodline was *ordained* to heal the sick. If they'd been church-going folk, they might have said their gifts were God-given. And if that was the case, Aubrey's ability to mend, rather than heal, was a blaspheme upon their family.

Carefully, Aubrey put both hands on the altar, his palms flat against the cool obsidian, and closed his eyes. He considered himself a patient man in all other aspects of his life, but this small ritual always left him feeling antsy. Perhaps it was the absence of belief. Perhaps he simply could no longer shut his mind off from the slow drip of his days, filled with monotony and boredom.

Perhaps it was knowing that if he left his mind to quiet itself, he'd be shown a truth he wasn't quite ready to admit to. Yet.

Your powers are simply different, his mother had told him. *We've always had those in the family whose abilities twist and turn. You can mend materials, Aubrey. That is a unique gift. Your father's disappointment is only that — disappointment that you are not more like him. He'll come around, and when he does, you will be stronger because you will have embraced your truth.*

Aubrey squeezed his eyes shut. What his mother had said would pass never did, and he'd been left with a broken heart and an urn he took with him to New York. Why couldn't his father have stayed alive long enough to see Aubrey's powers grow...and why was he so terribly selfish in his wish to have his father back?

Aubrey shifted his stance and curled his fingers over the plinth's edges, reveling in the bite of rough stone. Obsidian had to be unpolished when used in altars; a way to ground oneself to the Earth. The first time he'd touched the obsidian, the memories of the stone had flooded back — the smell of dirt and grass, the sensation of wholeness, then a great loss as it was pried from a larger piece of stone. Stone, dirt, trees...they didn't have *memories*, so to speak. But through his ability to mend, Aubrey could sometimes sense things. It had never been easy to describe when his parents pressed for more.

All Aubrey knew was that every torn page, every shattered bit of glass, every moth-chewed scarf could tell him *something*. But this extension of his magic wasn't stable, or predictable.

The glass again, he thought as he opened his eyes and stared at the twin snakes of the caduceus. *I should have touched it, when it shattered at my feet. It could have given me something and instead, I walked away.*

He pushed away from the altar, quickly throwing the sheet back over it, and walked back downstairs. Left wondering.

His last act before heading to his study was to pen a response to Ethaniel. Overthinking the matter would only leave him pacing the halls, chasing the ghost of sleep well past the witching hour. And Ethaniel wasn't coy typically. Smart, handsome, talented, but very forthright. It had been one of the first things Aubrey had been pulled to, that down-to-earth mentality that seemed burned into Ethaniel's bones. That man could have taken his patterning talents to anyone in the city and been offered a bounty in return, but Ethaniel had stuck by his uncle's side. Dedicated, loyal, honest.

And, to put it rather bluntly, Aubrey was terribly curious. Ethaniel wouldn't write such a message for no reason.

Aubrey wrote his reply and then sent it off with one of the evening messenger services. For all the availability of quick magic, he'd rather set the envelope into a person's hand. Slowly, Aubrey walked back upstairs to the bank of windows that graced his study and stared out into the dark city, watching as lights flared to life across its expanse; tiny torches of civilization against so much black. He let the melancholy sink in, scratching its way into his mind, into his body, until he couldn't stand it any longer.

Then he threw himself into the night's work, looking for any story in his family's books so he'd stop kicking himself for not having that shard of glass.

Seven

E THANIEL

"You must let me come with you."

Ethaniel tipped his head in acknowledgement as he sealed the envelope and passed it to the messenger hopping from foot to foot at his back door. Just an hour ago, he'd gone out this same back door for some fresh air and wound up with a minor English noble carrying a strange book crashing into his life. How quickly the tides changed.

"Perhaps," he demurred, letting the boy snatch the envelope and a few bills from him before bolting down the alley. "My friend doesn't trust easily. And he's already going to be wary due to the lack of specificity in my note."

Ethaniel shut the door, bolted it, then motioned Calix back down the hall to the stairs. Calix, however, didn't budge. He hadn't let go of the satchel for one moment. "No, I *need* to come with you, Ethaniel." Determination made a thin line of Calix's pretty lips. "There is something wrong with this damn book. This whole situation." His face crumpled with worry.

"Let's start with something easy." Ethaniel wanted to reassure Calix it would all be fine, even if the uncertainty of *everything* ate at him, the teeth of that worry blunt but persistent. "My apartment is secure. I need to check on my uncle, but let's get settled somewhere more comfortable." He gave Calix what he hoped was a smile void of concern, even shifting his shoulders away from his ears a tad. Just in case Calix had an eye for body language.

Ethaniel was also bearing in mind that he did not know Calix, and had already jumped to help a complete stranger. And may have put Aubrey in harm's way because of his own need to bloody *help all the time.*

"Right. No, of course....you're right." Calix sighed and slowly uncramped his fingers from around the satchel. "There's so much swirling about in my mind and I don't feed on chaos."

Ethaniel did let his smile warm at that. "Nor do I."

He led Calix back upstairs, but did the impolite thing and let the man linger in his small living room without refreshments while he dashed over to Jeremiah rooms. When Ethaniel cracked the door to peer in on the old man, he got a soft, "You can come in," in reply.

"I was hoping you were still asleep," Ethaniel said as he went to Jeremiah's bedside. His uncle was turned on his left side, his head cradled on his arm. This position and the way the light had faded from the room made Jeremiah's white hair look ethereal. Ghostly, even. It was a sobering thought.

"I was until a few minutes ago. Turned over and heard two voices outside." Ethaniel flinched but Jeremiah tutted at him. "You were more than quiet, son. But my good hearing hasn't given up yet, so let me have it while it's still fairly sharp."

"Still, Uncle..."

"No, no. I won't...*hear* of it." While Ethaniel groaned, Jeremiah laughed, the sound showing the rusty state of his lungs. "You brought someone home? That's surprising."

Ethaniel paused. Deciding. Letting Jeremiah think Calix was a suitor would keep him in the dark — which Jeremiah would hate but would hopefully keep him safe, should this whole mess be something more difficult than a consult with Aubrey.

And that alone was going to be challenge enough.

"It's a friend," Ethaniel finally said. "We're going to have tea and talk books."

"Ah, lovely then." Jeremiah patted his hand, eyes already fluttering closed once more.

"Dinner, Uncle?"

"If you're making tea, just that and some bread."

"All right."

Ethaniel got to his feet, kissed his uncle on the brow, and then returned to Calix. The man was still rooted to the spot before the fireplace. As twilight began to show itself across the sky like an iris unfurling, Calix was cast in half-shadow, dreamlike and almost hazy. The man was so focused on the flames that he jumped when Ethaniel said, "Sit, please. No call for you to stand."

Calix shook his head. "I was terribly cold all of a sudden, so I stoked the fire." His fine throat bobbed as he swallowed. "I heard it again."

Instantly, Ethaniel was at his side. Tomorrow couldn't wait. They should go to Aubrey *tonight*—

"Just a word." Calix held up a finger. "A single word."

He had to know. "What did it say?"

Ethaniel was surrounded by ghosts — the ghost of the man across the hall, and now the ghost of Calix's proper London roll. The man sounded hollowed out as he whispered, "I'm afraid to say it out loud. The word isn't odd...but how it spoke was the way the penitent say the name of God. It was horrible. Beautiful."

"Could you write it down?" It was crawling up Ethaniel's throat, curiosity's claws in his soft tissue.

"All right."

Ethaniel quickly grabbed a pen and old handbill from his tiny desk nearby, and they sat where they had earlier. He had to keep himself from leaning forward, to see, as Calix scrawled his terrible single note.

Ethaniel read the word once, twice, at least a dozen times before looking up at Calix, confusion marring his brow.

Convergence

"It means nothing, and yet apparently something," Ethaniel finally replied, confused and deeply troubled. "Does it mean anything to you?"

"No." Calix shivered and pulled his jacket tighter to him with one hand. The other hand rested possessively on top of the satchel. "But being near it makes the world feel as if it's spinning off its axis. I feel...unmoored, like a boat that floated away from the dock with no heading."

Ethaniel wasn't going to let the poor man shiver. He went to the closet and pulled out a thick blanket, the wool scratchy but warm and in a shade the color of winter pine needles. Carefully, he draped the blanket over Calix's shoulders. The way Calix looked at him with gratitude nearly rooted Ethaniel to the spot. Ethaniel felt useless in the moment, hovering over a man who looked like he'd been hollowed out by life itself; everything crashing down on him in one short afternoon.

But dinner he could do, and Jeremiah was waiting. "I need to make something up for my uncle, and you look like you could use some tea." Ethaniel tried for a small smile, even though Calix wasn't looking his way. "Or perhaps something stronger?"

Calix's laugh was raspy and devoid of joy. "Something stronger for certain. But I'm already imposing—"

"You're not." The words came easily. He wanted to help, even if all they could do right now was wait out their meeting with Aubrey. They *should* go tonight, but he didn't think wandering about the city in the dark while clutching a satchel with gods only knew what inside was a smart move. "You're welcome to stay here or you can join me in the kitchen. It won't be anything fancy, I'm afraid, but dinner will be warm. I can guarantee that."

With that, Calix got to his feet, setting the satchel aside to fold up the blanket. "Let me help. Please." His brown eyes bore into Ethaniel now and something about the sadness on the other man's face made his protective nature flare once more. "Doing something, anything, will keep my mind from swirling into a pit of despair and self-pity. I'm a decent cook, all things considered."

"Really?" Ethaniel leaned in, pretended to peer closely at Calix. It made the other man stifle a tiny chuckle. Good, at least Calix could still laugh. "Then the help is appreciated."

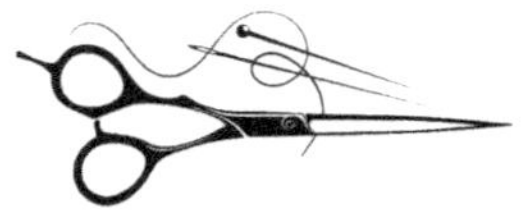

Before Ethaniel handed Calix one of the good kitchen knives, he paused, put the blade back down, and said, "I need to know something. Directly."

Calix lifted a brow but his expression remained smooth. "Certainly."

Might as well bite the bullet, as the expression went. "When we met, you didn't use any title. Yet your accent, your bearing, your manners say otherwise." Ethaniel waved a hand around the simple, but clean, kitchen. "This is not the proper place for gentry, Americanized or not."

Calix's retort was swift, precise. "Does it matter?" When Ethaniel jerked back, Calix softened his tone. "I mean that. Truly. Yes, I am titled but only because my father preferred to claim a bastard over having no male heir. I'm the only one left. I chose a different path, a different life, when I came to America about a decade ago. England might cling to the old ways, but I'd rather not, if it's all the same to you."

There were a lot of nobles in England. Many minor, some with great clout. Ethaniel still needed to know, if only for his safety and that of his uncle's. "And yet, there are enough people here whose heads will turn at a title. And even more who can be swayed by Marquis this or Lord that." Ethaniel moved closer to Calix, peering down and into the man's fathomless brown eyes. "I will help you, Calix. But my uncle is ill and needs a great deal of care. I won't risk him. I need honesty moving forward."

Calix's nostrils flared, his jaw tensed. "I've been nothing but honest with you," he replied. The very air between them simmered and it made Ethaniel suck in a tight breath. The tension wasn't...entirely unwelcome. And after Calix's panic and fear earlier, seeing some fight in the younger, slighter man set something roiling in Ethaniel's belly.

"Then be honest with me once more." Daring, perhaps stupidly, Ethaniel put his hand on Calix's shoulder. "But if you're somehow in line for the throne, let's just skip over it."

That pulled a startled laugh from Calix. "I'm not. I promise." He sighed and looked away and for a long moment, Ethaniel wondered if the man would answer. That would change things drastically between them, and he would hate it.

When Calix looked back at Ethaniel, all the tension had bled out from his face, his posture. "My mother, Lily Addington, was from a wealthy American family. She was left a house in upper New York when her parents died in a carriage accident. I loved it there, especially spending summers in the woods and in the gardens. But we always went back to England when autumn set in. Part of her arrangement with my father. To keep me close. But she and my father never married, and since I was the product of their little affair, Mother always said we should be grateful that he didn't throw us out." And like he'd practiced it for a play, Calix said, "I'm the Earl of Batherton. And if I have my way, I'm the last."

Relief flooded through Ethaniel. He wanted to sink into, to drop to the floor like a boneless puddle. Oh, any earl was wealthy enough to buy entire blocks of real estate in New York City, and the working class part of him would always squirm in discomfort around gentry. But as far as he knew, Batherton was in no way connected to the Patterners' Guild, or any guild, in London. No shipping magnate or purveyor of branded quick magic here. Just an Earl from the country. Rich, educated, probably spoiled and a little unused to the rougher side of life. But not someone who could pull the right strings and destroy the safety net Ethaniel had built over the last decade.

"You look relieved," Calix said quietly.

"I am, to be honest," Ethaniel replied, giving Calix a wan little smile. "My life here is...very carefully constructed. And the right — or, I suppose, wrong — person could destroy that."

Shaking his head, Calix said, "And I suppose I'm not this horrible person who would do such a thing?"

"So far, the worst you've done is crash into me."

Calix bit his lip. Oh, that was a fine expression on the man's delicate features. Ethaniel didn't have the time to get so distracted now but perhaps for a moment, he could visually trace the lines of Calix's brow, his cheekbones, before returning to the matters at hand.

"I brought a strange magical book into your shop. Into your home."

"By invitation," Ethaniel corrected, earning him another smile. "But that invitation isn't free, my good Earl." Calix groaned, playfully aggrieved, and Ethaniel felt like they'd been set back on mostly even ground. "Help me finish this soup and then perhaps we can have a look at that strange magical book of yours. I don't have the proper equipment to handle it, but we should at least make sure it isn't going to...set itself aflame or something awful like that."

"I don't think it will do that. Or, at least I hope not." Calix replied. "Though I'm surprised my friend didn't come looking for it." Doubt was an anchor around Calix's tone.

That didn't sound like an invitation to probe too deeply, so Ethaniel let go of Calix's shoulder and returned to the countertop where the onions that needed chopping awaited. "How exactly did your friend come to this book, by the way?"

"I've tried to figure that out myself. I *think* it was part of a lot he purchased at an auction last week. A new business venture of his." Calix came to stand next to him, hip propped against the counter and looking more at ease now that they'd cleared the air a bit. "He's...spirited, I suppose you could say. Most people who meet Lawton love or hate him, and it's easy to see why. He's a keen observer of people and has this kind of natural charm, but it can come off as flippant. He and I didn't fit in too well at boarding school, where we met. So we stuck together, supported each other. And when I left for the city, he followed."

Ethaniel set an onion onto the chopping board and cut its ends off before peeling the outer layer away. "I hear a *but* coming on."

Calix chuckled. "*But* his version of *spirited* sometimes gets him into trouble. He's vivacious and daring, and that can run afoul of the wrong people."

"Is he like you?"

There was a heavy pause and Ethaniel could feel Calix's stare. "How do you mean?"

Ethaniel cleared his throat, embarrassed. That had slipped out faster than he could reel it back in. "Nobility?"

"Ah, yes, very minorly. Most of his family are academics but there's some property and a few racing horses, that kind of thing. Lawton's always gone in the opposite direction as them." Calix looked down at the ground, scuffing at a worn spot in the floorboards with his shoe. "But his father always managed to ruin family finances with some scheme or another. If Lawton's father had stuck to being a shipping merchant, they would have been quite comfortable. But I think that left Lawton feeling 'less than' in some way. Monetarily or otherwise." He gave Ethaniel a weak smile. "He'd stuck to me like glue for a long time. It's an...odd relationship, the two of us."

Something about Calix's tone tickled the back of Ethaniel's mind. He could almost hear another layer underneath, like when he could see the base function of a pattern that made up something more complicated. The red carnation brooch the man had worn into his shop the previous week had been partially hidden by his scarves, but it had been there all the same. Common knowledge amongst people like himself knew that the brooch was a hat tip toward the queer community as a whole, but unless he saw Calix kissing another man in public, Ethaniel could only harbor a few educated guesses.

If there was anything deeper about Calix Addington, Earl of Batherton, Ethaniel was terribly curious.

"Let me," Calix said a few moments later as Ethaniel moved to cut carrots. "I can handle a knife, I promise."

Ethaniel stepped out of the way so Calix could take up his spot. He sat on the stool Calix abandoned and realized his mistake the moment Calix began to remove his jacket. The material was sumptuous but decidedly plain next to what he'd seen Calix in previously. Calix handled the garment with care and when it was dangling from his fingertips, Ethaniel held out a hand in silent offering.

In the few moments it took to place Calix's jacket over a chair by the window, Calix had rolled up one sleeve of his dark blue shirt and was working on the other. The man's forearms were shockingly muscled. Ethaniel stared. *Hard.* He shouldn't have. While shame battled with his own baser desires, Calix got his attention by clearing his throat.

Whether Calix was oblivious or playing along, Ethaniel had no clue. But he didn't hear a word of insincerity as Calix said, "Apologies. I didn't want to have my sleeves get in the way."

"No need to apologize. I was simply startled." *Amongst other things*, Ethaniel thought. "I should have offered you an apron."

"I'm perfectly content as is." Calix threw him a small smile then began to wield the knife with shocking precision against the tough fiber of the carrots.

"Right, well..." Ethaniel left Calix to his task so he could make Jeremiah a tray. He made sure to add a few extra sugar cubes into his uncle's tea; it was easier to hide the bitter taste of the pain relieving tincture the doctor had given him the prior morning. Jeremiah hated the stuff but agreed to take it only if Ethaniel came up with a way to hide the flavor. So far, the extra sugar had been working.

With his tray set and Calix slowly adding carrots to the soup pot on the small gas range, Ethaniel made his way back upstairs, only to find Jeremiah asleep once more. Clutched loosely in his right fist was a blood-flecked handkerchief. A bit of quick magic would keep the tea warm for another hour or so, but Ethaniel would feel better knowing his uncle had taken the tincture.

He woke Jeremiah up with a gentle hand at his brow. The old man snuffled and wheezed for a few moments; the sounds sent Ethaniel's heart racing. Jeremiah didn't sound well at all.

"Just some tea for now?" Ethaniel asked as Jeremiah blinked awake. "I brought the bread and some jam, but I know you're not always hungry when you first wake."

"You fuss too much over me," Jeremiah grumbled through a hoarse voice, and even though he sounded like he'd swallowed gravel, Ethaniel had to chuckle at that. Jeremiah wouldn't stop grousing about Ethaniel's *fussing* until he was gone, so any attempt on his uncle's part at his usual tone made him feel a bit better. "You dosed my tea again?"

"Of course I did. Extra sugar tonight, even."

"Ah, well." Jeremiah smacked his lips and slowly sat up, then reached for the cup Ethaniel brought over. "Let's get it over with." He barely winced as he sipped the tea, but followed every swallow with a bite of bread. It was good to see Jeremiah eating.

"Let me get you a clean one." Ethaniel plucked up the blood-stained handkerchief as Jeremiah ate. "I'll be right back." Jeremiah didn't protest, much to Ethaniel's relief.

Leaving his uncle's bedside to go to the linen closet gave Ethaniel a moment to pause. He leaned against the cold wall and closed his eyes, but regretted it the moment he did. The pattern he'd seen when he'd dropped his sight over Calix's book returned, swimming sickeningly in the dark behind his eyelids. Colors flashed — green, purple, red — and the seemingly infinitesimal pattern churned. Ethaniel's stomach heaved and he gasped, flinging his arms back so he could press his palms to the wall and grind his fingertips into the rough plaster.

Pain was good for shaking loose from a pattern; the bite of tiny points into his skin made Ethaniel suck in a breath and immediately, the flashes began to fade.

Logically, Ethaniel could blame the lack of sleep over the past few nights as he neared Jeremiah's bedside. He'd also been working more, taking on more projects. The stress of seeing Aubrey again. The stress of what — and who — had crashed into his life today.

Logic could explain all of it.

Ethaniel *knew* it was the book. He needed to try to look at it once more, and now that he knew what to expect, maybe he could get a little closer. Aubrey could admonish him on the morrow about lacking training in handling questionable magical items. Lord knew Aubrey was the city's foremost expert who had actually written the manual used by other artifact researchers.

Calix had been near the book for hours, and while it had made him rather dizzy and nauseated, nothing worse than that had happened. And he hadn't felt any ill effects himself. There were a few still-active dampening cloths in the back room, tucked away for when an embroidery pattern went awry and Ethaniel needed to undo the work. It would probably be enough.

Determination set in his step and in his mind, Ethaniel pushed away from the wall, got Jeremiah settled once more, and went into the kitchen. Calix was standing over the stove, wooden spoon in hand, peering down at the soup. Steam from the near-boiling pot left the hair at his temple clinging to his skin, and even from the doorway, Ethaniel could see the flush in Calix's cheeks. Calix was a beautiful man. Knowing Calix's peerage, and the conflicted feelings that brought up in him, couldn't hide the man's beauty. And Ethaniel could stare later, when there weren't so many questions hovering about in the air like troublesome fruit flie s.

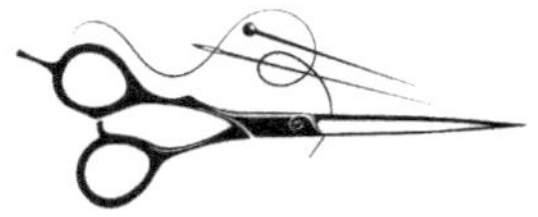

"Are you certain?"

Ethaniel shook his head. "Not entirely. But I do count myself lucky you haven't run off and left me with the problem and the question of the thing."

Calix looked scandalized at the suggestion. "I would never! I brought this trouble to your doorstep, I should be the one—" And he motioned at the satchel that now sat on the table between them. Moving to the small study had been Calix's idea and Ethaniel's aching body was grateful for the comfort of the big fireplace and worn but clean armchairs.

"I can see the patterns, Calix."

"But I should be able to—" Calix huffed and crossed his arms. "It spoke to me. Shouldn't I be the one to try?"

"What we should do is stuff the thing into the cellar and wait for Aubrey's reply," Ethaniel said, his tone more terse than he meant. "Apologies. It's been a long day."

"No, no. Don't apologize to me. But...Aubrey?" Now Calix sat forward, hands gripping the armrests. "Aubrey Lavigne? He's a curator of some sort at Darwin's Attic."

Amongst other things, Ethaniel thought. The bitterness of their argument had long faded into a soft yearning, but he doubted he'd be able to think about the place without that tiny taste of salt. "You know Aubrey?" he asked, startled.

"No, we've only met once. But we met at the auction Lawton won the books from." Calix's brown eyes were now glued to the satchel as his words dripped into the space between them. "That...thing was probably in that lot. And I met Aubrey that day and you know Aubrey and that's...honestly, that's a tad too much coincidence for me, Ethaniel."

Ethaniel covered his mouth with his hand as he thought. Coincidence wasn't something he personally believed in. The world and its idiosyncrasies, magical or not, were more than strange enough. But he couldn't shake the sensation that Calix had the right of it. This was all far too odd to be mere happenstance.

Ethaniel watched Calix twist his hands together as his gaze grew distant. "Coincidence or not," he said slowly, "Aubrey is extremely talented and knowledgeable. He'll be able to help. The other option, is of course, to simply return the book back to your friend."

The moment he made the suggestion, Ethaniel knew it was the wrong one. The question of those beautiful, terrifying patterns would haunt him, but ultimately, it wasn't his business.

Right?

"I can't do that," Calix replied. "Lawton's...I don't know what he's done but all this shady business. The book, the money, the woman I saw him talking to at the auction. Being chased by that man. Lawton not coming back around to try to find the book. Or me."

Ethaniel sucked in a breath. The pain in Calix's voice was evident. He felt betrayed, left to fend for himself by someone he called *friend*. That kind of wound stung more than most. "Then stay here tonight. I know it's not a plush apartment or brownstone, but the wards will hold until morning."

Relief seemed to hollow Calix out, making him curl forward and hang his head until his entire body drooped. "Thank you. You are..." He looked up at Ethaniel with those pretty brown eyes. "You are far too kind."

A few replies came to mind but the moment was snapped in half by the buzz of the back door bell. Ethaniel made quick excuses to Calix and took the stairs at a jog. He didn't want to leave the messenger outside for too long, or so he told himself. The eagerness in his steps belied something else, but Ethaniel dashed all that aside to carefully unseal the door's ward and poke his head into the alley.

The messenger was a tall, thin young man with dark hair, probably barely eighteen, and he wore a heavy black scarf around his neck that he fussed with while Ethaniel dug in his pocket for a few coins. There were no lights in most of the alleys in this part of the city, but the light spilling out from his doorway circled the boy's lean face like a halo.

Out of curiosity more than anything else, Ethaniel said, "Did you pass anyone as you came into the alley? A big man, perhaps, muscled like a boxer?"

"Nah. No one really out, guv." The boy motioned to the darkness around him. "Don't know. It's weird tonight."

"How so?"

The boy shrugged. "Don't know. Just a feeling."

Ethaniel couldn't do much with a feeling, but on some level he understood. He gave the boy an extra coin, thanked him, and immediately shut, bolted, and warded the door once more. He took the letter from Aubrey upstairs, not even glancing at it until he was seated across from Calix once more.

It was clearly Aubrey's hand that had so gracefully written Ethaniel's name on the front. He could almost feel every scratch of the pen on the page, how Aubrey never paused when penning his name and every word on the thick cream paper inside.

Ethaniel,

Your note intrigues me, as I'm sure you knew it would. And I'm honored you would trust me with something that seems to be a rather delicate situation. Please be careful with this 'strange magic', but I know you will. Because of your immense skill and your calm disposition and how much you care.

Because I know you, Ethaniel.

Let us meet tomorrow at the time and place you have chosen. If this strange magic is an item, I don't wish for it to be out in public for too long. Dampen it as best you can and bring it along, but also do what you can to hide it from sight. It is likely we'll need to take it to the museum. I'll prepare ahead of time, should that need arise.

I've missed you.

Sincerely,

Aubrey

"Any luck?" Calix asked after Ethaniel refolded the note and set it on his lap.

"He'll meet with me," Ethaniel replied as he rubbed his thumb along the edge of the note.

"With us, you mean."

Ethaniel didn't see a choice in the matter, not anymore. "With us."

INTERLUDE

LAWTON

Things with Tomas were going about as fine as Lawton had figured. Tomas was suspicious by nature. Every fence Lawton had ever met stared at the world through narrowed eyes, but Tomas was a different sort.

Prone to violence more than blackmail or sabotage.

But his muscled thugs were slow, big men reliant on their strength and not lean, agile creatures like him. And Calix.

This had been the backup plan all along, but seeing the fear and confusion on Calix's face as Lawton slammed the four-inch blade through Tomas's hand had sent a wave of guilt through him. Calix had been insurance against Tomas getting violent, but it hadn't quite worked.

Because of that damn book. The very one Cassandra wanted delivered to her at precisely eleven a.m. No sooner, and certainly not a minute late. And Tomas had agreed to meet, but only at ten. Everyone's fucking demands were standing between him and enough cash to pay off his gambling debts. Every last one of them.

But priorities first.

Lawton shoved the satchel into Calix's arms and told him to run. Calix was the only person in the world he would trust with the book, and now that Lawton had drawn first blood, he would be the one ducking fists and dodging blades. He was a lot of things, self-sacrificing not being one of them. But he wouldn't stand the thought of Calix being hurt.

Their gazes locked for a moment that felt like forever, but then Lawton shoved Calix toward the back of the shop while he went to the front. And then he lost sight of Calix as both of Tomas's thugs lunged at him while Tomas snarled and wailed in pain and rage behind him.

Losing all three men giving chase would take smarts. And Lawton had already mentally mapped an escape route, but it relied on good timing and a bit of luck. Being chased in the Village would lead to having the authorities summoned, and he wasn't about to chance that.

Instead, Lawton burst out of the shop and onto the rough cobblestoned street that was Babylon Boulevard, veering left, then left again down a narrow alley while heavy footfalls pounded behind him. Just as Lawton reached the west edge of the Boulevard, the distinct — and terrifying — sound of a gun being cocked hit his ears.

A gun? A bloody gun? How very...American.

Fear was a real thing at the back of his throat, pushing him to run harder, faster. Just as the first shot rang out. Guns were terribly inaccurate at the best of times, so while Lawton wasn't surprised to remain upright and whole, he wasn't nearly out of danger yet. All his carefully laid plans were crumbling with every second, so Lawton did the one thing he was good at, even more so than charming people.

Surviving.

Up ahead, a thick metal door creaked open and a bald man in a blood-stained apron stepped out, cigarette halfway to his lips. Lawton rushed forward and grabbed the man by the shoulders.

"Sorry, mate," he said as he shoved the man into the alley, giving a swift kick to the trashcan by the door for good measure. Anything to distract his pursuers would be useful right now. Lawton dove inside the building, taking in the sounds of knives on countertops and the murmur of conversation, then raced to the front of what turned out to be a butcher shop. The smell was truly terrible and Lawton sucked in a lungful of air a bit too hastily. His eyes watered as he coughed, but he dove into the crowded shop front, pushing past men in torn overcoats and women in bedraggled bonnets, ignoring the few people who shouted after him.

As Lawton dashed onto the busy sidewalk, he chanced a look back. He'd lost the two thugs but Tomas was quickly barreling through that same crowd in the butcher's.

Far too close for his liking. Foolish, perhaps, to continue to run and risk a collision with a carriage; a collision he'd certainly lose. But the carriages weren't his target.

"Sir! Sir! A man with a gun is robbing that butcher's!" Lawton yelled, hoping he looked frantic enough that the mounted policeman plodding along the street would stop. He pointed a shaking finger toward the butcher's and the policeman, a lean man with a thick, black handlebar mustache, whirled around, hand going immediately to the club at his belt.

Score one for the bravery of a policeman carrying only a blunt weapon, thinking of going up against a man like Tomas with a gun.

"Please help!" Lawton yelled, drawing onlookers. The timing couldn't have been better. A scream rose up from the butcher's and the policeman spurred his horse forward. Giving Lawton the out he needed as one...two...three shots rang out and a man yelled for help.

Ten minutes later, he was unlocking the back door to Dodge's ground-level apartment, pointedly ignoring the sweat trickling down his spine. A horrible feeling, truly, and it made him shudder as the cool dark of the kitchen enveloped him.

Dodge was an old friend, one of the first people Lawton had met down at the horse racing tracks a few months after he'd immigrated from England. Lawton had quit that habit when he'd finally found a few decent gambling dens in which to wile away the hours, but Dodge earned his entire living betting on the ponies. So while his friend was out trading bills for slips of paper and cheering on his horses from the sidelines, Lawton was finally alone. And safe.

Lawton sat on the floor, back to the wall, and sighed. He had fucked up royally, as Dodge would say. Now he had no deal for the antique books, which meant no money. And he had no book for the Golden Order, after spending their money. And Cassandra was expecting him soon.

He was fucked.

Lawton let himself wallow in his misery, a hippopotamus in a puddle of shit of his own making.

Time for a plan, one that would help him find Calix and that damned book.

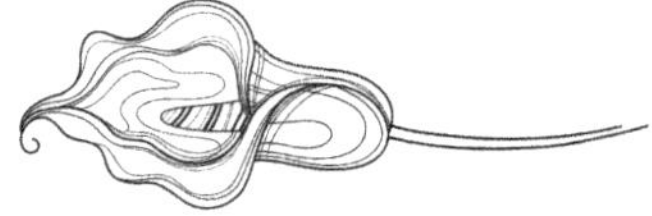

That same night

"What do you mean you can't find him?" Lawton forced himself to unclench his jaw as he stared at the blonde-haired man standing in his parlor. "You told me you could find anyone. I gave you Calix's scarf. You *assured me* he would be found."

The man shook his head. "I didn't give any assurances, Mr. Adler. You can talk to Ms. Spurrington about whatever she might have promised you. There's no trace of your friend, or the artifact, anywhere in the Village. I suggest checking other parts of the city."

The man paused, giving Lawton time to fume as his mind raced. Calix was a creature of habit. After the *mishap* with Tomas, Lawton knew the book would be safe with Calix. He had figured Calix would head home, because when his friend panicked, he fled to certain safety.

Or so he believed. Clearly something else was going on. And all Lawton knew at this point was that the Golden Order's mage had failed, which meant his handler would be displeased. Not at the mage, of course, but at Lawton.

He had failed. Spectacularly.

That damn book, he thought as he dismissed the mage with a wave. "Fine," Lawton bit out. "But I'm deeply displeased."

The blonde man laughed. "Good for you. Not much you can do about it, though." He walked out with a cheeky wave and the impertinence only fueled Lawton's rage. The temptation to throw something — that vase in the corner, the book on the table, his half-empty glass of brandy — was strong. But Cassandra would be here any moment and he couldn't afford to appear ruffled in front of her.

Cassandra Spurrington was terrifying. Lawton would never admit it out loud, of course. But the woman screamed *authority* with a single look and after he'd learned how close she was to the head of the Golden Order, well...he knew better than to cross her.

Which meant tonight he had to turn on all the charm and spin his story perfectly. Otherwise, the consequences would be his alone and he might lose any chance at being ingratiated even further into the Order. He only had so much leeway in his temperament for failure, and things of late had been pushing him to the edge.

His only relief had been Calix. Sweet, tempting, pliable Calix and his soft eyes and plush mouth. Lawton shuddered, remembering the feel of Calix's hair between his fingers and the heat in those brown eyes as Calix stared up at him. Lawton let his eyes close as the memory — and the sensation of it — rushed through him.

Calix's mouth, his lips, his sinful tongue. The dents in Lawton's skin from how Calix gripped him, holding him so tightly. As if Calix were afraid he'd leave. How the gas sconces flickered, casting them both in velvet shadow. The sweep of Calix's eyelashes against his cheeks.

"Lawton."

Lawton's eyes snapped open. Cassandra Spurrington stood in the doorway to the parlor, dressed in her trademark pinstriped suit, arms crossed and her gaze intense. Everything about Cassandra was intense, at all times. He'd personally witnessed people cross the street to get out of the way.

If only they knew who she was, and who she worked for, Lawton thought as he gave Cassandra a tight smile. "Please come in."

Without a word of acknowledgement, Cassandra strode into the room and took the chair to the right of the fire. It placed her back to the wall instead of the door; a move Lawton had noticed at their very first meeting. Cassandra was still an enigma to him, but some of her behaviors were highly evident of a person constantly on alert.

"Tell me what happened with the book," she said as Lawton sat across from her. "Don't leave anything out."

Lawton had thought long and hard about how he wanted to approach this story. Spinning his own version of events meant placing the blame at the feet of a few — that haughty man who tried to outbid him at the auction, Tomas and his thugs. He didn't want to involve Calix in all of this, but considering he had possession of the book (and hopefully did still), Lawton saw no choice.

Cassandra listened with a stony expression until Lawton mentioned the other bidder. "What did he look like?" she asked, tipping her chin up.

"Tall, lean, impeccably dressed if I might say so. Close-cut hair, high cheekbones, dark skin." Lawton tapped his fingers on the armrest for a moment, remembering. "He carried a teakwood cane—"

"Tipped with gold? Silver rings on his fingers?"

Lawton raised an eyebrow at that. "Yes. You know this man?"

Cassandra didn't look so much as nonplussed. She nodded and said, "Aubrey Lavigne. I'm not surprised. He's been an occasional thorn in our side, but usually doesn't get in our way."

"Perhaps not so much happenstance this time, Cassandra. He offered me double what I paid for the lot for one book."

Now he had her attention. "Did Mr. Lavigne mention which one he desired?" When Lawton shook his head, Cassandra sighed. "There's a chance he was after the grimoire, but we can't be certain. The lot we had you purchase contained more than one magical book." She made a circular motion with her hand, cunning gaze fixed back on Lawton. "Tell me the rest. And don't lie to me, Lawton. I want to know precisely how you lost the grimoire."

Something inside Lawton squirmed. He wasn't a man to fidget, but Cassandra managed to make him feel insignificant with a glance and a few words. And her request to know the whole story, instead of demanding to know what happened in the immediacy of the day's events, made his palms sweat.

With a deep breath in, Lawton continued his story. "Our appointment at eleven was at the forefront of my mind, so I was determined to finish my business beforehand. Taking Calix with me was a precaution, as the book dealer who accosted me — quite unusual for him, I must say — is best dealt with if a witness is there."

Cassandra held up her hand. "Get to the point, Lawton. You couch your words in a manner that removes you from the situation, as if you're only a bystander. You went to this bookseller to do your personal business. Fine. Why did you relinquish the grimoire from your care?"

Lawton tried not to show frustration. *She wants the whole story, then interrupts me. Fine.* "Tomas, the bookseller, has a quick eye. He spotted the grimoire in my bag and tried to take it. His thugs attempted to strong-arm my friend and I when I wouldn't turn the book over, so I had to think fast. I told Calix to run, gave him the book, and then split with him the other way."

Cassandra's one word rang out in the room. Even the fire couldn't abate the chill in the air. "Why?"

By this point, Lawton's nails were biting into his palms. The pain grounded him, even as panic started to set in. Cassandra could do anything to him, per the Order's rules. She was his handler. The retrieval of the grimoire had come from on high. Lawton took another deep breath and said, "Because I trust Calix. I know him on every level. I knew he would circle back to find me, or go to his home and send a messenger to track me down. When nothing of the sort happened, I called for an Order mage to find him. But the mage said—"

"I know what he said because he waited outside your building to tell me," Cassandra cut in. "Rian is one of our best. And he said there was no trace of your friend or the grimoire. It would take immensely powerful magic to block that book from a tracking spell." The look she gave Lawton cut right through him. "Does your friend have any abilities?"

The one thing Lawton swore he would never do was rat on Calix. Even after all these years, he was certain Calix hadn't been fully honest with him after explaining it as "mostly indecipherable near-dreams" that sometimes were useful in a pedestrian sort of way. But Lawton had no evidence to the contrary; if Calix ever had those "near-dreams" about Lawton, he'd never said a word.

"No," Lawton said with a sad little head shake. It was only mostly for show. He didn't *want* to lie to Cassandra, but any magic of Calix's wouldn't have been able to block magic like Rian had found. So the lie didn't hurt anything. "Other than being preternaturally beautiful."

Cassandra didn't so much as crack a smile. "Does he know anyone who could work that kind of warding magic?" When Lawton shook his head again, Cassandra's gaze narrowed. Lawton felt as though someone had dropped him into a meat locker. "That makes my job more difficult, but so be it. We can't keep track of everyone in the city, not without more funding."

While Lawton puzzled over that statement, Cassandra stood to stand before the fire, her back to the room and him. Her black-gloved hands were clasped at the small of her back, and with her ramrod straight posture, she was even more intimidating. "Tomorrow, you'll track down your friend and get the book back. Bring it to me immediately, with absolutely no delay. Do this, and we'll forget this cock-up of yours. Retrieving the book is your primary job."

Her tone brooked no argument. Lawton wasn't entirely sure he even had a good one, as much as some part of him was itching for a fight. *Something* to relieve the tension he could feel through his entire body.

"It'll be done," Lawton said. *Show her no fear. Cassandra latches onto fear like a hunting dog with a fox's trail. Well, old boy, you're the fox right now.* "But if I'm going up against wards, surely you have some way for me to break them or even see through them? As much as I adore you magical lot, I don't have an ounce in me."

Cassandra didn't move as she replied. "If your friend is as trustworthy as you say — and he must be, since you gave him the book — he'll have it. Don't forget your place, Lawton. You've yet to be fully ordained. Do this, and you will be."

Fury, whiplash fast and hotter than iron, made Lawton bite the inside of his cheek. The sharp pain made him focus, but no amount of pain would shake Cassandra's words out of his mind. Wasn't he already good enough, having dedicated the last year of his life to helping the Order? Courting influence at parties with the names on everyone's lips, getting pivotal Order members invited to other parties to do their own courting. Hells, even stooping so low as to run their errands, like with this damnable book. Cassandra had massaged his ego a little by saying the job had come directly from Vincent de Laine, the head of the Golden Order himself. At the time, Lawton had been proud, but now it felt cheap and bitter. And when he did find Calix tomorrow and got the book into Cassandra's hands, it would only be a hollow victory.

The withered hand of envy and jealousy threatened to scratch at old scars deep inside him. But maybe he needed it now, something to latch onto so he could be done with this entire fucking asinine errand boy job. Lawton's fingers sought out the gold pin on the inside of his jacket and remembered how Calix had asked after it.

Any thought of Calix right now besieged him with worry.

"Consider it done," Lawton bit out.

"Good." Cassandra left the spot before the fireplace to pin him with her stare once more. "If you arrive at the Bleeker Street office after noon, you can wait until I'm available. You cannot leave that book with anyone else."

Lawton stared hard back. "Surely they're all Order employees, considering it's an Order office?"

"Only me, Adler." She was serious, clearly, using his last name like that. "And this meeting is over."

Cassandra walked out of his house without so much as a terse farewell.

Lawton waited until he was certain she'd departed before walking over to the wall and punching it. He whipped around, breathing through the pain as he stared at the blood welling on his knuckles. Then he went upstairs to his bedroom with one goal in mind — the little black book locked away in his bedside drawer. Two decades of parties and faires, ballrooms and barrooms, had given Lawton plenty of chances to wield his formidable charm. The contacts he'd built up and maintained over that time gave him an in with almost every aspect of New York City society.

And right now, he needed a very special kind of magic user.

FOLIO TWO:

An Oracle's Binding

*"**Magic** can be learned, but it must be learned by those of sound **mind** and **body**, ones who seek to **elevate** themselves and others like them. Today's...conveniently magical world provides nothing but **frivolities** and fleeting **pleasures**. The Golden Order will **change** that, to secure peace and safety for **all**."*
- Vincent de Laine, in a speech to new graduates of The Golden Order

EIGHT

AUBREY

The next morning

Aubrey's colleagues hadn't questioned why their curator had cordoned off the storeroom of the Magnificus Collectio, and for that Aubrey was grateful. Only the researchers and junior curators, like Alon, even knew of the existence of their store room, since they were the only ones aside from Aubrey trained in the proper methods of indexing, labeling, and restoring the items.

And as the Collectio's first, and so far only, curator, Aubrey had the clout and favors to trade on when he told the Collectio's executive management that he would need to inform the staff to be ready to evacuate. Magnus Durnshee, the only person Aubrey reported to, had raised an eyebrow at that. But Magnus also understood that Aubrey would never ask unless it was necessary.

The only thing Magnus had wanted to know was if the item Aubrey was bringing in was alive. And Aubrey couldn't properly answer that. Magnus had nodded once, then pulled a sealed lead box from the safe and handed Aubrey a warding glyph. It was a piece of black tourmaline polished and shaped into a rectangle roughly the length of Aubrey's palm, and with it, Aubrey could activate every ward on the building. Or take them down, depending on the situation. Those wards were the museum's way of containing errant magic and could, from everything Aubrey understood, protect the entire block from any kind of magical explosions, fires, or other catastrophes.

And now, as Aubrey pulled on his coat and made to leave out the museum's back door, his hand went into his vest pocket. There beside his velvet-wrapped monocle was the warding glyph. Whatever it was that Ethaniel had to show him, Aubrey could only hope it was harmless. Aside from the obvious danger of dealing with any unknown magical item or artifact, the thought of putting anyone at risk made his stomach clench.

Thinking of Ethaniel in harm's way made Aubrey want to vomit. On the heels of that feeling was the one thing he'd uttered to himself every night since their argument last autumn.

You owe him a proper apology. On bent knee and begging. Because you miss him dearly and he deserves so much better, and yet selfishly you can't let him go.

Maybe he'd get that chance today.

Aubrey took the streetcar from the northeast edge of the Village to Bryant Park. He chose the one that followed along Sixth Avenue, instead of the more tourist route following Fifth. His entire body felt itchy and restless, and Aubrey was in no mood for a trolley packed with gawkers and hangers-on. Instead, as he watched the neighborhood slowly pass by from his seat on a hard metal bench, Aubrey was alone save for a man in a sharp blue suit at the front and two young women in brightly hued walking dresses near the back.

With no major distractions at hand, Aubrey closed his eyes to focus. Last night's meditation hadn't helped him sleep, but it had brought a sense of clarity over his morning tea and toast. The temptation to wear his father's medallions to meet Ethaniel had been almost too much as Aubrey dressed, but he'd shaken it off like an irksome insect. The medallions were gold and silver, oxidized copper and well-worn bronze, all meant to protect and provide. Maybe, at one point long ago, they had given his father strength or energy. But now they were reminders of the man Aubrey had adored as a child, and how bitter their relationship had become after that same man had turned on him.

You can do this, Aubrey reminded himself once again as the streetcar's bell rang overhead, signaling a track change. *Whatever Ethaniel has to show you, you can handle it readily. Ethaniel trusts you. Needs you. Be there for him.*

The bell rang again ten minutes later and Aubrey exited the streetcar before it came to a full stop. Bryant Park was a half a block away, and even from here the green of new grass blazed against the stone grays and mud browns of the city. Aubrey skirted a few puddles between the footworn boards of the sidewalk, eclipsing the strolling couples arm in arm and drawing a few looks as he hurried by. Most of the time, it was his height that drew such attention. If he were hurrying to the park at sundown, he knew he would draw looks from those wondering if Aubrey was on his way to a *raison d'etre* near the fountains; a well known meeting spot for men looking for male company.

None of that mattered at the moment, because just beyond the park gates sat the famous Bryant Park fountain. And to the west of the massive bowl-like fountain and seated on a bench across from it was Ethaniel. Aubrey's heart hammered, as if it had forgotten the sight of Ethaniel behind his shop counter last week. As if Aubrey's attempt at conversation hadn't been stilted.

But Ethaniel wasn't alone. His head was tipped down toward a shorter, leaner man with copper-streaked hair and dressed in demure navy and gray. When the other man tilted his face up to Ethaniel, Aubrey's heart nearly stopped.

He knew that man.

Beautiful. Young. Dressed in fairly formal attire but glinting with jewelry at his throat and on his fingers.

The Earl of Batherton.

They'd been at the same auction not a fortnight ago. And this man was friends with that odious malcontent who wouldn't take Aubrey's (or rather, the Collectio's) money for the diary of a court mage. Yes, the book had been merely historical in interest, but Aubrey had been excited to read it. The question of why Calix's friend hadn't taken Aubrey's offer had been a small one, and it had been temporarily forgotten when he had been too occupied with the near-perfect glass circle left when Calix had dropped a bottle.

Aubrey had always treated glass circles with the same amused vexation as things like the Death tarot card. Neither meant what most thought — clarity, or reflection in the case of glass, and death for...Death. That was where the amusement came in, as if the gods were having a laugh at poor humanity's expense. The Death card meant change, transformation. Not always the best time in one's life, but it rarely ever meant actually dying. And glass in a circle, especially spontaneous and random, rarely meant finding an answer. So much like that dreaded Death card in some readings, the glass meant reflection. Self-awareness. What was reflected wasn't always positive, but like Death, it gave the person looking for answers a warning and a path forward. Whether they chose to act on it rested solely on the individual.

But Cunning Folk, particularly healers, saw glass as betrayal. A broken glass was of no use to anyone, so his mother had said many times, and it signified the shattering of a whole. Of the self, of a relationship, of even one's whole identity. It was change, yes. A death, in some ways. But it was almost always negative.

Those meanings warred within him still as he watched Calix laugh at something Ethaniel said. Aubrey's stomach was full of razors then, jealous and bitter and angry at himself for not being better to Ethaniel.

He felt brittle. Glass on the edge of a table, waiting to be tipped.

Aubrey shoved his hands in his pockets, reaching for the black tourmaline piece as he proceeded through the park gates. Winter's chill had unclenched its fist from around the city and the first sprigs of spring green were pushing up through black-brown dirt around the tall elms scattered amongst the park's paths. Soon, the park would be full to bursting as spring courting began and the gowns and ascots would vie for the gaze of others next to lilacs and tulips and hydrangea. And Aubrey would avoid this place, and many others, like the plague while most strolled in the sunshine. The world may be advancing, but someone preferring his own company was still seen as some kind of...errant behavior.

Well, it wasn't the worst *errant* behavior he'd partaken in, but that wasn't anyone's business but his own and his partner's.

Ethaniel had been his last partner. That wound was open once more, flowing freely and unwilling to be staunched as Aubrey stared at Ethaniel. Surely one of them would see him at some point. But Ethaniel and Calix were so deep in their conversation that Aubrey got to within mere feet before he caught Calix's gaze.

Both men shot to their feet, but only Calix's face registered surprise. Ethaniel's expression remained neutral, but the fleeting edges of a smile he'd given Calix trembled at the corners of his lips. Aubrey wanted to see Ethaniel's smile once more, but not here, not now. Not with so much uncertainty clinging to the very air between them.

"You came," Ethaniel said. He sounded relieved.

Aubrey nodded, trying to appear unaffected by simply being in Ethaniel's presence. He could maintain the stalwart facade for a few more minutes, surely. "Of course I did. Intriguing mystery aside, I'm not someone to go back on my word."

"You are not," Ethaniel agreed, now letting Aubrey see a bit of that smile.

Calix sucked in a breath and stuck out his hand before saying, "Mr. Lavigne. It's good to see you again."

Aubrey took the proffered hand, not wanting to appear rude as he remained quiet. Attempting to unscramble his thoughts — spooling out, like insect feelers or the roots of a tree — made things even harder to parse. There were too many questions and not enough answers and they were out in the open.

"I admit I'm surprised it's you, Mr. Addington," Aubrey replied finally. "But you'll have to pardon my hesitance with this situation. It is nothing personal. This is one of those instances where the world feels quite small."

"Aubrey worries," Ethaniel said quietly. "And his cautious nature is a boon for us, especially now." Ethaniel's glance his way and how his shoulder brushed Aubrey's made Aubrey shiver.

He wanted to scoff at himself. A little bit of contact and he was biting the inside of his cheek, ready to prostrate himself at Ethaniel's feet.

"Well, I..." Aubrey trailed off, shoving his hands into his pockets once more and feeling for the tourmaline and the velvet bag where his monocle waited. "I'm not about to examine anything out in the open, but I can get an idea easily enough. Where is this item?"

Calix tightened his hand on the satchel over his shoulder. "Here. But..." He looked around and Aubrey saw panic there. Genuine fear.

"Stay as you are, Mr. Addington," Aubrey said, trying to sound soothing. "You could sit back down, if you like."

"Let's do that." Ethaniel drew Calix back to the bench, but Aubrey could tell his attention was fractured, too. His gaze darted around, as if daring someone to take too much of an interest in the three of them. Aubrey did notice one woman staring their way, but from her disdainful sniff in their direction, she was likely more worried about their proclivities than what Calix had hidden away in his satchel. Aubrey quickly slipped on his monocle, making sure to tighten the chain around his neck, and gave the woman a cursory glance. No magic. Nothing of interest.

"Why don't you tell Calix about the museum, Ethaniel?" Aubrey murmured as he adjusted the monocle's lenses. From the outside, anyone looking at the monocle wouldn't see a difference. The trick was in the pattern of taps he gave the monocle's gold rim; each one switched the lens, giving Aubrey different insights into any object.

One tap: a simple focused glass lens, for closer examination.

Two taps: a lilac-tinted lens to allow for observation of any curses or traps.

Three taps: forest green, to look for patterns.

Aubrey got no further than three taps. As soon as the lens clicked into place, he was blinded. Pain seared through his head and Aubrey cursed, ripping the monocle away and squeezing his eyes shut.

As he hunched over, palms pressed against the sockets, Aubrey heard Calix let out a shocked cry. But it was Ethaniel's hands on his knees (and they were Ethaniel's, they would be no one else's), that drew Aubrey back into the moment. His head ached and he felt as though he'd stared directly into the sun. He gave a casual bit of worry to his vision, but the tears streaming down his face told him at least something was still working.

"Aubrey," Ethaniel said softly. "I'm here."

"I know," Aubrey managed to choke out. He let his left hand drop and Ethaniel grabbed it. Ethaniel was a lifeline, a beacon, and with that single touch, Aubrey felt *safe*. It wasn't a feeling he was used to, or even comfortable with in most situations, but as the burning behind his eyes receded, Aubrey knew Ethaniel wouldn't leave his side.

He'd been so, so foolish. With Ethaniel, with their connection. He'd wiped away the trust they'd built with a single misguided statement that had, like the proverbial stone gathering moss down a hill, become something out of control and impossible to dodge.

Aubrey felt like a horrible cliche, having a moment of realization when the man he loved had saved him once again. But here he was. Here they were.

"Fuck," Aubrey bit out. "We need to get out of the open. Ethaniel, can you—"

Another hand wrapped around Aubrey's arm. "To the museum, then?" Calix asked. "We're drawing a bit of attention."

Aubrey nodded. His eyes were still clamped shut but with only his head ringing from pain, he thought he could chance opening his eyes. "Pretend you're comforting me," Aubrey said as he leaned into Calix's strength.

"Won't have to pretend," Calix replied and tightened his grip on Aubrey's arm.

For once, Aubrey had no reply, but the kindness felt like a shot to the heart.

He let Calix help him to his feet, took the handkerchief Ethaniel offered, and turned away to wipe his eyes. "I've never experienced anything like that," Aubrey said as he let himself be guided out of the park. Noticing how Calix steered them to a less-used path instead of through the front gates (and noting what that meant about the other man's familiarity with the place), Aubrey directed his next words to Calix. "I'm assuming you didn't just stumble across this item, whatever it is."

"In a strange way, I did," Calix replied, gently moving Aubrey to the sidewalk. Ethaniel was close, hovering at Aubrey's left shoulder, and it made Aubrey feel safer. But out in the open, Calix had to let Aubrey's arm go and the loss almost made him protest.

Aubrey may not have thought much of the man when they'd first met, but his care and concern was touching. And his comment about the item left Aubrey intensely curious. The thrill of the unknown rose up in him, swift and ready to bite, to clamp down on him.

Aubrey glanced over at Ethaniel, who nodded. "It's quite the story, Aubrey."

"I'm certain it is." His eyes still stung, but he could see enough to point left to the next street. "Here, then a right, then a left on Lexington. It's not far."

"I'm getting a carriage," Ethaniel said, his tone serious, deep-set hazel eyes gone dark and brow furrowed in a way that made Aubrey's fingers itch to *touch*. "You're exhausted and shouldn't be on your feet."

"I'm grateful for that," Aubrey replied. *And for you.*

Aubrey's eyes returned mostly to normal on the short ride over, though the jostling over uneven streets didn't help his headache. He and Calix were on one seat, Ethaniel on the opposite. And the satchel was still secure around Calix's torso, his death-knuckle grip even tighter now. Aubrey couldn't resist glaring a little at the cursed bag. He had his doubts about Calix Addington, but even more about the item secreted away inside that leather satchel.

Perhaps it was when Calix paid for the carriage — paying over Aubrey's rather terse objections, mind you. Or it may have been when, like some kind of spy from a dime novel, Calix hovered near Aubrey's elbow during the short walk from the carriage to the museum's back doors.

But it became clear as day to Aubrey that Calix felt a sense of duty, of responsibility, to both he and Ethaniel. For...bringing the artifact into their lives? For causing hassle for Ethaniel and pain for him? The exact motivation eluded Aubrey, but he was certain Calix wanted to *protect them*.

An odd thing, for a wealthy white man to feel so honor-bound to him, a black man, and Ethaniel, who was the son of a white man and a Spanish woman. The country had shifted course, and they benefited from living in a large urban area. But even in New York, white men ruled and Aubrey very much doubted the turn of the century would change that.

As Aubrey used a small iron dowsing rod to deactivate the first set of wards, Calix sucked in an excited breath. He never stopped looking around the alley where the two banks of service doors led into the Attic's back room, but at least he'd let his hackles relax a little.

"Does the museum deal much in magical artifacts, Aubrey?"

"Here and there," Aubrey replied as he made a square on the cold metal with his finger, releasing the personal identification wards next.

His reply to Calix was a lie, and not. Darwin's Attic did occasionally put a magical artifact on display, but they were always dead.

The Collectio was both the clearinghouse for Darwin's Attic and private clients, focused largely on the preservation and restoration of magical artifacts. A torn page in a grimoire written to ward off the Black Plague here, rethreading the tassels on George Washington's "invincibility coat" there. (Aubrey could find no evidence that the coat was actually magical. Washington had simply been extremely lucky to never be injured in any way. His coat bore the holes from four bullets he claimed never touched him. Nevertheless, the private collector believed it to be magical, so they restored the coat with a few clever patterns and sent the man on his way.)

The Collectio dealt with items of all kinds — dead, alive, sentient even. But they were not a museum. Even the "Collectio" part of the name was a bit of a misnomer, since most people of sound mind would presume a collection to be at the very least open by invitation. Collections, curiosity museums, cabinets of curiosity, and several other variations on the theme were all the rage over the last few years. The wealthy had their private collections of trinkets and weird artifacts, and a smaller few collected magical items, but those were kept under lock and key — by the Collectio's orders. There was no way to corral everyone under the Collectio's invisible but deeply influential political workings, but most collectors understood the consequences if caught with even one unlicensed artifact.

Dire, to say the very least.

The ward on the doors opened with ease under Aubrey's touch, and it left him relieved. Something deeply odd was going on, and the wards were sometimes temperamental around strong magic. He peered down at the satchel slung across Calix's lean frame. There was a boyish charm to the man, and he seemed to stay firmly rooted between the masculine and feminine, and that distinct lack of definition (whether intentional or not) poked about in Aubrey's psyche. His world was full of indefinites and mysteries yet to be unraveled. But so few had the grace, the magnanimity, the...well, the fucking daring to be so open about it. It was something he envied, being able to live honestly like that. He didn't dare leave his house in anything but a proper suit, but for someone like Calix, so much leniency was given. There were days, admittedly few anymore, where Aubrey daydreamed about wearing the flowing silks and bright colors of his home attire in the wide world, but he doubted that day would ever come.

"Let's head inside," Aubrey said to them both, catching Ethaniel's eye once more. "It would take me some time to set up all the extra wards I suspect we'll need, so we'll be using a temporary method for now." Here, shelves and shelves of items were racked up, ramshackle rectangles stacked on top of each other, and all the residents carrying their own strange stories. But everything in the Attic's back room was harmless. The same couldn't be said for what lay beyond the next set of doors.

"I've never seen so many strange objects in one place," Calix said as he lingered near a book on one of the shelves. The book itself was unremarkable, a plain navy leather journal closed by a leather cord wrapped around the middle. The bottom half of the journal was gone, replaced by a bite mark the size of Aubrey's hand. "What the devil…?"

Ethaniel had the same wondrous reaction when I brought him here the first time, Aubrey thought as he watched the two men gather close, heads bent over the book.

"It's an augury journal," Ethaniel said. "It's completely harmless, according to Aubrey."

Aubrey snorted. "You say that as if you don't believe me, Ethaniel."

"I believe you," Ethaniel replied softly, his gaze hooking Aubrey's for a moment before he turned back to Calix. "Aubrey says this is a bite of unknown origin, but apparently the story is that the dreamer who wrote this was so disturbed by what he recorded on the pages that he had his dog bite it."

"Rendering the book 'dead', as we call it," Aubrey finished. "It's complicated theory, but it did work as far as we can tell. And the bite mark makes for a good story for the display, or so Ethaniel tells me." In response, Ethaniel smiled. He'd *missed* that smile so much, all crinkling hazel-brown eyes and the small dimple on the left side of Ethaniel's mouth.

Aubrey remembered the stolen hours here, after everyone else had left. He should have taken Ethaniel home with him those times, but those old, half-buried fears had risen up and claimed stake on him once more. Bringing a man home…what if someone saw? What if they figured out who Aubrey was, where he worked, and told someone? If he lost his job, if he lost his *purpose*….then what?

The moment between he and Ethaniel passed and with it, Aubrey could breathe once more. But the air tasted bitter as he returned to unsealing the hidden doors that led into the Collectio itself.

"Here," Aubrey said as he held out two dark gray stone amulets on leather cords. "Keep these on while you're inside."

Ethaniel nodded and took the amulet, but Calix hesitated. Gods, he looked young even in the dim light of the Attic's storeroom. Calix had a youthful appearance no matter what, but the shadows clung to the hollows of his cheeks, the curve of his chin; they deepened the brown of his eyes and left Aubrey feeling unmoored. He didn't know what to do with the feelings sparking in his belly, but he hadn't the time to explore them now.

"You'll need it," Aubrey said as he dropped the amulet into Calix's hand. The weight of the stone probably felt like an anvil; it usually did to first-timers until they adjusted to the overwhelming magic in the Collectio. "Normally I'd set up all the wards but we're in a bit of a hurry."

"I know. Apologies. All this...strange magic has me uneasy," Calix replied, ducking his head to drop the amulet over it.

"Not at all. You're right to be suspicious." Aubrey wasn't beyond magnanimity, even though his hunch had been correct. "And now that you're settled we can go forth."

The thrill that traced a fingernail down his spine was present every time he opened these doors, but Aubrey felt a distinct *lack* in the air as the magically concealed doors silently slid open. As if the Collectio itself knew something was wrong.

Aubrey was split between caution and excitement — whatever this item was, it was incredibly well-protected. In the few seconds he'd been gifted, Aubrey had seen *thousands* of patterns latched, lacework and delicately complicated, around, through, across, and over each other until they became one near-solid mass. An impossible feat of patterning.

But maybe not for Ethaniel.

"Wait here," Aubrey said as they stepped into pitch-black. It was clearly off-putting to the others, as Ethaniel closed his eyes and waited while Calix stared around, mouth agape.

Aubrey smiled slightly. He loved showing off the Collectio. Visitors were so few and far between. But Ethaniel could sum it up better. "Ethaniel, could you regale our friend here with how this works, while I get us up and running?"

"Of course, Aubrey."

Ethaniel's knowing smirk clearly caught Calix's attention, so Aubrey took his leave. The electrical panel didn't need to be started, as their end goal was the far back workroom. So Aubrey started up the gas lights, the flicker and hiss of flames not enough to cover up Ethaniel's rapid discussion of the building's patterns.

Ethaniel would know. He helped build them.

Ethaniel Harkness was a part of the infamous Harkness family, very well-known in magical circles for having some of the most intelligent, skilled, and ruthless magic users in history. The family had long split off into sects, but Ethaniel's father had been born in the wilderness of middle America and hadn't known his family history until he was nearly an adult. So he'd told Ethaniel from a young age about their ancestors and living relatives — who to avoid, who to trust — and what to do if Ethaniel showed the slightest sign of magic. *Go to your Uncle Jeremiah,* Ethaniel had told Aubrey over wine and bread while they caught their breath; careful to not drop red on their cooling skin or the floor. *He'll set you on the right path, show you London and England and everything you need to keep yourself you, Ethaniel. To stay true to who you are and not be seduced by power, so you can remain loyal to morals and ethics.*

Aubrey let out a sigh as the last gas lamp flickered to life and the memory faded. He had work to do and distractions were controllable. And he could speak to Ethaniel privately after this was done.

Calix and Ethaniel were looking around as Aubrey returned to them. Now with the gas lighting their way, one could make out what looked like an office and a library had become some kind of strange hydra — rows and rows of desks, pin neat, flanked by floor-to-ceiling bookcases that went up...and up...and up. Technically there was no limit to the bookshelves, but they hadn't come close to pushing the bounds of the spell, even as the Collectio's artifact storage had been in demand of late. Too many Victorian explorers had thought the Collectio would be interested in magical tomes and scrolls, statues and amulets, jewels and containers stolen from other parts of the world. Part of the Collectio's job was to see these items returned to their owners.

Most people wanted their items back, of course, but every now and then the item would come back with the emissary and they'd have to work with it, from cleaning and repairing to deactivating any dangerous wards or patterns. Then came cataloging, studying, and sometimes experimentation (nothing permanent, mind you) to gain a better understanding of the item's makeup.

"The Magnificus Collectio is this world's largest storage and study facility of magical items," Aubrey said as he returned. "It is a modern-day Library of Alexandria for magic."

Calix held up a finger. "I'm sorry...*this world's?*"

"Caught that, did you?" Ethaniel replied lightly as he walked toward Aubrey. "He won't tell me what it means either, but I'm glad I wasn't the only one who heard it."

Hoping, daring that he wasn't completely out of line, Aubrey slid closer to Ethaniel and smiled down at him. A real smile, not that mask he wore to placate. "And I'm afraid I can't tell you," he said to them both. And then he ducked his head and whispered, "Unless you're very, very good. Then I'll think about it."

Aubrey didn't give Ethaniel time to react. He straightened and motioned them both forward. "Come, gentlemen. Let's see what your magical item has to offer."

Further back into the Collectio was the restoration room. The floor was plain concrete, the walls painted stark white and lined with thin lead plates. It gave the room a disjointed look, like a quilt made with a beginner's skill. But it served their purposes well.

Aubrey shut the doors behind them and activated the panel for the electric lights, which generated a low hum. Aubrey watched Calix wrinkle his nose at the sound. "You get used to it," he said to Calix as he pulled out his tool kit from underneath the massive table in the middle of the room.

"I've always been a little...sensitive," Calix admitted. His big brown eyes appeared hooded as he stood on the edge of the circle of light. Aubrey was intrigued by the way those eyes narrowed, almost cat-like, as Calix visually inspected the table.

"My sister was that way," Ethaniel replied as he moved to the right-hand side of the table. "Light bothered her more than sound, though."

Aubrey let the comment hang, choosing to focus on his supplies. It wasn't a cruelty, and Ethaniel wouldn't see his silence as such. Aubrey knew that story, too; about a sad little girl whose eyes saw a bit too much of the world. Whose magic never stabilized. Who disappeared on her tenth birthday, with no trace left behind. Not even a piece of clothing or bit of hair. Ethaniel's father buried Maria's doll behind the family home and never spoke of her again.

"You're welcome to stay there, if it's easier for you," Aubrey said as he unrolled the leather pouch. At first glance, it might appear like a chiseler's tool belt, all sharp blades and hooked picks, along with a pair of black velvet gloves. "The velvet helps disperse the magic," Aubrey explained. "The lead plates on the walls catch anything errant and trap it until it can be released safely. Keep your amulets on and you should be perfectly fine."

Ethaniel nodded but Calix bit his lip. He lingered, long-limbed and wraithlike, on the precipice of the circle of light, his hands balled at his sides. "How do I give you the book?"

Aubrey had suspected the item was a book, but he purposefully hadn't asked as to not cloud his judgment any further. A shaky tendril of trepidation was slowly winding its way along his spine since the park, but a book he could handle. Magical books were the bread and butter of the Collectio's business, after all. Paper was easy to enchant, easy to destroy, and commonly accessible. Paper was what every blossoming magic user practiced on.

He could handle a book, even one so heavily patterned.

"Calix," Aubrey said. The younger man snapped to attention. "I want you to simply take the book out of the bag and lay it on the table, then step back. That's it."

"Easy enough," Ethaniel said softly, putting a hand on Calix's shoulder. "I'm here, Calix."

If only that hand would be so gentle with me again, Aubrey thought, biting back his jealousy. There was no time to be so...absurd. Aubrey motioned to the table, then held his breath while Calix unlatched his satchel and pulled out the book.

Aubrey drunk in the sight of the book. The size of a journal and practically coated in silver foil. It was both pristine and had the appearance of something one could find in a higher-end bookstore, where foil-stamped covers were made by hand, with great care.

And to the naked eye, there was nothing remarkable about the damn thing.

Calix suddenly flinched, reeling back. Ethaniel caught him by the shoulders, pulling him close.

"What happened?" Ethaniel asked.

"It spoke again," Calix replied, his voice gone hoarse, as if he'd been shouting for hours.

Aubrey quickly pulled on his gloves and pried a small hook from his kit. "Be on alert, both of you." Ethaniel made to pull Calix back into the shadows, but Aubrey shook his head. "I need you close, Calix. If the book has already formed a bond with you—"

"A bond?" Calix sounded alarmed and his wide eyes flared even wider.

"Aubrey, he has no idea what's going on," Ethaniel said as he tightened his grip on Calix's shoulders. Calix was half a head shorter than either of them, but in Ethaniel's hold, Calix looked even smaller. Ethaniel had long-fingered, broad hands that seemed to wrap all the way around Calix's bony shoulders, his tawny skin almost golden in the dim light outside the examination table.

"The book clearly has an affinity for you, Mr. Addington," Aubrey explained, his patience waning. "If the book was a danger to the populace, he would have felt it, or the wards would have gone off, or any one of the Collectio's fail safes would have alerted him. But instead of anything he'd expected, the book — whatever, or whoever, it was — had latched onto Calix.

"I don't want it to," Calix said, his breathing now faster. "I never asked for that!"

Ethaniel gave Aubrey a dark look of warning. It should have held him back, but it only spurred him on. "Then we'll attempt to break the affinity. That's what it's called: *affinity*. Intelligent and sentient objects sometimes seek it out."

"Aubrey." There was that look again, his former lover trying to pin Aubrey down with a glare.

Curiosity was the thing that would kill him eventually. Aubrey was sure of it. But he wasn't planning on dying tonight. He needed more insight into this affinity between the book and Calix, to at least put it into stasis while he took the case to Magnus—

"Convergence." Calix swallowed hard, then gave Aubrey a look. "That's what it said. Again."

"Unexpected," Aubrey replied slowly as he leaned over the book. "That's not a normal reaction."

Ethaniel gave a forced chuckle. "Only you would have a mental catalog of what's considered 'normal' for an intelligent object."

"There's no normal here." Aubrey hovered his gloved hand over the book. "But I have to ask a favor, Ethaniel."

"Anything."

Something burrowed far down in Aubrey's heart awoke at that one word. "Use my monocle while I work with the book and tell me what you see." When Ethaniel didn't reply, Aubrey looked up. "You can see more than I can with patterns. The book is drowning in them and your patterning control is nearly impenetrable." Aubrey ignored the look of awe on Calix's face to add, "And I don't want to be caught in some siren's trap."

"Of course." Ethaniel let go of Calix long enough to step forward and reach across the table. Aubrey fished the monocle's bag out of his jacket, gave it to Ethaniel, and then waved him away once more.

When Ethaniel had the monocle affixed to his right eye, Aubrey took a deep breath and reached for the book's front cover. The creak of pristine binding was the only sound in the room, other than Calix's rapid breathing.

"Try to breathe evenly, Mr. Addington" Aubrey said quietly. "I'm afraid you'll faint." And Aubrey set to work.

He knew what Calix and Ethaniel saw — a tall, proud man in an impeccable suit placing his hands on the spread pages of a...

...curiously blank book.

Aubrey felt deflated for a moment. Well, if it wasn't going to let him have its secrets, he'd just have to pry them out. This wasn't his first stubborn artifact. He slid his hands off the book, placing them on either side of the gilt edges, and looked up at the two men. Specifically at Calix. "I can assure you, Mr. Addington, that you're perfectly safe," Aubrey said, watching with silent glee how Ethaniel sucked in a breath. That dark tone always *did something* to Ethaniel.

Aubrey *pushed* his power into the stone table. Into the glass-smooth surface and then further in, past layers upon layers of sediment, down crooked tunnels and through swerving channels. He felt every pebble, every chip, every smooth corner leading into tight paths that took him to the edges of the stone and out. To bounce off the lead panels that only reflected that power back, magnifying his abilities to mend into something *more*.

It had been an accident the first time this had happened. Now, with a decade at the Collectio under his belt, Aubrey knew where to push, where to pull, and when to pull back. He understood his power on an intrinsic level, down to the molecule, the atom. On a plane beyond thought and recognition, out past the point of return for many magic users.

He did not follow in his family's footsteps, healing the sick and delivering babies and mending broken bones. He could see magical objects on a level unparalleled with reality. To mend, you had to understand an object, how its parts fit together. How those parts were made.

This book, paper and board, velvet and ink, foil and cloth? It was unlike anything he'd ever laid hands upon. Aubrey knew he had to go deeper.

He would be glowing now, a soft cobalt that bled into green. His eyes, like glass so many said, would be blank. But the third eye on his forehead would be glowing, beckoning. Aubrey couldn't see Calix and Ethaniel, but he could feel them, that presence, those heartbeats. Rapid but steady, one a little faster, a little louder.

Calix reacting to him. To his magic.

Ethaniel had called him a torch. Warm and safe, golden and glowing. That comment had lit Aubrey up from the inside, and did to this day. For so long he'd been a lighthouse. A warning about magic mutating in families. A warning about being *different* and *difficult*.

You're supposed to stay away from lighthouses. They mean danger. A light flashed in the dark, in hopes of preventing tragedy.

Would Calix see a lighthouse, or a torch?

Something new is here.

The voice rang in Aubrey's head, turning him into a clapper inside a bronze bell. He pushed back, feeling for grips inside the stone. The stone yielded so easily, but that...voice stopped him cold. Aubrey's power stayed put, no further progress was made.

The stone helped cycle his power, tap into a thread of it inside him that was so rarely tugged on. No one understood why him, why this big hunk of unnamed black stone. *Whywhywhywhy.* He'd let all that go to learn how to use the stone, to make it his. And this thing had stopped him dead in his tracks.

You're not the other one.

You found a path through.

Who are you?

Aubrey stood on the edge of some black oblivion and wondered if there were teeth below. He could see everything. Nothing. He existed and didn't. He became, he unraveled.

Aubrey was suddenly, sickeningly thrown back into his own body, his own mind, aware of nothing and everything at the same time. His head swam with it all, so much that he wondered if he was drowning.

"Aubrey!"

Aubrey blinked and then there was Ethaniel, all wavy brown hair a few inches too long and his brow beaded with sweat. Big hazel eyes flared wide in worry. Day old stubble on his jaw, framing Ethaniel's perfect lips.

I should have told you before, Ethaniel. Everything about how I feel.

Regret ate alive at him again, like a freshly uncorked horror burrowing into his heart. It made Aubrey forget how much being thrust out of an object's aura *hurt*. Ethaniel's magic was a cool breeze on his skin, gentle but persistent. The pattern Ethaniel had used glowed on Aubrey's jacket —a simple thing, something Ethaniel always had on hand, but it was welcomed all the same.

"Here." Slender, pale hands thrust a teacup full of water under Aubrey's nose. "You should probably drink that."

Aubrey's gaze dropped to the blue and white teacup before taking it with a slow nod. "Is this…" His vision was still hazy, little bits of it floating in and out of darkness. "I think this is Alon's."

"Oh, Aubrey," Ethaniel whispered as he sat down near Aubrey's knee. They were on the floor. No wonder his back ached. "Can you tell me your name?"

Aubrey scoffed, but there was no heart in it. "Don't patronize me, Ethaniel." He sipped at the water, which was cold and clear and felt like an oasis in his throat. "I'm fine."

"You look…" Calix came into view, kneeling at Aubrey's feet. A man who looked like that, wearing expensive silks and brocades, sitting on the cold floor and looking at Aubrey with deep concern. "I don't know."

"Distant." Ethaniel's tone was like thunder in Aubrey's ears.

"Maybe I am a bit dizzy," Aubrey admitted.

"You sound not like yourself." Ethaniel took the cup from Aubrey's now-cold fingers. "How do you feel?"

"Strange," Aubrey said before everything went black.

NINE

E THANIEL

    Ethaniel couldn't fully breathe until Aubrey was awake and talking. His former lover had been out for only a few minutes, but they'd been the longest of Ethaniel's existence. Between him and Calix, they were able to carry Aubrey into the small office off the Collectio's main rooms. They managed to avoid knocking Aubrey's head or limbs into any of the impossibly neat shelves (and the organizational structure was impossible through human effort — the organizing pattern wasn't Ethaniel's, but he could feel its hum in his bones), and gently lay him down on the small cot in the office.

Staring at Aubrey now, seeing how his feet dangled off the end of the cot, admiring how perfectly rumpled he was? Ethaniel could only chuckle a little. The man was completely endearing when he didn't mean to be.

"I'm supposing that's a good kind of laugh," Calix said as they stood over Aubrey's prone form.

"It is," Ethaniel admitted. He resisted the temptation to shove his hands into his pockets, just to give himself something to grip onto; even if it was the lining of his jacket. "He...I..." Ethaniel sighed and looked around. The office hadn't changed a bit. "I've memories here. Nice ones. And Aubrey will be pissed when he sees how wrinkled his clothes are."

Calix stifled a chuckle of his own. "He seems the type."

"He is."

Calix gestured to the lone chair in the room, the rickety one Aubrey refused to replace because it wasn't broken. Yet. "You should sit."

"I'm fine." He wasn't, but that was to deal with later. Ethaniel felt overwhelmed and underprepared, as if they'd all stepped into something much larger than their limited comprehension. He turned to Calix, brow furrowed and mouth pursed. "The book...or whatever it is, said that word to you again?"

Calix swallowed hard. "Yes. But it showed me something. Or..." He trailed off and something slick and oily began to form in Ethaniel's stomach. *Worry* didn't cover the deep concern he suddenly felt. Calix himself looked pale and worn but he was steady on his feet. "I told you I can see glimpses of the future? The book, or my sight, showed me something I can't quite decipher." Calix swallowed hard. "Only darkness and what looked like a gravestone. But it didn't feel like a threat."

Ethaniel waited in the silence that followed, but it was difficult. Calix was clearly distraught, Aubrey was barely awake, and Ethaniel worried about leaving his uncle for too long. Leaving the shop for too long. Losing income, which meant not being able to take care of Jeremiah. What if all of this spiraled? What if it cost too much?

Should he walk away?

If he did, would he lose Aubrey again?

Would he lose any connection there might be with Calix?

"Sit." A firm hand steered him to the chair and Ethaniel went willingly this time. "I think we all need a rest, and as charming as this office may be, we're all exhausted."

Ethaniel sat down with a muffled thump, ignoring the pain in his lower back as Calix knelt before him. The man was entirely too pretty. It was a nice distraction to stare at such a pretty face, those big brown eyes full of concern, but even that left Ethaniel feeling guilty while Aubrey eased his way into consciousness.

After a few quiet minutes, Ethaniel said, "When I fixed that monocle to my eye, do you know what I saw?" Calix shook his head. "Darkness, at first. Only a black void. And then like a fire coming to life, ember by ember, I saw the patterns. They were *beautiful*. There was this pulse of something under all of it, under all those lines and shapes and delicate swirls that made no sense to me. But I couldn't do much other than feel it, like a heart beating."

Ethaniel sat back in the chair with a sigh and scrubbed his face with the heel of his hands. "Aubrey is incredibly powerful. If that...*thing* disrupted his magic, I shudder to think what it truly is."

Calix's hand flew to his mouth, face now drained of any color. Even his hair seemed to pale. The change was so sudden, it sent Ethaniel's heart racing once more. "That book...Lawton had it. He hid it. Kept it secret. And we were supposed to stop somewhere else before our final destination that day."

The pieces clicked into place. "He was bringing it to someone?" Ethaniel asked. The nod Calix gave made his stomach drop. "Do you know who?"

"No. He's been so odd of late, so tied up with finances and running off to meet people." Calix sounded torn between confusion and despondency. "I kept telling him to not worry about money, that I'd help him, but over last summer something changed. That's when the late nights started, the sneaking about. I thought he had a lover, someone married perhaps."

Ethaniel badly wanted to pry the information about Lawton out of Calix, but that would get them nowhere. Calix looked devastated, like every word that fell from his mouth beget another revelation, and none of it good. He understood, on some level; it was clear Calix and Lawton had a close relationship, and sometimes that closeness made betrayal easy to hide.

"Does your friend have any talents?"

They both startled, nearly jumping up from their seats as Aubrey's hoarse voice floated to them from the cot. He was awake now, looking at them both through half-hooded eyes.

"Do you mean magic?" Calix asked.

"Most certainly. Magic, divination, augury?"

Calix shook his head, hair falling in his face. Ethaniel wanted to push it away, to give Calix comfort. "Only a quick mind and a silver tongue."

One eyebrow went up, giving Aubrey an oddly charming, rakish look. *His looks were always devastating*, Ethaniel thought as he watched the two men converse.

"Does he know about your abilities?"

"Only a little. I..." Calix trailed off, looking even more despondent.

"You downplay them," Ethaniel hedged, earning him a nod. "That's wise. The world isn't kind to Oracles."

Silence filled the room once more, only broken by Aubrey slowly shifting to a seated position, his back against the wall. "This is a tad more complicated than some magical trinket," Aubrey said softly, letting his gaze drift from Calix to Ethaniel. "It should stay here, under strict safety controls."

"It's not mine, though," Calix said, his tone steeling suddenly. "That's half the difficulty, Aubrey. Lawton *will* come looking for that book. He's likely been around my place already, and would have been turned away."

"You seem confident in that," Aubrey said.

"I *am*, because Richard, my valet, is that good, and Lawton is that persistent."

The finality in Calix's words dropped like an anvil. And with it came a wave of exhaustion that swept over Ethaniel, threatening to pull him under completely. The words Calix and Aubrey exchanged faded to a dull roar.

"I could drop off here," Ethaniel mumbled. Calix and Aubrey's attention snapped over to him. "Though I don't think that cot can hold all three of us."

"Unfortunately, no," Aubrey replied before shifting slowly to his feet. Ethaniel jumped from his seat to assist and to his shock, Aubrey didn't wave him off.

The contact between them was anything but casual. Ethaniel gave a fleeting thought to Calix bearing witness to this — how Ethaniel sucked in a breath the moment Aubrey's skin brushed against his, how Aubrey's beautiful eyes locked onto him, how they both froze as the moment ensnared them.

Ethaniel didn't care. All that past regret and anger was *past*, and now, in the middle of uncertainty and barely-controlled chaos, Ethaniel remembered. And he wanted.

Aubrey's hand slipped away, taking part of Ethaniel's heart with it. "I need to put Convergence into storage. Then we can discuss what to do with it."

"Not here, perhaps?" Calix asked. "I'd invite you both back to mine but with Lawton surely roaming about, that seems…" He trailed off but Ethaniel heard the unspoken.

Dangerous

It seemed dangerous.

While Ethaniel wracked his mind to come up with a neutral place, it was Aubrey who had the solution. "I know where we can go. It's unconventional, but as private a place as almost any." Ethaniel's shock must have shown on his face, because Aubrey shrugged. "I know it well. It's safe. And the heavens know I've paid them well over the years."

"Color me intrigued," Calix said, getting to his feet as well.

"I would say the same, though I've a terrible suspicion Aubrey's about to shock us both," Ethaniel replied, his tone lightly teasing. He didn't want Aubrey to take offense, especially not now that their bond could yet reform.

He hoped it would. He could forgive Aubrey the transgresses he'd committed months before; in some way, Aubrey had been looking out for him. Aubrey wasn't always the most emotive but over the course of their *relationship*, Ethaniel had been privy to the molten core Aubrey hid away, and hid well.

Perhaps there was room for something more once again.

They waited while Aubrey wrapped the book in what appeared to be tea-stained linen, then wrapped a heavy iron chain around it. The chain was padlocked, the key added to Aubrey's already immense ring he carried at all times, and then Aubrey disappeared for a few minutes into what he simply called "the vault". When he returned, Aubrey was still ashen but he'd righted his coat and now had his hat and cane in hand.

"Are you ready?" Aubrey asked Ethaniel and Calix, his gaze scrutinizing.

"As much as I can be," Calix said while Ethaniel nodded.

"Ethaniel?" Aubrey asked.

For a brief moment, Ethaniel wondered if Aubrey would extend his arm, a silent ask for Ethaniel to take it. But the moment passed and Ethaniel was left to reply, "Yes, of course."

Ethaniel spent the entire walk wondering if he'd missed an opportunity.

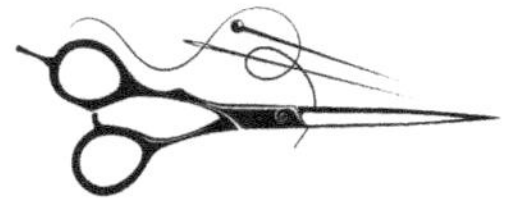

"Well, you did say unconventional," Ethaniel muttered as the three of them entered a glossy, clearly expensive building. "A bank?" He stared up at the high ceilings from which bright glass light fixtures hung. It was a beautiful building, clearly well cared for — freshly waxed marble floors and shining panes behind which smartly dressed tellers sat. The customers were of the wealthy sort, decked in furs and jewels even though it was barely noon.

Aubrey gave him a soft, secretive smile. "Not in the least. We're headed downstairs."

It was perhaps foolish of Ethaniel to whisper, "All right, I trust you," to Aubrey as they walked past the customers standing in line and wood paneled offices holding loan managers deep in conversation with well-dressed clientele. Aubrey didn't appear to react, but a single glance at how tightly he gripped his cane told Ethaniel everything.

Ethaniel hid his smile by turning to Calix and saying, "I'm glad you're here, Calix."

Calix ducked his head, eyes averted. Perhaps it was Ethaniel's imagination, but the man seemed to be *blushing*. "Thank you. I appreciate the invite, especially because I'm the one who caused all this trouble."

They'd reached a heavy iron and wood door, something one might see at the front of a church in London. A man dressed in all navy blue with no adornments but the gold buttons on his tightly tailored jacket waved them forward. Aubrey strode ahead, shoulders back and head raised high while Ethaniel and Calix followed in his shadow. Watching Aubrey tower over the man in blue, seeing his confidence radiate out and turn a few people's heads? It was opium to Ethaniel, heady and unadulterated. It made him *yearn*, made him *ache*.

He didn't care where they were going. All he wanted was to be near Aubrey, somewhere quiet and soft, where they could talk and...

Ethaniel shook his head to clear it. They had much more to worry about right now. The man at his elbow, this young, wealthy earl who had careened into his life, and then into Aubrey's, was in distress and possibly danger.

But all that logic did nothing for the slow burn simmering in Ethaniel's chest.

"You didn't cause anything," Ethaniel replied softly, looking down into Calix's big brown eyes. "By luck or fate, you found two people willing to help. Perhaps it was meant to be."

"Maybe." But Calix looked unconvinced, his brow pinched and mouth tightly pursed. "I've never put much stock in fate. Or any god, to be honest."

"We're of similar minds in that regard," Aubrey said as the uniformed man opened the door and stepped aside. "Come. We'll discuss all that once we're somewhere more private."

Aubrey led them down a wide, winding stone staircase, which curved and curved again. The lower they went, the damper the air became, until the walls were slick with moisture and the scent of salt made Ethaniel's nose tingle.

"I've heard of this place," Calix breathed out as they came to the bottom of the stairs.

"Somehow I'm not surprised," Aubrey said, his tone lightly teasing. Ethaniel made note of that — Aubrey wasn't one to warm up to others easily, but when he did, it was like watching a painter finish a masterpiece. Those final brush strokes revealed the painting's full nature, in all its glory. "I envy you both, seeing the Minotaur Baths for the first time."

The room opened up in a massive chamber, at least three stories tall and ringed with walkways across which figures moved. His head swam with the scent of salt and the tingle of magic; a place like this would be impossible on its own, but every day that passed convinced Ethaniel even more of magic's capabilities. The stone walls, dripping with condensation, were a soft coral brown, like the sandstone cliffs of England, but instead of dropping into the ocean, they sloped and zagged into multi-tiered hot springs. There were no gas or electric lights down here, only magical lanterns gently bobbing in the air and casting a golden glow. They reminded Ethaniel of the lanterns he'd seen in places like Acadia Gardens; places where direct, bright light often attracted the wrong kind of attention.

He turned his gaze to the hot springs, astounded by what he saw. All around the pools of steaming water were bathers, bold in their various states of undress and utterly unconcerned about themselves or those around them. Stature, color, appearance...none of it seemed to matter. Some bathers were bare-chested and decked in fluffy blue towels, dangling their feet into the water or walking arm in arm with another, sometimes two. Others lounged near the pools' edges, their glistening skin and shifting muscles impossible to look away from. And others frolicked in the water, small groups of bathers in tight circles chatting and hanging off each other while others sank to their necks and rested, eyes closed.

It was an incredible, *impossible* sight.

The glistening walls. The inlaid slate flooring, in more pinks and browns and touches of copper. No, wait...Ethaniel peered closer at the stone beneath his feet. Those were actual copper veins running through each and every dinner plate-sized tile, as if they'd been ripped from the Earth whole and only sanded into shape. And with the gentle bob of lanterns overhead, Ethaniel wondered if he hadn't stepped foot across some invisible veil to an impossible *demimonde*.

But fairy worlds would likely have women, and this place did not. Every single person in view appeared male, and they ranged from those with bulging biceps and beautifully sculpted legs to the more lithe, almost dainty fairies whose red lips and slicked back hair accentuated the dangling earrings and sparkling rings they wore.

Ethaniel could hardly believe what he was seeing.

"The Minotaur Baths are some of the oldest in the city, and they're well protected," Aubrey said as he turned to face them. Something like *pride* stood out on Aubrey's face. Pride, mixed with the headiness of a close-kept secret. "I've been coming here for years. It's survived every police raid, every attempt to shutter its doors permanently. It's as private a place as we might find anywhere else."

They were interrupted by an attendant carrying a folded bundle of cloth dyed such a deep red it looked nearly black in the dim lights. "It's good to see you again, Mr. Lavigne. Cahill up front told me you'd brought friends." The attendant's eyes were a verdant green, shining darkly in the flickering, golden light; the paint on his lips was a shade lighter, but only a shade. He was sharply featured, from the point of his chin to the cheekbones that shifted under sun-golden skin. So sharp Ethaniel thought he might cut himself.

Aubrey was quick to wave the man away, taking the bundle from his hands. "Get them situated, Basil. Which room?"

"Four, sir." Basil paused, spreading his hands wide in a gesture toward Ethaniel and Calix. "Unless you're wanting the third level."

What glittered in Aubrey's glass-hued eyes shifted. Darkened. Not anger, Ethaniel had seen that before and this...gods, this was far from it. It made him shiver, that look, and a glance at Calix found the younger man enraptured by the sight, too. Ethaniel could hardly blame Calix. It was impossible to resist Aubrey when he broke down his staid veneer for even a moment.

They were the best moments, in Ethaniel's humble opinion.

"I'll meet you both in room four," Aubrey said as Basil held out both his arms in offering. "Let Basil help you and then we can partake."

Ethaniel swore he heard the *click* of Calix's throat as he swallowed hard. "I'm so sorry. Could someone explain what's going on?"

Ethaniel shot Aubrey a rather pointed look. "I've some notion but Aubrey..."

One of Aubrey's dark, thick eyebrows rose. The playful glint was still in his eyes, but from the way Aubrey was stroking the collar of the garment in his hands, he was clearly distracted. "Basil will help you find robes, towels, and the like. Then he'll bring you to me and you can partake in what the baths have to offer, for as long as you'd like. You're on my tab."

"Aubrey, that can't be..." Ethaniel shook his head. "I thought we were here to discuss our next moves. That's very generous but I've already been gone too long."

"I can go back with you," Calix said softly as he put his hand on Ethaniel's arm.

"And that's quite kind," Ethaniel replied, smiling slightly. "But we'll be fine."

"Ethaniel." Aubrey's voice was steel now, rough-cut and raking across Ethaniel. "Even the world's most dedicated nephew needs a breather now and again. You can't properly take care of Jeremiah if you're not seen to. We are here to discuss our plan. A harried, anxious mind and tense body do not a good plan make."

That old *rage* boiled inside Ethaniel at that single comment. He snapped his head up and met Aubrey's gaze with the knife-tip of his own. Calix's hand tightening on his arm, each fingertip like a brand even through his clothes, was grounding enough to let Ethaniel draw back into his common sense.

Aubrey *was* right, and Ethaniel knew it. But his instinct was to jump forward, to protect, to hurl himself into problems and work the solutions as things progressed. Aubrey was calm and collected, never missing a beat of his own song. Ethaniel was the one who felt unmoored, even more so now while standing in a place too opulent for him, his life.

"Ethaniel." Aubrey was before him now, bundle neatly tucked under his arm while he stared straight at Ethaniel. "Could you two give us a moment? Basil, perhaps take Calix on to pick out a robe."

"Of course. This way, sir."

Calix and Basil drifted out of sight and no sooner were they out of peripheral vision did Aubrey steer Ethaniel to an open doorway and into a small chamber. It was barely more than an offshoot of the springs, a private little pool for intimate conversation.

"Can we sit?" Aubrey gestured to the gently curved stone bench to the left, just inside the room.

"Of course." But Ethaniel was biting his tongue. Snarking at Aubrey would get him nowhere, and would be unfair. So Ethaniel sat and Aubrey settled to his left.

Ethaniel waited. They were close enough that their shoulders and knees touched, soft bumps of cloth and flesh and bone.

"I'm so sorry, Ethaniel."

A million responses came to mind, but what Ethaniel eventually said was, "Why now?"

"Because I'm a fool." Aubrey pressed into him, solid and real and already glistening from the humidity in the air. "Because I should have repaired things sooner than this. Because I should have come to find you, to beg at your feet."

Aubrey's response, so beautifully simple and incredibly raw, made a knot form in Ethaniel's chest. "I don't need that," Ethaniel replied, voice thin. "It wasn't all your fault, Aubrey."

"Perhaps. Perhaps not. But I know I didn't give you time or space. I was thinking only of myself." Aubrey's right hand now drifted down Ethaniel's back. Ethaniel's throat went dry. "Because I want...no, I *need* to make sure you're safe. Taken care of. And I made an error in judgment thinking my offer of assistance for your uncle would be seen as just that. I assumed, when I shouldn't have." The hand drifted lower again, light pressure now just above the small of Ethaniel's back.

I used to shiver every time he did this. It was always after we were together, tucked away in his office or in the back of the shop. So gentle, that Aubrey. So vulnerable, as though I could see every piece of him laid bare, able to admire its rigorous symmetry and its glittering heart.

"I made many mistakes before our parting." With the softest touch, Aubrey turned Ethaniel's face so their eyes could meet. "I should have invited you over, damn what the neighbors think. Taken you out more. Gone with you to Acadia Gardens to see that dance troupe you love so much."

"Aubrey." Ethaniel could barely choke out the name. Aubrey was *here, now,* staring into Ethaniel's damned soul and asking for forgiveness.

"I only wish to help. Truly. But I am deeply sorry for what I caused between us last summer." The side of Aubrey's thumb traced across Ethaniel's cheek. Ethaniel felt weak, lightheaded. Every touch, every glance, every word Aubrey had for him...it all conveyed genuine sorrow. Genuine kindness.

Genuine regret.

"And I will not ever apologize for looking out for you." That thumb traced lower still, Aubrey's fingers curling up behind the hinge of Ethaniel's jaw.

He *wanted.* Burned with it. Had told himself over and over again that accepting help wasn't weak, wasn't giving up on Jeremiah. But when Aubrey had insisted on helping, it had turned Ethaniel's vision red.

"Charity? I don't need your charity, Aubrey! I've taken care of my uncle for years now, and run the shop, and made every order with my own two hands! And you dare to suggest—"

The knot in his chest tightened again, a fist of past mistakes and failures growing larger with each second. "You've apologized plenty," Ethaniel whispered, letting his head drop so he could turn his face into Aubrey's shoulder.

"And yet it feels as though I've come up short." Aubrey's long, agile fingers sunk into Ethaniel's wavy hair, making them both shudder.

Time apart had only made the longing worse, it seemed.

They sat in silence, listening to each other breathe. The tension eased out of Ethaniel's body; he imagined it slipping away like an afternoon shadow at dusk. He needed to go home soon. And he wanted to be here. The stress of the day wasn't gone, only pushed aside to make room for old hurts, old concerns.

Here, perhaps, the things that kept him up at night needn't loom so large. He could put them to bed for a moment and see the world through another set of eyes, ones bright and shining and not dulled by every tiny stressor.

And he could be with Aubrey. His light at the end of the tunnel. His waypoint. Surely there was more to their story than a handful of spectacular months followed by incredible pain.

Surely there was more.

Calix's face, his gentle care, his soft voice, pushed their way to the surface. That little thing made Ethaniel feel like a dirty traitor; but was that right? Was finding another man attractive seen as a wrong to Aubrey?

Did it matter?

Those long fingers kept combing through Ethaniel's hair, the pressure against his skull so divine it made Ethaniel sigh. "I know what you're thinking," Aubrey said quietly. "That we've landed in quite a mess."

"A mess I brought to your door," Ethaniel replied.

Aubrey huffed. "True, but a mess I willingly then brought into my work."

"Also true."

Another huff, more like a laugh now. "And you brought along with it someone who...I mean, your Calix fills the role of plucky young hero rather well."

Now Ethaniel raised his head, staring hard at Aubrey. Aubrey met his gaze but something on his face looked damn near *vulnerable* now. "He's not *mine*," Ethaniel said, his throat dry now. "He literally ran into me."

"But he'd been in the shop the prior week. Leaving right as I came in."

Ethaniel had spared more than a few thoughts toward those seconds where all three of them had stood on his shop floor, not even remotely aware of how their fates would intertwine mere days later.

"You say that as though every person who comes into the shop is mine," he groused.

Aubrey laughed. Actually laughed. His face broke into a rare, full smile and the sight of it made something in Ethaniel crack open. "Only the beautifully handsome ones, with large brown eyes and copper hair."

"I don't know what you're getting at," Ethaniel replied. Some part of him *did*, but it was a fleeting notion. Right? Aubrey couldn't be...

"Don't you?"

God, how he'd missed Aubrey's playful side. Ethaniel swatted at his shoulder, drawing out another laugh. "I thought you dragged me in here to apologize."

"So I did."

Quick as a fox, Aubrey swooped in to cup Ethaniel's jaw once more. He *loomed* now, dark and dangerous and as changing as a tide brought in by a storm.

"Aubrey," Ethaniel breathed out.

"I've missed you." Aubrey's thumb brushed Ethaniel's bottom lip. "I've missed this. And I will continue to apologize, because I was wrong."

"So was I."

"Then perhaps..." Aubrey leaned in closer still, tilting his head. Tantalizing Ethaniel with possibility. With promise. "Perhaps you'll let me apologize like this, too."

Ethaniel melted into him, into that touch, that promise, that chance...and when it became reality, when Aubrey's lips brushed his, Ethaniel's *soul* shivered. All the old hurts were salted over, stitched but scarred so they might be gone but not forgotten. Meant to make room for the new, the open, the honest.

The way Aubrey gripped him, cradled his face, pulled him closer? It spoke of repression, yes, but more than that, of an unbridled *need* that rose above all else. Aubrey's passion wasn't told in small touches and furtive glances. It was in raw, carnal physicality. Ethaniel knew that well.

Aubrey's tongue touched his, sweetly begging for entrance, and Ethaniel let him in. He groaned as heat flushed through him. Not every bead of sweat at his temples was because of the humid air.

Aubrey kissed him hard now, his grip near to painful but perfectly balanced on that edge. The way Aubrey knew Ethaniel liked. That touch, this kiss, tipped Ethaniel headlong into pleasure, leaving his breath bottled up in his lungs and begging for release and yet Ethaniel denied it. He wanted the burn of it, welcomed it openly, and returned Aubrey's kiss with tongue and teeth and a palm to the back of Aubrey's head.

When Aubrey finally pulled away, they were both gasping. Ethaniel's thoughts, so chaotic before, were now filled with *Aubrey*. His taste, his scent, the way his corded muscles gave under Ethaniel's touch.

For that moment, in the quiet, humid dark, they found their bond again.

"I've missed you," Ethaniel whispered, too choked up to say anything else as he stared into Aubrey's eyes. "And I forgive you. Can you forgive me? I know it might take time to mend us fully, but I want to try."

Aubrey's stoic face melted into something soft and earnest. It made Ethaniel's heart flip in his chest. "There are no trespasses if what we did was out of concern.

Misguided, yes, but concern nonetheless." Aubrey carefully brushed the hair out of Ethaniel's face. They'd emerge from this little nook looking all the more damp and mussed, but Ethaniel had a feeling no one in this strange place would care.

Ethaniel laughed. "I'm afraid mine was more out of pride and ego."

Aubrey drew them together once more, his hand firm and warm on the back of Ethaniel's neck. Their foreheads touched and Ethaniel closed his eyes. "It doesn't matter anymore."

TEN

CALIX

Calix had never seen so many beautiful robes in one place. He adored a fine robe — how the material swirled around his ankles, its slip against his skin. His robes were all at home, tucked away in their drawers like perfectly pressed squares of luxury waiting on his return. He should be there now, instead of standing before a massive granite and wood table while the attendant Basil stood off to the side, ready to assist.

He should be at home. Safe. Secure. Home, where he never had such conundrums arise. Home was quiet and easy, the very place where his anxieties about the world at large bled out into a state of calm.

But if he went home, would Lawton be there? How would he explain the book, Calix wondered. What excuses would his *dearest* friend make?

Questioning their friendship was part and parcel for being a passenger in Lawton's life. Calix often wondered why he kept Lawton's company after boarding school, after Cambridge. Surely he could find other friends, other connections. Edna, his guardian until his twenty-first birthday, had despised Lawton with gracefully concealed grimaces. She never spoke ill of him to Calix, but her disapproval wasn't difficult to discern.

Lawton's quick mind and silver tongue did him well in many situations. He was much more adept at navigating tricky social circles with their finicky politics and snide asides, so Calix benefited from that. And to Lawton's credit, Calix never heard any whisperings of his friend talking behind his back. Lawton had stuck by his side at countless parties and balls, had known when to usher Calix outside when the press of people and the heat of their bodies was too much.

But he was also...*challenging*. Particularly when they were alone. Lawton had a unique ability to make Calix feel like the center of the solar system. When Lawton focused his attentions on someone, they tended to *glow*. Calix had certainly felt that way many times.

"I'd recommend the peacock silk, sir. The blue would look fine against your hair."

Calix suppressed his startle at Basil's smooth voice interrupting his thoughts. "Ah, yes. I had been leaning that way myself but..." He traced the lace collar of a robe so black it seemed to defy the definition of color. Instead of robust velvet or slippery satin, this robe was delicate and sheer. It twisted something inside Calix's gut, made him suck in a breath.

He knew he would look very good in this robe. So why shouldn't he wear it?

Wasn't he trying to attract *their* attention? What would it be like to sit with Aubrey and Ethaniel and discuss their plan for that cursed book and see if their gazes strayed? Why shouldn't he tempt them to drink him in, to wonder if the fabric might be a little more sheer if Calix were to only pull it taut?

They were both incredibly attractive men. And had clearly been together at one point, and still longed for each other. But there was a simmering energy there when Aubrey looked at him; Calix had at first thought it was disapproval, but he soon realized that Aubrey was *calculated*. Ethaniel was all heart, molten to the core and as sweet as penny candy. He was gentle but mindful. Aubrey, on the other hand, was thrilling in a domineering sort of way.

Yes, this robe was the right one. Perhaps he was losing his mind thinking of more...intimate situations in which all three of them could partake, but it was also the only thing keeping him from worrying away the skin on his lower lip. A bad habit, for sure, but difficult to put aside when it felt like the weight of the world rested on him and that damn book.

"This one," Calix said, rubbing the lace between his fingertips.

Basil nodded before coming around to Calix's left and plucking the robe up with both hands. "I'll be waiting for you after you change, sir." He motioned to an area of red velvet-curtained stalls.

When Calix hesitated, Basil gave him a bright smile. It disarmed the thread of sudden nerves in him and Calix relaxed. "I assume this is your first time at a *proper* bathhouse?"

Calix nodded. "I'm afraid so."

"It's nothing to be concerned about, sir. Many of the people who come here are a bit hesitant before they understand the lay of the land." Basil's pretty smile evened out and he began to unfold the robe with easy movements. "The main floor is the bathing chamber. As you saw when you came in, it's for lounging and bathing. Many who come to the Minotaur Baths prefer to stay there, soaking in the mineral waters and enjoying the company of other men and those who do not wish to categorize themselves."

"But there are floors above?" Calix asked.

"There are." With the robe unfolded, Calix could see delicate red embroidery along its hem and pockets, clearly done by a skilled hand. It wasn't to the level of Ethaniel's work, to be sure, but it was beautiful. "The second level has small private areas for conversation and entertainment. There is a staff waiting to take your order for anything from cocktails to cigarettes. It is the only floor that requires some form of coverage from the waist down."

Calix tried not to goggle at that. "I'm sorry?"

Basil's expression remained placid, but his eyes glittered. The man had a vulpine face, all sharp, narrow angles that seemed a tad...*sinister*. And Basil's stare was thorough, as though he were taking stock of Calix inside and out.. "The springs are naturally clothing-optional. The second floor requires some form of dress from the waist down, so that no one is uncomfortable traversing there." He leaned in as if sharing a secret. "The third floor is a bit...different."

Calix couldn't possibly flush any more but oh, no...yes, that burning in his cheeks was, in fact, intensifying. Wonderful. "Different, how?"

"Ah, well, it requires reservation, for one. And it's quite popular, so typically the wait is at least two to three months. And that floor plays host to more sensual sights." Basil gave him an apologetic smile. "I'm afraid I cannot divulge more. But Mr. Lavigne may have some knowledge he wishes to share."

Calix swallowed against a dry throat. "He does?"

"I cannot confirm that, sir, but you may wish to ask him, as he is a member of our establishment."

Basil was quick to move Calix into a curtained stall after that, but before he flicked the heavy velvet curtain closed, he gave Calix a keen look. "And please excuse me for the forwardness, sir, but if you ever find yourself curious about the third floor but want to be more discreet, I am available for private tours. Now, once you've changed to your level of comfort, please leave your clothes and shoes inside the stall and I'll retrieve them. They will be cleaned and pressed while you're in the bathhouse, and returned to you once you've partaken in all you wish."

The curtain fell from Basil's fingers and Calix was left to stand in the stall, robe in hand, wondering what in the hells he'd gotten himself into.

Carefully, he undressed and folded his clothes, resting them atop his shoes. The choice to leave his undergarments on made him freeze up. Could he truly be so bold as to wear nothing underneath a sheer robe? What would Ethaniel and Aubrey think? Would they see him as too forward, too assuming? What if...well, what if neither of them desired him in the same way?

Was he fooling himself?

Sighing, Calix picked up the robe to give it another look. He could stand here all day and waffle about, or he could be the person Lawton said he was.

Brave, sweet, tempting Calix, with your honey hair and chocolate eyes. Gorgeous in every way, but especially your soft heart. What a darling, what a treat you are.

Calix shucked the last stitch of clothing, slipped on the robe and tied it tight. A glance in the standing mirror revealed the robe's clever design; the embroidery around the pockets was patterned to serve as a kind of opaque shield around the groin area. Calix turned this way and that, trying to make the robe reveal any part of his intimate areas, but it didn't work. A silent sigh of relief escaped him and he finally felt confident enough to be seen by others. When he emerged from the stall, Basil was folding more robes, his back turned to Calix.

"Do I pass muster?" Calix asked.

Basil's expression upon turning to Calix was worth its weight in gold. The man set aside the deep plum robe he'd been folding, not noticing or not caring when it fell to the floor, and walked to Calix. Calix stepped back as Basil's taller, broader form towered over him.

Calix found he *liked it*. This strange man, in this strange, wonderful, freeing place, was staring at Calix as though he hung the moon. Basil looked besotted.

Lawton used to look at him like that.

"You are some fey creature come to tempt all who see you, I think," Basil said. His tone was warm, almost casual, but an undercurrent of *darkness* rattled something loose in Calix. "I think your friends will be unable to look away." Basil swallowed hard, leaving Calix to track the movement. There was the tiniest bit of stubble under Basil's chin, likely a miss with a tricky straight razor. The sight left Calix feeling itchy for contact. Even a single touch.

"I've not known them so long," Calix replied, staring up into Basil's eyes. He really did have beautiful ones, all emerald green with a touch of brown near the irises.

"If I might be so bold..." And Basil reached out to touch Calix's collar. When Calix didn't object, Basil leaned in more, angling his head until his lips were at Calix's ear. "If they do not treat you the way you deserve, come and find me."

Then Basil stepped back, walked over to the counter, and resumed his folding.

"You....you utter *tease*," Calix sputtered, unable to wipe the grin from his face.

Basil smiled back, as placid as a lake on a summer morning. "Room 4 on the first level is where your companions will be. If you need guidance there, I'd be happy to take you."

Calix shook his head. "Thank you anyways."

He left Basil to his folding, amused and not a small bit excited for what lay ahead. Yes, the book was priority; no number of teasing smirks and knowing glances could distract entirely from such a serious problem. But this place was, in Calix's opinion, a minor miracle. Even the time with Basil had felt like proper flirtation, instead of perverse exchange. Basil had *appreciated* Calix, and hadn't seemed the least bit concerned it had been untoward. Calix had never felt as though Basil wouldn't adhere to his wishes, whether on robe choice or the flirting. It was...remarkable.

Gay and queer masculine people proudly presenting themselves authentically, with no fear of scrutiny or repercussion? It boggled the mind, and even more so now that he knew this was a place Aubrey frequented.

Head held high, Calix strode out of the changing chamber and into the bathhouse proper. And like with his interaction with Basil, Calix was aware of *attention* cast his way. But even when he met the stares of other men, from their rocky perches in the mineral waters or as they walked past him, their steps silent on the stone floors, he never once felt ogled. And he didn't mind the little smiles and handful of winks tossed his way.

There was nothing wrong with being appreciated, and here, deep underground, far removed from the anxieties of the world above, Calix understood acceptance. He understood admiration. And he felt appreciated in a way he'd never before experienced.

Up ahead, the natural stone walls created several hollow spaces which the bathhouse had turned into private rooms for small groups. Numbers were painted in black on the walls; Calix found number 4 but neither of his companions. The space was surprisingly plush, given it was a literal room made of rock, but the hard slab seats were covered in cushions and pillows. The room could seat around four people comfortably, but the sharp curve in the wall would force inhabitants to budge together.

Calix started to lean toward number 3 when a voice behind him said, "We needed to get Ethaniel a robe. Apologies, Calix."

Aubrey's voice sent a shiver down Calix's spine. He had a lovely voice meant for candlelit dinners and smokey libraries; for lounging in dressing robes while sipping fine whiskey or port. Soothing, vibrant, and deep.

Slowly, Calix turned and found Ethaniel and Aubrey standing rather close behind him. The intrinsic intimacy of the lack of space was thrilling. But even better was how the two men looked in their robes: Aubrey, properly imperious like a pampered king in oxblood red, his glass-colored eyes softer in the flickering lantern light; and Ethaniel swaddled in deep gold with navy trim, his very profile arresting like an artist's subject to which no paint or brush could do justice.

But for all their beauty, all their appeal to Calix, what he found most intriguing — and most titillating — was how they stared at him. Aubrey disguised it better, but Ethaniel's open appreciation was shockingly forthright. Something in Calix itched to drop the robe and let them look at him. Let them see the muscle he earned in fencing classes, the trail of dark blonde hair down his stomach, and even the old scars from childhood accidents.

He was certain they'd see him in a way Lawton never did.

"Shall we?" Aubrey said, motioning to room 4.

Calix followed him and Ethaniel inside and watched, fascinated, as Aubrey pulled a small lever tucked down by the bottom of the rock bench.

"For privacy," Aubrey said as something *snapped* into place over the room's entrance. It was magic, it had to be, from the way it fizzled and popped under Calix's skin.

"I'm surprised they allow that," Ethaniel said as he settled in the room's hair-pin-like curve. Immediately, Ethaniel hugged a bright yellow pillow to his lap, learning forward slightly. "Seems an excuse for the authorities to claim ignorance of crimes."

"I was just thinking it seemed a good way to disguise criminal activities," Calix mused. "But in a place like this...I see your point." He sat down, his worry suddenly triple what it had been when they'd arrived.

"It's not a privilege one can simply buy here," Aubrey said delicately, sitting to Ethaniel's right, leaving the left seat open. "And we don't have it for long before they will need to recollect the shielding ward."

As Aubrey turned his focus onto him, Calix couldn't help but see the way Aubrey and Ethaniel seemed to curl into each other. He narrowed his eyes.

Wait. Something's different. They look...they look...

Calix shook off the sudden revelation. Of course they looked more intimate, even though their hands were in their laps — Aubrey's in the robe's deep pockets, Ethaniel's fussing with the tasseled tie about his waist.

Something had certainly shifted.

Calix sank into the pillows at his back, closed his eyes, and dug his fists into his eye sockets. "I've been trying to summarize all of this in my mind. It's not easy." When Aubrey hummed in thought and Ethaniel nodded, Calix continued. "The book was in the lot Lawton won at auction, which he won with money a dark-haired woman gave him. The auction was the one he beat Aubrey out for. The next day, Lawton asked me to accompany him to a man named Tomas, who seemed to be some sort of smuggler. Tomas was not Lawton's buyer for the book

I'm going to call..." Blearily, he opened one eye and looked at the others. "Any suggestions?"

"I uh...hmmm." Aubrey tapped his finger against his lips. "Well, certainly not its *real name*."

Ethaniel began to chuckle. "You two have absolutely no imagination. And I feel as though I'd been hit on the head with a baton even suggesting this, but what about Pandora?"

Aubrey nodded. "That'll do nicely, I think."

"All right, so...*Pandora* wasn't being sold to Tomas, but to the person we were to see next."

"Do you know where that was?" Ethaniel asked.

Calix racked his memory. "Babylon Boulevard, then Bleeker. No, there was something else there." He let his eyes drift shut once more, trying to recall. Everything had been such a blur, feeling as though days had passed when it had only been a few dozen hours. "Ah! 3rd Avenue! That was the spot between. I know it wasn't Bleeker because Lawton said he'd gotten us reservations at the White Lotus, which is on Bleeker."

"Very good." Aubrey's low voice rumbled, resonating off the small chamber's walls. It was like adrenaline in Calix's heart. "And Tomas is the one who got aggressive, which is why Lawton had you run?"

"Tomas was trying to take Lawton's bag. He seemed the sort to strong-arm someone. Then Lawton shoved the bag at me and told me to run." Calix flicked a smile up at Ethaniel. Ethaniel's fussing with the belt stopped and he smiled back. "I ran into Ethaniel, and he helped me hide."

Ethaniel's smile widened. "I wouldn't turn away anyone seeking help."

Silence lay heavy on them, broken only by the sound of Aubrey drumming his fingers on the rock beside him. After a long moment, Aubrey leaned in, gaze gone sharp. Calix felt the weight of that scrutiny, heavier than any silence.

"The book talked to you."

Memory was an insistent tug on Calix's mind now, letting him drift deeper into those moments. They'd been painful and terrifying, but the messages had always been clear.

I know you hear me

You heard me the first time
You hear me now
I understand you better now

"'Like the voice of a god', you said," Ethaniel whispered. One of Ethaniel's beautiful hands balled into a fist amongst the voluminous fabric of his goldenrod robe. "That's...horrifying."

"Any psychic feedback? Headache, nausea?" Aubrey asked, his voice soft once more. When Calix nodded, Aubrey's mouth turned into a mue of pity and sympathy. "When it lashed out at me, my head felt as though it was on fire. And then I fainted."

"Did it speak?" Calix asked.

"'Something new is here.' And then it asked me who I was, because I'd been able to 'break through'. But I wasn't 'the other one'." Aubrey was back to tapping his chin with his finger, the expression pensive and pinched. "The book has an affinity to you, Calix. It didn't fight me when I locked it away, but I expect it may not be pleased when we return."

"We?" Ethaniel asked, just as Calix said, "Return?"

"We have to. That book cannot stay in the Collectio's vault without formal record. I'm letting it slide now due to safety concerns, but we need to go back tomorrow."

"I need to return home to check in with my valet," Calix replied quickly. "I can also find out if Lawton's been around."

Ethaniel nodded. "And I need to go back to my uncle tonight. Perhaps you should stay with me, Calix? I can go with you to your home, and then we can meet Aubrey together in the morning?"

"I think that's the best course of action." Aubrey's eyes glittered in the low light. "I have some research to do tonight once we depart from here."

"Aubrey has the finest research library," Ethaniel said as he now curved toward Calix. Calix swore he could feel the other man's warmth, even though there was space between them on the bench. "He's a sight handy with books, but he's even better with magical items."

Aubrey shifted slightly, frowned, then reached behind him to pull out a dark blue pillow. "Bloody thing was poking me in the back," he grumbled before replying. "My abilities rest in healing, but not people. My family is from a long line of Cunning Folk, as far back as the 15th century. They were rather well-known and held for a few centuries, and then the church got involved. It's a long story, but suffice to say my family is *very* well-steeped in healing magics and that turned out to not be my path."

Calix was intrigued. "So you heal objects?"

Aubrey gave a shrug. "In a way. Magical objects present the most challenge, but are the most rewarding."

"But you can mend things, like a broken chair?"

Aubrey nodded. "Easy enough."

A glimmer of a thought sparked in Calix's mind, like a flashbulb behind his eyes. "Do you work on privately held objects?"

That got him a narrowed gaze and to his right, Ethaniel shifted as if uncomfortable. Well, there was no stopping a runaway train. No sense in backtracking now. Stars, he was starting to sound like Lawton.

"Perhaps, though my work for the Collectio, and now the mystery of this book, hold the bulk of my attention."

Calix smiled. A man like Aubrey wouldn't be able to resist his mother's collection. "What about an entire collection of dead magical objects?"

One dark eyebrow slowly raised. Calix saw Ethaniel bite his lip, then their gazes locked. Ethaniel was curious, that much was certain, but there was a coyness to the look he gave Calix, as if to say, *Ah, good. You've found one of Aubrey's buttons. Well done.*

"My mother was a collector in her own right. But she was adamant that anything she collected be dead before crossing the threshold of the house." Calix smiled softly. "She was sensitive, particularly to magic, but she loved sitting at her big drafting desk and staring through a set of magnifying lenses, admiring all the details on every object that came into her hands. She had reliquary chambers, wax death masks, something a buyer told her was a copy of a 'utopian machine', which turned out to be bunk. But she loved every item equally, said they showed love and devotion and madness in equal measure."

Aubrey looked as if someone had struck him across the face with a glove. "Every object is non-functional?"

Calix nodded, then because Aubrey and Ethaniel were both staring at him, he rubbed his palm across his jaw. Ethaniel made some kind of *noise*, something that could be mistaken for a muted groan.

Calix kept his expression gentle, even though he so badly wanted to grin. "Are you all right, Ethaniel?"

Ethaniel's eyes shot wide. "Oh, I...yes. Yes. I'm fine. Just rather warm. Seems I picked the wrong robe." He plucked up part of the collar and held the neck of the robe open slightly.

A yearning took hold of Calix then, sweet and lovely, and he wanted to help peel Ethaniel's robe off and revel in the glistening skin below it. All this magical talk, all this threat of danger and the fog of confusion, was making Calix antsy. The energy inside him felt bottled up, looking for release. It was as though his body didn't understand the difference between the tensions warring in him.

After a deep breath, Calix eyed the magical shield ward over the opening to the nook. "How long do we have, Aubrey?"

"Just a few minutes."

Feeling brazen, Calix laid a hand on Ethaniel's arm and said, "As neither of us wants darling Ethaniel to overheat, let's simply plan for tonight and tomorrow morning."

"I'm going with you," Ethaniel said immediately.

"All right, then we will meet up with Aubrey afterwards?" Calix looked down at his hands and sighed. "This is all some horrible mess. I wish I could just pay Lawton for the book and leave it in your capable hands, Aubrey."

Aubrey seemed slightly chuffed by that, a smile playing about his face. That smile made fine lines appear around his mouth and Calix was utterly charmed. "As far as plans go, it's not a bad one. But I'm going to guess your friend is in deep with whoever that dark-haired woman is connected to or works for. He may ask for a lot, or for something else entirely."

"Lawton's always asking for something else," Calix muttered. Twin looks of surprise got his attention. "Apologies. I've known him for so long, and he can be wonderful one day, and terrible the next. I've only ever seen him be truly kind to me, and even then I knew he was using me. I've not been strong enough to break away."

"You are, though," Ethaniel replied as he put his hand on Calix's knee and squeezed. "You've already stood up for yourself."

"That's kind of you, Ethaniel, but I think it's going to take more than one instance of me doing that to get through to him." Calix huffed out a humorless laugh. "And that would involve more than me running away from some Babylon Boulevard thug."

To Calix's utter shock, Aubrey swiftly leaned over Ethaniel, coming so close to Calix that he could smell Aubrey's cologne or soap. The sweet, slightly bitter scent of lemongrass cut with heady, dark jasmine made him breathe in deeply. And Aubrey noticed.

"Don't cut yourself short, Calix," Aubrey said as he carefully placed his hand on top of Ethaniel's, so both rested on Calix's knee. "You've done several very brave, very forward-thinking things to date, and we haven't known each other that long. Don't cheapen your intelligence, or your skills. Lawton might want that from you, but we don't."

Calix found himself trapped — he wanted *so badly* to wedge himself between them, so he might trace Ethaniel's square jaw or Aubrey's cheek with his fingertips. The kindness called to him as much as their physicality did, and Calix felt as if he were floating.

"Thank you," he whispered, leaning so far forward his robe gaped.

Two sets of eyes darted to where a bit of his chest was exposed.

"Perhaps," Ethaniel said, "we should partake in the mineral baths. Since we're here anyways. And we can talk about things that aren't as frightening as a sentient book."

"I would love that," Calix said, daring to lean forward a tad more. He almost smiled at the way Aubrey stared. It seemed the man had a few human weaknesses after all. "I just need a moment alone, to sort my thoughts out."

And in truth he did. The appeal of these two men, the question of Lawton's loyalties, the Damocles' sword of the book...it made his head spin. Calix wanted to enjoy the baths with a clearer head.

At his nod and smile, Ethaniel and Aubrey got to their feet and slowly made their way out, leaving Calix alone in the room to breathe in the fragrant air and wonder how in the world this had all happened.

INTERLUDE

LAWTON

Earlier that morning

If Lawton's irritation could manifest into physical form, it would look a lot like the massive gorilla he'd once seen at the Central Park Zoo. Huge and hulking, with rippling muscles and deep brown eyes that glared at anyone who came too close while it paced in its enclosure.

He hated waiting.

"If you tap your foot one more time, Mr. Adler, I will find cause to have you escorted from this room."

Lawton bit the inside of his cheek and huffed, but he did as the mage instructed. "Well, then I shall tap no more."

"Excellent." The older woman didn't look up from the jade-green bowl into which she gazed. She likely couldn't, Lawton assumed through his limited understanding of divination, but he did know that Irene Blau was one of the best trackers in the city. He'd used her for far more piddly things than tracking his dearest friend, and Irene had been correct every time. Lawton fully expected the *very* good money he was paying her now would turn up results.

"Hmmm. Well, he hasn't gone home," Irene said as a flash of light came from the bowl. Or her hands. Perhaps both. Lawton couldn't quite tell, but the light was bright enough that it made little sparks dance before his eyes.

Lawton averted his gaze as he said, "Strange. Calix is a creature of comfort. He's not been home at all?"

"I said he hasn't, so he hasn't," Irene replied. Her voice was snarled from years of cigar smoking and living near the factories that churned out machine parts and sent black smoke billowing over the rooftops of Queens. It made her sound angry even when she wasn't. Lawton wasn't quite sure if he'd tipped her past the point of irritation, but then again, she'd kept him waiting for almost half an hour while she stared into her little bowl.

Half an hour, and no results yet other than to find out that Calix hadn't been home.

Lawton sighed, then immediately clamped his lips shut when the guard in all black who hovered just inside the door made a move forward.

"No need, Samson," Irene said, waving a hand at her bodyguard. "He's just being a little shit."

Lawton bit the inside of his cheek harder, then winced as his incisor sank into the sore he'd worried there over the last day or so. All because of *fucking Calix.*

Godsdammit, Calix, where are you?

"You need to think a little quieter, Mr. Adler," Irene said as she held up a finger. "I understand you believe your thoughts should stand out above all others, but I can guarantee you aren't the only pissed-off Englishman writhing around in my bowl. But most of them have real reasons to be angry, like hunger or uncertainty about where they may sleep tonight. Now, be quiet, or I will let Samson escort you out, despite my words a moment ago."

Lawton hid his smile behind a cough. He liked the old bat even when she was testy, and Irene usually gave half of a fuck on a good day. If she hadn't ripped into him, Lawton would have wondered if she was ill.

So he sat in the red leather wingback chair in the corner, crossed his legs, and waited.

And waited.

"Ah, there he is." Lawton's moment of jubilation at Irene's exclamation instantly shifted to something more concerning when she added, "No wonder I couldn't get a bead on him. Whoever he's with is quite good at Sight warding. They even managed to block me for a time. But I also wasn't expecting...*that.*"

Something in her tone made Lawton's blood cool. "Expecting what?"

Irene leaned back from the bowl with a deep inhale, then she slowly turned in her chair to lock him down with her steel gray eyes. The light from her divination Sight was fading, but bits of it still glowed within those cold irises. "Your Calix has not one, but two people in quite close proximity who reek of desire. Practically coated in it. I'm almost jealous." She eyed him closely. "Two men, complete opposites in appearance. One is coated in patterning magic, the other is...colder, somehow. I only get a glimpse of a walking cane and strange eyes."

Lawton's mind whirled, a dandelion seed on a vicious wind.

"I take it you know at least one of these men," Irene said with a smirk.

Lawton got to his feet, feeling unmoored, as if the very floor were shifting under him. Like when he and Calix had taken ferries around the small port near their boarding school. Thirteen years old and every day seemed new, bright, bold. He'd looked at Calix one day and saw someone new in his friend's place; someone devastated by his mother's death and void of himself. Lawton had wanted to comfort Calix but didn't know how until Calix had leaned into him, sighed into Lawton's neck, and cried silent, shaking tears.

The wind had been brutal that day, and the ferry had bobbed. No more than a toy to the wind, something the ferry driver had no power over. He had no power over Calix's sadness. And the ferry had bobbed on.

Somewhere along the way, it had all gotten twisted up. And somehow that damn museum curator was involved in all of it. The man was *close* to Calix, lusting after him. Taking up the spot that Lawton had rightfully won so many years ago.

"Where is he?" Lawton bit out.

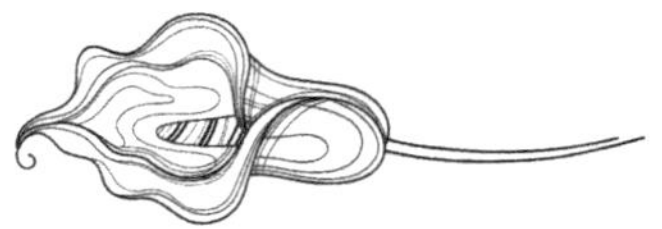

The tall, burly man at the wide wood and steel door stopped Lawton with a hand. The door hadn't been the easiest to locate, even with Irene's rather specific directions. So Lawton's barometer of ire for the day was high already, and now this massive man was saying so insouciantly, "No entrance."

Lawton was having flashbacks of just a week before, when he and Calix had been stopped from going into that blasted salon in Acadia. But this man was well-dressed and coiffed, whereas the salon guard had been some thug hired off the street. He might not be so easy to buy off.

Lawton narrowed his eyes, recalculating his attack. Claims of an issue with membership renewal slipped in between a few hearty handshakes stuffed with bills likely wouldn't succeed here. So the next natural answer was the one that could lead to more problems, but he'd rather Calix be incredibly angry at him than cause a scene that could catch the attention of the Order.

Lawton thumbed the little golden circle pin under his lapel, gave the guard a sheepish smile, and said, "Honestly, mate, I'm not a member, but a friend is." He held his hand a few inches above his own head. "Aubrey Lavigne's his name. Rather tall bloke, close-cropped hair, impeccably dressed, pale green eyes?"

The man clicked his tongue, ran it over his teeth, and said, "Are you asking me about his features or describing them to me?"

What was it with doormen in this blasted city? Lawton bit back on his frustration. Today was going to end in spectacular fashion, whether he lost his temper or not. Truth be told, he didn't have much of a plan outside of "find Calix, get the book back", but the presence of Aubrey Lavigne and another man had mucked everything up. He had one idea, and it was a terrible, brilliant one. Lawton wasn't ever in denial about his looks, or the heads he turned with regularity, and weaponizing those to get what he wanted was usually rather simple.

He didn't suspect for a second that a man like Aubrey Lavigne — tall and proud and unbending — would be an easy target.

So Lawton smiled at the man, ignored his flat expression, and leaned in close to say, "Aubrey's the kind of man with a bit of influence to fling around, and he tells me that this is the most premier club this side of the city. I want to join."

The man shrugged. "Membership's closed for the foreseeable future." He sucked on his teeth and the sound made Lawton want to rip the man's tongue out of his mouth and watch it wriggle. "There's another place a couple of blocks over—"

With a snap of his wrist, Lawton had the man's chin in his hand. The soft flesh under the man's jaw puckered slightly where Lawton pressed a tiny blade against it. He sighed, knowing the claw ring was going to be hell to replace. The transforming spell that allowed the big ruby signet ring to slide down his finger and seamlessly become a hooked claw that fit around his fingertip was long lost to his family. But such was the risk with patterns, Lawton supposed.

"Walk with me," Lawton said softly, making sure to lean in and block the sight of any passerby with his body. They were at the back of the building, off a long hall, where footsteps would echo loud and clear across the gold-veined marble. No one had yet walked by but Lawton wasn't going to chance Fate at this moment. Silencing patterns weren't uncommon, after all.

His hand clenched tightly, warningly, around the man's beefy upper arm, Lawton steered them to a shadowed alcove he'd noted on his initial approach. Uncertainty on how he'd approach Calix was unique; he was always aware of his surroundings otherwise.

"There," he snapped, giving the doorman a solid elbow to the kidney before rushing forward to press his claw under that fleshy chin once more.

The man's eyes were backlit with defiance, but his brain must have caught up with him because he said, "Pass is in my pocket. Won't work after today, cause they'll notice the queer entrance patterns—"

With a vicious snarl, Lawton snapped his elbow up with a wide arc. There was no need for the blade to go into the man, after all. The doorman took the blow with a huff of air before he dropped to his knees, eyes rolled up in his head like a dime novel lackey. Lawton stepped backwards as the man's unconscious form crashed to the floor, his lip curled as he stared down at the man.

"Well, lovely." Lawton made quick work of patting through a finely cut jacket, finding a decent wad of bills, a gold pocket watch, and...ah. *There.* A thin metal wallet, no thicker than a few sheets of paper, and inside was a pass to the Minotaur Baths. The thing was likely enchanted up and down and sideways, but Lawton only wanted to borrow it. Really, if the idiot now out cold at his feet had listened to him, his wad of cash would have been a little thicker for no more work than the turning of a door handle.

Lawton snatched it all up before staring down at the man. Specifically at the strip of skin under his ear. Without any more measured consideration, Lawton split that bit of skin with his little gold claw, and before the blood could drip onto a starched white collar, he flicked the now-broken ring into a handkerchief and tucked it away, coming back out with a small, square compact. It was a pretty thing, pure silver and dotted with strange little runes Cassandra refused to explain to him. "All that matters is you use this on anyone you have to be…aggressive with," she'd said when he'd first been recruited. The compact was a new invention of the Golden Order's leader, Vincent de Laine, but apparently not everyone received it. Not everyone could be trusted with such a powerful tool.

Well, Lawton had never been someone with a strong moral fiber, but even he wasn't going to run around wiping everyone's memories. Morality was the stuff ginned up by the churches, and with so many of them now, suddenly, railing against the "fags and fairies"? A pox on their so-called "morality". Everyone knew the priests were made of ill repute, too. He'd not yet had cause to use the compact, and now relished the feel of it in his palm, cool and serene like a springtime lake.

He flipped it open, then rubbed his thumb across the cobalt ink inside the compact, making sure to get it all on the cut he'd made. Instantly, the skin glowed with a sickly green light, then faded to reveal unblemished skin. He got to his feet, tucked away the compact, and headed back down the hall.

Job well done, me, Lawton thought as he used the door pass and followed the dark, steep stairs into air that lay heavy with humidity and the scent of salt and lavender. *Now to figure out what the fuck to do about Calix.*

Eleven

AUBREY

"I should have brought us here sooner."

Ethaniel smiled down at him. "Maybe. Or maybe we're here exactly when we should be."

Calix had asked for a moment alone in the small pool room, which afforded he and Ethaniel some time in the fragrant steam in one of the near-empty pools in the middle of the hot springs. Aubrey had immediately sank up to mid-chest, but Ethaniel lingered on the edge, dangling his feet in the water. They were both gloriously nude, neither one of them concerned about modesty. There was no need for it in such places, and that particular brand of casual intimacy was why people kept coming back to the Minotaur Baths, and helped to keep it open despite the raids and lockdowns. Society was already bending in a way that concerned Aubrey, and while he hoped to be proven incorrect, he doubted such would be his luck.

The Minotaur Baths were sacred for men like him and Ethaniel, and apparently Calix. It hadn't been a total shock to discover the man's proclivities through a red carnation brooch when they'd first met, but the blatant hunger in Calix's eyes when he'd seen them in their robes?

That had been a thrill, even if some part of Aubrey wondered where in the hell this sudden attraction to young aristocrats had come from.

"You are too quiet," Ethaniel said, giving Aubrey a friendly nudge with his foot.

Aubrey snorted. "Not a sentence I expected to hear from you."

"Well, you're hearing it now." Ethaniel's toes poked Aubrey in the ribs. "I can hear your mind churning, Aubrey."

"Something about this doesn't add up," Aubrey slowly admitted as he rubbed his hand over his chin. "I feel as though we're missing something."

Ethaniel had reached up to undo the thick leather band that held back his hair, but now paused to give Aubrey a thoughtful look. "I admit my sleuthing skills aren't yours, but I agree. I don't think Calix has the answer, though."

"He truly stumbled into the entire thing," Aubrey said, "and dragged us into it."

Ethaniel's stare turned canny, his lips twitching as though holding back a smile. All right, perhaps he'd played into Ethaniel's hands *a little* on the subject of Calix, but Aubrey needed to know. Because for all the questions about this damn book and who was funding this Lawton fellow, Aubrey knew he'd been given a gift because of those same questions. He'd been given Ethaniel again, and this time he wasn't going to muck about.

If Ethaniel wanted him, and wanted Calix, Aubrey was more than happy to accommodate. The fact that Calix had a keen sense of curiosity and a sharp pair of brown eyes was a rather nice bonus.

Ethaniel now leaned down more, pressing his forehead to the top of Aubrey's head. His hand drifted onto Aubrey's shoulder and that single, innocent touch made Aubrey shiver. "You say one thing, but I hear another."

"Do you now?"

"Mhhhm." Ethaniel slid into the water, catching himself with a strong arm around Aubrey's shoulders. "Should we be doing this? Calix will come back at any moment—"

"Maybe the boy should know what he's getting into."

Before Ethaniel could say any more, Aubrey kissed him. This kiss didn't have the previous one's sharpness and tang, even with the salt air on their lips. This felt more true, more real, in a way that had Aubrey palming the back of Ethaniel's head in hopes of bringing him closer. Ethaniel curled sweetly against him, gifting Aubrey with a soft groan.

They couldn't do any more here, nor would Aubrey want to. Too many things hung in the air right now, and for all he felt like a puppet getting jangled about, Aubrey could put it all aside to show Ethaniel how he felt. With one glorious kiss.

A polite cough made them pause, just as Aubrey was smoothing his hand down Ethaniel's side. Aubrey bit back a smirk. He didn't bother to lift his head or look in Calix's direction to say, "You're staring. That's rather rude, especially coming from an Englishman."

"I'll have you know I'm the picture of mannered perfection, when I want to be."

Ethaniel went completely still in Aubrey's arms. *That is not Calix.* The voice was smoother, more honeyed, and Aubrey knew it immediately. The realization was like gravel in his throat.

Slowly, he let go of Ethaniel, even when his instincts screamed to pull him closer. Aubrey lifted his chin and gave Lawton Adler a look of cool neutrality. "Apologies, Mr. Adler. I mistook you for someone else."

Lawton's smile smeared across his face, and it made Aubrey's gut churn. The man stepped into the water, pale skin instantly going pink at the heat, but he unexpectedly kept his distance. It gave Aubrey a moment to put a reassuring hand on Ethaniel's shoulder.

Ethaniel bit his bottom lip, nodded, and slowly turned, putting his back against the wall. Aubrey mirrored Ethaniel's pose. It left a wide chasm of water between them and Lawton, like combatants with secretive goals across an uncertain field. At least from this direction, he and Ethaniel could hopefully catch Calix's attention before Lawton noticed him.

"I've never been mistaken for someone else, Mr. Lavigne. How delightful," Lawton finally said as he leaned back, arms laid out in a long line on the pool's edge. There was something feline and lanky about the man, and for all Calix was certain his friend had no magical abilities, Aubrey could still sense danger. Intuition, perhaps. Or simple dislike. Lawton wasn't helping himself by smiling at them in such a way.

"I see you know each other," Ethaniel said calmly.

"We've met before," Lawton drawled as he dipped a hand into the water. The move of a completely unbothered man.

It was a good act. But Ethaniel was no fool, and Aubrey was eternally grateful for his ability to read others. "How interesting," Ethaniel said, leaning in as if he yearned for more information. "And in a city this large. So how did you meet?"

Lawton's honey-colored eyes latched onto Aubrey, the grip of his gaze like the snapping of teeth. A threat. A question. "How *did* we meet, Mr. Lavigne? Don't be stingy, do share with your friend."

"At an auction," Aubrey replied smoothly. He could feign being unbothered as good as anyone. A mite like Lawton Adler was no match for him. "We bid on the same lot of old books."

"We did, indeed." Lawton's smile was no less canny, but it dipped as his left eyebrow arched. "I wonder if we were after the same title in that dusty lump of old leather and crumbling pages. Most of them were worthless, if that eases your *academic* conscience at all."

"It doesn't. And we weren't," Aubrey replied. "At least, not at first."

At that, Lawton went completely still. Beside him, Aubrey felt Ethaniel bristle. They were all dancing around the same thing, and the tension in the air cut through the salt. Aubrey was good in emergencies, but this scenario was beyond any of his experiences. All he could do was trust his own intuition and intelligence, and trust that Ethaniel was ready to play his role. Thankfully, Ethaniel could claim willful ignorance of some things, but even that knowledge wouldn't help keep Aubrey's worries at bay.

The canny smile was back in place. "Well, as fun as this strained silence is, I have a proposal for you and your friend, Mr. Lavigne." Lawton floated toward them now, making Aubrey wish he had the space in which to back up. Ethaniel didn't move, strong and still at Aubrey's left. They couldn't show weakness or fear, and Aubrey knew deep down that Lawton was just a pawn.

But Ethaniel had been attacked. And the book was deeply troubling. That *voice* still had its hooks in his mind, as if distance and time were mere obstacles over which it had to hurtle.

Aubrey drew himself up as tall as he could, staring down at Lawton. "And that is? We have no business currently, Mr. Adler."

"Oh, but we do. See, the two of you are connected to something of mine, due to a mutual friend. This mutual friend took that object. And I would like this object back." Lawton gently flicked a hand in Ethaniel's direction. "So it's quite simple. The other of you toddles off to fetch Calix — young fellow, gorgeous copper hair, bit of a wet blanket — while you and I talk, Mr. Lavigne. Because out of the two of you here now, I think I know where the power is."

Aubrey had never known such *rage*. It boiled under his skin, as if it might spew forth, all volcanic sludge and fire, and wanted to only bury the absolute ass standing in front of him. Bury him and never again let him curse the world with his guileful smile and little head cock, as if everyone who ever met Lawton Adler owed him.

Over Lawton's head, Aubrey saw Calix slinking back into the shadows, the line of his mouth grim and his brown eyes full of fear, and it only fueled the fire of Aubrey's anger.

All pretense evaporated, like mist in the air. Aubrey lunged for Lawton, fury incarnate. His fingertips brushed wet, damp skin and there was a surprised yell from somewhere beyond the pool, and then Aubrey was held still. Suspended. Eyes wild and rolling, Aubrey saw Lawton was stuck in the exact same position.

"That's enough," Ethaniel hissed, one hand outstretched, fingers spread wide. Just out of his periphery, Aubrey could make out the glittering lines of a pattern hanging in the air. "Both of you."

Aubrey couldn't move, but he could speak. "Ethaniel, not here."

"Too bad." Ethaniel circled around to face Lawton. His skin glistened with water and the strong, proud lines of his shoulder muscles shifted as he leaned forward. Aubrey could barely make out how close Ethaniel was to Lawton, whose eyes were near to bulging out of their sockets. For once, the man looked *afraid*.

"I'll say this quickly, before someone calls an attendant on us," Ethaniel continued. "You are here to retrieve the book you left with Calix when you got into a bit of a pickle in Babylon Boulevard. Fine. But that book is dangerous, and I'm guessing whoever you're working for is a bit dangerous, too. Which puts you, Mr. Adler, in a sticky situation." Something cunning flashed over Ethaniel's face and Aubrey watched, spellbound, as his lover took the situation firmly in his grasp and twisted it until he was satisfied. It was...well, rather *glorious* to watch. If he wasn't suspended by magic, Aubrey might have had to will away tendrils of desire.

Ethaniel snapped his fingers and dropped the pattern. Aubrey and Lawton drifted back into place, both scrambling to grab onto the sides of the pool and replaced the chasm of water between them. Lawton looked pale and wan, and Aubrey could feel the blood rushing back into his body. Being touched by Ethaniel's magic was an intense experience, and he was grateful for Ethaniel's intervention even in the face of such a strange sensation.

Ethaniel rounded on Lawton, but not before giving Aubrey a slight nod. That nod made the churning in Aubrey's gut lessen. "So while you're here being rather sneaky about the whole thing, I'll have you know this. You left your friend alone and scared, and we've been taking care of him since. You made a mistake, maybe trusted the wrong person. And now Calix, who never asked to be wrapped up in your shady business, needs care and attention."

Lawton's face had lost some of its surprise, and in its place was a crackling anger, draining his voice of any emotion but that promise of *danger*. "So you know where the book is. Perfect. Tell me where, and I'll pay you anything—"

Ethaniel snapped his fingers and the first few lines of a new pattern hovered in the air. Lawton froze. *Smart man*, Aubrey thought. "I don't want your money. I care only that you put a strange, dangerous artifact out in the world. You should count yourself fortunate it is in our hands, and not with those who force you to act as courier. My advice, Mr. Adler? Break your contact with these people and return to being a spoiled rich man living in the city. Find a hobby, go walk in the parks, take on a lover or two. Leave Calix alone, and forget the book."

With his last few words, the pattern hovering around Ethaniel's fingertips faded, and Ethaniel slid back in the water until he was resting against the wall, shoulder to shoulder with Aubrey.

Aubrey's first instinct was to wrap a protective arm around Ethaniel's shoulder before saying to Lawton, "I think you now know who the power is here, Mr. Adler. I recommend you leave. But before you go...who are you working for? The Robed Brotherhood? Twin Spires?"

Lawton was staring hard at them both, and Aubrey could almost see the cogs turning. Lawton was recalculating, weighing his options and trying to predict an outcome. Well, they had time, as long as Calix stayed in the shadows, out of sight.

It wasn't lost on Aubrey that Lawton never once had asked if Calix was well. The man was slavishly devoted to that damn book, but beneath Lawton's tone and buried deep in the faint lines of his skin, was a terror. There were plenty of strange magic organizations dotting the city, most of them benign stains. The Collectio had even done work for some of them, but never outside the bounds of disenchanting an artifact or taking something dangerous into custody.

But there was one group bold enough to be at fault here. The one no one wanted to acknowledge but anyone with magical powers had heard of.

Heartbeat now kicked up a few notches, Aubrey pushed through the water, closing the space between him and Lawton. Ethaniel made a noise of protest behind him, but let him go. Aubrey waited to see what Lawton would do, as the man's polished veneer was wearing thin.

"It's the Golden Order, isn't it?"

Every hint of color drained from an already pale face. Lawton immediately crossed his arms over his chest and stepped back, only to find himself pinned against the pool's rocky wall. "I don't know what you're talking about," Lawton said faintly, expression gnarled up like an old tree root.

Aubrey felt Ethaniel's hand skim down his back. It was steadying, that faint pressure. Aubrey needed the reassurance. If Lawton was working for The Golden Order, they might well and truly be in a bad spot.

"Allow me to help clear the air, since you're so uncertain," Aubrey said not entirely uncharitably. "It's fairly well known amongst magic users that there are..." He turned to Ethaniel.

"Guilds," Ethaniel finished. "Some on the level, others not so much."

"Indeed," Aubrey continued. "But the Golden Order is a whole other beast, isn't it?"

Lawton's lips had all but disappeared into his face, pressed so tightly as if he was willing himself to not speak. But the tremble in his fingers gave him away as he pointed at Aubrey. Close to touching but not quite. "You couldn't possibly understand," he whispered.

"A keen almost-admission," Aubrey replied. "But your business with this *group* has put people I care about in danger."

"Aubrey...time and place." Ethaniel's hand turned possessive on Aubrey's back. "Time and place. This is neither."

Aubrey unclenched his jaw, willing the tension he felt vibrating through his body to still. He would be of no use to Ethaniel and Calix if he stayed strung-taut like a bowstring. "Right. Well. You can meet us somewhere safe, then."

"He can meet me at midnight at my home."

Calix came to them on silent footsteps, still draped in his robe but looking like the furious crack of Zeus's lightning. And for the first time in Lawton's presence, Aubrey saw the man's face flash with real regret. The man was a selfish, thoughtless cad for certain, but perhaps he relied on Calix for more than money and social clout.

None of that kept Calix away, though. He walked right into the water, robe now diaphanous, a graceful sea creature swirling around his lithe body.

"Don't speak," Calix snapped as he came face to face with his friend. "You will meet me at my home at midnight. Six hours from now. And we will sort this mess out. You will walk away with more money than you've ever had in your hands at one time, and then we are done."

"You're meeting *us* there, Mr. Adler," Ethaniel said quickly. "And you'll be alone."

Aubrey watched as Lawton swallowed hard, his pale face pink only due to the water's heat. His own anger had died down to a slow boil, but it lingered. Waiting. If Lawton didn't walk away in the next few moments, Aubrey would give real consideration to bodily tossing him out of the pool. It wasn't one thing or the other, it was *everything* he'd done...but the worst of it was his connection to a zealot group like The Golden Order. Lawton had all but confirmed it with words, but Aubrey wanted to hear it out loud.

The Golden Order was more than a religious organization. They were superstitious, rigorous, and, by many opinions, cruel. The Golden Order was responsible for the pamphlets floating around the city about the dangers of magic and its potential connection to "perverts". They paid street preachers — mostly homeless men and women looking for work — to stand on rickety wood-slatted boxes and yell out hateful screeds in the middle of Wall Street and The Village. Those people weren't to blame; taken advantage of and left still downtrodden. Another black mark against The Golden Order — using those fallen on hard times to their own purposes.

Everyone involved in magic even tangentially knew groups like The Golden Order had an agenda to push. But The Golden Order was something darker, more sinister. It had started years ago via advertisements in the papers, playing a message of "faith and order" in a city dominated by vice and money. Aubrey had instantly been suspicious, but no one knew who ran the group, or what actual influence they had. And like so many other shadowy groups flitting in and out of the city's saloons and tenements, The Golden Order faded to the background. For a time.

Then the raids started. Beatings, jailings, stories of more humiliating, more violating acts tunneled through the queer and bohemian and magical communities. Aubrey had nearly been caught one autumn night, barely managing to escape from a party where city council members were vying for re-election and looking to court influence. That had sent sparks flying, but it had also fueled the fire of their opponents.

And the covert whispers became loud cries for change echoing across the cobblestone streets of Acadia Gardens and down the narrow, smoke-clogged alleyways of Babylon Boulevard. The Golden Order made more statements publicly, but still ringed its leader in shadow. Rumors of magical artifacts being bought at high-end auctions — in cash, to figures wearing golden circle pins proudly on their lapels — circled, vulture-like and starving for more. There was no *proof*, of course. Just whispers and sidelong glances.

The city pushed back. More importantly, the safe enclaves for queer people used their networks, and some help from the magical population, to conceal themselves. The bathhouses the police raided looking for vice found nothing but dock workers cleaning up after a hard shift. (And dock workers were never happy about having their bathing rituals interrupted, since the smell of fish often made it difficult to socialize in the nicer saloons.) A few failed raids and a handful of newspaper articles against the police force later, and things calmed down.

The pins disappeared. The rumors quieted. The raids lessened. The Golden Order went underground. And many never forgot the havoc they'd wreaked on the gay enclaves, how they'd made queer people feel lost and small in a city that largely accepted them, or at least tolerated them. Aubrey certainly hadn't, and ever since then, had been waiting for the Order to reappear with a new message and the same old targets.

Yes, there was only one group possibly at fault here.

Mind made up, Aubrey pushed forward in the water until he could tower over Lawton Adler. That meant he towered over Calix as well, but his ire was aimed at one target. "Bring anyone else, and you will answer to more than us," Aubrey said softly. "I'll make sure of it."

Calix's cold anger was a sight to behold, but some small part of Aubrey wanted to chuckle at how quickly Lawton cowered below him. "Fine," Lawton spat.

"I wasn't finished. We're meeting at my apartment. I won't put any more weight on Calix with this," Aubrey continued. "I'll send a carriage for you, Adler. With a driver I trust."

Calix's single, curt nod of approval made the greedy part of Aubrey want to preen.

Lawton gave Calix a helpless look. "You've known them for days! I've known you for years! How could you take their side when I'm your oldest friend? Surely you're not going to leave me to their mercy, Calix. Please."

Calix's smile was thin. "No. You're left to mine. Now go."

They watched Lawton scramble out of the pool, his pale rear marked by where he'd been pressed up against the stone. When he was gone, Calix slumped forward only to have Aubrey catch him.

"Breathe," Aubrey said, leaning in as Ethaniel drew near on his left.

"You did a brave thing," Ethaniel said quietly, reaching out to put a hand on Calix's shoulder.

"Possibly an ill-rationalized one as well," Aubrey grumbled.

Ethaniel cuffed him gently on the shoulder. "I could say the same for you! You're offering your apartment for tonight?"

"I can safeguard it easier than Calix's place. And I wouldn't ever put that on you and your uncle, Ethaniel."

Ethaniel's eyelashes, glittering with damp, seemed to glisten a little more. "And I'll have time to check on Jeremiah before we meet."

From below them, Calix sucked in a sharp breath, coughed, then looked up with red eyes. "Apologies. I simply couldn't let him...use people again. It's too much. He's become so reckless, I barely recognize him."

Keeping Calix in the dark wouldn't help matters. "It's worse than you know," Aubrey replied softly.

TWELVE

CALIX

Few words were exchanged between the three of them on the carriage ride. The unspoken sat heavy in the air, but not as much as Aubrey's dire words back at the baths. They rattled through Calix's mind like marbles. He couldn't keep his fingers out of the tassels of his scarf, the silky threads slipping between his fingers as he combed through them. Ethaniel kept his hands in his lap, fingers laced together tightly, his head bowed so his long, wavy brown hair fell across his face. Across from him and Ethaniel, Aubrey peered out the small window, his chin on his fist, jaw clenched tightly. Calix ached to say something, but no words could convey how he was feeling, and what he assumed the others were feeling as well.

The only clear thoughts he had were diametrically opposed in so many ways, including all manner of sense, but they sat firmly in his mind. On one hand there was Lawton, and Calix's sheer anger at his friend and occasional lover. God, he'd been *so blind*. He'd known Lawton's fickleness, his flitty sense of loyalty, first-hand but for some reason, Calix had never expected it to turn against him. How many times had Lawton said, "You're the only one I can trust, Calix. Darling dearest. My one true friend."

Yes, and how many times has he left you out in the cold? Left you at a club or a dinner to follow after a pretty set of eyes? Left your bed empty, so when you rolled over in the morning, the weight of how alone you were sat like an anvil on your chest?

How long were you going to trust that, no matter what, Lawton would always be there for a laugh, for a good time?

How many times were you going to let him touch you, kiss you, fuck you against a wall or in your bed and leave you breathless and still yearning for more? How many times were you going to let him crush you and then come back as though nothing had happened but a good time?

When were you going to be stronger than that?

When his eyes burned and tears threatened, Calix didn't try to hide how he wiped them away with the back of his hand. Nor did he try to hide his sad smile when Ethaniel put a gentle hand on his knee and when Aubrey looked at him with concern before silently handing over a handkerchief.

"Thank you," Calix said quietly. "I'm simply feeling sorry for myself. It will pass. We have work to do." He shook his head. "*I* have work to do."

Instead of the rebuke he was expecting, Aubrey said, "What did you have in mind?"

Calix leaned back against the seat, glad for the both of them. Lawton was no real threat, Calix was certain of that. But whatever this Golden Order was, Aubrey had certainly been worried, but had refused to speak on it further until they were safely at his townhome. They would drop Ethaniel off at his home ("It's plenty warded, Aubrey, so you needn't worry so much"), and then he and Aubrey would cross town to The Village to prepare for whatever might walk through the front door at midnight. He needed to stop at home as well, to check in with Richard and grab his mother's diary.

Calix had an idea, one that had coalesced in a bright moment, steeling his fear into anger like a blacksmith might turn a lump of iron into a sword. It had happened when he'd seen Ethaniel's magic on full display, beautiful and powerful and dizzyingly breathtaking. Ethaniel hadn't been afraid of who he was, *what* he was, and he hadn't hesitated. Suddenly, Calix had known his part in all of this mess. It had meant saying out loud a truth he'd buried for so long, and that terrified him.

But he could do this. He *had* to do this.

Calix cleared his throat and said, "With a bit of time and a few simple items, I might be able to divine what Lawton's planning and if he's going to betray his own word."

Aubrey's eyebrows couldn't arch higher, and Ethaniel's hand on Calix's knee tightened. "I thought your visions were unpredictable," Ethaniel said.

"They are," Calix conceded.

Aubrey's expression couldn't be more serious as he said, "Except?"

Calix gave him a weak smile. "I can try to tap into the power. It's tricky, and it doesn't work most of the time."

"But it's worked in the past?" Ethaniel looked utterly bewildered and Calix couldn't help but think how adorable he was in the moment.

"A few times." Calix couldn't bring himself to say what lay on his tongue.

"More importantly," Aubrey said quietly as he leaned forward and braced his elbows on his knees, long fingers interlocking under his chin, "was what you divined in those times *correct*?"

Calix nodded. "Twice. Out of a dozen or so attempts. Many of them were...rushed due to circumstances."

For all Aubrey was staring at him like a specimen under a microscope, those glass-colored eyes fixed in interest and wonder, Calix saw sympathy written in the lines of that sharply-featured face. "And?"

"Aubrey." Ethaniel's reprimand was gentle and it made Aubrey blink. Calix was still understanding their dynamic, but it was impossible to hide how that one utterance made Aubrey pull back a little. The man was so intense, Calix feared his hair might catch on fire, and he was thankful for Ethaniel's ability to balance Aubrey out. He understood their dynamic at least that much.

Calix held up a hand. He might as well spit it out. "The first time it was right, I was under my mother's strict supervision. She prepared the ritual, taking days to cleanse the house and ensure our timing was exact with the rising of the moon. I was fifteen and home for holiday break. I focused on something small, the health of one of the horses who had suddenly taken ill. I saw her..." He cleared his throat, the memory rising not like the moon had that night, but like spark in dry tinder. "I saw her die, in agony. But it didn't show me the stable catching on fire from a lantern that she'd kicked over."

He couldn't meet their eyes now. Not Aubrey's penetrating gaze or Ethaniel's steady stare. Empathy rolled off them both in waves, threatening to pull him under. Calix focused on his hands and waited for the inevitable question about the second time he'd forced a vision. Not even Lawton knew about that horrible truth.

Ethaniel was the one to break the silence. "You don't have to tell us, Calix."

"I think he does," Aubrey said, making Calix jolt upright, an indignant reply already metal-sharp in his mouth. "While it may be the polite thing to do, Ethaniel, we need to know. I need to know what we're walking into."

As the carriage rumbled to a stop, Aubrey leaned into Calix's space and tipped his head up with two fingers. His touch was gentle, more a suggestion than anything else, but it went through Calix like lightning. He was sucked into the whirlpool of Aubrey's gaze, helpless in that grasp.

Calix reveled in succumbing to it..

"The second time you saw something, it was another death, wasn't it?" Aubrey asked softly.

"My mother's." The reply was dragged from him but not unwillingly. Calix let the words go. Holding them for so long, for a decade of pain he'd avoided, finally felt wrong. He should say more out loud, should speak up even when it hurt. He shouldn't let others take and take and take and never give him back the things he so desperately needed and deserved.

Aubrey didn't pull the words from him. He gave Calix the space to let them go.

A bit dazed, Calix let out a shaky breath. He let Aubrey give a slow nod of understanding and he let Ethaniel pull him close, the tailor's strong body warm against him in that dim space of the carriage. He wasn't judged for what he'd seen and what he had done, and they didn't ask for the sordid details.

They both let Calix breathe until his head cleared and he was able to open the carriage door.

"We're going to figure this out," Ethaniel said in his ear before he exited. "Both of you, please be cautious."

"We will," he and Aubrey said it at the same time and it made Ethaniel laugh.

"Well, since you're both on the same page…" Ethaniel gave Aubrey, then Calix, a canny look and, smirking, leaned in to swiftly kiss Aubrey on the lips.

Then he turned to Calix, eyebrows raised in anticipation.

"Oh." Calix swallowed hard, then nodded. Ethaniel took it as permission to place a soft kiss at the corner of Calix's mouth. It left Calix tingling all over, and the only thing he could do was sit back and let Ethaniel close the door. Leaving him and Aubrey alone in the carriage.

Their ride rattled around a corner, the cushioned interior of the carriage muffling the street noise just beyond their fragile shell. Calix forced himself to look up at Aubrey, only to find the other man cheekily smiling at him.

"You knew he'd do that," Calix said, flustered and blushing.

"I did." Aubrey's smile grew and it only made the man more infuriatingly handsome. Calix's heart beat harder. "That was our little plan in the bath house, you know. Before we were so rudely interrupted."

"The plan?"

As graceful as anything, Aubrey slipped from his seat to take up the spot at Calix's left, leaning back with his long legs elegantly crossed at the ankle. Calix suddenly found himself obsessed with Aubrey's ankles and legs and everything they attached to. And that gaze sucked him in once more.

"We were interested in sussing out *your* interest," Aubrey said softly, his words practically curling at the edges inside Calix's mind. He knew logically that Aubrey was talking about intimacy and physicality, but Calix couldn't help but be charmed at Aubrey's gentle approach. It was clear the man *wanted*, like Ethaniel wanted, but no one had said the words outright.

Maybe he should. Just to be absolutely certain.

You are braver than you know. Even if thinking about…sex right now is impractical. We could all be harmed grievously doing this. I don't want to have missed out on a moment in the here and now.

"My interest?" Calix reached out until he could put his hand on Aubrey's bicep. Aubrey made the tiniest sound but didn't pull away. "In…both of you?"

Aubrey was so still and that made Calix's heart pound beneath his ribs. "Admittedly, Ethaniel and I are just finding our footing again, but if you're amenable…"

Calix didn't give himself time to think, to question if it was wise or right. Every single thing that he'd held close or hid away, every bit of pain and stress of the last few weeks, every thought of Lawton using him once again for his own ends, came crashing down on Calix's head.

People like him, like Aubrey, like Ethaniel...they made connections quickly, fell in with people of similar inclinations at a pace that would defy all social norms. They had to, because it could all be stripped away by a street preacher as easily as the stroke of a mayor or governor's pen.

He *wanted*, and it burned so hot he couldn't bear it any longer.

Aubrey was so much taller than him but Calix didn't let those long legs or broad shoulders get in his way. He climbed into Aubrey's lap, planted his hands on the carriage seat, and kissed Aubrey hard. Immediately, there were palms sliding down his back, holding his quivering body still in that calm, collected way Aubrey had about him.

The man's kiss, however, was pure fire. Aubrey met Calix's flame with one of his own and Calix clung to that warmth. He welcomed Aubrey's tongue into his mouth, let Aubrey mold his body with his touch, and when he tipped his head back to breathe, Aubrey didn't relinquish his hold. He *pursued* Calix with such beautiful tenacity and needy lips against his jaw, his neck.

Calix didn't shiver because he was cold. No, now he understood how to properly burn, blazing like a wildfire that couldn't be put out.

The carriage jolted to a stop just as Aubrey reached up to cup Calix's face between his hands. "You are a constant surprise," Aubrey whispered in the growing warmth of the cabin. "And you'd best kiss Ethaniel like that or he'll be sorely put out that you kissed me first."

Calix fought not to smile and lost. His entire body tingled, and he felt alive on a level like he'd never experienced before. *Maybe kissing is supposed to feel like this*, he thought as he stared down at the stunning symmetry of Aubrey's face.

"I kissed you first because I thought you'd be the higher hurdle," he replied, not trying to sass the man but...he sort of wanted to.

"Is that so?"

The sudden twist of darkness in Aubrey's voice made something squirm deliciously deep in Calix's belly. "Perhaps," he teased.

Aubrey rumbled something that sounded like wordless consideration, his gaze heavy on Calix now. Calix felt studied once more, but this time, it was with a level of care he'd only seen directed at Ethaniel. "Shall I come inside with you?"

"Are you worried about me?"

"Even if you hadn't just kissed me as though your life depended on it, I would be," Aubrey conceded. "Be quick. I'll tell the driver to wait."

Calix bit back on the urge to say *Yes, sir*, and carefully slipped off Aubrey's lap and stepped outside.

"Take this." Aubrey's hand appeared out the window, a velvet drawstring bag dangling from his fingers. "Just in case. Check your doorways in and out of the house with it."

Calix took the bag and opened it to find a small set of spectacles, the half-moon kind that sat low on the bridge of one's nose. "Do I need to do anything with them?"

Aubrey chuckled, the sound low and deep as it rattled through Calix. "Other than wear them and look over your doors? No. If there's any errant magic, you'll see runes or a glow."

"All right. Thank you, Aubrey." Calix smiled up at where Aubrey's face was just visible through the carriage's curtains. "Give me ten minutes."

"Not a moment over, or I'll be forced to come in and rescue you." Aubrey's tone was serious but Calix heard a bit of amusement buried within.

"Well, we wouldn't want that," Calix replied. "Ten minutes."

With that, he hurried around the side of his building, fumbling with the tiny spectacles. Calix paused before the back entrance he sometimes used, scanning the doorway. It was nothing but seafoam green paint chipping on the old wood, and the heavy black door Richard hated because it would swell and stick to the doorframe when summer came along.

Calix shook his head, smiling fondly, and took the stairs up to the main level of his townhome. "Richard?" he called out as he paused in the small foyer, his hand immediately going to the table on which a picture of his mother sat, the silver frame glinting in the late afternoon sun.

Thunderous steps heralded Richard's approach, and Calix was blindsided by a hug so forceful it threatened his lungs. "Oh, thank God," Richard said as he squeezed Calix tightly. "I've been looking *everywhere* for you."

Calix was startled by the physical affection for only a second before he let Richard cling to him. "I'm so sorry," he replied, meaning every word tenfold. "It's been a hellish few days but I'm safe."

Calix pulled back to give Richard a once-over. As usual, not a black hair was out of place and his suit was perfectly pressed. The only hint of something amiss was the flush in Richard's pale face, making his freckles stand out. "Are you all right?" he asked, heart pounding.

Richard nodded. "I'm fine now that I know you're whole. What happened? Where have you been?"

Someone not accustomed to his relationship with Richard might have been aghast at a "servant" speaking to Calix thusly. But Richard was family, like a brother to him, and Calix had no trouble speaking plainly to the man. Except for now — the knowledge he had, the things he'd seen and experienced over the last few days? It could put Richard in harm's way.

"I can't explain fully," Calix said slowly, stepping back so they could both take a much-needed breath and he could safely return Aubrey's spectacles to their bag. "And before you argue, I'm saying this because there's a...few shady personages roaming about and I don't want you involved. The less you know, the better."

Calix motioned for Richard to follow as he took the stairs to the second floor library. The library was across the hall from Calix's quarters, so he asked Richard to fetch his suitcase and a valise while he gathered a few objects from his desk. Richard came back with the luggage moments later, a question clearly written on his face.

Calix huffed out a sigh as he sat down at his desk. "I have to be quick, I've a carriage and a friend waiting outside. But it's imperative you do two things for me, Richard."

"Anything," Richard replied with the kind of earnest loyalty Calix would never, ever betray.

Calix gently ran his hands under the lip of the desk, fingers searching for the button that would pop open its secret compartment. With a *click*, the desk's left drawer opened, then with a whirl of enchanted gears, the drawer grew twice in size. It was an old pattern of his mother's and now, more than ever, he needed her secrets stored within.

Once his mother's diary, pattern book, and ritual grimoire were in his possession, Calix tucked them all away in the valise and came to stand before Richard. He put his hands on his old friend's shoulders and said, "One, I need a few bits of clothing thrown into that suitcase while I retrieve a few more things. Enough for two or three days, it doesn't matter what you pick out."

Richard nodded after swallowing hard. "All right. And two?"

"Pay yourself and Marie for the rest of the month, and send word to the estate that we need to open Rosehill early. You're welcome to go there, but I'd prefer you take a nice visit to go see your family in Rhode Island or....anywhere not here."

The concern that wrote itself across Richard's face could have filled a novel's worth of dramatic speeches. "Calix, what in the bloody hell is going on?"

Calix shook his head. "Nothing good. And it involves Lawton, so if you see him, stay far, *far* away. Please. Promise me you'll do this."

"Yes, of course, but—"

"The questions you want answers to? I can't give them now. Just....please leave the city. You will be welcome at Rosehill if you wish, but I would never ask that of you. I know you hate those hills the carriage has to traverse."

Richard looked down at his shoes, cheeks going even more red. "I don't know what you're talking about."

"You do and you know it, but I won't tease." Calix gripped Richard's shoulders tighter now, looking him dead in the eyes. "Get out of the city by tonight. And take this." He dug in his pocket for his billfold, but as he pulled it out, the knuckle of his right index finger caught on something that *scraped* across his skin. Calix hissed and yanked his hand free to see a tiny scratch already welling with a thin line of blood.

He took your blood, boy
The blood he took it
Why don't we let him reap the harvest
Harvest the blood
No not yet

We've waited for so long
Oracle

The voice he'd heard, the voice of that blasted book, now grew inside Calix's mind, echoes upon echoes of a vast chorus that never *stopped*. It would surely drive him to madness if it didn't stop the damn *ringing*, over and over and over again like the most beautiful bell and the most terrifying dirge and it kept ringing

Over and over and over and over again again again

Somewhere, in some other time or on a distant island, Calix heard his own screams. They rose and fell in line so quickly with the chorus of voices that had somehow become one and yet never ever *stopped*—

He was on the floor now, voice gone hoarse from the screaming, and Richard was trying to fight off an irate Aubrey who was insisting—

"—I KNOW HIM. I was waiting outside in the carriage, now let me through—"

"You bloody will not touch him!"

Calix looked up, head still ringing and eyes watering as if he'd been at a funeral, to see Richard and Aubrey grappling with each other, Aubrey looking deeply annoyed and concerned at the same time while Richard was huffing and puffing for all his worth.

"Stop, both of you," he croaked. "Richard, I know Aubrey. Let him pass."

The words hadn't hardly left Calix's mouth before Aubrey spun neatly out of Richard's flailing grasp and dropped to his knees beside Calix. "What happened?" Aubrey asked, his fingers gentle on Calix's face and neck.

"That damn book again," Calix said, coughing as something caught in his throat. "It was like a fit came over me."

Richard looked utterly baffled and helpless, but he did pause as Calix spoke. "After you cut yourself. This happened after you took your hand out of your pocket."

"Let me," Aubrey said, and Calix held out his right hand to show the small cut on his finger. "How did this happen?"

"I was reaching into my pocket for my billfold and something scratched me."

Aubrey motioned to Richard. "Help me get his jacket off."

Calix tried to move but any twist of his neck made him nauseated, so he let Richard and Aubrey move him around like some kind of ragdoll. Aubrey carefully turned the right pocket inside-out, bringing the material up to his face to better examine it. He squinted, then frowned. "Here," he said. "There's something metallic stuck in the lining."

Calix watched as Aubrey pushed on the fabric until a thin gold pin dropped to the floor.

"Is that a needle?" Richard asked, leaning down for a better look.

"We call them stingers," Aubrey said quietly, his expression gone sour. "Needles like this, long and made from precious metals, are used ritualistically. Cunning folk use them to draw blood, of course, but they have symbolistic meaning, too."

Something akin to horror was slowly blooming on Aubrey's face, and Calix felt its twin spreading over his own. There was only one person who had handled his clothing and who had tried to insert himself into Calix's personal life. Who had tried to seduce him.

"Do you think Lawton paid that attendant, Basil, to do this?" Calix said, his words shaky as he tried to breathe.

"It doesn't matter anymore," Aubrey said as he plucked up the needle with a handkerchief. "They got what they wanted. Blood is used in many spells, but I can only think that someone meant to find you. And whatever they did opened you up to...*it*."

"Then you need to leave here, and do it now." Richard was on his feet instantly, picking up Calix's suitcase and holding his free hand out to Calix. Calix felt a wash of gratitude as his friend and valet helped him up while Aubrey tucked away the needle into one of his many pockets. "I'll be downstairs with your suitcase in two minutes.".

"Thank you," Calix said. Words beyond those seemed too difficult, too complex for his lips to form, but Richard seemed to understand, nodding before stepping across the hall to Calix's room.

"We need to get you somewhere safe," Aubrey said in his ear as he guided Calix down the stairs. "If Lawton or someone from the Order did this, they'll be on their way here now. I've no doubt."

"But the book's at the Collectio, so they'd only find me." They rounded the last few stairs in silence, but it was a silence that weighed heavier with each second. "Aubrey?"

"The book is not at the Collectio."

Calix stared at Aubrey, aghast. Aubrey's face was ashen and as he reached down to pick up the valise and cane he seemed to always carry, his hands shook. Calix's head had been spinning so much that he hadn't noticed Lawton's gray satchel looped over Aubrey's long torso.

"You were upstairs and I felt something...like thunder rock the carriage. I think it must have been the same time you were pricked by the stinger." Aubrey's grip on the satchel's soft gray leather could have dented steel. "The book doesn't want to be out of your company, it seems."

Richard clattered down the stairs and immediately looped an arm around Calix's waist, for which Calix was grateful. "We'll call a carriage from the servant's entrance. No need to attract attention."

"Smart man." Aubrey straightened and rolled his shoulders back, as though the weight of the valise was greater than his own. When Calix reached for the satchel, Aubrey shook his head. "I've a feeling you will be handling the albatross in the very near future, so let me bear it for now."

Calix nodded. He wanted to embrace Aubrey, or perhaps kiss him once more, in an attempt to soothe the bubbling tar in the bottom of his stomach. Everything was *wrong*, and even more so, that Lawton was involved and willing to throw away years upon years of friendship and companionship.

But was that really what they had? How many times had Lawton used him, gave him glimpses of bliss, only to snatch them away when something prettier crossed his path? How many times had he willingly played the fool?

Maybe it was the stress of everything that had taken place. Maybe it was the question of that damnable book. Or perhaps it was simple heartbreak. But as Calix leaned back on the velvet seat of the fine coach Richard had called for them, he was left to wonder if this chaos was permanent, or if it would live only in these moments, bright and terrible, and yet still capable of so much damage.

THIRTEEN

Ethaniel

Uncle Jeremiah was awake when Ethaniel rushed through the back door of the shop.

He was awake. And fully dressed. And pacing.

"God, boy, where have you been?" Jeremiah rushed toward Ethaniel with an energy he hadn't seen since before tuberculosis had sapped it all away. "I've been worried sick. Even walked the block a few times hoping you'd turn up."

Ethaniel stared in amazement at his uncle. "How are you...what happened?"

Jeremiah shook his graying head, bushy eyebrows drawn down to give him a professorial look. The rumpled but clean suit helped as well. "I don't rightly know, to be honest. I had the strangest dream about tea and when I woke up, I felt better than I have in years. Years!"

Ethaniel reeled. Jeremiah was ill. He knew that much. It was as sure as the sun rising in the east every morning. But this Jeremiah was the one of his youth, of Ethaniel at eighteen and terrified of living in the city but so, so eager to learn from an expert like his uncle. This was the Jeremiah he remembered from that time before, and even now, in an old suit a decade out of style and his hair wispy and stuck to his skull like a cheap wig, Ethaniel saw life in him once more.

It was a miracle. Or a trick. Time near Aubrey and mixed up in strange magical questions had left Ethaniel a tad suspicious.

"No one's been here since I left?" Ethaniel asked, craning his neck to look around the store. "I made sure to lock up, but I know sometimes Dr. Heddington likes to stop by to check on you."

"Not a soul," Jeremiah replied. "I woke up and you were gone and I figured while I had the energy, I'd wander out into the world once again."

The slight smile dropped off his uncle's face. Miracle or trick or not, his uncle was clearly elated to again experience the city he loved. Who was he to take that away from the man who'd taken him in, been nothing but kind to him since Ethaniel had been a gangly teenager with a rebellious streak a mile wide and bearing the worry of his father on his back?

"Well, I'm beyond thrilled you're up and about," Ethaniel said, trying to match his uncle's enthusiasm. "Are you hungry? I can reheat yesterday's soup—"

But Jeremiah was already moving toward the coat rack near the back door. "I thought I'd go out for a bite," he said sheepishly. "It's not that I don't want to be here with you, Ethaniel, but I've missed this damn city so much." Jeremiah paused, gaze tracking down to the floor. "If this is my last gasp before the eternal night takes me, I want to see the city lights one more time."

Ethaniel swallowed hard against the lump in his throat. With everything moving so quickly, so suddenly, and his life upended by a copper-haired noble and a strange book and the return of the only man he'd ever cared for, he'd lost the plot a little. Remembering who his uncle had been and still was hadn't been a priority in any way, and now that same man stood before him, vibrant and bright.

"Please be careful," Ethaniel said as he clasped his hands in front of him. "The city's only gotten more dangerous and I...please promise to be careful."

"I will. I swear it." Jeremiah took down the only coat of his Ethaniel had left on the rack (a gesture of frail hope, he supposed). Ethaniel silently held out a few bills, more than enough to buy his uncle a nice steak dinner and a bottle of wine at some place around the corner. Jeremiah grinned this time, and then drew Ethaniel into the kind of hug he remembered from that first night he'd spent in the city. Whatever this was, Ethaniel knew they were both grateful for Jeremiah to have a chance to see the world once again.

"I'm just going over to Scully's for some food," Jeremiah said. "And then I might swing by one of the clubs, listen to whoever's on stage. I'll stay close to home, I promise."

"I know," Ethaniel said. "Enjoy it, Uncle Jeremiah."

Jeremiah winked, threw Ethaniel a salute, and stepped out the back door, disappearing into the gathering shadows in the alley.

Ethaniel waited for a few long moments, his gaze fixed on the back door as if Jeremiah would come back through it, pale and weak and needing help once again. He didn't wish it at all, but how could he not expect it to happen? After so many doctors and treatments, tinctures and teas, they'd both known the battle was long lost months ago. With every bit of blood on a handkerchief and every coughing fit that left his uncle winded and fatigued, they both *knew*.

And now here he was, upright and walking and aching for life once more.

It was a cruel joke of Fate to put hope within reach like this.

"He can have it all back, if you want."

The voice came from behind him, startling Ethaniel back into reality from the dark place his mind had wandered. But the voice was known to him, even if it was the last one he'd expected to hear any time soon.

Ethaniel let his eyes close for a moment before he took a deep breath and turned around. "Brother."

Vincent smiled at him with perfectly white and even teeth. "Brother. It's good to see you. You look well."

Ethaniel wasn't about to ask how Vincent had gotten past the shop's security patterns. Vincent was highly skilled and, as far as Ethaniel knew, still associated with the more shady elements of the city. It could have been his magic, or something he bought from an arcane dealer, the kind that sold stolen patterns on the black market.

Suspicion prickled in him once again, but now it crawled up the back of his neck to rest at the base of his skull. "*We're* doing well," Ethaniel said. "The spring season always brings in new business."

Ethaniel wasn't about to address Vincent's first words to him — the first words they'd exchanged in two years, in fact. Vincent showing up meant he wanted something, and the last time they'd seen each other, it had been a simple goodbye and farewell as Vincent was leaving for shores unknown. *Somewhere in the Mediterranean, perhaps,* Vincent had said.

Two years had passed, and now his half-brother stood tall and proud just inside the back room to Ethaniel's shop. Vincent looked well, more than in fact. He practically glowed, his skin golden, his dark brown hair slicked back with precision, and his black suit worthy of the finest funeral parlor.

And then Ethaniel spotted the glint of gold peeking out from under Vincent's lapel.

"You didn't," Ethaniel said, voice choked with a rush of realization, followed by fear. "Please tell me you didn't."

His head was swimming. After the reveal of Lawton's allegiances and the way Calix described the pin his friend wore, now Ethaniel knew. He *knew* and it made him want to thrust Vincent out of the shop and into the burgeoning night, never to be seen again.

His half-brother standing here, in a shop he'd never so much as helped with even a single time, and slyly flaunting his new allegiances and the money tied to it was too much to bear.

The hammer of Vincent's smug response crashed down upon Ethaniel's head. "If you're referring to The Golden Order, that's why I'm here. And it's why Uncle Jeremiah is up and about, living his golden years out in this beautiful city instead of bound to that rickety bed."

The words were fire up his throat, his anger curdling in his stomach. Ethaniel couldn't quite believe what he was hearing and yet...he'd known. Somewhere in the very back of his mind, that quiet, secretive corner where his worst fears and suspicions grew like mushrooms in the dark...he'd known.

Ethaniel had known, deep down, that this all tied to something powerful that his brother was involved in. Vincent had always strived for the greatest, the highest, the brightest. Half-brothers and yet they looked so much alike; like their mother, with a strong jaw and wide hazel eyes that gave them all an innocent appearance. Ethaniel had his mother's nose, except his was slightly crooked from a few fist fights in his days as a rowdy teenager in a city full of possibility. Vincent took after her in a similar way.

Half-brothers and yet so similar they were often mistaken for full-blooded, sometimes even twins. But they couldn't be more different in personality, in desires and ambitions. Vincent wanted *power* and he chased after it with rabid intent. Ethaniel had never wanted anything more than the quiet and his work and a life gently fulfilled by using his skills to benefit others.

So different. So alike. He was Vincent's shadow, and Vincent was his.

"You gave my uncle something," Ethaniel managed to spit out between gritted teeth. "Some concoction your new friends sold you?"

Vincent acknowledged the truth with a bow of his head. "He can have that new lease on life permanently, Ethaniel. Or, at least until old age takes him. Your father's brother doesn't have to suffer so. Let me help him."

Ethaniel shook his head. "In exchange for what?"

Please don't say the book or Calix. Please let this be the worst stack of coincidences ever known to a single mortal soul. Please.

All pretense slipped from Vincent's face, and when Ethaniel glimpsed the monster under the mask, everything in him went cold. "You've touched the book. I can see its magic dancing across your palms, in the very air around us." Vincent stepped closer, and one step forward felt like miles to Ethaniel. "Brother, that book was rightfully purchased by a representative of the Order. It is my property. It belongs with me. If you know who has it, I would ask for their name so I can reclaim it."

Ethaniel's heart couldn't beat harder in his chest, and yet it kicked up another notch at the coldness threaded through Vincent's voice. He'd known the gentle brotherly talk, the *favor* that was his uncle's health, had all been a ruse. But for a moment, one shining moment, Ethaniel had pictured Jeremiah in full, robust health once more, never needing to suffer another tonic or tincture again.

Vincent had offered him hope, and Ethaniel wanted desperately to take it.

And he couldn't.

"I can't tell you what you want, Vincent." Ethaniel met his brother's gaze with his own, hardening his heart as much as he could. Ripping his uncle's hope away was the cruelest thing to do, but even worse was the contingency on which that hope had been placed. Like a child's seesaw slowly being weighted to one end, and eventually everything would come crashing to the ground in spectacular, awful fashion.

Vincent stayed perfectly still, but his gaze hardened, his voice now dripping with sarcasm. "Can't you? You won't think of your uncle? In exchange for a single book?"

"You know it's not merely a book, brother."

Vincent smiled, and all Ethaniel saw was a shark. "I do. And I know you do as well. How fortuitous for me."

Vincent's hand flashed at his side and Ethaniel braced himself for the unknown, but instead Vincent pulled out a small brown bottle and set it on the nearby counter. "A few more days of hope, I think. Because we're family. So you can really think it over."

Vincent left Ethaniel standing in the back of his store as the shadows of twilight gathered. The single light above his head swung gently in the spring breeze welcomed in by his brother's exit.

With no other recourse and no one near with whom to share his thoughts, Ethaniel quickly left a note for his uncle, placed the bottle on top, and packed a bag. With the wards secured and the CLOSED sign facing the street, Ethaniel knew customers would be held at bay for a bit. And his uncle might have a newfound lease on life, but he wouldn't go gallivanting off to new accommodations. The store would be safe and, hopefully, so would his uncle. Plus it was getting more difficult to rent in the city, and certain areas didn't like the "look" of two men many mistook for Italian-Americans, even though they were part Spanish and had been in the country for nearly a century.

He had to leave. He needed to resolve whatever the matter was with this damn book, and he needed to be there for Aubrey. For Calix. And for whatever Fate seemed to have in store for them all.

Fourteen

CALIX

Auburn, New York

1880

Ahead of him, Calix's mother ran through golden fields. She trusted he would follow, and follow he did, watching as she trailed her fingers over the long stalks of grass. When he would lay down on his back in those same fields, he thought the grass to be giant trees, endlessly reaching toward the sky while he looked on in wonder. But when his mother touched the grass, the plants seemed to sway in unison with her. As if she could talk to each one and teach it her quiet rhythms.

Calix had always known his mother was magical. He'd inherited her dreams, she would say, and then sometimes darkly add, "And none of my terror." When Calix turned seventeen, he began to understand the full weight his mother carried. He'd seen that terror, too. Little things, at first. A dead fox on the edge of the woods, the bite marks on its body bigger than any predator nearby. Hazy shadows clinging a little too hard to the dying of night for the sunrise; they seemed to follow him when he paced the Rosehill grounds in fits of insomnia.

Then, the worst: the form of a pristine lake marred only by white cloth and auburn hair floating just on the surface, her soft fingers that had once touched the high grasses so reverently now wrinkled, pruned by murky water and death's touch.

His mother's visions had driven her to madness. Calix often feared a similar fate for himself, but being around people, especially Lawton, quieted that mess. Maybe Lawton's drama had kept his own at bay for all this time.

But right now, as his mind's eye cast him into the past, to a happier time when being an Oracle's son didn't hamper some part of his life, either through physical or emotional pain. It wasn't all doom and gloom then; they were better moments where his mother ran carefree and Calix knew nothing of magic except what his mother carried in her soul.

"Mama! Wait!" Calix ran faster, pumping his legs harder in effort to reach her. But she had, somehow, drifted away from him. She now stood at the tree line, the heavy afternoon shadows demarcating the land as if drawn by a godly hand.

"I'm here, darling!" She held out her arms, her blue dress swirling about those golden stalks, and Calix ran to her. His grin evaporated when she did; an errant plume of smoke on wind that now smelled of dry earth and ozone.

"You wait for the third lightning strike, Calix. You wait, and then you'll see."

"Mama?" Calix spun around, panic gripping his heart with a heavy hand. "Mama!"

"The third strike. Wait. You must wait."

"Mama!" Tears streamed down little Calix's face as he cried out for his mother.

"You must wait!"

"Why didn't you make him wait until we were both here?"

"He's a grown man, Ethaniel, not a child. I can't stop him from doing anything –"

"You could have talked some sense into him!"

Calix heard the anguish in Ethaniel's voice, but couldn't get his eyes to open so he might see the handsome tailor, so he might rake his eyes over the crooked nose and hazel eyes and long, wavy brown hair he wished to sink his fingers into.

I owe you a kiss, Calix thought as Ethaniel's face finally, *finally* swam into view. He reached for Ethaniel and was met with a warm, firm grip. "Thank god," Ethaniel said as he tightly squeezed Calix's hands. "Calix."

Aubrey's stare, while disapproving to say the least, was no less warm. Calix stared in wonder at how those glass-green eyes could hold so much emotion without Aubrey saying a word.

"We keep losing you to unconsciousness," Aubrey murmured, passing his hand over Calix's brow. "I'd prefer this be the last time."

Calix chuckled but his throat was dry, so the sound came out rusty. "In my defense, before that blasted book came into my life, I'd been unconscious exactly one other time."

Aubrey's lips twitched; a near-smile that drove Calix mad. He saw Ethaniel staring, too, and had to hide a smile of his own. "And that was caused by…"

"Cracking my head on the ground after falling out of a tree. When I was seven."

Ethaniel huffed out a laugh. "So a normal childhood activity. Well, that's somewhat more pleasant than, as you call it, that blasted book. And speaking of, Aubrey was filling me while you were on your…journey, I suppose. Though I do wish you'd waited until I'd arrived."

Ethaniel gestured to the salt ring around Calix, and then to the small altar he'd set up according to his mother's notes. Everything looked fairly harmless in the day, but at night, the casting stones, black glass orb on a silver pedestal, and pink chalk (albeit, chalk infused with pig's blood) all took on an ominous aura.

"I didn't get anything," Calix said, upset at himself for breaking the connection so early. "It wasn't…it wasn't what I was aiming for. I was looking for Lawton and found…something else."

Ethaniel's face dropped and took a bit of Calix's heart with it. He struggled to prop himself up on his elbows, but once there, leaned forward into Ethaniel's space. He watched the man's pupils widen slightly as Ethaniel took in the sight of Calix — hair mussed by the wind the spell had kicked up, the white paint down his hands still glowing gold. Some part of Calix wanted to preen under the attention.

"I did warn you," Aubrey muttered.

"Warn him about what?" Ethaniel shot back. "What did I miss?"

Aubrey actually *snorted* at that. "Just this one launching himself into my lap after I—"

"After you teased me and told me you two wanted an *arrangement!*" Calix protested, near to laughing already.

As Ethaniel squawked in indignation, Aubrey simply held up a finger. "I said *interest.* There's a difference."

Ethaniel managed to recover enough to say, "I apparently can't leave the two of you alone, can I?"

"No," he and Aubrey spoke at the same time, leaving Ethaniel to stare disbelievingly at them.

Calix began to laugh. The joy rolled over him in waves, and he felt giddy and weightless from it. These last few days had been so awful, so confusing and frightening, and the moments between the terrors needed to be cherished. He didn't think things were over and done with by a long shot, and so Calix laughed. Soon, Ethaniel and Aubrey joined him. They sat on the bare wood floor of Aubrey's front sitting room, in his truly beautiful townhome, and laughed until tears formed and their sides ached with the enjoyment of it, and of each other.

Calix eventually lay back down on the floor and laced his fingers behind his head. "To think, if I hadn't gone with Lawton yesterday morning, things would be very different."

"If you hadn't, the Golden Order would have the book now," Aubrey said.

Ethaniel stayed quiet, but lay down on the floor beside Calix.

"Are you all right?" Calix asked, putting a hand on Ethaniel's arm.

"No and yes, and...perhaps. I've no good answer for that, I'm afraid." Ethaniel turned his head until their gazes could meet. "But I've a request before I lend my own part of this story to what Aubrey told me while you were in your trance."

"A request?" Aubrey's voice was liquid silk touching Calix's mind and he shivered. Aubrey noticed and replied by putting a hand on Calix's knee.

"Hmmm, yes." Ethaniel propped himself up on an elbow, now looming over Calix. Calix sucked in a breath at the beauty above him, and even more beauty to his right, and wondered if it all came crashing down tonight, or tomorrow, if he could ever have another moment that glittered quite like this one.

"I told you," Aubrey said softly, now also looking down at Calix. "I told you he'd want to be kissed the way you kissed me, Calix."

Ethaniel glared at them both. "I knew you two had been..."

"Canoodling?" Calix offered.

"Yes, fine. That. There was an energy around you two when I walked into the room a few minutes ago, even through the..." Ethaniel waved his hand toward the paint on Calix's knuckles and fingers. "What you were doing. *Alone*. Which I'm sure Aubrey told you was ill-advised."

"To say the very least," Aubrey muttered.

"I wasn't alone, and I think you're jealous," Calix shot back. The hand on his knee tightened and Calix had to force himself to hold still.

Ethaniel loomed over him even more, blotting out the candlelight and firelight and the way Aubrey's skin glistened. His vision now full of Ethaniel, and Calix rose up to meet him halfway, exquisitely aching for it.

Every single thing about the way Ethaniel kissed was elegant and skillful, but it was the quiet passion in his touch that left Calix panting. Aubrey was fire incarnate, but Ethaniel…Ethaniel was the wind fueling the fire. A fire could burn down a forest, but wind could literally break the earth. They were each other's catalyst, sometimes merely walking circles around each other, and then at times, combusting on impact.

Calix craned up into the kiss, pushing himself up on his palms to get closer. But as much as he drowned in Ethaniel's kiss, he could still tell when a new hand slid up his right thigh.

"This is insane," Aubrey whispered, half in Calix's ear and half to himself. "I'd call it magic, but I know it's not."

Ethaniel broke away to say, "Aubrey. Stop thinking. Kiss him. We'll sort this other shit out in a moment. Just kiss him already."

The moment Ethaniel's lips left his, Aubrey's sharp-angled features took up the whole of his vision. Calix felt Ethaniel's grip on his hip, sure and steady, but everything else was full up on *Aubrey*.

The man was magnetic, sucking in helpless but willing victims with those eyes and that countenance. "Are you sure?" Aubrey asked, low and soft.

Calix nearly scoffed, but managed to swallow it down. "Please tell me you're joking," he grumbled.

Ethaniel wasn't nearly as swift in cutting off his own response, but Calix heard that laugh stop abruptly when Aubrey took hold of Calix's chin — like he had in the carriage only an hour or so ago — and stared at him hard. "I rarely joke. Ethaniel can confirm that. But especially not when it comes to any kind of intimate affair. Not between myself and anyone in the past, and especially not when it concerns *this*." Aubrey gestured with an elegant hand to Ethaniel, then to himself, and finally came to rest on Calix's chest. The material of Aubrey's vest glinted in the firelight and Calix realized it must have been patterned to reflect light in such a way. It was subtle, but beautiful; clearly Ethaniel's work.

"Between us, you mean," Calix hazarded.

"Yes. The three of us. And because we're *men*," Aubrey said, sitting back on his haunches. "You live in this city. You know how it is."

Calix did. He wagered they'd all run afoul of some kind of trouble. Calix's money was more than enough to pay off any police officer, though he'd never wracked up any tickets. *Lawton*, on the other hand, had a few times before he'd gotten sick of being threatened with court and fines and even jail.

But even *sweet, proper Calix* had gotten caught outside of a safe zone once or twice. He'd been able to bribe his way out of legal troubles. From the look on Ethaniel and Aubrey's faces, it was clear his penance had been paltry to what they'd seen or experienced themselves.

They both waited on him to speak, their stares measured, but there was a stiff urgency to the set of Aubrey's jaw that made Calix speak up. "I do. I won't spit in the face of our safety, but I won't deny what I see before me, either. Or what I want."

Aubrey worked his jaw, nodding, while Ethaniel said, "Good. That's good. Because we certainly don't need to add trouble to this mess with that damn book."

"Agreed." And suddenly Calix's chin was held by Aubrey once more. "Now, where were we?"

Something about Aubrey made Calix want to launch himself at the man, apparently. He restrained himself enough to keep from knocking Aubrey over, but it was a near thing. Now Ethaniel laughed, delighted, but that laugh lived for only a moment as Calix poured the passion he'd saved for Aubrey into their kiss.

"Jesus wept," Ethaniel whispered, hoarse and harsh, sending waves of gooseflesh over Calix's skin. A hand — whose, he didn't know — snuck in under his rumpled shirt to find his spine and Calix tore out of the kiss with a moan.

"Focus." A hand in Calix's hair forced his head down, with a touch that was firm but gentle. He found himself staring at Aubrey once more as the hand on his lower back slid up, and the one in his hair tightened. "Be here."

"I am," Calix bit out as he tried to angle forward and find Aubrey's mouth again.

"You're not completely, though," Ethaniel said in his ear.

Calix shut his eyes against the adrenaline and pleasure surging through him. These two were going to tear him asunder. "You've done this before," he panted out, turning his head enough to catch sight of Ethaniel's pleased little smile. "That's completely unfair."

"Even if it were true..." Aubrey rocked up against him and Calix fell forward with a groan. Too much more, and he'd be embarrassingly hard. It felt too early for *that*, and yet Calix wanted it badly. "Would you be upset by that?"

"Not at all," Calix replied, eyes fluttering shut once more as Aubrey kissed him. Deeply, this time, and slowly; a fierce contrast to the hot kiss Ethaniel pressed inside his wrist. Clever fingers worked Calix's left sleeve open and more kisses were placed on his skin.

Calix let himself be swept away by these two fascinating, passionate men who only a few days ago had been strangers to him.

In their world, couplings were usually hasty, fumbling things, fear of being caught driving the senses higher. But so often, those moments were ultimately unsatisfying. They had been for Calix. And Lawton had his own selfish reasons for seeking Calix out; he claimed he wanted to find pleasure in Calix's body, his kiss, but Calix couldn't think of a time with Lawton that hadn't been at *his* beckoning, his urging.

It had never been about desire or intimacy. It had never been about learning someone else so completely. The scent of them, their taste, what sounds they made, how they liked to be touched. Undoing, and being undone. Lawton had only been interested in himself, and had taught Calix that any coupling between those like themselves would be fraught with denial and insincerity.

Surely there wasn't more to it than animalistic satisfaction.

But what if there was?

The low throb of pleasure in his belly was magnificent, but it was nothing next to how badly Calix wanted to *know* both of them.

They would get through this. They had to.

Calix broke away from Aubrey with a gasp, then yanked on Ethaniel until the other man fell into them both, half-laughing, grinning like mad.

"Kiss each other," Calix demanded.

"Not an issue," Ethaniel said swiftly before hauling Aubrey to him, practically pulling the taller man on top of him. Limbs now tangled with theirs, Calix let himself be dragged down, half laying on Ethaniel as the tailor kissed Aubrey hard.

Giddiness swept through him, light and airy and a source of unexpected pleasure. Gods how Calix wanted to drag them both to bed and let the rest sort itself out. It didn't matter *how* — hands or mouths or even frottage would be more than enough. He wanted to delight in them both, watch them both fall apart, sweaty and sated and gorgeous.

Calix slid his hand down Ethaniel's chest, entranced by the vision before him. They fit together so beautifully, so perfectly, and yet he knew he wasn't forgotten by the way Aubrey reached for him, the way Ethaniel curled an arm around Calix's back. Bringing him closer and closer, until they could fold him into their epicenter.

And then it all crashed down on them.

"No," Aubrey gasped. Calix froze, worried he'd done something wrong, but Aubrey said it again, his gaze now sharp as he looked around. "Someone's broken through the wards."

"How is that possible?" Ethaniel looked both startled and worried and Calix felt the arm around him flex protectively.

"I don't know but..." Aubrey got to his feet, hauling them both up with ease before running for a tall mahogany cabinet on the far wall. Calix hadn't much of a chance to look around Aubrey's abode, as focused as they'd been on other issues. A quick glance now told Calix that Aubrey liked dark wood and gilt, all of it tasteful, nearly sublime.

It hit him all at once. *What about the book?*

As if reading his mind, Aubrey said, "It's locked in my personal vault. But the wards on that share a link to the wards on the apartment. Someone breaking through one—"

"Means the vault clamps down on security. But the book jumps to Calix, you said so, Aubrey." Ethaniel sucked in a deep breath, seemingly more disturbed by the book wanting to be near Calix than the bloody *sword* Aubrey had just handed him.

"You can fight?" Calix asked as he closed the distance between him and Aubrey.

Ethaniel gave him a wan smile. "Amongst other things."

"Shit." Aubrey sighed before turning around with a revolver gripped tightly in his right hand. "Another ward down."

"What do we do?" Calix held out his hands. "Aubrey?"

Aubrey scanned the room, and Calix saw his gaze lock on the mussed rugs and pillows they'd left behind mere moments ago. "You take this," Aubrey said as he handed Calix a jeweled knife. "If you have to defend yourself, just throw it at your target. Grab your mother's things, so we have those, too."

Calix immediately went cold but did as he was told. Had they both used weapons before? Harmed someone? *Killed someone*? "I don't know how to use this knife."

Aubrey shook his head. "It won't matter. The knife follows intention, not skill. Aim to maim, not murder. The arms, knees, shoulders. If you think about defending yourself, the knife will follow that."

That helped some, but not nearly enough. Bile rose in his throat and Calix swallowed against it, resisting the urge to vomit. "All right," he said softly, taking the dagger from Aubrey.

"It's okay, Calix," Ethaniel said as he pulled Calix close. "Trust me. Trust us." Then he turned back to Aubrey, determination setting his jaw. "Aubrey?"

"There's a way out, but it won't be warded." Aubrey led them over to the closed study door and pressed an ear against it. "Well, from the sounds of crashing and stomping about, whoever it is is likely destroying thousands of dollars of antiques. Lovely." Aubrey shook his head. "We need to retrieve that book. The vault's in the library up the hall, and the guest room next door has a hidden door. There's a back staircase down, out to the alley. We'll go on three."

All Calix could do was grip the dagger harder and watch as Aubrey held up one...two...three fingers, then yanked open the door. Revolver pointed first, Aubrey spun into the hallway, graceful as a dancer. "They're still downstairs, go! Second door on your left, Ethaniel!"

Ethaniel grabbed Calix by the hand and ran into the dark hall. He and Aubrey hadn't bothered to light any of the sconces on the walls on their way through Aubrey's apartment, and Calix now regretted that lack of foresight.

While Ethaniel pulled him forward, Calix's mind whirled with questions, none of which mattered in the moment.

Right now, all that mattered was getting out safely. As far as he was concerned, that damn book — *Convergence* — could burn.

I can't

I won't

But those who broke through wish for much darker things

Vile

Fire

Judgment

I am safer with you

"No, you're not!" Calix screamed as he pushed his palm into his temple. "Get out of my head!"

Take me with you

Your mother's roses have the answers you seek

Her wards could have stood against a god

If such a thing existed

Calix's hands ached. His body sang with pain, as if he'd been tossed down several flights of stairs. This felt like every time his powers had acted up, but it was like all of it was combined into one ball of misery and confusion. He let Ethaniel pull him into a room that smelled like leather and wax, stumbling forward to make room for Aubrey.

Aubrey wasn't behind them.

"Aubrey!" Ethaniel yelled as he stuck his head back into the hallway. "Come on!"

Aubrey appeared before them now, but it was Aubrey from the Collectio. Eyes glowing and cracking with power. But now Calix could see thin lines of magic coursing up Aubrey's neck, across his cheeks and up over his head. That power pushed on Calix, crooking an inviting finger at his own magic...as if asking for it to come and out play. He pushed back against it, willing it to stay put. Now would not be a good time for him to lose control.

Ethaniel shook his head, mouth set in a grim line. "Aubrey, no."

"I'm giving you an escape," Aubrey said. "I'll hold them off so you can get to the street. I can tap into the door's memory of being whole and repair it faster than they can break it down." Aubrey tipped his head back, sniffing at the air. "They've set fire to something downstairs."

A series of crashes, then indecipherable yelling, filtered up to them. "Take Calix and the book and *go*." Hand like a viper, Aubrey snagged Ethaniel by the chin, kissing him hard. Calix braced himself and a moment later, found himself in Aubrey's grasp. "I'll be right behind you," Aubrey said softly. "I promise. I'm no martyr."

Smoke wafted up to them, seeping through the floorboards and curling up the staircase at the other end of the hall. "Go," Aubrey said, pushing Ethaniel back into the room, then entering himself, closing the door and locking it. "I'll ward this and stay near until I sense you're both outside. Pull on the second book, third shelf down on the left bookcase on the western wall." Aubrey pointed to the far wall, to a bookcase banking a large marble fireplace. "The room's through there, the vault's behind the painting over the bed." Aubrey's eyes flashed and the shockwaves of his power rippled over Calix's skin. "The wards on it are down. Go!"

"Goddamn it. All right." Ethaniel moved back, taking Calix with him.

"Don't I get a say in this?" Calix asked, but Aubrey only shook his head. "Aubrey! Just come with us!"

But Aubrey didn't reply. In his stead, Ethaniel said, "Come. He'll be all right. He's got a *gun*, for fuck's sake."

"But—"

Ethaniel marched them over to the bookcase, pulled on the correct book, and the entire wall swung open to reveal a bedchamber beyond. "Aubrey, I swear to all the saints, if you die..." Ethaniel muttered.

"You can line up behind me for that," Calix said before shoving his way through the opening. He chanced a glance back at Aubrey and saw the man standing before the large library door, one hand splayed out as power danced around his fingertips. The air in front of the door had a ghostly aura to it, and Calix could feel the ward's strength.

The other hand held the revolver steady, aimed for the door and whatever or whoever might come through it.

The darkness did them no favors, but thankfully the bedchamber was small enough to stumble through easily. Ethaniel went right to the painting over the bed, some innocuous pastoral landscape that looked pretty enough but wouldn't arouse suspicion. Ethaniel tossed the painting to the floor, his usual caution and care peeled away to make room for haste.

On the wall was a plain iron square.

Calix reached out to it, but Ethaniel stopped him. "Let me," he said, putting his hands on the wall, just to either side of the square. "You've both handled this book too much already. Let me take some of it on."

Calix didn't like the idea one jot, but he understood it. That innate sense to protect those close to him wasn't just a part of his personality; it was who Ethaniel *was*, in every manner. The protective arm he'd curled around Calix and how he kept pace with Aubrey. His care for his uncle. Ethaniel would give until the day his own heart gave out. It had been a slow slide of realization, but now it struck Calix with the power of a storm.

It made him want to protect them both. Aubrey staying behind was the height of stupidity.

"Take it and go," Calix said as Ethaniel slid the square's cover up. Inside was only the book and a simple velvet pouch. "Take them both and get a carriage. If we're not outside in two minutes, give the driver this and tell him to get you outside the city. There's an enchanted carriage company in Marble Hill, or buy a horse, and take the north trade route to Auburn. Ask for Nelly at the Greenrise Boarding House when you get into town. She'll get you to Rosehill."

Calix shoved his billfold at Ethaniel, knowing he had more than enough money to cover it all. "Don't argue," he said just as Ethaniel opened his mouth. Something fierce, like a fight breaking out, lit up Ethaniel's eyes, but Calix shook his head. "I can smell the smoke, Ethaniel. I'm fetching Aubrey, and worse comes to worse, we'll have to meet you at Rosehill. I already sent my valet on with word to expect us. Hell, that stubborn fool might be on his way there already."

Calix took a deep breath, leaned in, and kissed Ethaniel. Ethaniel immediately kissed him back, hot and hard and *perfect*, and if they'd had all the time in the world, Calix would have pulled Aubrey into that little moment.

A sudden, sharp pain flared in his temples, in his hands, and he knew they were out of time. Someone or several people were working strong magic. Aubrey wouldn't be able to hold out against them for long.

"Be careful," Ethaniel said as he shoved both items from the vault into Calix's satchel.

"I will," Calix reassured him.

He didn't have time to watch Ethaniel leave. Calix bolted from the room, bursting into the library as the hall door shook in its hinges.

"Calix," Aubrey muttered, even with his eyes closed and power swirling about him. "What the hell are you doing?"

"Making sure we both live through this," Calix said as his hand went into his pocket, fingers closing around the small diary within. A moment of reassurance before beginning to channel.

In theory, he'd done this a hundred times. He used to recite the deceptively simple steps to himself to get to sleep. His mother had practically ground into him *most* of what she knew, but the one thing permanently etched into his mind was how to channel magic.

Calix understood, as he watched a bead of sweat slide down Aubrey's temple, how much magic could eat away at a person. Edna, his caretaker after his mother's death, had fully believed that Lily Addington had suffered a "bout of madness" and drowned herself in the lake south of Rosehill. Calix knew better; he'd known better then, and he knew it now, as solid as truth and as harsh and cold as reality. His mother hadn't gone mad, as if it were some infection. She'd let the magic get too deep inside her mind, her body, and it had broken her down from within. Her visions, her night walks, and as the years passed, her slow, aching inability to touch anything even remotely magical, had all been evidence.

The vault below Rosehill existed because she couldn't handle the raw essence of magic, even the remains of it that lingered on dead artifacts. She had wanted to learn all she could from their makeup, in some attempt, Calix suspected, to reverse engineer her own condition. Magic had overpowered her, then pulled her under. Her death had been the final say on Calix's understanding of her powers. Oracles, exceedingly rare and usually not long lived, eventually succumbed to the magic that was part of their reality. It wore them down, bit by bit, until the erosion was unstoppable.

Aubrey was battling his own magic, his own skills, and the ones on the other side, with their raised voices and whatever patterns they were using to slowly tear away at the door. But he wouldn't last much longer against it all.

That understanding, that knowledge, forced Calix to do the very thing he swore he'd never do.

With a firm hand, Calix clamped down on Aubrey's shoulder. "Give it to me."

"Whatever you're suggesting, absolutely not." Aubrey was sweating and disheveled, but he was still *Aubrey*. The man had a stubborn streak a mile wide.

"Give me the magic. I'll lock them out, and we will escape."

"I can't," Aubrey said, his words strained as another blow shook the door. On the other side, they heard a voice yell something about controlling the flames and Calix's blood went cold. "Any disruption might give them an edge."

"Trust me, you can do this," he said, tightening his grip on Aubrey's shoulder. Aubrey stared at him hard, but rewarded Calix with a slow nod before he closed his softly glowing eyes once more.

It started with physical contact.

Establish touch

Then Calix closed his eyes and breathed Aubrey in.

Establish bond

Aubrey's citrusy scent was buried under sweat and smoke, but it was there all the same. Calix leaned into Aubrey's warmth and *breathed.*

In the darkness behind his eyes, a flame sprung to life. One flicker, as though someone were holding fire in their palm. Calix reached for it eagerly, knowing this was Aubrey trusting him deeply. Channeling was a highly intimate thing, too personal for any casual relationship.

Establish trust

"Breathe with me," Calix muttered, willing his own heart to slow.

The darkness pulled at him, plucking at his senses, but eventually the frenetic energy twitched into an even pattern. A musician figuring out his part in the orchestra.

"Breathe," he whispered.

A second flame appeared, greenish-blue like the glow of Aubrey's mending magic.

Calix knew Aubrey felt his rush of gratitude when the other man shivered, and he had to smile. The room, the smoke, the pounding on the door had all faded to a distant hum, somewhere far out on the horizon. But they were here, now, and nothing was more important than the final step.

Find the balance

Everything about channeling was dangerous, but the final step left Calix completely vulnerable. It's why one never channeled with someone they didn't trust — Aubrey could easily reach in at this very moment and shred Calix's power to fragments.

It would take nothing at all for him to do.

Calix felt that rush of gratitude grow, warming him all over, and he let go.

He opened himself up fully to Aubrey's power, and it felt like nothing he'd ever experienced. *This* was why his mother never stopped her channeling, even when it slowly obliterated her.

This

This power

This incredible rush

Calix was flying, soaring, riding a wave of magical essence unlike anything else. Aubrey's power was brilliant, bright and burning and yet somehow orderly; just like Aubrey himself. Calix tasted Scotch on his tongue, smelled lavender, could feel the comfort of plush rugs and well-polished floors under his feet. The satisfaction of a solid day's work vibrated through his being. And then what followed was deeper down, but still Aubrey; his foundation, his very being. Order and knowledge, but never without a tiny bit of risk. A small willingness to push past his limits, to see what he was truly capable of. Duty and stalwartness, yes, but under that was a man and his magic and the sense that if he'd truly wanted to, Aubrey could have it all. He could take power, topple establishments, run companies, and court influence.

Aubrey didn't want that. It wasn't his legacy or his family's legacy.

Aubrey was a healer. A mender. Someone who repaired, who restored, who made whole the things most others gave up on.

So Calix pushed all of that out, against the now splintered door, and out again, to where he could sense the mages throwing patterns against Aubrey's wards. Out further still to where a man in a black as night suit stood on the opposite street corner, cigarette in his mouth as he watched flames punch out the windows on the first floor of the apartment. Calix stared in shock as the man, who looked far too much like Ethaniel, suddenly locked eyes with him and gave a slow nod, then stubbed out his cigarette and walked away.

That stranger's hooded hazel eyes burned through him, as if they could find all of Calix's secrets and spill them like marbles from a jar.

Calix let out a guttural yell and *shoved* that power forward, as if he could spit in that man's eye and make him regret rising from bed that morning. He was healing and mending, and power, and pure spite, and it all slapped against that library door as if to say, "Your move".

Calix let his head fall forward as the last bit of Aubrey's magic ran its course through him. And in his ear, Aubrey said, "You bloody brilliant fool. Come on."

Calix wasn't entirely sure if he was walking or stumbling, but Aubrey must have managed to get them out, because the next thing he knew, he was slumped against Aubrey's side as the smell of horse and city streets assaulted him.

"Marble Hill," he muttered into Aubrey's sleeve. "I sent Ethaniel there."

"Good. We're not far behind him, and he'll likely stop for supplies while there." Calix felt his hair pushed off his neck and then powerful fingers were kneading into the base of his skull. "Stay with me, Calix," Aubrey said quietly.

"Bit stuck now, I think."

Aubrey sputtered a laugh. "I think we both are."

Calix closed his eyes and breathed, feeling a tendril of Aubrey's power touch his mind with something like *peace*.

FOLIO THREE:

Convergence

My heart is hardened; I cannot repent.
Scarce can I name salvation, faith, or heaven.
Swords, poison, halters, and envenomed steel
Are laid before me to dispatch my self,
And long ere this, I should have done the deed,
Had not sweet pleasure conquered deep despair.
— "The Tragedy of Doctor Faustus" by Christopher Marlowe

FIFTEEN

ETHANIEL

"Marble Hill's just up ahead, sir," the carriage driver yelled out. "You got a specific spot in mind, or you want me to drop you off wherever?"

Ethaniel opened his eyes and forced his hands to unclench. He was sick with worry over Aubrey and Calix, even though logic told him they were likely fine, if not soot-covered and exhausted. But the thought of leaving the city behind without them made his stomach burn with acid. Hell, even going to Marble Hill had been trying; it had been far too tempting to wait across the street from Aubrey's apartment.

But he'd caught sight of a few people dressed in dark clothes fleeing the building, headed toward a single man walking up the sidewalk, sticking to the shadows. Ethaniel had tucked himself into an alleyway to catch his breath, but it had been punched right out of him upon seeing Vincent again so soon, and so close to the fire his people had clearly set in an attempt to smoke them out.

If Vincent was here, no one linked to the book he now carried was safe. Dread had bloomed in him, forcing Ethaniel out of his low crouch so he could slink along the side of the building, out of eyeline of anyone from the Golden Order.

"Fuck, fuck, fuck," he'd muttered as he'd clutched the satchel close and, when he was sure he was safe, had broken into a dead run for the nearest well-lighted area, hand out to hail a carriage.

Ethaniel needed to gather his thoughts and his strength. He needed to set his mind right. And he needed to contact Calix and Ethaniel. For that he'd need privacy; working complicated patterning in view of others, even when it was completely legal, would make others instantly suspicious. He didn't need that kind of attention. "Do you know of any good inns nearby?" he called out to the driver. "A clean place? There's a hearty tip in it for you. "

The driver chuckled. "I didn't think you was the whorin' type. Yeah, Lacey's is good, mostly travelers and a few local tipplers."

"Perfect," Ethaniel replied as he leaned back against the carriage seat and put a protective hand on the satchel.

Lacey's looked like a decent place even from the outside, which was an accomplishment given most of the roads in Marble Hill were barely roads at all, but packed dirt and a bit of gravel. The winter melt had turned most of that into puddles and ruts, and Ethaniel's bones ached as he climbed out of the carriage and handed over the fee for the drive and the promised tip. The driver, an older man with graying stubble along his chin, was kind enough to wish Ethaniel luck before snapping the reins and disappearing into the night.

Ethaniel stared up at the brick building. The green shutters were a nice touch amidst all the mud and water, and past them he could see a few shadows moving about, backlit by flickering only candles could produce. The rain that had started on the way over was now a fine mist and it clung to his hair, his clothes. Ethaniel tightened his grip on the satchel and strode inside.

Warm air hit his face and Ethaniel breathed in the scent of herbs and firewood. A roaring fire to his left, a small but very clean check-in counter to his right, and coming down the stairs was a woman dressed in all dark blue, her blonde hair elaborately braided and hanging over her shoulder. She had wide, expressive eyes that widened even more when she saw Ethaniel's bedraggled state.

"Oh my goodness, I'm so sorry!" she said as she walked around the other side of the counter. "We had a few last minute arrivals and I was getting them situated. I'm Rose, the owner. Did you need a room?"

"If I'm not too late," Ethaniel said with a small wince. "I got a bit caught in the weather." He sniffed at the air, stomach growling. "Is there anyone still in the kitchens?"

Rose nodded. "Our cook's working on bread for tomorrow, but she has some dinner leftover. Or the tavern down the street serves late." Her gaze flicked to the rain-dashed windows. "Though I don't imagine you fancy going back outside."

Ethaniel gave a small laugh at that, but when it threatened to bubble up inside him — a symptom of the day's challenging events and the lingering pulse of Aubrey and Calix's kisses — he could only shake his head. "I'll stay here, thanks."

Rose showed him to a small but very tidy room and promised a warm meal would be brought up soon. Ethaniel sat in the single chair by the window, put the satchel on the floor, and stared down at his boots.

Tracking patterns weren't completely unknown to him, but he'd need more than someone trained in that magic. Ethaniel had half a mind to ask a policeman for help, but that would draw too much attention. They could likely find Calix and Aubrey, but that would endanger many lives, and none of them wished to pull more innocents into this mess.

He drummed his fingertips on the table. A plan. He needed a plan. And supplies. This late in the day, many shops wouldn't be open, but small towns like Marble Hill usually had someone willing to reopen for a few extra dollars.

Before he left the room, Ethaniel gave a fleeting glance to the satchel. He could hide it, or keep it on him. Keeping it on him might draw attention. Hiding it might draw The Golden Order to those in the boarding house.

Shit.

Ethaniel slung the bag back over his head and headed downstairs. He caught Rose as she turned the corner with an armful of blankets. "I was just coming up to give you these," she said, smiling. "Did you need anything else?"

Ethaniel put on a smile for her sake and said, "Do you happen to have a map of the city? It doesn't need to be terribly recent."

Rose nodded and immediately went over to her little counter, setting the blankets aside and digging around in a drawer. "I've got one from last year, I think. You heading into the city?"

"Out, actually, but I also need to give a friend directions here." Ethaniel was surprised at how smoothly the lie tumbled from his lips. Maybe the day's events had rattled him enough that nerves were no longer an issue. "And do you happen to have charcoal and perhaps a few blank pages of paper?"

Ethaniel slid a few bills across the counter, but Rose waved him off. "You aren't asking for anything terribly difficult. I'll bring it all up with the food, if that's all right."

By the time Ethaniel was settled in his room — as much as he could while damp and still shaky — there was a knock at the door. Rose passed him a tray packed with a tureen of soup, a bottle of beer, half a loaf of still-steaming bread, and a bowl of cooked carrots. Then she ducked past him to set his requested supplies on the small, chipped table across from the bed.

Ethaniel thanked her profusely, saying, "This is honestly too much. But I'll eat every bit of it, and thank you again for the supplies." Memories of Aubrey's kiss, Calix's touch, made him suck in a harsh breath. "Your kindness serves you well, and it is appreciated more than I can begin to explain."

"No explanation needed." She sniffed and gazed out the window. "New York's not very friendly to most, especially those of us trying to make a living on the edges." Rose gestured to his scarred knuckles — all the times he'd poked himself with enchanted needles or had minor patterning mishaps. "You work, like I do. We're not for Manhattan or Wall Street. So the most we can do to get along is show each other kindness."

Rose left him with a mountain of food and more than enough to think through.

Ethaniel only stopped to strip out of his sodden outer layers and, with the fireplace heating the room to almost uncomfortably hot, set to work on tracking Calix and Aubrey. He grabbed a few mouthfuls of soup and bread in between removing articles of clothing, but his focus was on them.

He didn't want to think about it.

Losing them

Ethaniel swallowed hard, the taste of misery and worry heavier on his tongue than the soup. But with the map spread out on the small table, some tiny reassurance swelled in him. Distance on foot or by horse was one thing; on a map, great distances, miles upon miles, could seem miniscule in comparison. Marble Hill to the Village seemed a mere pittance. And he could work with that, even knowing what little he did about tracking patterns.

With care, Ethaniel rubbed the charcoal stick over his index and middle finger, and drew a line on the path the carriage had taken him. That was his route, and it established the first part of the pattern. The rest was a mess of guesswork and intent, since the only times he'd ever done anything like this was years ago, when Jeremiah had taken him hunting in northern New York state. Jeremiah had always thought of patterning as "intent made corporeal", since good patterners could strictly follow a pattern with impeccable preciseness, but they also had to learn to improvise. Jeremiah also likened it all to "messy mathematics", where sometimes the number two really meant two and a half if you wanted the end result to function correctly.

Thinking of Jeremiah in the middle of all of this seemed to open a new fissure in his heart, so Ethaniel refocused. "Here, and here," he whispered as he drew two more lines from the Village to Marble Hill, this time with his middle finger. Routes Calix and Aubrey might take. He couldn't ask the pattern to scour the city for them, but if he let it follow a few direct paths, he at least would have some answers.

Calix's satchel and the little velvet bag that had been in Aubrey's vault held the final pieces. Ethaniel pulled out his needle kit from deep inside his coat and carefully plucked a fraying thread from the string that closed the velvet bag. Whatever was in it wasn't his business, so he turned to the satchel.

Temptation lay in letting his sight focus in on the book's patterns again. *After you find Calix and Aubrey*, he told himself. But even touching the bag's flap to pull away a loose thread sent a shiver down his spine. It made his hands tremble as he carefully tied the two threads together, then placed them in the middle of the map.

With his palms on the map, Ethaniel closed his eyes and waited. Every pattern was different, but for him it was about connection. Ethaniel would put his hands on a shirt, or a jacket, or a set of handkerchiefs purchased for someone's newly betrothed, and he would use his connection to the garment — and the work he'd invested in it — to forge a bond with it. A trusted bond, a sacred one. Blacksmiths made connection with metal, bookbinders with paper and leather, modistes with lace and ribbon. And he with a bit of clothing and some needle and thread.

A map was just paper and ink. But for him, in this moment, it meant so much more.

He remembered the twist of Aubrey's lips when he was amused but didn't want to show it. How Calix's eyes lit up when he encountered Ethaniel's patterning magic.

Aubrey's strong arm over his shoulders.

Watching them kiss, how it burned in his belly.

The way they felt, how they smelled.

How they'd turned his little world upside down.

Ethaniel trusted they were alive, and trying to find him.

Behind the darkness of his eyelids, Ethaniel saw the flash of power. It started as little tingles running up and down his fingers, his hands. Then, like a magnet, his right hand was yanked forward, index finger shooting out like an arrow to land squarely on the New York Botanical Garden.

Ethaniel's eyes flew open and he looked down at the glowing lines of the map, how the threads he'd bound together had unraveled to chart a course from the Village, up along the East River, to Soundview and then north.

The Botanical Gardens were a newer addition to that part of the city, a massive undertaking Ethaniel had only heard about. But if they were in or near the Gardens, Ethaniel figured they were safe. It wasn't the most direct route to Marble Hill, but their path made sense if they were trying to evade anyone tracking them.

"Now the hard part," he murmured as he refocused on the map. "Let's see if I can contact them."

He'd never done this before. It was honestly far out of the reach of his own magic, but he had to *try*. Vincent used to say that all magic was capable of all things, if the caster believed strongly enough. That there wasn't just "patterning" and "enchanting"; that humans had given certain spells those names to make better sense of a force much stronger, and much more foreign, to the natural order of their world. To mold, then wield the magic for their own purposes. Even when handled with care, magic was really only suited for a select few.

Ah, Vincent. What have you gotten us all involved with? Your beliefs about magic have been there since we were young, but I only now have come to understand how that's driven you to such hateful delusions.

"I hope you can feel me even from here," Ethaniel muttered as he ran his index fingers down the threads. If some tiny part of his lovers lived within those single threads, he would feed it his care, his devotion, his loyalty. And hope that they paid him back.

Ethaniel pictured their faces.

Staring back at him were two sets of eyes, one like cool glass and the other decadent amber. But they lingered only for a moment, and then he saw another set. Like his, but slightly wider set, a few more lines around his eyes, despite Ethaniel being older by four years.

And then came the pain. Like an ice pick through his skull, sudden and sharp and so, so cold. Ethaniel yelled, reeled back in his chair but tipped it too far, and he crashed to the ground. He was blind from the pain, unable to focus on anything but the agony carving out his skull. Even through that pain, Vincent's voice came to him.

It shouldn't have been possible. But then again, that damned book was rewriting the rules he thought he knew about magic and connection. About reality. Yes, Convergence was definitely to blame for opening him up to Vincent's pull.

I'm sorry, brother. But you shouldn't have been in that house. Now a fire blazes through a block of the Village. Why would you make friends with such a wealthy twat? He can't understand your life, your struggles. He's always had everything handed to him.

Calix Addington. Earl Batherton, Calix Addington.

Did you know he was nobility? I won't repeat my arguments to you about how the 'ruling class' should be eliminated entirely. That their wealth should go to the people. And the church. And places like mine that help others. That promote goodwill and grace, and the rightful truth about magic. You've heard it more than enough by now.

It's why we stopped speaking, after all.

So did you know who he was? Or did you like that someone of Earl Addington's so-called stature had come to Uncle Jeremiah's shop? Did you like the attention? Did the Earl look at you with his big doe eyes, softening you up so you'd do as he needed?

Has he whispered sweetly to you? Make you feel seen? Heard?
Is he yours?

Yes, I know. I've always known. But you've always been discrete. Until your most recent lover. It's hard to miss Aubrey Lavigne, tall and broad and so well-dressed, well-mannered. A proper gentleman in their dying age. Or, so he wants the world to believe.

Did Aubrey take you to the third floor of The Minotaur's Labyrinth? Did he show you the....perversities that go on there? Did he ask you to join him?

Nowhere is private, not completely. My spies see many things. They've seen Mr. Lavigne.

And tonight they saw you, fleeing a burning building carrying a gray satchel.

Turn it over to me. And I'll never bother you, or Mr. Lavigne, or Earl Addington again. If you meet with me, you can return to your life, and help our uncle return to health.

The pain flooded out of him all at once and he was left on his back, hands clenched around his head, his sight barely returning by inches while his ears rang. He wasn't able to answer the knock at the door, but heard Rose call out. He couldn't answer, couldn't get his tongue to work, to form the words he needed to put off the innkeeper.

Too late, too late, he thought as a key scraped in the lock, and then she burst inside, a look of worry on her face. That look morphed into real concern when she saw him.

"Oh no," Rose said as she rushed to his side. "My goodness, what happened? Are you all right?" Ethaniel's mouth wouldn't work, so he just nodded. "You don't look all right," Rose said, her tone drenched in worry, as if Ethaniel must truly be addled. "Let's get you up."

Rose helped him to his feet, then steered him to sit on the edge of the bed. His head hurt terribly and Ethaniel had to work his jaw a few times to spit out, "Thank you."

"Don't thank me. I heard a yell, gave me quite a start, and had to check with everyone. I'm sorry I didn't find you immediately." She glanced around the room with narrowed eyes. "Are you injured?"

Ethaniel didn't like lying, but here it was necessary. "A bad headache came on all of sudden. I get them sometimes when the seasons change."

Rose clucked her tongue in sympathy. "Ah, I'm sorry to hear. I'm glad you're all right otherwise. Can I make you some tea?"

Ethaniel put on a brave face and shook his head. "I think I'll just lie down. My thanks to you, though." He paused, remembering what Calix had said about an enchanted carriage business in the area. "Is there a carriage business nearby? Or a stable? I'm in need of a horse."

Rose nodded, and Ethaniel nearly sighed with relief that she kept her gaze on him, instead of tracking to the table and the evidence of his magical experiment. "There is! Strauss and Co., not a half a block north, has fine carriages and they also take on passengers. There's a stable there as well, though I don't know if they have many horses for sale at a time."

Ethaniel thanked her profusely, handed her another dollar for her troubles, and waited until her footsteps faded before sinking back on the bed again. A horse was his best bet; he was a good rider and knew how hard to push himself and a horse across the few days it would take to get to Auburn.

Head still ringing, Ethaniel quickly made a list of things he'd need, then turned the gas lamps off except one by the door. Before he let sleep claim him, he disenchanted the pattern he'd cast on the sword while hiding in an alley before hailing a carriage. Shrinking patterns weren't difficult, and were quite useful in his line of work. It had been tricky casting it on a fucking *sword*, but he'd managed to get it down to the size of a crochet hook, which let him shove it in his tailoring kit. New York City was a lot of things, but he'd likely not get away with carrying a sword about.

Ethaniel very carefully slid the blade under his pillow before settling on his back and closing his eyes. He had to get out of town, but he needed rest. Vincent's jabs at him, at Calix, and at Aubrey lingered on the edges of his mind. If his brother was reaching for personal insults, then he was frustrated. He would scale back and examine his plans, then come back with a new approach. Setting fire to the building was likely *not* planned; it wasn't Vincent's style of sticking to the shadows and knifing enemies when they were most vulnerable. A fire was splashy and would make the papers. It would bring attention too close to home. That would make Vincent uncomfortable. He'd need to leave tomorrow, and stay disappeared. Trusting that Calix and Aubrey could get out, could meet him at Calix's estate up north.

Ethaniel was putting a lot on trust these days. He hoped that approach wouldn't fail him just yet.

Sixteen

A**UBREY**

Mud-splattered and soot-streaked was the standard uniform in this part of the city, so he and Calix had that part of the unintentional disguise in hand. But Calix's clearly expensive clothes and his upscale but still common suit didn't earn them any congenial looks as they limped along the streets in some part of Lenox Hill. Very little of the old farms that had once flourished there remained, and now the streets were packed mud, the buildings thin and crumbling. Construction equipment and massive piles of stone blocks sat waiting for blueprints to be finished, perhaps signaling change for the neighborhood.

In the cloying dark that settled around them, the wide shadows between the few enchanted lanterns made those stones look rather ominous; like squat monsters simply waiting for him and Calix to walk into their gaping mouths.

Morbid and macabre, perhaps, but Aubrey's thoughts were no darker than the incoming night. Calix's arm carefully looped through his, which allowed him to keep Calix close, made Aubrey feel a little bit better. But they were both battered and exhausted, and Calix stayed quiet so as not to aggravate his throat. He'd inhaled smoke as they'd scrambled to leave Aubrey's apartment; hearts racing and blood pumping, the selfless man at his side had all but shoved him out the door and down the stairs first as gray smoke engulfed them.

Calix had held Aubrey's grip on the door until the last moment, then ripped himself out of the tether they'd shared. Something of Calix's power lingered in Aubrey's veins and strangely, it left the scent of roses in his nostrils.

"We should be able to meet Ethaniel at Marble Hill, if he hasn't moved on already," Calix rasped as they turned the next corner. Aubrey roughly understood where they were, but Marble Hill was still a ways off, and he doubted any carriages were selling their services in this part of the city.

"We'll need to get somewhere with more people, more services," Aubrey replied as he pulled Calix closer. A figure was stumbling toward them and while Aubrey didn't want to overreact, he wasn't about to get caught unawares.

"Right." Calix turned his head this way and that, then pointed left, to the spot near where the stumbling figure had appeared. "Might be a tavern there."

"Perhaps." But Aubrey suspected they were as likely to find an opium den as they would a tavern. The drug still ran rampant in certain parts of the city, and depending on how privileged the area, it could be simply addicts. Or it could be addicted magic users. The latter was worse by far; hallucinatory drugs and compounds were very popular with a certain subsect of the magically inclined and they were prone to violent fits of mania. "Let's move to that side of the street to check."

The moment they set foot in the sticky mud, the stumbling figure Aubrey had been watching paused midstep, turned toward a ramshackle tenement building, and leaned slightly forward. "It's a good piss here," they muttered. Out of politeness, Aubrey averted his eyes and moved them up the street a little more before crossing. The drunk kept muttering, but Aubrey lost track of the words as the distant sound of hoofbeats echoed toward them.

The hopeful look on Calix's face made Aubrey say, "Let's just see who it is. I have money enough to pay. Even if it's a personal carriage, we might be able to purchase a seat from them."

Calix nodded and picked up his pace. "We look terrible."

"As though we just ran out of a burning building?"

Calix's sigh held a note of exasperation and it made Aubrey chuckle. "Ethaniel didn't tell me about your dark sense of humor."

Aubrey shrugged. "We would have gotten around to it eventually."

The approaching carriage slowed and in the dimness, Aubrey could see a liveried driver, the silver trim of their uniform winking. He raised a hand in greeting and Calix did the same. "Let's hope we look desperate enough," Aubrey muttered.

"Or wealthy enough to bribe them for a ride," Calix answered.

Aubrey nodded but was unable to keep his tone light as he said, "Or that." He stretched his arm overhead and nudged Calix so he could out, "Please! Over here!"

The horses softly whinnied and the carriage slowed, then stopped. The driver looked down at them and gave a curt nod, then a voice from inside the carriage said, "Bit of an odd place for two gentlemen dressed as yourselves to be out. At night, especially."

Aubrey leaned forward to get a better look at the person speaking. "I agree, though it wasn't our intent to get stranded."

"Thieves chased us," Calix said. "They took my friend's cane and my billfold and we had to duck into buildings and hide behind…" He shivered, only dramatically enough to look completely honest. Aubrey nodded along, hoping his acting skills were half as good as Calix's. "Tire fires! Can you believe it?"

There was a pause and Aubrey wondered if they'd tipped their hands, but then a woman stuck her head out of the window, looking aghast. "My goodness! Calix Addington? It's been an age."

Calix visibly deflated. "Sophia, thank god. I'm so sorry our paths had to cross again on such a night. Could we bother you terribly for a ride?"

But this Sophia was already opening the door and motioning them inside. "Come, come. Don't worry about the mud, this is my third-best carriage."

He and Calix stepped in and the carriage jolted forward at a hurried clip, not one second after they'd sat down. Immediately, Calix took the older woman's gloved hands in his and squeezed. "It's so good to see you. May I introduce my friend? Aubrey, this is Lady Sophia Devonne. My mother was part of her social circle, for a time."

Lady Sophia smiled, an impish expression on a thin, sharp-featured face. If she'd had pointed ears and long flowing hair instead of a simple twist at her nape, Aubrey would have thought she'd dropped out of a fairy story. Aubrey gave a small bow and she waved him off. "You noticed Calix called me by my name? I don't like honorifics, they feel sticky in the mouth. Sophia, please."

"Then you must call me Aubrey." Calix was beaming at him and Aubrey didn't want to think long on how devastatingly handsome he was, even covered in soot and mud. "Thank you for the assistance."

"Bah, you're with Calix. I watched this little apple thief grow up."

At Aubrey's raised eyebrows, Calix chuckled. "I was six. Your apples looked better than ours."

Sophia laughed as well. "Well, even at six you always did have good taste. So why in the world are you out in Lenox at this time of night? The entire block is a den of thieves and con artists. It's where old Doc Slither used to work out of, you know."

They both went still at that. Doc Slither, or Perry Sizemore as everyone learned from his mugshot, had gripped the city in terror last year when he'd suddenly closed up shop after his "patients" began dying in agony. He was the worst sort of huckster, who saw no value in the lives of others, and convinced people through his knowledge of herbal remedies that he could cure anything that ailed them. And for a time, he acted as a kind of local Cunning Folk for Lenox Hill and the nearby neighborhoods; none of the impoverished factory or dock workers living there could afford real doctors and medicine, and many of them were immigrants who had brought over folk traditions of their own. Doc Slither had taken all that trust and bankrupted it by slowly convincing very ill people to keep buying his tincture. Hell, his catchphrase had been, "One More Bottle'll Do Ya!", which was a catastrophe in all regards (including to the English language).

And slowly over time, Doc Slither had, from what the police could tell, used some combination of ingredients and medicinal patterning to make the tincture addictive. So even if you were vomiting and shitting yourself, you'd keep drinking it. Only after he was caught did everyone understand why he'd picked *that* name: the man kept live snakes in his apartment. Fifty of them. In every nook and cranny. The mere thought of one snake made Aubrey's skin crawl; fifty was a nightmare.

"I didn't know that," Calix said as he leaned back. "That's awful."

"The police kept it out of the newspapers, but people talk. It's done a number on the people here. I was just dropping off another few bundles of clothes at St. Maria's." Sophia gave Aubrey a more solemn smile this time. "St. Maria's seems to be the only place trying to help these people. I help the reverend with arranging clothing donations." But Sophia didn't let Aubrey give her the politely appropriate compliments as she kept going. "So why are you two out here? Tire fires? Did you really get robbed?"

Calix gave her a highly sanitized version of the night's events, keeping the robbery story but twisting it to say they'd run by a building on fire and gotten turned around in the smoke. "You know me, I don't leave my apartments much," Calix concluded. "I'm so glad you were nearby."

Sophia looked properly stricken with worry. "My dear boy, you name it and I'll get it to you. Where are we going?"

"Marble Hill," Aubrey replied smoothly, even though he was touched by the woman's concern and willingness to help them. "The plan was to leave town tonight on one of those horseless carriages."

Sophia shuddered at that. "I know the place. Good on you both for enjoying the marvels of new technology, but I admit those things frighten me." She tapped on the roof of the carriage and called out, "Stuart, Marble Hill, to that carriage company that has the beautiful Morabs."

"Yes ma'am," came the call back. The carriage soon took one corner, then the next, and the heavy scent of mud and trash soon faded. It was only then that Aubrey allowed himself to lean back against the seat.

"He'll be okay," Calix murmured. "I'm sure of it."

Aubrey wanted to touch Calix, to pull him close and reassure him, but he didn't know Sophia's tolerances and they couldn't afford to be tossed from the carriage. "I know you're right, but my concern feels like a vise," Aubrey replied. Sophia was watching them but not overly interested in their interaction, so Aubrey allowed himself a small, sad smile. "Let's just get to Marble Hill and get our bearings."

Aubrey was grateful Sophia wasn't the chatty sort. Though considering how they looked and smelled, she might have been taking pity on them. As the carriage rolled along and the sounds of the city picked up, Aubrey started to plan. He couldn't say much, if anything, to Calix, but he knew leaving New York was needed. If they didn't...well, that wasn't a line of thinking with which he wished to engage.

Sophia flicked a heavy blue velvet curtain aside and brightened. "Oh, we're near the botanical gardens! It's too early for many of the flowers, but their hothouse is truly magnificent. Have either of you been? The orchids—"

Aubrey didn't hear the rest of what Sophia had to say about the garden's orchids. His vision went black, but there was no pain. He braced for it to come, but instead what he saw was a ghostly image of Ethaniel. He was sitting at a rickety table, hunched over what appeared to be some sort of map, and the blue glow of his power beckoning as he traced his fingers over it.

Aubrey tried to say something, anything, but his jaw refused to move. Then Ethaniel looked up.

Aubrey's power rose to the surface. He imagined it was like being struck by lightning, but without pain still. When their gazes connected, Aubrey understood.

His magic was answering Ethaniel's.

The headiness of the moment made Aubrey's entire being ache, but he refused to move, to do anything that might break the connection. It was unlike anything he'd ever experienced before, and unprecedented as far as he was aware.

Magic in humans didn't *connect*. They weren't like electricity arcing between contact points. Magic didn't *work that way*.

Didn't it?

As quickly as he'd been hit with it, the connection broke. And beside him, Calix gasped and whispered, "Ethaniel", and fumbled for Aubrey's hand.

After a long moment, where he watched Calix seem to go through the same thing he just had, Calix turned to him, blinking as if to clear his eyes. "Did you know he could do that?" he asked slowly, as if his tongue were numb.

"No. I've never heard anything about..." Aubrey paused, remembering they weren't alone.

"Neither of you have anything to worry about," Sophia said, looking completely unrattled. "I've got magic users in my family aplenty. Hell, my husband, God rest his soul, was one of the first to bring unbreakable horseshoes to market. They still wear down after a bit, mind you, but at least horses now don't have to throw shoes and go through all that pain. Poor dears."

Aubrey had to chuckle despite the fog cloud nestled over his mind. "You are a very welcome surprise, Lady Sophia."

Sophia patted his free hand. "You're a friend of Calix's. That's enough for me."

By the time the carriage slowed to a stop, Calix had fallen asleep and Aubrey was well on his way there. The questions whirling in his mind wouldn't stand in the way of exhaustion. Night had firmly settled in around them and it was late enough that even the main street on which they halted was barely lit; some of the magical lanterns flickered as their charms slowly fizzled out with each passing hour.

Sophia waved off he and Calix's profuse thanks with a simple, "Just be sure to invite me the next time you have a party at Rosehill, my dears." She was the epitome of generous and cunning, and reminded Aubrey very much of some of the women in his family.

"Should you ever need my assistance," Aubrey said, fumbling for one of the few cards left in his pockets that had survived their adventure.

Sophia's sly but delighted grin told Aubrey everything he needed to know.

They stumbled out of the carriage, taking in their surroundings. Across the street was their destination, a humble brick building with a large stable attached. Beyond the horses, Aubrey could see the glint of carriages and sighed. "We're close," he said to Calix. "But we should check for Ethaniel."

Calix pointed up the road. "There's lights and a few people. Maybe it's a tavern?"

"Agreed. Let's check."

They stuck to the side of the road, ducking under awnings and balconies. Aubrey could still feel the grip of Ethaniel's magic, but it only did so much to calm his nerves. Nowhere in the city was safe, and the longer they stayed, the more they risked another encounter with the Golden Order. All he could hope was that Ethaniel was safe, and the book was still in his possession.

"I definitely think that's a tavern," Calix said, his expression growing hopeful.

Aubrey struggled to find the energy to reply as they approached the building. A few people stood outside, cigarette embers casting red shadows over their faces. But lights blazed inside and the promise of warmth was too alluring to resist.

Something like an unscratchable itch at the back of Aubrey's mind made him pause, then turn to face the little boarding house across the street. Somehow...somehow he knew Ethaniel was inside.

Aubrey shook his head, trying to unscramble his thoughts.

No, Ethaniel was most *definitely* inside.

Before Calix could ask him what he was doing, Aubrey pried a small stone out of the mud and threw it at the window directly above.

"Aubrey!" Calix hissed.

"He's in there," Aubrey said. Truth was a drumbeat in his brain. Maybe it was that shared connection, maybe it was intuition.

When no one answered, Aubrey picked up another stone, this one slightly bigger, and hoped he wouldn't shatter the window. He still threw it, however.

"They're going to call the police on us!" Calix now looked stricken on top of the exhaustion wearing down his features.

The window above them slid open and Ethaniel stared out, mouth agape. "You've got to be fucking kidding me," he rasped, voice hoarse.

"Grab everything and come down," Aubrey said. "We're leaving. Now."

Ethaniel paused, as if processing the information, then nodded. "Two minutes."

Aubrey passed Calix his billfold. "Get a carriage. A proper one. No markings. Two horses, nothing showy."

Calix looked torn, so Aubrey took him by the shoulders. "We have to leave."

"I know, Aubrey."

"Good."

With the few smokers staring at them, Aubrey reached out to swipe soot from Calix's cheek. He'd fight all of them if he had to, should his tiny moment of affection for a man he'd only met a fortnight ago make them incensed. Aubrey didn't care.

Calix didn't move away, only bit his lip and stared up at Aubrey, complete trust thick in his gaze.

Ethaniel was with them moments later, throwing his arms around both of them, the satchel containing the path to their futures bumping against Aubrey's side.

"We have to get out of the city." Ethaniel looked like death warmed over, but he was alive and whole and for that Aubrey was thankful. At that, Calix took off for the carriage company, he and Ethaniel following in his wake.

"We'll make it," Aubrey replied, feeling the truth of his words settle in his bones. "We will."

SEVENTEEN

CALIX

Exhaustion was a thing buried deep in his bones, but Calix needed to stay awake. He needed to get them out of the city.

"Absolutely not," Aubrey said, taking the reins from him the moment they left Marble Hill. They'd both agreed that Ethaniel should sleep in the carriage while they fled the city, and neither of them was going to chance waking him. Ethaniel had looked the worst out of all of them by far, but it hadn't escaped anyone's notice that the moment Calix took the book from Ethaniel, he easily dropped into sleep.

Now the book rested safely with their few bits of luggage inside the closed — and locked — compartment below their feet.

Aubrey was staring at him so intently it made Calix blink. "Absolutely not..."

One eyebrow went up. "Absolutely you're not going to stay awake. I can drive, I know my way north for at least a day. Go rest."

Oh no.

Apparently Aubrey had the same realization, at the exact same time. Truth's hand might have been discarnate, but they felt it all the same.

"You heard my thoughts," Calix said. *Please don't agree with me—*

"I did. Sort of."

Shit.

Calix jerked his head up. "Sort of?"

Aubrey's brow furrowed so much Calix feared his eyebrows would become one. "I would appreciate it if we stopped having so many odd things happening all at once," Aubrey muttered before clearing his throat. "I didn't hear your thoughts. It was more like I understood your intentions roughly when you did? I think."

Aubrey shook his head, his jaw working, and Calix reached over to run the pads of his fingers over the ticking muscle, which immediately softened under his touch. "Rosehill can be our respite," Calix said softly, unable to think of much more in the moment other than that safety. "But I am now deeply concerned at what that bloody thing is doing to us."

Home

Safety

Peace

Connection

Yes, connection for me. For you. For US.

The very thing he always craved. The sloping roofs and thick glass windows, the plush rugs and soft leather chairs, and the rambling rose garden after which the house was named were more than a construction meant to hold things and people. They held memories.

The big oak bed in the second largest bedroom where he'd first kissed another boy. The stone hearths decorated with thick pine boughs and bright red holly berries during Christmas. His mother's candlelit study, smelling of leather and beeswax and roses.

Always roses. It's why the rose garden was her resting place.

"I get to see her when we arrive," Calix said, suddenly beyond exhausted, and yet he worried what might happen if he closed his eyes.

Aubrey only hummed in response.

Before him stood a figure wreathed in shadow.

"I've been here so long," the figure said, "that I've forgotten so much."

A strange sound, like broken whispers flung into the air by a careless hand, filled Calix's ears.

"Tell me, oracle," the figure continued, staring at Calix as though they could see through him, "do you hear them as clearly as you hear me?"

There was a hand on his shoulder. His leg. Grasping at his arm. There were hands everywhere, their touch light and then not.

One curled cold fingers around his neck and squeezed. Calix coughed, fought against its grip but it held firm.

"They hear you more than you them, I think," the figure said. Its shadow wavered for only a moment, but Calix swore he saw a suggestion of femininity in its shape. Its voice, though, was still echoing pain and smug satisfaction, turning over and over again, preventing him from learning its intent.

The hand at his throat squeezed again. A warning, he thought.

The words left him in a rush of thorns and vertigo. "Just whispers," he rasped, twitching against the hands that held him in place. Calix was cold all over, a wave of aching sensation that sunk into his flesh like teeth. "Who are you?"

The figure chuckled. "The final one. The only one. The one who rose to the surface like a nightmare, and a dream. But then, just like that, after so long in the dark, you appeared. A beacon for me to latch onto. Don't you see, Oracle? Don't you see what we can do together? I hold the wisdom of so many trapped within this book before me. What do you want? I can give it to you. I won the struggle for dominance and consumed the rest. Imagine what you could do if you let me in. If you give me a home, a proper one."

Calix's mind reeled, the ground beneath him spun. "What are you offering?"

"Everything," the figure said, and that one word echoed in the space around them. "I am Convergence, and I am him. I used to raise the dead, charm the living, and speak the language of the angels and the heavens above. I offer all that, and so much more, little Oracle," A hand floated to Calix out of the darkness and stroked his cheek. "I waited so long for someone like you to open a door." Then the hand passed over his brow, almost gentle. "Sleep."

Calix startled awake as the carriage stopped.

Ethaniel was beside him, doing his evident best to not look concerned. But Calix saw his brow smooth out as he smiled. "Good. You're awake. I told Aubrey we had to stop. We need food, clothes, and proper rest."

Calix rubbed his eyes. The day was too bright and the carriage cabin was stifling. "It smells like mud and smoke in here," he said, sitting upright. "How did I get in here?"

Ethaniel jerked a thumb toward the window. "Aubrey."

Ah, of course.

"But he's gotten us to a proper town." Ethaniel sighed and squeezed Calix's hand. "We're safe now."

Dread pooled in Calix's stomach. They weren't safe as long as Convergence was with them. It was a truth as sure as the spring sunshine outside and the warmth and strength of Ethaniel's hand on his.

Calix slowly climbed out of the carriage, his clothes stiff with mud and his entire body one massive ache. The inn sat on the corner of a quaint street, flanked by a general store and a few freshly painted homes. It was the kind of town he was used to outside of New York, hastily slapped together as new arrivals to the States pushed on the available resources. Many immigrants pooled their money to buy land or buildings, to open stores or boarding houses or stables or even schools. A quick glance around told Calix this was that very kind of place.

Their arrival would not go unnoticed by locals, but Calix trusted Aubrey had led them somewhere secure. For a night, at least. Calix helped Ethaniel gather what little they had, and slung the satchel over his shoulder. He hated having the book so close, but he couldn't make it an albatross for anyone else.

Aubrey appeared on the clapboard walkway outside the general store, a canvas bag on each arm. He nodded in greeting, then motioned to the inn. He looked...well, rather normal, considering the circumstances and his muddy clothes.

"Is he all right?" Calix asked as Ethaniel led him around the back of the inn.

Ethaniel sighed. "Aubrey is very good in times of crises. But you and I need to make sure he rests. Will you help me with that?"

Calix felt honored. "Yes, of course."

The room into which Ethaniel led them was surprisingly large. The bed was crisply made, the militant corners of the navy bedspread making Calix long to slip underneath. A large oak dresser sat to the side, and the oval white and blue rug covered the middle of the floor. And off to the other side of the room was a very large bathtub.

Relief was a wave through his entire body. "I will fight both of you for the tub," he said, making Ethaniel and Aubrey laugh.

"We're all disgusting. I think we can manage." Aubrey set the bags down before slumping against the wall. The placid expression he'd worn on the street was now gone, replaced by a weariness Calix was certain the man felt in his soul. "Go on, then, but give the water a moment to heat up. I've been here before, and I figured a place known was better than the three of us coming into a town unknown. We should only need to stop for tonight, and if we take turns with the reins, we can shave off roughly half a day."

Ethaniel chuckled as he unpacked the bags Aubrey had brought in. Plain trousers, plain shirts, and simple socks were set aside from one; the other contained pouches of jerky, dried fruit, bread, and hard cheese.

Calix was suddenly torn, as he realized he was ravenous. But Ethaniel nudged him to the tub, then tossed him a towel from a nearby shelf. "We'll manage. Go."

Calix hesitated. They both looked so worn. He knew there was no one to blame but himself for this entire mess. Or, at least he had been the catalyst down this road full of potholes and fire and smoke.

Aubrey's hiss of pain as he began to unbutton his shirt spurred Ethaniel into action. "Let me see," Ethaniel said as he crossed the room, leaving Calix to pull the wood screen around the tub.

Calix left his filthy clothes in a pile and didn't wait for the tub to fill completely before dumping in an obscene handful of bath powder and slipping in. The hot water felt like a blessing against every bit of his weary body, and while the dirt flaking from him was absolutely disgusting, he instantly felt better. He slid his hands along the tub's curled edges and watched his body disappear under cloudy water.

When the last bit of tension had eased from his body and the tub couldn't hold any more water, Calix finally willed himself to relax. This wasn't Rosehill, but it was out of the way and safe enough that Aubrey had trusted their wellbeing to this little inn. It was enough, for now.

Beyond the screen, Calix heard hushed murmurings — likely Ethaniel trying to help Aubrey — and those small sounds made him sigh. He had all but careened into these two men's lives and yet, they hadn't left his side. It was remarkable. And a tad frightening.

And then there was Lawton.

Calix blew out a hard breath and scrubbed his hands over his face. Lawton wasn't a problem for now, even though his heart thumped in an unsteady but very familiar way.

"That was a mighty breath." Ethaniel was near the screen again, his shadow stretched long across the floor. "Are you all right? Are you injured?"

"Best let Ethaniel see to you," came Aubrey's call from deeper in the room. "He's only had a bit of fun poking me. I can tell he's not satiated."

Aubrey's words carried a hint of mischief, and they made Calix feel emboldened. Why yes, maybe he did need help.

Or maybe I'm losing my mind. Maybe I'm so exhausted I'm still dreaming, except now it's about the hands of a handsome tailor.

Calix shivered despite the warmth of the bath. Anticipation — and need — walked fingers up his spine. But he felt guilty, constantly taking from both men. Men who had saved his life and kept him close despite the obvious danger he posed.

"I can hear you thinking," Ethaniel said, and Calix looked over to see him pop his head over the screen. But the blasted man had a hand over his eyes. Calix sputtered a laugh. "I'm not trying to be inappropriate here!" Ethaniel said, indignation curling through his words.

"I am," came Aubrey's dry-as-bone reply.

Calix laughed again, louder now, and Aubrey joined him. "Well, if you two have had your fun," Ethaniel fussed, disappearing once more. "Then maybe I won't help you wash your back, *Earl*."

Calix was laughing too hard to properly retort.

"Bloody hell, Ethaniel, just go. If he doesn't want your assistance, I'll be right here and quite willing," Aubrey said, chuckling.

A moment later, Calix felt a presence at his right shoulder. "You're going to bruise spectacularly, I'm afraid," Ethaniel said. He was so close that his breath stirred the hair at Calix's neck. "Is that from the carriage?"

Something about Ethaniel's words, his tone...his *softness* made Calix open his eyes. He was up to his shoulders in steaming, sudsy water, but he suddenly felt rather bare. Laid out before Ethaniel's scrutinizing gaze, Calix could only slump deeper into the tub.

"You don't have to hide from me," Ethaniel said quietly, reaching for a washcloth. "And I'm afraid we don't have much in the way of medical supplies, but Aubrey did pick up a bit of aloe balm. It should help with the bruising." He held up the faded but clean yellow washcloth. "Do you want some help?"

A knot formed in Calix's throat at the simple, honest offer. He didn't trust his voice at the moment, so he leaned forward and braced his arms on the tub's edges. He hadn't even been aware of the bruise on his right shoulder, but under Ethaniel's gentle fingers, Calix's skin prickled. It wasn't *pain*, necessarily, and he was certain the pain would come later. Now it was more of an awareness — of both the injury and the man helping him wash his back. It was a deeply intimate thing to do, and yet Ethaniel had offered it with nothing but surety, and honesty.

The water sloshed as Ethaniel wet the cloth, and Calix stared down at the knobs of his knees poking up through the water. He marveled at how, instead of feeling small or child-like, he felt *cared for*. It had been years since anyone had offered something so simple, and done so with no selfish intention. The knot in his throat tightened.

"Let me know if it's too much?" Ethaniel's voice, like his touch, was soothing. Calix let his eyes close so he could sink further into this strange, welcome sensation.

Trust yourself to let someone else in like this. To let them touch you in this way. You've already kissed both of them. Why can't you let yourself go?

Whatever had built up inside Calix broke. A sob tore out of him, and he put his forehead on his knees and cried while Ethaniel touched him so sweetly and whispered gentle things in his ear.

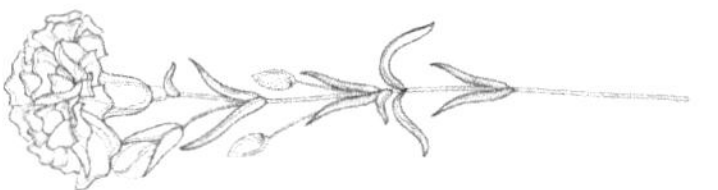

Ethaniel rubbed his back until the water cooled, leaving Calix feeling like an emptied oyster shell, then helped him up and out. Swaddled in a towel, Calix shuffled back into the room to find Aubrey sprawled on the rug, shirtless and snoring gently.

Calix froze, then felt Ethaniel come up behind him. "I had a feeling that might happen," Ethaniel said, fondness in every syllable. "The man sleeps like the dead, it's truly remarkable." He nudged Calix to the bed, which Calix was realizing was a perfectly normal sized bed...for three of them. "I'll get him up, don't worry."

Calix turned back to Ethaniel, to the man's unwavering hazel stare and soft smile. "I'll help," he said, shaking his head when Ethaniel made noises of protest. "You helped me. Who helps you? Don't think for a moment I haven't noticed the selflessness, Ethaniel."

Maybe it was daring. Maybe it was the vulnerability Calix could feel draped over him like a shroud. The towel around his waist was tied tight, leaving his chest bare to Ethaniel's sight, and something in Calix trembled at the thought of those long fingers trailing over his skin with no water to ease the way. Lawton had liked how pale and thin the Calix of their youth had been, and over the years Calix had taken up fencing and calisthenics, hoping it would drive him away. It didn't work, of course, but he had tried.

A strange thing, to transform yourself in order to keep another at bay, but the way Ethaniel looked at him now, Calix could only feel *wanted*. It was a want he welcomed.

Calix stepped into Ethaniel's space and whispered, "You don't let yourself want for much, do you?"

Ethaniel shook his head. "It's not...I can't. Or, I couldn't. My uncle needs care, and now I don't even know where he is. For all I know, he's with..." Ethaniel's pause seemed his own personal albatross, and Calix didn't want to pry.

"We're the only ones here," Calix said, reaching up to trace the corner of Ethaniel's mouth with his thumb. "Aubrey and I had a moment together, after the fire."

Ethaniel was fixated on him now, staring down slightly at Calix as if they were seeing each other for the first time. And...it was true. The first meeting had been as tailor and customer. Then as pursued and rescuer, followed closely by both of them turned into cogs in the wheel of some strange, magical machinations.

Never like this.

"I smell terrible," Ethaniel said, which Calix ignored in favor of plucking out the little bit of leather that held back Ethaniel's thick hair. "Calix..."

Calix slid his fingers into Ethaniel's hair and kissed him. Ethaniel immediately melted against him, and while Calix had prepared to back down the moment Ethaniel expressed a desire for anything but Calix's kiss, this was decidedly better. Ethaniel was taller by a bit, but still shorter than Aubrey, so Calix was able to wind his arms around Ethaniel's neck and push up on his toes. Ethaniel's fingers bumped along Calix's upper spine and then Ethaniel let one hand drop down Calix's back. His touch was gentle but encouraging; a delightful contrast to how Calix clung to him.

Ethaniel followed Calix's lead in their kiss, only daring to deepen it when Calix made a desperate noise in the back of his throat. Ethaniel would be a generous lover, a kind one; the type to never back down from another's needs, and someone who delighted in *giving* so completely. The revelation of what that might feel like, sound like, made Calix shiver.

"Is it too much?" Ethaniel asked after they broke apart.

"God, no," Calix managed to breathe out. When he dug his fingers into Ethaniel's hair, and then against the man's scalp, Ethaniel's eyes fluttered shut, his mouth dropping open. "Oh. That must feel good, then."

"Incredible." Ethaniel was still gripping Calix as if he feared letting go would make Calix disappear. "Never stop."

Calix bit his lip hard enough to make him wince, but he didn't stop massaging Ethaniel's scalp. He did carefully draw Ethaniel's right arm down, until he could guide Ethaniel's hand down his ribs. Then lower, until the towel stopped them.

At that, Ethaniel opened his eyes and Calix got to properly stare into them. He didn't have to speak to communicate the *want* his body nearly vibrated with. He was a tuning fork under Ethaniel's control, and he wouldn't push for anything Ethaniel didn't want.

Ethaniel very much *wanted*, apparently.

Clever fingers tugged at the towel around his hips while Ethaniel crushed Calix into a blistering kiss. This was raw and rapturous, all-consuming in the only way Calix wanted from every lover and had yet to experience. The bits of the room faded — the drip of the bathtub faucet, the quiet murmurs from the street below, the sound of a carriage bumping along the rutted road. Everything was Ethaniel.

He should have been embarrassed at how he pushed up against Ethaniel, practically rutting his hardness against Ethaniel's hip. But the sparks dancing behind his eyelids, the tongue in his mouth, the fingers skating over his now-bare skin only demanded his attention, and his desire. Calix let his worries fall to the wayside just as Ethaniel slid his other hand beneath the towel and pushed it to the floor.

"You're gorgeous," Ethaniel whispered as he pressed kisses into Calix's jaw. "Can I touch you?"

Heat washed through Calix, like nothing he'd ever felt before. This was what he'd ached for for so long. He gently pulled back to look Ethaniel in the eyes while saying, "I might combust if you don't."

Ethaniel nodded and let go only long enough to strip out of his shirt, leaving his suspenders dangling as he didn't bother to remove his trousers. And the entire time, he stared at Calix with desirous appreciation. His eyes didn't linger on any one place, but instead took Calix in as himself. Whole. Pale and freckled across his shoulders and down his arms, a trail of those same dots across his upper chest. Ropy, lean muscles and only a smattering of hair on his chest, leading to a thinner trail that traced down his stomach. Calix fought not to ball his hands at his sides, his lungs seized up in a power play between vulnerability and desire.

Ethaniel recrossed the space in one big stride, crashing into Calix. What could he do but melt against Ethaniel, give in to the mouth on his, the hands exploring his skin? And how could he not whimper when Ethaniel's palm slid down his back and lower yet, following the curvature of his body? Their first kiss might have been lodged in Calix's memory, but it was sure to be supplanted by *this one* and how it embraced them both so completely.

There was a soft noise, then movement, to their right, and Ethaniel tried to break away, but Calix pressed against him, desperate for friction, for *anything* that might ease the fire in his veins. "Let him come to us in his own time," Calix whispered against Ethaniel's mouth.

To his surprise, Ethaniel's laugh bubbled up between them. "Oh, Calix," he murmured, his touch to Calix's backside more brazen now, squeezing and caressing. "He likes to watch. I can assure you he's more than content."

Ethaniel guided Calix's chin between two fingers, just like Aubrey had in the carriage, so Calix could take full stock of the man in question. Calix didn't know where to look, his sight full with the lines of Aubrey's body as he had propped himself up against the footboard of the bed. How his chest heaved and his hips flexed; how his long feet were planted firmly on the floor, but his toes were curled against the rug; and how Aubrey's muscles jumped as he palmed himself through his trousers. That glass-green gaze had gone dark with desire. It only accentuated the sharp lines of his face and Calix found himself snared in Aubrey's orbit again.

"He's beautiful, isn't he?" Ethaniel said as he gently took Calix by the shoulders so he could slip behind him. "Aubrey's always been lovely, but I daresay age is kinder to him than us mere mortals."

Calix bit his lip hard when Ethaniel's touch, still so gentle, slid down his hips. He had wondered where all this would lead, after the uncertainty and danger of the last few days. Where their strange, heightened energies would take them. Both of them had caught his attentions immediately, but Calix couldn't have anticipated *this*.

He yearned, like anyone else might, but this was different. New and heady and it made Calix want to give in. Let Ethaniel direct his body while Aubrey watched.

"I want to touch you," Ethaniel said, astutely reading Calix's need. Maybe it was Ethaniel in his head now, skating so effortlessly across the waves of desire. "I want to pull you off."

"And I want to watch," Aubrey said, voice gone husky as he stared at Calix. "But it's your decision. We won't think anything –"

"Yes. God. *Please.*" Calix easily leaned his head back against Ethaniel's shoulder and took Ethaniel's hand in his own, guiding it down.

The softness of earlier was dashed away, and Calix could only watch as Aubrey quickly unbuttoned his trousers and pushed them off, leaving him completely bare. Stunned by the beauty in front of him, Ethaniel's first touch to his cock made Calix buck forward, leaving Ethaniel to grip him by the hip to hold him in place.

"Be good for Ethaniel," Aubrey said softly as he spread his thighs apart. His legs were, like the rest of him, gorgeous, but the power in them as Aubrey shifted left Calix dizzy.

"Be good for us," Ethaniel said in his ear.

Calix threw his arm back to grab at any part of Ethaniel he could reach, and his touch made Ethaniel hiss appreciatively. "God, please *touch me*," he panted.

Ethaniel hooked his chin over Calix's shoulder and planted a kiss under his ear. "We'll go slowly," he said as he wrapped his fingers around Calix's cock.

"Fast, slow, I don't care," Calix moaned. His knees were trembling and he was dizzy and short of breath. And then Aubrey began to stroke his own cock, his beautiful mouth twisting into a snarl that only made Calix's heart beat faster. Of course Aubrey would be beautiful even while doing something so *intimate.*

And Aubrey's little chuckle at Calix's desperation only made the need under his skin beat a heavier, more urgent tattoo. As did the hardness that pressed up against his backside, and the way Ethaniel's movements mimicked those of his hand.

"You're exquisite," he heard Aubrey say, and the revelation of it made Calix tremble.

Calix lost himself in the hazy blur of it — the rawness of his nerves, his skin, the way Ethaniel crooned breathlessly in his ear, and how intensely Aubrey focused on Calix while pulling himself off. At one point, when Ethaniel pressed another kiss into his skin, Calix swore he felt that kiss's twin ghost over his cheek, as if Aubrey were on his other side.

But Aubrey...for fuck's sake, the man was *glorious*. Sweat beaded at his temples and he'd spread his legs even wider, heels ground into the floor. Aubrey looked as lost to it all as Calix felt, and the urgency between them seemed to find the right tempo. As Ethaniel stroked him, from tip to root and back, Aubrey followed. Some wild part of Calix's mind understood they were both being conducted by Ethaniel, but he didn't *care* who was leading so long as the fire in his skin was abated, and soon.

"Ethaniel...fuck, god, *please*," Calix said, not caring how desperately he was begging.

"I think you'll wait," Ethaniel said in his ear, "until Aubrey's found his release."

The power play of it, knowing he was safe and being cared for, only made Calix push back against Ethaniel's little thrusts, making Ethaniel swear. It had never been like this...ever. Calix wanted to drown in the trust and the pleasure being shared. He wanted to roll around in it and never leave.

"Wait," Ethaniel whispered when Calix shuddered against him. Ethaniel's hand stilled on Calix as Aubrey looked up at them.

"Let yourself go, Aubrey," Ethaniel said before curling his tongue against Calix's jaw. "Let it take you under. It's only us here. Let go, darling. We want to watch you."

And Calix watched as that stubborn, stalwart, intelligent man fell apart with a rattling groan and a full-body quiver. He was gorgeous in his destruction, and Calix found himself enraptured by the sight.

"He's beautiful," Ethaniel said in his ear, "and so are you."

Ethaniel stroked him quickly now, both of them full of the sight and sound of Aubrey's shivering from aftershocks and softly groaning as he slumped against the bed, spent and flushed but looking *directly at them*. Ethaniel used the downstroke to press his thumb against Calix's cockhead, seeming to delight in how Calix keened as he shook through his release.

Calix lost track of everything except how *light* he felt in the moments after orgasm, but he did register Ethaniel's gasp as he spilled over his hand. It seemed Ethaniel had enjoyed himself as well from the way he was panting in Calix's ear, so Calix shelved daydreams of dropping to his knees and putting his mouth to good use on Ethaniel's overheated flesh.

Calix's slow rise to the surface made him realize how exhausted he was, and one look at Ethaniel and Aubrey told the same story. Calix fell face-first into the bed the moment after he'd cleaned up, lost to the sensation of loose-limbed relaxation and the sounds of the others washing and changing.

The bed dipped to his right, so Calix turned on his side to come face-to-face with a smiling Aubrey.

"Sleep," Aubrey said before leaning in for a kiss. "Ethaniel will be here in a moment."

When the bed dipped again, Calix let himself be moved until the others were comfortable, leaving their limbs tangled together and Ethaniel's breath warm on his neck.

Eighteen

EThaniel

Waking to warm breath on his neck and soft skin under his palm made Ethaniel never want to leave the bed. Calix was curled around him, one leg shoved between his knees and a limp arm flung over his waist. And when Ethaniel managed to pry his eyes open, he saw Aubrey staring at him over Calix's tousled curls.

With liquid grace no human should have at God-knows-what time of the morning, Aubrey slid out of bed, only to cross the room and crouch at Ethaniel's side. "We'll need to leave soon," Aubrey said quietly as he stroked a hand down Ethaniel's bare arm. "But I'm going to bathe, since I don't think we should stop again before arriving at Rosehill."

Ethaniel wrinkled his nose at Aubrey, trying not to chuckle at his lover's steadfastness to cleanliness. If he laughed, he might wake Calix up, and he didn't have the heart to do that quite yet. "Go," he whispered, unable to resist putting a possessive hand on Calix's bare hip. "I'll pack up once I can extricate myself."

Aubrey shook his head but gave Ethaniel a fond smile. "I think you can spare a few minutes for him. We don't have much with us." Aubrey's eyes flitted to the corner where their few bags — including Calix's satchel — sat. "I have thoughts on what to do with the book. As you might expect."

"I anticipated that." With the book now looming again in his mind, Ethaniel had to look away from Aubrey. The memory of Vincent wouldn't be put aside any longer, but the guilt that came with it made a sour taste rise up in Ethaniel's mouth. "We need to talk when we arrive at Rosehill. There are...complications I wasn't expecting. We were so hurried in leaving the city and—"

"Whatever it is can wait," Aubrey replied, still stroking Ethaniel's arm. "We'll figure it out."

He left Ethaniel only after placing a gentle kiss on his mouth. Ethaniel knew the truth of Vincent's reality, and his betrayal, would be a shock, but Aubrey would understand how deeply it wounded Ethaniel. Aubrey knew some of his past with Vincent, knew how distant they'd become over the years. And he would have questions to which Ethaniel would have some answers, but not all.

With a sigh, Ethaniel turned back to Calix, trying to settle himself by pushing those copper-brown curls out of Calix's face and studying the lines of his jaw, his nose. Ethaniel breathed in the man curled so tightly against him, and wondered if this journey, and their destination, would provide a satisfying conclusion to so many questions that rambled through his mind.

When Calix stirred, brown eyes fluttering open, Ethaniel didn't hesitate in kissing him until he was fully awake. Calix was loose-limbed from sleep, cheeks flushed a gentle pink, and it took everything Ethaniel had to not roll the man on his back and kiss his way down that wiry chest. But it would have been a distraction, and Ethaniel needed to stay clear-headed. They all did.

Whatever waited for them rested in the fate of the book sitting twenty feet away.

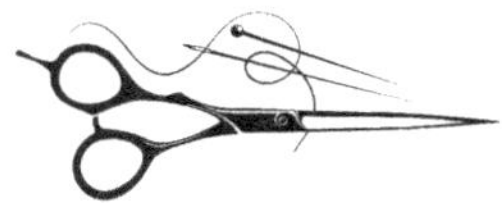

The day in the carriage felt as if it lasted a week, and Ethaniel felt every rut in the dirt roads as if they were trying to realign his spine. He switched places with Calix when the afternoon sun began to finally warm the spring air, giving Calix and Aubrey a chance to rest. They were riding straight through the night and rest would be in very short supply.

Ethaniel spent the time at the reins trying to figure out how to reveal what he knew about the Golden Order, and his half-brother's involvement, to them. On one hand, it made all the sense in the world that Vincent's hunger for power would have led him to a group like the Golden Order, but the ambition was what stunned Ethaniel more than anything else.

The Vincent he knew of their youth had often been angry, but it had been the type of anger young people who grew up in poverty carried with them. When you fought for everything you had, from oil for lanterns to the meager food on your plate, anger was easy to lean into. The clarity of anger could be refreshing, letting you ignore the hunger pains and the backbreaking work, the abusive supervisors and holes in your shoes. They'd spent more time apart than together as the years passed, but every time Ethaniel saw Vincent, he saw his younger sibling's fury written clear in the too-soon lines decorating his face. The factory work, then the slaughterhouse, and always the same stories of twelve and fourteen hours days for little pay.

When you were born into poverty, there was no way up or out. Not for most people. Some were lucky enough to marry money, or catch a break due to natural talent or skill — magical or mundane. Ethaniel would never forget when he told Vincent about helping Uncle Jeremiah in the shop and working on his patterning guild apprenticeships, studying for the tests that seemed to only grow more expensive each time he passed into another rank.

Ethaniel gripped the reins tighter, trying to shake loose from the memory of Vincent in that moment. How he'd told Ethaniel how *lucky* he was, how *fortunate*, how it must *feel so good to be the chosen son in a family of fuck-ups.*

But you have skill, too, Ethaniel had protested. *Why not harness it for your own ends? Why not use your magic to make your life better?*

God, the absolutely righteous fury on Vincent's face. Even now, it made Ethaniel's hands clammy. *Why should it all fall on the poor to fix their lives? Why do we get the added weight of uplifting ourselves, when the rich snobs that fill this damn city can't be possessed to look beyond their gold and gilded edges? Why? Why, Ethaniel? Tell me!*

Ethaniel let out a hard breath and stared out at the fields and small farmhouses that dotted the landscape. Everything was newly green and hopeful, and yet his stomach was all lead and acid.

Ethaniel stopped the carriage near a river and unhooked the horses to let them drink. Aubrey ambled out of the carriage and handed him a few strips of jerky and a canteen of water. "Calix is asleep. We should swap out here," Aubrey said as they both stared out at the river. "But your expression tells me there's more on your mind than the remaining journey."

Ethaniel shook his head, but the movement only made him dizzy. The exhaustion written in his bones had been temporarily forgotten in the midst of passion, but now the road forward felt endless and aimless. "What are we going to do, Aubrey?" he said as he turned to face Aubrey head-on. "Even if we can somehow lock this book away, the Golden Order will still come after us. Calix's *friend* could easily lead them right to us. And that book...why is it even bothering with any of us? What does it want?"

Aubrey sighed. "I wish I had the answers. I do. Calix has been talking of some kind of plan, and I fear he's far too clever for his own good."

That made Ethaniel snort. "Don't let him hear you say that. He's young, you know. It might inflate his ego."

To his surprise, Aubrey's expression grew serious. "He's not that young. And after our...time together, I think it would behoove us both to remember there's another danger here. More than how emotionally entangled we're all becoming."

"You're being shockingly forthright," Ethaniel said, brow now furrowed. "What's going on?"

"I've realized my many mistakes, Ethaniel." Aubrey took Ethaniel's hands in his own, holding them tight. "And I will keep apologizing for how I treated you, how I disregarded your present, and your past. Now we have someone else in the equation, and he's not..."

"Like us," Ethaniel finished. "Or, at least he doesn't come from a life of hardship." He squeezed Aubrey's hands, then linked their fingers together. "Or one of family disappointment."

Aubrey smiled sadly at that. They had shared a fair bit about their pasts between bouts of lovemaking, and Ethaniel remembered the stories Aubrey had told about his family, how the cloud of *fatherly disappointment* had hung over his head for so long.

"And I'm so sorry about your apartment," Ethaniel continued as he stepped into Aubrey's space. "I know you kept very personal mementos there."

"Perhaps it was for the best," Aubrey said, looking down and away. "I kept clinging to those old rituals, even when they did nothing but dredge up the worst memories." Then he glanced back at the carriage, his tone not nearly as superfluous as his words. "Perhaps it's time to move on. And besides, you brought along the only thing I really would have kept out of it all." When Ethaniel furrowed his brow in confusion, Aubrey said, "That little velvet pouch in the vault? It's a sending stone. A gift from my grandmother. They're very rare Cunning Folk artifacts, and mostly passed down from grandparent to grandchild. It's a fair bit faster than a letter."

Ethaniel brightened at that. "Could we use it to talk to my uncle?"

"Maybe. It would be a very short message, and we'd need to do some adjustments to attune it to you." Aubrey's tone went thoughtful in a way Ethaniel recognized and it made him smile. "But at the very least, I can use it to get a message to my superior about what's happening. He may have some advice for us concerning that damn book."

"Good. That's good. It'll be a relief to have someone else to rely on," Ethaniel replied, already feeling a bit lighter now that Aubrey's brilliant mind was working on their predicament.

Above their heads, the bare branches of an elm creaked as the wind picked up. One of the horses raised their head, then the other. A chill ran down Ethaniel's spine, and from the expression on Aubrey's face, he was thinking the same thing.

Something on the air promised more than a simple spring storm.

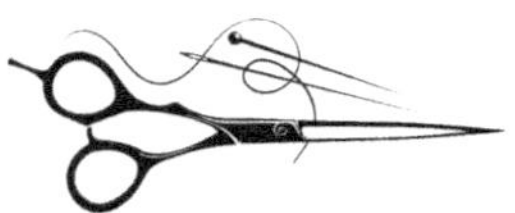

Ethaniel slept rather soundly in the carriage, his body finally becoming adjusted to the bumps and ruts of the road. Calix proved to be a deft hand at steering around the worst of it, and being curled up next to Aubrey on the hard bench helped even more. When the sun broke over the horizon, Ethaniel woke to take up Calix's place at the reins. He found the younger man smiling to himself, and that smile was quickly turned on Ethaniel as he swung up into the seat.

"We're close," Calix said as he pointed out to the shadowy jut of low-slung buildings to the west. "A few hours out, now that we can see the village. It's not Auburn proper, not yet, and the road home doesn't take us there, but I can adjust our route if you wish to see it—"

"Calix."

Calix turned to him, biting his lip in that way Ethaniel had come to understand as nervousness. "Yes?"

Ethaniel rubbed his thumb over Calix's cheek. "I think I can speak for Aubrey and myself when I say we will go where you wish. Rosehill seems a special place, and a safe one, and if that will make you feel better, that's where we go."

Every bit of tension seemed to leave Calix's body and he leaned into Ethaniel's touch, his smile grateful. "Thank you," Calix said. "I truly mean that. Some part of me was…"

"Afraid we'd leave you alone?"

Calix didn't answer. Ethaniel didn't need him to. He understood how vulnerable Calix must feel; he felt something like its cousin echoing in his own bones. They were all on fragile ground, and the quaking beneath their boots wasn't composed of a single source. Ethaniel only wanted them all safe, so they could sort out the tangled knot of Convergence in peace.

He doubted Vincent would leave them alone to do that, however.

"When we get to Rosehill, we must all talk," Ethaniel admitted.

"I agree," Calix said as he snapped the reins, steering the horses around a particularly deep hole in the road. "But you sound like you're…."

Calix cut off as the sound of hoofbeats thundered behind them. A single set, moving too quickly — and too urgently — to be a rider out for a morning trot. Immediately, Ethaniel was pulling the still-shrunken sword from beneath the carriage seat and leaning down to alert Aubrey. As he did, he caught a glimpse of the figure on horseback behind them, the sunlight striking red-orange curls. As Ethaniel registered this, he realized that the figure was also slumped over the horse in a way that looked painful.

Lawton might be either bone-tired or injured, from the way he clung to the horse's neck. But his body jostled hard with every beat of the creature's hooves, and the strange limpness of his movement made dread pool in Ethaniel's stomach.

If he's dead… Ethaniel thought as he straightened up to say to Calix, "You might not want to look back, dove."

Calix's face brightened at the new pet name, but then realization struck him. "No. No. He *can't.*"

"I don't think he's well," Aubrey called up as he leaned out of the carriage window, his monocle affixed to his right eye.

"Fuck." Ethaniel stared hard at Calix, knowing the other man would be torn. And he was. Calix's face was a mirror of panic, his knuckles white where he gripped the reins. "Calix. It's your call."

"It could be a trap," Calix croaked. "He could just be bait."

"I don't think so," Aubrey replied as he turned to them. The hand holding his revolver was as steady as anything, and that sight made Ethaniel relax a little. Aubrey's surety was a balm, even as his own nerves began to jangle with the threat of danger. "Someone's used magic on him. He looks very wounded."

"Wounded?" Calix echoed.

"Blood. Bruising." Ethaniel heard the click of Aubrey's throat. "Burns. Magical ones."

"No, no, no," Calix muttered. He had grown even more pale, so Ethaniel took the reins from him and began to pull the carriage over.

"I don't think it's a trap," Ethaniel said as Calix leaned into him, breathing hard. "We need to help him."

"This is so stupid," Calix said, his eyes now wet with tears. "I shouldn't care about him. Not after what he did."

Ethaniel's heart twisted as he watched Calix try to pull himself together. His friendship with Lawton was clearly a complicated thing, and when loyalties ran that deep, it was nearly impossible to completely cast them aside.

"It's not stupid, Calix. We will do whatever you wish," Ethaniel said. "Aubrey?"

"Hmmm?"

"Is there anyone else on the road?"

"No."

Ethaniel turned back to Calix and said, "What do you want to do?"

Calix took in a deep breath, then another, then straightened to his full height and threw his shoulders back. "Stop the carriage."

As soon as Ethaniel guided the horses to a spot off the road, near a bank of elms that swayed in the wind, Calix hopped down, his expression grim but determined. Ethaniel wasn't about to let him go up to the horse - and a clearly injured Lawton - on his own. While Aubrey took charge of their horses, he and Calix made their approach.

Ethaniel had no defense in this situation, aside from the sword still in dagger form. Any protective patterns he knew took time and energy; they were meant for warding buildings and possessions, not people, and not at a moment's notice. And there was nothing tangible for Aubrey to mend or use in their defense.

But he would not let Calix go on his own.

The horse slowed as they approached, and as Lawton weakly raised his head, Calix gasped and ground to a halt. The man's right eye was swollen shut, a bruised mass under which a crusted-over wound split his cheek. The hand Lawton had tangled in the horse's reins was bruised and cut as well, and Ethaniel would bet there were more contusions under Lawton's stained and ripped clothes.

Calix rushed toward his friend, hands trembling as he reached up. With a groan, Lawton slid from the saddle and crashed into Calix, taking them both to the ground. Ethaniel ran toward them, yelling for Aubrey as he did.

Lawton rolled his one good eye upwards, locking onto Calix, then Ethaniel. "I wasn't followed," he rasped. Anger swelled within Ethaniel's chest, but his words were lost to the wind as Lawton pulled his grimy shirt aside. "It's a traitor's brand," he whispered before he lost consciousness.

The jut of Lawton's collarbone was marred by a burn roughly shaped like a circle bisected horizontally by a thick line. "It's the same symbol I use in some castings," Calix whispered, his expression full of horror. "Salt."

The implications of that one word made Ethaniel shudder. Salt was for binding, but also for curses. One could not grow crops on land that had been salted. Salt was a part of unhallowing sacred ground. It was powerful. And permanent.

Salting a body, and the soul inside it, shouldn't be possible.

Calix's arms failed him, so Ethaniel dove forward. "I've got him," Ethaniel said. Calix shot him a grateful look as Ethaniel bundled Lawton into his arms. The man was far lighter than he'd anticipated, and the shock nearly sent them to the ground, but Ethaniel regained his footing just as Aubrey dashed up.

"I'll handle the horse," Aubrey said, giving Ethaniel — and Lawton — a worried glance. "Calix, use what supplies we have on Mr. Adler. Ethaniel..."

"I'll get us there," Ethaniel replied, feeling the weight of those few words bury themselves deep.

Nineteen

A UBREY

The frantic beat of Aubrey's heart didn't slow until the gates of Rose-hill were visible in the distance. Calix's estate was a beautiful Tudor-style brick manor with elegant wood shutters painted a soft green and a deep emerald front door bearing a magnolia-leaf wreath. The grounds were lined with perfectly trimmed hedges; the curling arch of a large trellis was easily spotted to the right, where black-thorned rose bushes waited for spring's kiss. The sound of the carriage and horses over the gravel path to the manor's front sent that very front door flying open, and pounding down the concrete steps was Richard.

"Thank God," Richard said as he rushed forward while Aubrey swung down from their newly acquired horse. Ethaniel managed to get to the carriage door first, and Aubrey watched the other man's face flicker with annoyance. "Calix!"

Calix carefully opened the carriage door. "Lawton's inside, " Calix said. "Richard, Ethaniel, can you help me get him to a room? His wounds need tending to."

Richard fell quiet after peering inside the carriage, then nodded. "Yes, of course." The nod he gave Aubrey was silent with the heavy weight they were all bearing. Aubrey knew Richard would do whatever Calix needed, and that knowledge made the squirming fear in his stomach settle a mite.

As Richard and Ethaniel carried Lawton's limp form between them, Aubrey drew Calix aside with a hand to his shoulder. The younger man was sweaty and disheveled, his shirt streaked with dirt and blood and gods knew what else from his friend's injuries. "Calix, look at me," Aubrey said. He recognized the wild look in the other man's eyes, that panic and worry and helplessness that all bound up into a Gordian knot. "Is there a doctor in that village we passed? Or in the next town over?"

Calix blinked slowly, his brow furrowed as he thought. "I um...yes. Dr. Bilstein. She lives just down the road with her family. Her husband runs a dairy farm. But can we trust anyone else?" He swallowed hard, gaze going to the open front door, as if he could still see Lawton through the layers of wood and brick. "Lawton's injuries are very clearly not normal."

Aubrey knew it would come to this eventually, but having the decision made for him in this way was nothing he could have expected. He *knew* his family's recipes and treatments. He *knew* their magic. His power shared the same roots, even if it had branched off into its own tree. It had been a very long time since he'd done anything but minor healing on anyone outside himself.

Aubrey had made the decision during the last hour or so on the road. Trusting Lawton's injuries to anyone else would draw attention. They might have a few days, or a few weeks, to decide on next steps, but an injured man sporting a strange burn and multiple other wounds *would* become gossip. No, they couldn't trust anyone outside the manor, that much was certain.

He turned back to Calix, determination set in his tone. "If I draw up a list of what I need, do you think the doctor would sell me the supplies?"

At that, Calix cocked his head. "What kind of supplies?"

"Bandages, of course. Some herbs—"

At that, much to Aubrey's surprise, Calix smiled. "We have all that."

"Really?"

Calix nodded and began pulling their few belongings from the carriage. "I'll have Richard handle the horses while we go check on how Ethaniel's fairing with Lawton. Then I'll show you the greenhouse."

Aubrey couldn't help it. Something about Calix's joy, in the midst of constant tragedy and danger, drew him in. He cupped Calix's face between his hands and when Calix made a soft sound, Aubrey kissed him. Like a yew in the wind, Calix bent to his touch, and it was the easiest thing to drop one hand so he could run his fingers down Calix's throat.

"Well, that's unfair," Ethaniel said from behind them. Aubrey only drew back a little to yank his other lover in by the collar, kissing Ethaniel hard as well.

"It's only unfair if I were to start playing favorites," Aubrey murmured after they broke apart. "And that's not going to be an issue."

With Lawton safely tucked away in a guest room, Ethaniel and Richard began making an early dinner while Calix walked Aubrey through the rest of the house. It was beautifully decorated in jewel-toned wallpapers and plush rugs, and, to Aubrey's delight, almost every living space had at least one floor-to-ceiling bookcase practically groaning under embossed leather tomes. Calix seemed much more relaxed here, too. He'd finally let his shoulders pull away from his ears and he talked to Aubrey as they passed through the house, noting the various rooms with clear fondness.

"It's usually just Richard and I here, plus Marie, the housekeeper, and Martha, a woman from the village who comes up every few days to cook." They paused in the open doorway to a beautiful kitchen, where copper pans gleamed from their hooks and the massive fireplace put out enough heat to fill even the hallway in which they stood.

Aubrey found himself entranced by the fire's glow, but instead of comforting, the flames only reminded him of what he'd so recently lost. Material objects meant little to him, but the obsidian and marble altar and the glazed jar of his father's ashes were irreplaceable. In those flames, he saw more than what had been destroyed; he saw his father's hands carefully shifting a bowl of bright red feathers, his movements slow and measured as though the feathers were as fragile as glass. That image shifted, blurry and hazy, until Aubrey then saw his father's body outside the meticulously kept horse stable, crumpled on the ground like a discarded corn husk.

You've disappointed me again, son. You always disappoint, and the passing years have not changed that. You couldn't even protect me after my death. My only son.

Aubrey grit his teeth against the intrusive thoughts. On a normal day, the thoughts might have risen, but he could have swept them away with an errant flick. Now, after days of exhaustion and stress and the sudden reappearance of someone who clearly caused a large portion of the chaos? He wasn't strong enough to ignore it.

"Garden, you said?" he asked, twisting to see Calix watching him with a concerned expression. "I'm fine, only tired."

Calix nodded. "We all are. But you looked so...lost for a moment." Calix ran his fingers down Aubrey's sleeve and somewhere deep in his bones, Aubrey felt a pang of longing. Not lust, not carnal desire. Only the thick, heavy *want* of touch. Connection.

"I might have gotten distracted," Aubrey said softly as he leaned in. Calix immediately, instinctively bent to him; every time he did, it made Aubrey's head spin. Calix was the opposite of Ethaniel in so many ways, and yet in them both Aubrey saw the strength, the resilience. The intelligence and open hearts. He was the strong, tall, stalwart one. Cold, sometimes. Was it so wrong that he sought another's warmth, craved it in a way for which he had no words?

"I think you're even more distracted now," Calix teased, his voice barely above a whisper. "Now's not the time but..."

"Calix?" Aubrey chanced a touch to Calix's cheek, just the backs of his fingers.

"The gardens. Right." Calix gave him a wobbly smile but didn't turn away from Aubrey's touch. He did put one hand on the satchel still around his torso. "I should put this in the vault. But perhaps the safe is better? There's nothing in the safe except some old papers of my mother's."

"I think the safe is best, for now. You said the house was warded?" Aubrey asked.

That earned him a smile. "You didn't even feel it, did you?" Calix's long fingers dipped into his tunic and he pulled out a silver medallion on a sparkling chain. "The wards...learn, for lack of a better word. I think I felt something similar when we arrived at the Collectio." Aubrey nodded, and Calix continued. "The wards are my mother's invention. She dabbled in many arcane and esoteric arts, but her wards are the strongest I know. I fully believe we'll be secure here. So I suppose the safe will do until I can show you both the vault."

Calix led Aubrey into a small hallway, then to the right, where a simple wood door stood shut. When he opened it, Aubrey felt the *pop* of a ward releasing, the magic old but strong and leaving little tingling waves moving up and down his skin.

The study itself was largely inobtrusive, dominated by a beautiful mahogany desk, heavy bookshelves of the same wood built into the walls. The thick velvet curtains were drawn, and the scent of dust lingered in the air. Calix snapped his fingers and two sconces on the wall leapt to life, their merry orange flames providing just enough light to navigate by.

"Give me a moment," Calix said as he headed for one bookshelf. Aubrey nodded, ready to help if needed, watching as Calix pulled a large handkerchief from a small end table, then opened the satchel with his uncovered hand. He looked up at Aubrey for a long moment and said, "I don't suppose we should simply toss this thing into a fire and spend the season curled up in my bed together?"

A very tempting idea. The mere suggestion of it brought to life hazy images in Aubrey's mind, the three of them tangled together in dark red sheets. He could finally relearn Ethaniel's body while memorizing Calix's, leaving them both shaking and moaning and pleading for more.

It was a very good idea. One he'd like to find time for later.

"Fire might only anger it, to be honest," Aubrey finally replied. "Sentient objects are incredibly rare. Very little is known about them. I've only ever read reports of their existence." He had to chuckle before saying, "It's why I was at the auction. There was a diary of a court mage from the time of John Dee and his tenure with Queen Elizabeth I. Rumor had it the court mage had documented many of Dee's so-called predictions, and had written extensively about Dee's fortune board, as he called it. A simple wooden board Dee swore could help him prognosticate answers the Queen posed." Aubrey pinned Calix with a look. "A *sentient*, fortune-telling wooden board."

To his surprise, Calix burst out laughing. "That's...surely that's fake."

Aubrey shrugged. "That's what I wanted to find out. I can read the history of an item, and I was hoping that book had something to tell."

"I wonder if we would have met again, had you won that lot," Calix said, his expression suddenly, painfully sad. "But no matter. We're here now."

He bunched the handkerchief in his hand and slowly pulled Convergence from the satchel. Calix wasted no time in pressing his free hand to the bookshelf, palm flat against three books. With a grinding sound, a section of the bottom shelf popped open. Calix carefully wrapped the book in the cloth, then set it into the drawer that made up the false shelf. Another press of his palm made the drawer slide back, and the bookshelf was whole once more. There was a faint *click* from the drawer, but it was vastly overshadowed by the pulse of **POWER** from the safe itself. Temptation lay heavy on his brow, making Aubrey itch to take up his monocle and examine the vault's patterns, its very construction. He didn't want to be rude, however, and he highly suspected he'd want and need time and proper mental capacity for such an endeavor.

"Well," Calix said, brushing off his pants, "That's done. Somehow I feel better already, knowing that blasted thing is locked away for a bit." His eyes rolled up to look at the ceiling. "Now to Lawton. Can I help you gather what you need? My mother was a bit of an herbalist, so there's yarrow, mint, rosemary, calendula, and almost anything you might want."

That made Aubrey breathe a sigh of relief. "Yes. Help would be most welcome."

Calix led them back to the kitchen for a basket and shears, then had Aubrey follow him into the back of the house. The hothouse was attached to the manor's east-facing sitting room, closed off by a door of thick glass that, when he touched it, sent radiating warmth up Aubrey's arm. "Ah, the wards are sometimes temperamental," Calix said, pausing as Aubrey shook out his hand. "But I'm with you. It won't be an issue."

"That's good to know," Aubrey said as he gazed around in awe at the neatly ordered raised bed jammed with herbs and medicinal plants. It was a beautiful space, and he could imagine a young Calix kneeling beside his mother, gently taking stalks and stems and flowers and leaves and placing them in the very basket Calix now carried.

Together, they slowly made their way through each bed, Aubrey snipping off what he might need while Calix carefully added each piece and adding it to his basket. They didn't speak over those quiet minutes, surrounded by the fading afternoon sun and a bevy of sweet-smelling plants and humid air.

Something like *peace* washed over Aubrey and from Calix's little sigh as they rounded the last garden bed, he was feeling a similar way.

"I'll go see to Mr. Adler," Aubrey said, gently taking the basket from Calix as they re-entered the sitting room. "You should rest."

Calix shook his head. "If I lie down now, I won't get up until morning. Or perhaps I'll be terribly lazy and not rise until the afternoon."

Aubrey had to smile at that. Calix managed to sound both very responsible and wistful at the same time. "That sounds lovely," he admitted.

Calix smiled, but it only lasted for a moment before he broke eye contact to gaze down at the floor, his body curling in on itself; a signal Aubrey was learning to read as unconscious but clear doubt or sorrow. It was perhaps a little of both, in the case of his friend.

For good luck, he rubbed his fingertips over Calix's cheek, allowing himself one grazing touch to the younger man's jaw before saying, "I'll do my best for Mr. Adler. If the wounds are superficial, then he'll heal with time and rest and the right salves."

"If?"

"If," Aubrey replied firmly. "I simply don't know yet." He gave Calix a little nudge with his shoulder. "I'll send Ethaniel down to you. In the kitchen for tea, perhaps?"

"Oh! Yes. Right." And to Aubrey's surprise, Calix leaned in and kissed his cheek. "Thank you."

Aubrey watched Calix leave, his heart twisted into a two-headed beast of admiration and desire. Getting to know Calix would not be boring in the least.

Aubrey made his way upstairs, following the sinuous curve of the mahogany staircase carpeted by thick oxblood red, and found the small guest room in the south hallway. The door was cracked and from inside came the *drip drip drip* of water inside a porcelain or ceramic bowl. Aubrey inhaled deeply to clear his head, then knocked.

"Aubrey?"

Aubrey poked his head inside, squinting against the room's dimness. The only light came from two gas sconces on the wall which were turned down low. Ethaniel sat in a cushioned chair beside the bed, one hand holding a wet cloth as pink water dripped from its end. "I didn't want to leave him lying here in his own dried blood," Ethaniel said, fully rinsing out the cloth, folding it, and setting it aside. "But I'm afraid outside a proper dunk in the tub, some of it won't come o ff."

"I'll focus on the wounds first. Everything else can wait." Aubrey noted with approval that Ethaniel had managed to peel off Lawton's shredded clothes and pull a blanket over him. "Did you see any wounds worse than the burn?"

"No. His legs are largely untouched." Ethaniel's throat clicked as he swallowed hard, his expression going flat. "But the burn is quite bad. They *branded him*, Aubrey. No one deserves *that*."

Unlike Ethaniel, Aubrey could think of a few people who deserved severe punishment, but he agreed that burning someone like cattle was the act of a sadist. Or someone very, *very* angry. "I shouldn't have asked you to come up here," Aubrey said, trying to find the right words to express how badly he felt. He crouched by Ethaniel's chair after setting his supplies to the side, and took Ethaniel's right hand. They stared at Lawton — covers pulled up to his belly, skin ashen against dark green sheets, his hair like fire atop his head. Rapid movement behind his eyelids and the occasional shift of his jaw made Aubrey wonder if the man was dreaming, or if his mind was taking pity on his body and keeping him unconscious because of the pain.

He finally looked at the burn properly and winced. It was brutally done, ragged and raw, the skin bubbling and purple in some spots, sunburn pink in others. As Lawton breathed, Aubrey swore he could see the tiniest bit of dark red muscle and bone just below the skin.

"Calix is in the kitchen with tea. He's expecting you," Aubrey said as he nudged Ethaniel from the chair. "Let me take care of him. We still have the salves I purchased in town, and plenty of clean bandages. I'll do what I can to keep him unconscious while his body heals."

"All right." Ethaniel made it to the door before turning back. "Aubrey?"

"Hmmm?"

Ethaniel's expression flickered with something unreadable, then he shook his head. "Just be careful. I'll go find Calix, but we'll be just downstairs. In case."

As soon as Ethaniel shut the door, Aubrey went to work. He knew the recipes well, able to pull them from his memory with ease, but the motions of grinding herbs, adding oil, then creating the packing paste for Lawton's burn felt...strange. It was almost as if it were another Aubrey doing all of it; an Aubrey from the past, whose path would have been very different had his magic manifested like everyone else in his family.

The part of him firmly rooted in the here and now wanted this done quickly. Lawton didn't move the entire time, and Aubrey was careful with his touch so as not to disturb him more than need be. But the burn he saved for last, his gaze flicking to it every now and again. It was a truly awful wound, and one that would leave a scar that would pull every time Lawton moved his arm. It would take months to heal properly, and the risk of infection was fairly high.

Dammit. Lawton needed a healer, a proper one.

But Aubrey could *try*. Even without myrrh or mistletoe, he could *try* to heal Lawton's wounds. The worst that would happen would be nothing at all. Something inside Aubrey squirmed at the thought, though. He should retrieve Calix and ask permission. Or ask Ethaniel to come back and bear witness. *Something. Anything.* So he wasn't alone.

But maybe alone was better, so no one could watch him fail.

Aubrey clenched his fist against the softness of the blankets Lawton had been swaddled in and closed his eyes. *Failure* was natural. He needed to remember that. Striving so hard for perfection until it had made him ill had probably shortened his life by a few years, and had made him dour for too long. He was not his family. He was not his father. And he was something unique, something different, in a bloodline so tied to earth and root and flesh and bone; but he could see the past of the earth, the fibers of the root, the disease in the flesh and the break in the bone. And so much more. Every object had a past and if Aubrey focused, he could hear their stories and let them ring their truth in his ears, his body, his heart.

Aubrey opened his eyes and looked down at Lawton; so still, so fragile, so wounded. Perhaps it was a simple burn that had charred his flesh, but if Aubrey had been head of the Golden Order, he would have burned the man with magic. After all, they'd metaphysically salted the wound so it would never fully heal. Why wouldn't one ensure extra pain on top of that?

He let his eyes close once more and put his fingers into the thick gray paste he'd slathered on the burn.

Let me try. At least let me try. The man's so still, he might as well be an object. Let me find the burn, find the magic below, and erase it.

Something in Aubrey's mind *pulsed*, power that tasted of cold metal...leather...parchment. The taste grew thick on his tongue and his stomach convulsed, but Aubrey held on. He imagined he was back at the Collectio, surrounded by the strange and mysterious, and on that massive obsidian block lay an odd artifact. After all, that's all the burn was...an odd artifact to unravel, catalog, and repair.

Aubrey felt his power push forward, seeking the root of that burn, and he imagined it sending tendrils through Lawton's body, seeking the smaller wounds, too. Closing, restoring, mending. The taste on his tongue turned to rosemary and he sighed into it.

And in the dark, his power found a bizarre little flicker of brackish purple light buried deep under the torn skin and charred flesh. Aubrey reached out for it, snapping it up with a spectral hand, and turned it over. It was perfectly round and smooth, growing solid in his palm.

You don't belong here, he thought. His power pulsed again and with it brought a sharp pain. He needed to work quickly. He was already butting up against the reaches of his own ability, and this was no torn book or broken clock to mend. Aubrey wrapped his hand around the sphere and squeezed. What was once solid became malleable, making the sick feeling in his gorge rise even higher. The energy from it squished between his fingers; fighting him, pushing back. It was fighting to stay buried under Lawton's flesh.

Aubrey brought his other hand up and pressed against the magic with his own. As the magic jerked and writhed between his palms, Aubrey grit his teeth, snarling in response. *You don't belong here. Leave.*

NOW.

The mass between his fingers squealed, nipping at his skin with blunt teeth. It was trying to find another host, a way in to save its own life. Aubrey laughed, knowing the sound was cruel, but how could he not laugh at the demise of such foul magic? It had been implanted under Lawton's skin like a disease, or a worm. It had turned Lawton into a time bomb, because buried underneath all of it had been the taste of fire and ash.

The Golden Order seemed to like their fire. Maybe in the future, he'd have the opportunity to return the favor. It was a horrid thought, but some part of Aubrey crowed in relief as the mass between his hands let out an ear-piercing shriek, then popped.

Aubrey opened his eyes and looked down to find his fingers covered in medicinal paste, but below it, Lawton's skin glowed a soft gold. Not healed, but better, and no longer booby-trapped. The man would likely make a full, but slow, recovery.

The door cracked open and Ethaniel stuck his head inside. "Aubrey? What happened? We heard a strange noise—"

Aubrey got to his feet, not caring he smeared paste down Ethaniel's shirt or across his neck as he hauled him into a kiss. Ethaniel instantly kissed him back, gripping Aubrey hard by the waist. After everything, Ethaniel was *here, with him,* and as lovely as ever. This kiss didn't make him dizzy or take Aubrey's breath away; it grounded him.

"He'll heal," Aubrey said after they broke apart. "The Golden Order essentially booby-trapped the man, but I found it and destroyed it."

Ethaniel stared at him for a long moment, his grip still tight on Aubrey's shirt. "Wha— Aubrey, that's incredible."

"It's not perfect," Aubrey said, unable to ignore the fierce surge of pride in his chest, "but he's better than before. I think we can manage his care from here, without doctors poking about."

With a heavy sigh, Ethaniel leaned in to rest his forehead on Aubrey's shoulder. "You constantly amaze me. Do you know that?"

Aubrey snorted, still lightheaded from the rush of power but glad to have Ethaniel to cling to. "I have lost time to make up for," he said, lifting Ethaniel's face with his still-sticky hands. "Don't sing my praises just yet."

When he and Ethaniel followed the sounds of Calix and Richard to the front parlor, they found the two men sitting across from each other, full wine glasses in hand, fireplace roaring.

Richard smiled as they walked in, his brow only dipping in brief confusion at the drying gray paste on Ethaniel's shirt and Aubrey's trousers. "I managed to get him to sit," Richard said with a note of pride, which immediately made Calix pout. "How is...how are things upstairs?"

"Better. Only just, but it's an improvement." Aubrey sat to Calix's right with a wince, still feeling rather jostled from their frantic carriage journey. But from here, he could put a reassuring hand on Calix's knee. "He'll live."

Calix looked down at his hands and nodded, but didn't speak. The silence carried them into more wine and fireplace contemplation, interrupted only when Aubrey asked, "Did Calix get you caught up, Richard? I know we disrupted everything."

Richard waved him off. "I've known Calix for many years, and while more...*exciting* than normal, it's nothing I can't handle. And yes, he did."

At that, Calix raised his head. "Mostly. We didn't get bogged down in the details, but he understands the risk."

"And since I'm a stubborn ass, I also refuse to leave 'for my own safety', as it were." Richard sipped his wine, then said, "Besides, if there's trouble to be had, I won't leave Calix alone. And I won't entertain questions on that." He tipped an imaginary hat toward Aubrey. "But I do apologize, again, for trying to tackle you at Calix's apartment. I didn't know what was going on."

"Not a worry," Aubrey replied. "I'd have done the same in your place."

Aubrey turned to Ethaniel to ask him if he wanted more wine. But Ethaniel was staring at the floor, nearly bent over in his chair, one arm wrapped around his middle. It was only then Aubrey heard the man's shaky breaths. "Ethaniel? Are you all right?"

Ethaniel seemed to almost jump forward, with how quickly he moved, dropping to his knees beside Aubrey's chair and looking up at with such raw trust, it made Aubrey stop breathing for a moment. "This is all my fault," Ethaniel choked out. He gripped at Aubrey hard now, his fingers digging into Aubrey's thigh. "When I stopped at home, Uncle Jeremiah was moving around like he was healthy again, and my...*Vincent* showed up."

Dread dripped into Aubrey's stomach. "Your half-brother?"

"The very one," Ethaniel growled. "He must have given Uncle Jeremiah something to make him feel better. He made all these threats and then he told me...Aubrey, Vincent's the head of the Golden Order. And he wants the book back, above anything else."

Through the static of truth that made Aubrey's head buzz, there was the satisfaction of feeling a final puzzle piece click into place. It all made a strange kind of sense, to be honest, and immediately Aubrey started to plan. None of it was Ethaniel's fault. The connection to family ran deep and so often it was a knife that could cut both ways. Aubrey certainly knew that. He had so many words for Ethaniel, but the man looked so broken and betrayed that Aubrey did the only thing he could. He slid from the chair to drop to his knees before Ethaniel, putting them on the same level, and gathered him close. Ethaniel's inhale shook, and then he buried his face in Aubrey's shoulder and cried.

Ethaniel was not a small man, and his weight combined with Aubrey's exhaustion finally collapsed them both. Aubrey managed to wedge them against the couch on which Calix sat while Ethaniel all but crawled into his lap, silently asking to be held while his sobs ebbed and flowed.

"We'll figure this out." Calix was on the floor at their side now, running his hand soothingly up and down Ethaniel's arm. Aubrey was eternally grateful for Calix's lack of judgment. None of them could judge the other, not now. Not with everything that had happened. "We will. We're safer here than anywhere else, and that gives us time. Please don't blame yourself, Ethaniel."

Aubrey gave Calix a grateful look, hoping it spoke the depths of his appreciation. When Calix didn't move and didn't speak, Aubrey said, "We'll need time. And each other." He freed his left hand so he could pass the backs of his fingers over Calix's cheek. Their own secret language, built one touch at a time. This younger man had careened into Ethaniel's life, and then his, but had shown nothing but care and compassion, and was clearly all right with tangling his life, and his romantic notions, with them both.

Ethaniel's tears slowed and his grip on Aubrey eased, so it only made sense to shift around so they could all sit comfortably on the floor in front of the fire. Aubrey realized that Richard had quietly left the room; for the first time since the fire, they were alone and in a place where no demands were made, no fear consumed their bodies, and, if Aubrey had any say in it, no worry would consume their minds.

A moment's peace.

An idea rose in him, both soft and fierce, built on a foundation of trust and longing. Aubrey pushed Ethaniel's hair out of his face and turned to the other man. "Calix?"

Calix had leaned his head on Aubrey's shoulder and now looked up, eyelashes fluttering. "Yes?"

"You have a room here, right?" Aubrey arched an eyebrow. "With a sizeable bed and a tub?"

Calix's mouth twitched into a smile. "I do."

"Good." Aubrey got to his feet and helped Ethaniel to his. When all of them were standing, he dragged Calix in for a kiss, making sure to hold Ethaniel close so he could hear their lips moving together. It didn't take long for Ethaniel to press against him, his hands wandering Aubrey's chest. Aubrey took that as a sign to say, "Show us where you sleep, Calix."

INTERLUDE

L AWTON

The night of the fire

The last place Lawton ever wanted to find himself was in front of Vincent de Laine. But going with Cassandra's guard, an intimidatingly broad man with a stunning black goatee named David, as he left the Minotaur Baths had been inescapable. David had been waiting for him, and with one of his big hands, managed to snag Lawton's arm before he could dance out of reach.

"Cassandra's got a carriage for us," David said, his square jaw working as he chewed on and spit out each word. The New Jersey accent was thick, and had this been any other moment, Lawton would have charmingly teased David about misunderstanding him.

Not now. Not if Lawton wanted to make it out of this alive. Because Cassandra sending David — her fixer, for lack of a better word — meant she was more than serious. The woman was *always* serious, so much that Lawton often wondered if her face ever relaxed. Even now, standing to Vincent's right, hands behind her back and spine rigid, Cassandra's face was a perfect mask of diluted anger mixed rather strangely with fear. Lawton spared a brief wonder at what such a woman like Cassandra feared, then remembered whom before he stood.

He'd shown his hand by letting his desperation to get that book back show. And there was no recovering from such humiliation. But in the end, it was all his fault. He'd let Calix and his new friends escape without so much as an empty threat or penetrating glare.

He loved Calix. And he'd betrayed him. He should be absolutely bloody *terrified* of what Vincent might do to him. But Lawton refused to let go of his sadness, and yes, his own self-pity, for what he'd done to Calix.

"Cassandra has kept me apprised of the growing situation over an item you were asked to retrieve," Vincent said, folding his hands together on his desk. "Fortunately for you, I know that you didn't purposefully draw my family into this."

Lawton inhaled sharply at that. *I might be well and truly fucked at this point. Family?*

His mind scrambled through memories of the past few days: snatches of color and sound; of Calix's big brown eyes hardened in anger while he wore a lacey robe that made Lawton's prick stir; the magic that had held him and Aubrey Lavigne at bay, being cast by a man with hazel eyes exactly like Vincent's.

Genuine fear, cold and slippery, wound its way through Lawton's stomach and then down further, into his guts, and curled up like it had a right to live there. He couldn't move, couldn't speak, could barely think enough to shake his head, hoping Vincent would accept that for now.

But that fear was deeper than a heartbeat under his skin, pulsing with the sound of the name *Ethaniel*. He'd heard it once, not even an hour before, and now — with so much regret it was likely to choke him — Lawton understood terror.

"But Cassandra tells me you had them within reach, and let them slip away." Vincent stood, his black suit fitted perfectly to his body, and walked around the desk to lean back against it. The casual pose did nothing but stoke Lawton's fear higher. He was frozen to the spot, and Vincent could have done anything, *anything* to him. Lawton doubted he would even make a sound, to be honest.

Maybe he deserved it.

Lawton's eye caught on the gold trim around Vincent's white marble desk. Everything in the room was either black, white, or gold. Under his feet, the circle and arrow of the Golden Order gleamed. He was in a house that belonged to Vincent de Laine, and he had no defense for anything that had happened.

With the bitter citrus of fear on his tongue, Lawton said, "I did."

Vincent pursed his lips and nodded. "Admitting your mistake is a good start. So I suppose it's my turn to admit that I also made a mistake. By not giving you a better understanding of *why* the book is important, I let you assume this all was a…" Vincent waved his hand in the air. "A simple endeavor."

"It should have been." Cassandra didn't move, but her voice echoed in the hollow spaces of the office, content to worm around the books and knickknacks and strange little objects that Lawton had to assume were magical or something of the sort. Vincent was *exactly* the kind of person to cloak himself in the vanity of his chosen interests.

"But your little retrieval job grew complicated and here we are. It's a shame, really, but then again, Cassandra was convinced you'd fail from the beginning." Vincent drummed his fingers on the edge of the desk, examining Lawton like a fox with prey. Not a wolf, a *fox*, slick and vulpine and cunning and so quiet in the shadows and then there were teeth and claws and the sound of flesh ripping. "But it's not all for a loss, Mr. Adler. I understand you fell in with my brother, yes, but also his old flame and your current one. And while I know my brother's skills, Mr. Lavigne's are only rumored and your Calix seems to… well, he's got a glow about him that's hard to ignore."

Vincent's little shudder when talking about Calix made Lawton want to vomit all over that gold-veined white marble floor.

"Curious, then," Vincent continued, "how I'm to extract the book from their possession without…" Vincent paused, cold, flat gaze punching through Lawton, "damaging something important. But we always add in an acceptable risk of loss."

Lawton tried to open his mouth to speak, but couldn't. This wasn't fear, though. This was magic. It held him in place as though he'd been wrapped in chains and now, dangling over the wide black chasm of the ocean, Lawton knew his fate was to be devoured.

His only thought before he heard Vincent say, "Take him to the back office," was, *Calix, please forgive me.*

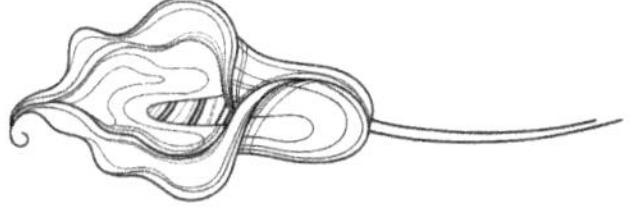

Lawton was not bound or blindfolded, simply walked down a long hallway with Cassandra at his right and two guards at his back. Somehow, this made everything that much worse — they expected his acquiescence to whatever tortures lay in store. As if he were no more than a mindless drone working on part of something grand, something greater. After all, that's part of what Cassandra had sold him when she'd recruited him from one of the many smoke-hazed nightclubs of Acadia Gardens.

A chance to be better. To bring about much-needed change. To make a name for himself, while being a part of a whole. And she had him down pat from the start, appealing to both his grandiosity and his insecurities. Worst of all, Cassandra had found the tiny part of him that Lawton had only let Calix see — miniscule as it was, it squirmed in pleasure of recognition when Lawton had admitted he wanted to be *needed*. The third son of a perpetually-drunken merchant who frequently lost whole shipments at the card tables wasn't relied on for anything, and even less so than his gimcrack brothers and father. Lawton had raised himself, taught himself, and when opportunity presented itself, took it with both hands and held tight.

The Golden Order was supposed to be *his* opportunity. *His* chance. The promise of wealth and societal ladder-climbing had been factors in his decision, but it had been the *passion* behind Vincent's ideas. Magic for all, doled out by those who were studied in its ethereal, oft unknowable ways. The chance to change and better all lives through the distribution of magic's gifts. Establishing proper channels through which to learn magic, because Vincent was convinced anyone could learn.

He'd spent years and years watching Calix fight against his own abilities, the ones he'd inherited from a truly unstable woman who was the picture of an unfit mother. Not that his own had been much better, but she'd *tried*. Lily Addington had everything at her fingertips — money, status, clout, respect, and a young son who adored her. And she had power; Calix had told him of his mother's seemingly endless abilities, how magic lived in her veins.

She'd had so much, and yet she'd never lived up to her full potential. And in Calix, she'd instilled fear of his own powers. Lawton had long suspected Calix took after his mother with more than simply "prophetic dreams", as his friend so often called them. Even to someone like Lawton, without a bit of magic in him, Calix *glistened*.

So much wasted potential. So many chances to be better treated like refuse.

When The Golden Order had immediately put him to work, Lawton had reveled in it. He easily garnered favor with the right ears, pressed bills into hands that would put his name at the top of certain lists. *All the way up to the mayor's office, for a start,* Cassandra had said when Lawton had inquired about how high this could all go. *But that is only a start. You'd best be thinking bigger than the city, Mr. Adler. We do.*

And now here he was, tossed into a dim room devoid of any basic comforts like a chair, and left to sit on the cold stone floor. Time passed in a dreamlike way, heightening his senses until every little creak made Lawton jump to his feet. It was the tenterhooks on which he'd been strung, even as invisible as they were, that served a particularly cutting brand of torture. Cassandra knew him enough to understand Lawton's mind was his worst enemy — not his bulging appetites.

So he waited.

When the single door to the room opened, Lawton got to his feet once more, only to be immobilized. But this time, it came with pain. It made him hiss through his teeth and desperate to thrash in an attempt to alleviate any of it. The pain ricocheted through him, never staying in one spot long enough to cause damage (or so he hoped), but enough to make him wish it would. Localized pain he could work through, like when he'd fallen out of a lover's window and badly bruised his tailbone.

This...this was a razor's edge, singing through his body with such expert wielding Lawton thought he might pass out.

After a minute, or maybe an hour, the door opened and two figures entered. There was a hush of conversation, and Lawton swore he saw the glint of Cassandra's coat buttons. Then pain coursed through him again. "Handle it," he heard Cassandra say before the door shut and he was left alone with a man he'd never seen before. A slight man, all button nose and smiling mouth and smokey gray eyes like a storm, came right up to him. No preamble, no conversation, only a stare-down from a man half Lawton's sized and dressed like a dandy. Which was saying something.

"Mr. Adler, I'm Mr. Smith," the man said in the most ridiculous southern accent to grace Lawton's ears. "I know you can hear me, since the pain isn't so bad it's made you nonsensical. Just nod for me." Biting back bile, Lawton nodded, still unable to fully look up at the man. "Good, good. Now, Cassandra has put me in charge of your banishment. She advocated for your execution, but Mr. de Laine's a bit of a soft touch when it comes to the quick and—" Mr. Smith made a slicing motion across his throat. "So, instead, we're going to excommunicate you. Sound good?"

Lawton laughed weakly before it was cut off by another course of pain shooting through him. "Never been one for the Church," he said, laughing and coughing and absolutely certain he'd live long enough to take Vincent de Laine's head off with a butter knife. It was only this thought that kept him from blacking out as the pain hit again and again and again.

Time meant nothing when he could feel everything. Surely the human brain wasn't capable of processing *this much* at one time, which was why Lawton's memory of the hours or perhaps days that had passed between Mr. Smith's looming visage and the horrendous agony through which he was put was...hazy at best.

But at some point, Lawton had been struck, cut (bled?), and was now bandaged across his right shoulder and collarbone. He had no memory of any of it, and the area under the bandage was completely numb when he pressed his shaking, bloodied fingers to it.

The door to his room opened on a creak, and Lawton curled in on himself despite the pain.

The man who approached was blonde haired and green eyed and gorgeous and very familiar. "You daft prick," Basil hissed, quickly stepping toward him and snapping his fingers. Lawton dropped to the ground as if his strings had been cut, left panting and tear-streaked, but the pain had stopped. "What would you have done if Cassandra had sent Mr. Smith in again? He's the worst of the scourgers."

Lawton gave over to the shivers coursing through him; his body reacting belatedly to the stress and trauma, he knew, but it didn't provide any comfort. "I was figuring on death, to be honest," he whispered through vocal cords that felt abused from all the screaming he hadn't been given permission to do. "Basil, if she catches you…"

Basil scoffed and got him to his feet, practically holding Lawton up with one powerful arm, and said, "The Order's a lot of things, but they're not terribly perceptive about their most trusted. Still, I'm not sticking around to find out."

Lawton turned his head, feeling like a flopping fish on a shipyard dock. Basil was beautiful as always, but tonight he wore dour black and gray and it washed him out to a shade of ashy that made Lawton think about vomit. Basil got down on the floor with him, pulled Lawton into his lap, and shoved a canteen between his lips. "Drink. You have to," Basil said, not unkindly. "They've been keeping you on the edge of consciousness for a day. Do you remember anything?"

"No," Lawton rasped.

"That's good. I wouldn't want to be you if your memory ever comes back." Slowly, Basil let him drink until the canteen was empty and Lawton could rest his head on Basil's thigh again. With some hesitation, Basil petted Lawton's now-matted hair for a few moments before saying, "I hate to rush you, handsome, but if you want to get out of here, now's the only chance. The guards are rotating shifts and I told Cassandra I'd handle the mess of your care."

Lawton snorted, but the breath was dry and harsh and he was back to coughing again. "Some aftercare," he said. "Where's my blanket and chocolate?"

"No time." Basil paused, listening. "We have to go."

The rest was a blur of Basil half dragging him through a dark hallway that smelled of cold stone and standing water, stopping every so often to gauge their surroundings. Lawton floated on a strange numbness that only was slapped from when Basil patted his cheek. "We're outside," Basil said. "You have a bag of provisions and a horse. I can't do much more."

Once Lawton's slurry brain caught up with Basil's words, he choked out, "Why?"

Basil sighed, shifting their combined weight until Lawton could be seated on the horse's saddle. "Because…shit, Lawton, because! You might have gotten yourself into this, but I didn't help. I…I helped the Order find your friend and the others after they left the bathhouse. I knew it was wrong and I did it anyways." Basil's green eyes flashed and Lawton saw real anger there, but had seen it enough in his own reflection to know how much it hurt when that anger was turned inward. "Because I want out, and you need to be out, and the Golden Order is power-hungry and dangerous and Vincent's got such a hard-on for that goddamn book that he can't see anything else. He'll sink the entire goddamn ship just to get his hands on it, and I don't know about you, but working for a man obsessed with one thing and one thing only is not what I was promised." Basil huffed, nostrils flaring, and Lawton could only watch the younger man's hands flutter over his coat. As if smoothing it down would make him feel better. "Leave. Don't come back. Go somewhere, anywhere. Start over. And if your dreams lead you..."

Basil paused and that sense of dread returned again. "Basil?"

Basil shook his head. "If your dreams lead you to how you got that bandage, and the wound underneath, don't follow the path. I'm serious, Lawton. It will do you no good to remember how it happened."

The warning sank into Lawton, a thing with hooks and sinew, and all he could do was nod. "What will you do?" Lawton asked.

Basil actually smiled at that. "Don't worry about me. I'm leaving tonight, too." His gaze tracked up to the dark sky and he sighed. "If you ever come to Canada, find me." He pushed himself up on the saddle to brush the briefest kiss over Lawton's slack mouth, then looked away before nudging the horse forward. Lawton was barely able to cling to the reins as every hoofbeat jostled him, and soon Basil and that muddy street and the sound of the city faded.

Over the next two days, the drive to survive pointed Lawton north and east, toward a place he'd been to a handful of times over the years and looked on with a fuzzy, warm kind of fondness. Rosehill Manor was not in Calix's name, not directly; it was held in a trust by his mother's long-term partner, but the paperwork was only for show. Edna Monroe hadn't lived in the States for several years, and Calix made a yearly sojourn to Auburn to spend time in those halls, visiting his mother's grave in the rose gardens and getting tan under the summer sun. Calix always came back from Rosehill relaxed and sweet, even more pliable than normal. It was a sacred place for him, and for the few times Lawton had been able to visit, he could understand why.

So he went there now, hoping Calix would be just on the other side of the manor's bright green door and not completely unhappy to see him. Otherwise, well...he'd figure it out. He always did. Lawton had learned a long time ago how to survive.

TWENTY

E**THANIEL**

"We should...figure this out," Ethaniel rasped between breaths. Aubrey's lips had been on his since the moment they'd all stumbled into Calix's bedroom. The air smelled like wood and wine and if Ethaniel thought of nothing else but the lips on his and the hands on his body, he would never have another care in the world.

But the real world was never so simple. They were squirreled away in a manor in upstate with a malicious group headed up by his brother potentially on their heels. And on the personal side, he had reacquaintances to make with Aubrey, and new things to learn with Calix—

"Look at him" Aubrey said softly, mostly in Calix's ear, but the words were snarled with so much lust Ethaniel had to let out a hard breath. "Do you want him, Ethaniel? He wants you. Look at how tightly strung..."

Aubrey ran his hands down Calix's sides, every heaving breath making Calix lean closer. The berry-pink temptation of Calix's lips was right in front of him. Ethaniel was grateful for the wall at his back as he reached for Calix, his entire being feeling unsteady.

"Look at how Ethaniel trembles, right at the end of his fingers," Aubrey murmured in Calix's ear as he placed a hand on Ethaniel's arm and trailed it down, until their fingers touched. "That's how you know he's wound up. Like he's trying so hard to hold back—"

"Aubrey." Ethaniel slammed his eyes shut.

"— but he wants *so badly* to touch you —"

"Aubrey, god." Ethaniel grabbed a fistful of Aubrey's shirt, mind now made up. Everything was a mess, they shouldn't squander their time in safety and yet...and yet...

Ethaniel pulled hard, yanking Aubrey forward until Calix was squashed between them, Aubrey caging them both in from the side. This kiss was everything Ethaniel remembered from Aubrey, biting and slick, the physical manifestation o f *wanton*. Even months after their parting, Ethaniel hadn't been able to look at that word without thinking of warm skin and clever hands and the way he'd felt *important, cared for* when Aubrey took him. With Calix here, it felt magnified. Aubrey was still taking care of him, but doing so with Calix as well, and having someone to share that with was beyond anything Ethaniel could have imagined.

Ethaniel broke the kiss only when Calix whispered, "I want this, but I don't know how."

Aubrey laid a kiss on Ethaniel's jaw before replying. "We managed quite well back at the inn."

That sent a bolt of lust snapping down Ethaniel's spine. He smiled at Calix and reached out to him, linking their fingers together while Aubrey watched. "Did you like what we did at the inn?" he asked, voice quiet. "We can do that again."

"No! I..." Calix swallowed hard. From the corner of his eye, Ethaniel saw Aubrey bite down on a smile. "Fuck. I mean *no*, I want to do something else."

The implications rushed to Ethaniel in a dizzying array, images of limbs tangled and mouths swollen red and fingers linked together, clenching. He and Aubrey had gone to one party on the third floor of the Minotaur Baths and it had been...unlike anything he'd ever experienced. A night of satin and sin and he remembered in vivid, beautiful detail how Aubrey had held him while men in gorgeous gilt masks took him apart with their mouths and hands.

"What do you want?" Ethaniel managed to ask, his throat gone dry.

Calix bit his lower lip and looked down, only to have his head guided back up by Aubrey's gentle hand. Christ, Aubrey's hands were big enough to palm the back of Calix's head and the sheer *power* of it made Ethaniel's cock jump. "I want to watch you two," Calix whispered, a blush staining his cheeks. His left hand grasped Ethaniel's sleeve while the other planted onto Aubrey's chest.

Calix didn't move his head from Aubrey's grip and the entire scene was goddamn intoxicating.

Doubt tugged at Ethaniel's mind, but he wiped it away. *You're safe. They're safe. Lawton is alive. Your uncle is…hopefully living it up on the town. Vincent doesn't matter right here, right now. You can only do so much.*

Be alive with them now.

"Ethaniel?" Aubrey cocked an eyebrow at him, and the bastard looked so good doing it, Ethaniel almost dropped to his knees right there.

"Yes," Ethaniel gasped out, reaching for both of them, frantic now in his need to be touched.

Aubrey was right there, his glass-colored eyes like the endless depths of some vast ocean. Ethaniel thought he might see all the way through them, right to Aubrey's core. As he clutched and clung, stealing kisses from both of them, Aubrey and Calix worked to remove their clothes and peel Ethaniel from his. The warm air of the bedroom was freeing on his skin, smothering the itch that had burrowed there since the fire.

Ethaniel knew Aubrey to be fastidious, but the man was in a damned hurry to get rid of their clothes; the tunics and trousers dropped in piles to the floor, their trail of breadcrumbs leading to the bed. He pressed kisses to any bit of skin he could, entranced by the curve of Aubrey's muscular shoulders and the freckles splashed across Calix's long neck.

"Will you lie on the bed with us?" Ethaniel asked Calix, holding out a hand to him as Aubrey tugged him to the bed. They were both so beautiful and Ethaniel yearned so much.

"Yes. Yes, of course." Calix scrambled up on the high bed piled with recently-fluffed pillows and fresh blankets. Everything was done up in sapphire and emerald and butter yellow, tasseled to within an inch of its life and so plush Ethaniel wondered if the bed would swallow them whole.

Aubrey tossed a few pillows onto the floor, making him and Calix laugh between their moans as Aubrey's hands wandered. "What is so humorous?" Aubrey teased, taking the chance to press his lips to Ethaniel's neck as they settled chest-to-back on the bed.

Ethaniel started to answer, but Calix crawled up between his legs. His breath left him in a gust. "I don't...I don't know now," Ethaniel stuttered, fully entranced by the fluid movement of Calix's body. Calix pushed Ethaniel's legs further apart with his knees, pale, slim hands warm and firm on Ethaniel's skin. The entire world had narrowed to where Calix touched him, and how Aubrey was kissing his neck. Ethaniel fully believed he could have passed out from those simple pleasures. He felt pampered, luxuriated upon. He never wanted to leave.

"You said you wanted to watch, Calix," Aubrey said. Ethaniel felt his lips spread into a smile where they were slick against his neck. "That's not watching."

Calix sucked in a sharp breath but stopped, his entire being frozen as if on command. He was so entrancing to watch, almost delicate. But there was fire in his eyes as he stared up at Aubrey. "I do." Teeth sunk into Calix's bottom lip and Ethaniel groaned. Aubrey only chuckled and ran his tongue along the shell of Ethaniel's ear. "I need to learn."

He blinked and Aubrey had Calix's chin in that long-fingered grip and they were kissing. The few kisses they had exchanged before and which Ethaniel had borne witness paled in comparison to now. Calix's eyelashes fluttered and his throat worked, as if he were trying to surround himself with Aubrey. Ethaniel knew that desire well, felt something like its kin swell in his chest and make his belly swoop pleasurably. And Aubrey...he looked utterly focused, pouring all his energy into that kiss, somehow able to still scratch his nails across Ethaniel's scalp while kissing the breath from Calix.

When they broke apart, Calix was smiling. Aubrey looked besotted. They were both far too beautiful. "Not like any lesson I've ever learned," Calix said, grin growing. "Incredible."

"Ah, I see," Aubrey said as he settled back behind Ethaniel. "We'll have to watch out for him. I think your *dove* is a bit sneaky."

Ethaniel tipped his head back onto Aubrey's shoulder. He usually let Aubrey take control but with Calix so close and looking like he needed to be cared for, he decided to chance it. "Lie beside me," Ethaniel said, patting the open space to his left, which Calix quickly occupied. "You can watch from here. You can touch yourself, but not me or Aubrey." When Calix nodded, Ethaniel continued. "Remember what I said at the inn?"

When Calix only stared at them with a delightful blush staining his cheeks, Aubrey took the opening. "Ethaniel told you to *be good for us*, didn't he?" Aubrey's hand skated down his chest and Ethaniel groaned. "If I have to worry about you, Calix..." Aubrey circled clever fingers around his right nipple. "Then I can't give Ethaniel all my attention. And my best work."

"Christ, Aubrey," Ethaniel bit out as Aubrey pressed a little harder. Already he was rattled and shaky, but the way Calix was staring at them was just as heady. "You going to leave me straining like this?"

"Only a little." Blunt teeth nipped his earlobe. "I like watching you struggle for it. You make the most *beautiful* noises when you're desperate."

Both he and Calix moaned at that and Aubrey laughed. Bastard *loved* winding Ethaniel up as much as possible, got hard on watching him fight against the need for immediate gratification. But Ethaniel was tenting his boxers something terribly and Calix was shimmying out of his and Ethaniel thought he might *burst*.

"Such a cruel man," Ethaniel whispered as Aubrey curved around him for another kiss. "Playing into what you know I want. We're not alone."

"He wants to learn. And I want to venerate you," Aubrey said between their lips.

The bed dipped, breaking their concentration, and Ethaniel leaned away to watch Calix, naked and gorgeous and damp with perspiration, climb back on the bed to settle on his back in the spot he'd been allowed, pillows propping up his neck so he could watch. His cock strained upwards and Calix reached for it, only stopping to look at Ethaniel for permission.

"Touch yourself," Ethaniel said, trying to sound stern. It was a difficult feat when Aubrey was busy pushing his fingers under the waistband of Ethaniel's boxers, but he managed it.

"Authoritative is a good look for you," Aubrey said, biting down on Ethaniel's shoulder. The sweet, sharp pain of it made Ethaniel's hips roll. Aubrey took pity on him and shoved at his boxers, tossing them to the floor..

"I'll practice it later. Please touch me."

Aubrey heavy and warm against his back. Calix staring up at them, adoring and aching and pleasuring himself. Ethaniel had never known such bliss. The sounds of heaving breaths and gasps and slick skin on skin began to find a rhythm. It filled Ethaniel's senses, made his skin prickle and his nerves sing.

Calix was loose-limbed and flushed from his cheeks to his groin, biting his lip in that way he had. It had been moments, or minutes; impossible to tell when pleasure seemed to sink into the air around them. Ethaniel watched him thrust up into his fist, the muscles in his legs flexing with power. He was *beautiful*, like a painting brought to life.

Aubrey's fist around Ethaniel's cock was exactly as he'd remembered, the skin soft but the fingertips callused and catching. Aubrey's abortive little thrusts against Ethaniel's back were telling; he was such a master of control, but how could anyone not be affected by the beauty pleasuring himself feet away, the feel of Ethaniel's cock in his fingers?

Ethaniel could feel the end nearing, the way his stones tightened and his entire body flushed with heat. He flung his hand out, fingertips grazing Calix's calf. Calix groaned in response and stroked himself faster. A pace Aubrey matched. "Don't stop," Ethaniel panted. "Ah, fuck. *Please don't stop.*"

His pleasure fed them, theirs looped back to him, and again and again the sensations cycled, rocking through Ethaniel until he had to succumb. He kept his eyes open through force of will when Calix cried out, his leg jerking under Ethaniel's hand as he spilled. Through their connected gaze, Ethaniel felt Calix's pleasure wash through him, leaving him gasping and thrusting up into Aubrey's fist, then stilling.

"Aubrey," Ethaniel said weakly, reaching back to grab at anything he could. Aubrey shivered under his touch. "Be with us in this."

Aubrey pressed his temple into Ethaniel's and rutted against him, finding his release with a shuddering sigh.

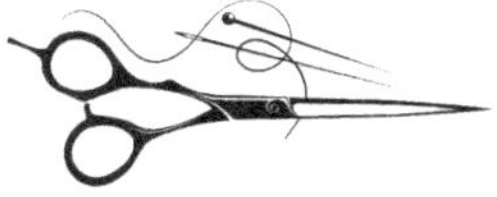

He'd fallen asleep curled between Calix and Aubrey, and awoke untold hours later to a darkened room backlit only by a low fire in the grate. The room was cold and the last thing he wanted to do was leave the warm bed, but he needed to get a fire going once more. He carefully disentangled himself from them and walked over to the fireplace, deeply disliking how the cold floor bit into the soles of his feet.

A few more logs and some nudging with the poker forced the flames to build, leaving Ethaniel shuffling back to bed as fast as he could. That was when a sensation, like sudden sea sickness, washed over him. It stopped Ethaniel dead in his tracks, torn between the need to lie back down and the demand of hot bile rising in his throat. He slammed his eyes shut and waited, hoping it was only exhaustion.

He should have known better.

Patterns in bold pink and green and yellow danced before his eyes, whirling and spinning. Ethaniel couldn't follow their motion without wanting to vomit, but when he tried to open his eyes, his body resisted.

I have a wonder for you, pattern-seer.

I wonder what you might glean from the collected knowledge inside my pages. Knowledge that could help your uncle.

Could you heal him? Completely cure his illness, banish it from his body forever?

What if you could do that, and help your Oracle quiet his mind? What if, inside these pages, one of the many I've consumed over the years could teach the Cunning Man how to heal properly?

Would you help them gain what they lack, what they need?

What would you be willing to give?

Ethaniel slammed back into his body with enough force to send him scrambling for the bed. He landed on Calix, who awoke with a start, which in turn roused Aubrey. Their shock instantly bled away when they saw how panicked Ethaniel looked.

"What happened?" Aubrey asked quietly, holding out a hand to help him into bed.

"It was the book, wasn't it?" Calix said. When Ethaniel nodded, he swore and said, "We need to get that thing in the vault. I've never put such an active object in it, but my mother had cast all kinds of wards to block any objects that wanted to be, er...rowdy, I suppose. The vault usually won't open immediately after I arrive, to safeguard me and the items, but we can try."

He felt shaky all over. Aubrey gathered Ethaniel's hands in his and it helped. He shot Aubrey a grateful look before continuing. "I've never...heard that thing in my head before. If that's even close to what either of you have gone through, the sooner we can put that thing away, the better. And it...offered me all manner of things."

"A devil's bargain, to be sure," Aubrey said. "What kinds of things?"

"Help for my uncle. For both of you." Ethaniel couldn't bear to look at either of them now. The shame was too much, thick and oily and he thought he might be sick again. "It knew what to offer and how."

Aubrey gently let go of one of his hands to drum his fingers upon his bare knee. "*Convergence.* I wonder..." He caught both of them staring and smiled, mercury-quick. "Oracles are rare, we know this. There are other strange objects and abilities I've read some tales about. Even that blasted book I tried to acquire at auction was rumored to have some stories in it from a court mage who had been given access to a royal vault. It stands to reason that any magical item that can speak in our minds and unwind our deepest desires would have, for lack of a better word, a rare ability or two of its own."

"That makes sense," Ethaniel replied, trying to see where Aubrey was headed. The man was *brilliant,* but so often his thoughts jumped in ways that defied logic. He could see it now, living on Aubrey's face and in the *tap-tap-tap* of his fingers; Aubrey's intelligence manifesting through something otherworldly in its own right. "So it's potentially what?"

Aubrey's tapping stopped. "Sentient," he said. "I think it's sentient. And more than that, I'm thinking it needs something from us. And I fear what that might be."

Calix jumped in, shocking Ethaniel with how *sane* he said, "It latched onto me. An affinity, I think you called it? My mother's powers were strange and rare. It seeks to reason mine are as well. What if it's been looking for someone like me, to help it..." He sighed and pushed his hair out of his face. "I don't have a bloody fucking clue, to be honest."

"I have more thoughts on that, but they're worth nothing without confirmation."

"And I hate to interrupt," Ethaniel replied, making them both stop and look at him. "But I want to help. I just don't know how."

Aubrey squeezed his hands. "Neither of us can see patterns. That makes you the scientist with the microscope, love."

"Oh, well, when you put it like that..." Ethaniel smiled at him. Aubrey always knew how to make him feel better, and the last thing he wanted to do was hold them back. Maybe he wasn't dead weight in this situation, after all.

"Let's get it down to the vault," Calix said as he turned his head this way and that before snatching up his discarded sweater.

"I agree," Aubrey said, concern buried deep in the lines around his mouth. Ethaniel reached up to smooth them out and Aubrey leaned into the touch. "Do you feel up to it, Calix?"

Calix nodded. "I think with both of you here, I can get through the wards easier." He cut his gaze to Aubrey. "I may need to...borrow again."

That was new. Before Ethaniel could ask what was going on, Aubrey explained how Calix had managed to to amplify his healing abilities, mending the door faster than anyone could break through.

It was an astounding magical feat, and like nothing Ethaniel had ever heard of or read about. "Calix, that's incredible." Calix flushed under the praise. The man was made to go pink at the drop of a hat, and Ethaniel couldn't tell if he found it charming or strangely enticing. "But are we taxing you in any way? I worry."

Brows knitted together, Calix crawled into Ethaniel's lap, forcing him to rest back against the pillows and steady Calix by the hips. Calix gazed down at him, sure and steady and as beautiful as the moon outside their window. "You are very sweet," Calix said as he leaned down, hands planted on either side of Ethaniel's head. "And I appreciate your concern. But you needn't."

But Ethaniel couldn't shake that voice, offering him so many things that would make his worries cease. "It's difficult to get past," he admitted. "Both my worry for you two, and the things that book wanted to give me."

"A devil's bargain," Aubrey said again as he laid down on his side, one hand propping up his head so he could look at them both. "And anything so untrustworthy tends to walk away with everything. The house always wins, and all that."

"I had thoughts on that," Calix said softly before brushing his lips over Ethaniel's. "The vault is exactly what we might need."

"Lock it away and pray my brother never finds us?" Ethaniel asked before lifting his head while pulling Calix down, eager for the distraction of a kiss.

"No," Calix said after they broke apart. He fixed Aubrey with a sharp gaze layered with meaning Ethaniel couldn't quite parse. "The item is sentient, right?"

"I believe so," Aubrey said. His hand found Ethaniel's and Ethaniel took comfort in how it felt to intertwine their fingers.

"I think it's more than one voice," Calix said as he sat back on the bed. "The tones…change sometimes, when it speaks. When it first spoke to me at the auction house, there were more voices. Discordant. Disturbing. Now it's like one voice with echoes off it."

Aubrey squeezed his hand and Ethaniel looked over to see calculation written all over his face. "Aubrey?" he asked, wondering what was churning in the man's mind.

Aubrey blinked rapidly a few times, then graced them with a smile writ large in the language of cunning. God, the man was far too intelligent and it was deeply attractive. "More than one voice," Aubrey said, sounding more and more certain with each word. "An affinity with you. It's either looking for an owner, someone to wield it, or it's looking for a new source of power. Those would be my top suspicions, anyways. We might be able to coax the main voice out."

Pieces clicked into place in Ethaniel's mind. "Are you wanting to *negotiate* with this thing?"

Their replies came at the same time. "Yes."

"That's madness," Ethaniel sputtered. "It's clearly intelligent! It could do anything!"

Calix snapped his fingers. "Exactly. It wants something. We can use that to our advantage."

He was involved with two madmen. Ethaniel looked between them, flabbergasted and more than a little worried. "And…do what? Give it what it wants?"

Aubrey shrugged. "What do most intelligent beings want? Safety, comfort..." His glass-colored eyes glinted. "Freedom. Negotiating with it is only part of the plan, if I understand Calix's intentions."

"You weren't wrong, Ethaniel," Calix replied. There was a similar gleam in his eyes and Ethaniel could only stare. It was mildly terrifying and...admittedly, rather attractive, even if they had both lost their minds. Perhaps that said more about him than them, though. "The vault can hold anything magical. It's what my mother built it for. What if we give this voice, or being, its freedom, but on our terms? What if I know of an artifact in the vault that used to be a soul phylactery?"

The air rushed out of Ethaniel's lungs, but Aubrey beat him to the punch, only with more practicality than Ethaniel capable of in the face of such a rare (and some thought bogus) magical artifact. "You think I can mend such an object." Aubrey leaned in, eyes alight with a bright hunger.

It wasn't a question.

"I saw what you did the night of the fire, Aubrey," Calix said. He wasn't pleading or stating his case. He was, just like Aubrey, merely airing out facts. It was a bit of a shock to see how quickly Calix understood Aubrey, how to coax him out with logic when necessary. Their younger paramour was a quick study. Ethaniel would only interfere to halt an argument, but from the look on Aubrey's face — perplexed but intrigued — it wouldn't come to that.

Finally, Aubrey said, "That's a terrible amount of trust to put in one person."

Calix broke their mutual stare to look over at Ethaniel, then down to his hands. "You've trusted me this far. You're in my home, with the man who is arguably most at fault for all of this mess just a few rooms down the hall. You trusted me to handle him. To bring you somewhere safe. Trust me now that I *know* you can do this, Aubrey. I've had your magic in my veins and it's unlike anything I've ever felt before."

Ethaniel rose from his spot on the bed then, intent on dealing the finishing blow to Aubrey's hesitance. "I think you're both completely mad, but mad doesn't mean wrong," he said as he approached, drawing Calix near as he moved. Calix went willingly, seemingly happy to be touched once more. "Calix's channeling, your mending, my ability to watch over the patterns. It *could* work. Or explode in our faces."

When Ethaniel looked up at Aubrey, the man's final wall of resistance melted. Aubrey had doubted his abilities for so long, it had forced him into a kind of complacency, leaving him to mend old books and reshape broken blades, all in the name of making the wealthy and powerful happy. Ethaniel had always known Aubrey had so much more in him.

"All right," Aubrey said softly. "All right."

After a long pause, Ethaniel said, "There's still the issue of my brother. That won't go away any time soon."

"He won't, that's true. But we can give him the book once the strongest voice is stripped from it," Aubrey said, his tone a bit gentler as they rounded the issue of Vincent. "I've been trying to parse out what the Golden Order might want from such an object, and it stands to reason that voice has some knowledge or power they wish to gain from. We might still have an enemy after that, but from what I understand about the Order, scrutiny isn't what they want right now. They don't have a large enough, or established enough, power base in the city. We would gain the chance to regroup and plan for the future."

Ethaniel scrubbed at his face with his hand and sighed. "If we can get this to work, it's a fine plan. But it hinges on a lot of unknowns."

Calix's expression turned sad. "That's very true," he admitted. "And there's no guarantee we can work fast enough. The manor is held in the name of a trust which would track back to my mother's partner, then eventually to her and me. But that kind of digging can take months and the lawyers who drew up the trust were well paid for their discretion."

Even with his head spinning, Ethaniel had to chuckle a little. "Woe is the two of us then, to be trapped here with you, Calix."

As he'd assumed, Calix laughed with him while Aubrey watched on with what Ethaniel would call a mix of fondness and *interest*.

Calix eventually went downstairs to find Richard and let him know what was going on, leaving him and Aubrey alone in the large master bedroom, the rumpled sheets and slightly humid air a delightful reminder of how they'd spent some of the afternoon.

Ethaniel stared at Aubrey for a long moment, simply remembering. The suddenness of it all, the spectacular way they'd all been pushed together, and how they'd each held on fast caught up with him. He was *exhausted*, but jubilant in it. Ethaniel hoped Aubrey felt the same way, and gazing at the man now told him just as much. His body, from the proud line of his shoulders to the looseness of his jaw and the soft lines around his eyes, was what Ethaniel had been hoping to s ee.

"I've missed you," Ethaniel murmured as Aubrey drew close. "But this is a hell of a mess."

"I've missed you as well," Aubrey replied before kissing Ethaniel gently. Aubrey's hands framed his face and it made Ethaniel feel seen and cared for, all at once. "I think this might work. Putting the book in the vault so I can better examine it will be very useful, but I haven't the tools like I would at the Collectio." Aubrey's expression soured. "Pulling a disappearing act will not reflect well on my next performance review."

"I know you're only joking—"

"I am," Aubrey said as he rubbed the edge of his thumb over Ethaniel's cheek. "And I'm doing so because I know in actuality, Magnus and Alon and the others will be in an uproar looking for me, and then they'll discover the burnt ruins of my home. Magnus is a very skilled mage and researcher. He may find us before the Order does, which would be helpful."

"But you won't drag them into this, right?"

"Not willingly. Like you wouldn't with your uncle."

God, his uncle. Ethaniel didn't want to think about it. Jeremiah would be beside himself with worry, and Ethaniel had no way of getting word back to him without pulling him into the strife and danger of their current predicament.

"So we do this as quick as we can, and try to set things right," Ethaniel said. He took strength from Aubrey's warmth, his touch, his surety that their plan stood any chance at being seen through to the end. If only his worries could cease entirely. "You and Calix seemed to be of a similar mind when it comes to that book. I think you're more alike than either of you realize."

To Ethaniel's surprise, Aubrey slid his hand down his chest while pulling Ethaniel's up until he could cup Aubrey's cheek. Aubrey closed his eyes and sighed; so many emotions layered into that single noise. But it was Aubrey opening his eyes and staring down at Ethaniel, saying, "I think you're right. Stubborn and skilled, to be sure. We both drew to you like magnets, didn't we?" Ethaniel gave a dry laugh that quickly died as soon as Aubrey ran a thumb over his bottom lip. "And there's you," Aubrey said, "the heart in the middle. You call Calix 'dove'....what should I call you?"

There was only one answer. "Yours. Call me yours."

TWENTY-ONE

C ALIX

Calix left Aubrey and Ethaniel in Richard's capable hands, knowing his valet would ensure they were fed properly. There was an anxious energy around all of them, fueled by far too little rest and far too much drama. He hated popping the bubble of peace around Rosehill, his one respite from the city.

And Lawton.

Lawton had come to Rosehill a few times before, always at the end of the season. His appearance wasn't always unwelcome, but it was always unannounced. And the household always felt a tad colder when he did arrive with his one too many bags and curls flopping in his face. They operated like normal, of course, but something about being under the same roof changed their dynamic during those August days. He'd never been able to put his finger on it before now, but hindsight was a terrible thing.

He felt sorry for himself and for Lawton. Two misguided souls stuck in an ouroboros of need and dependency. One would start it, the other would fuel the circle, and around and around they went. In reality, he should be so, so angry. And perhaps he would be in the future, when they weren't dealing with frightening magical books and some strange cult whose ways and purpose felt incorporeal and yet all too consequential.

Calix pressed his forehead against the cool wood of the guest room door and breathed. Some part of him would always love Lawton, but now that he'd been shown real affection, real desire? He questioned whether it was love, or something like infatuation fueled by loneliness. And in the wake of Lawton's betrayal, how could anything ever be the same?

Did he want it to be the same? Was there room for Lawton in whatever new life Calix might forge?

Did Lawton deserve it?

Calix finally opened the door, unsure whether he hoped Lawton was awake or not. As the sun moved toward setting, the room had darkened, the shadows long and climbing over the walls. The blanket-covered lump under the bed stirred. Just a single soft sound, but it drew Calix's attention like a cat after a mouse.

"Lawton?" Calix came into the room, closed the door gently, and then sat at Lawton's bedside to wait. The only part of Lawton visible was a single pale hand, poking out from the spring green covers. Lawton's palm was clean but shiny with some kind of salve. The skin was bright pink and angry, like a burn one might get from accidentally touching a hot stove. Without giving it too much thought, Calix plucked up the corner of the blanket and lifted it until he could see fire orange curls, then a long sweep of reddish-brown lashes framing a vicious black eye, down to Lawton's bruised lips.

He wanted to feel like iron or steel: unforgiving, unyielding. He wanted to feel anger or even pure bewilderment. Not his oldest friend! Lawton could never betray him. Would never betray him. But he had, in so many little ways, some swirling miasma of never repaid loans doused in expensive cologne.

"I should hate you," Calix whispered as he tucked the blanket in around Lawton's shoulders, mindful of the large bandage over the right one. "And I can't. I don't know who I'm more angry at, you or me. But I would never want to see you like this." Calix pushed a limp curl off Lawton's forehead, watching it fall back against the pillow, then turned for the door. In a romance book, Lawton would snag his hand and plead with Calix, teary eyed over how he'd acted. He'd confess that he'd been so selfish, so careless, and that he could only hope Calix would forgive him.

It didn't happen. Lawton slept, and Calix left the room, letting the door shut without a sound.

Calix retrieved Convergence from the auxiliary vault's drawers and with it safely back in his satchel, found the others in the kitchen huddled over steaming mugs of tea and talking. The lack of rest was getting to all of them, if he was reading Ethaniel's hunched posture and the bags under Aubrey's eyes correctly. Even Richard looked a tad askew, his vest off by one button and his hair sticking up around his ears.

"He's still unconscious," Calix said as he entered, grateful for the mug of tea Aubrey pressed into his hands. "I feel better knowing that."

Ethaniel nodded. "It's more than understandable, Calix."

Which Aubrey followed up with, "But we're ready when you are."

If he weren't so bloody tired, Calix might have marveled at how well Aubrey and Ethaniel made up both sides of a coin, the logical and the emotional. Especially since he'd seen them be the opposite, for him and for each other.

Calix led them all into the rose garden, where thorny vines and stems still tainted black by winter's touch spread out at all angles. He'd let the garden grow a little more wild than his mother had kept it, but there were still clear pathways through to the back, where the manor's outer wall rose up in forgiving sandstone. It had started to rain while they'd been...otherwise occupied, and the wet seeped beneath his thin jacket. Calix shivered as they came to stop before three stone mausoleums.

The ones in the middle and on the right bore family names, Smythe and Richardson. They were left by the manor's previous owners, some strange custom Calix couldn't quite understand. But his mother had felt the pull of it, like a shared history, so the left one bore her family name, Addington. She'd never married, and despite insisting Calix take the boon of his father's name and lands when they were offered after his death, she'd never wanted anything but the solace of Rosehill. Even Lily's need for Edna's companionship had withered toward the end. Edna still wrote, and she was sent a healthy stipend every quarter, but Calix hadn't seen her since he'd started living in New York a decade ago. The moment he'd arrived in America, Edna had left for Montana, where her family had a ranch. None of that burned quite so badly now, but then it had felt like a betrayal.

Lawton had been extra attentive during that time. Calix had lost himself to pleasures that now wouldn't appeal, and Lawton had been there every step of the way. Enjoying it all while Calix paid for it, then crawled into Lawton's bed and let him have his way.

"Dammit," he muttered, feeling as though he was finally understanding things clearly.

"Calix?" Richard was at his left, lips pursed in concern. "What is it?"

"Just realizing some things about Lawton," Calix mumbled, having to force his gaze up to look at them all. Shame was a thing scrabbling up his throat now, threatening in its grip.

Richard put a hand on his shoulder and squeezed. "One thing at a time."

"Right, well...." Calix approached the left mausoleum and put his hands out, hovering just before the small stone structure's iron door. The pull of his mother's power was still there, twisted up in some complicated pattern that felt like no other magic he'd ever experienced. The moment his palms neared the door, Ethaniel sucked in a harsh breath.

"It's the strangest thing," Ethaniel said. Calix looked back to see Ethaniel squinting up at the angel perched above the mausoleum's door. "I swear I saw that rose in her hand spin. Maybe a quarter of a turn? So odd."

"Calix, may I..." Aubrey gestured to the mausoleum. "I'll only touch the outer wall. I admit to a curiosity, after what you've relayed about your mother's powers."

"Of course." Calix felt the first set of wards slowly melt, then was rocked back by a blast of pain, icepick sharp and right behind his eye. It had felt like this right before...

He saw Aubrey touch the mausoleum's moss and vine covered walls, then a bright flash...then Aubrey on the ground, his arm buckled under him at an odd angle. The white of bone jutted out from torn fabric and flesh and Aubrey's cry of pain rang in his ears.

"Aubrey, no!" Calix rushed at Aubrey, whose hand was *so close* to the wall. He tackled Aubrey to the ground as a sharp *crack* sounded and a bolt of pure white light shot out. Ozone filled the air and Calix felt his hair dance with static electricity. He looked down to see Aubrey staring up at him, a dazed look on his face. "Aubrey, are you all right?"

Aubrey blinked, worked his jaw, and said, "I'm assuming you didn't know that would happen."

Calix flopped onto his back, the satchel hitting him in the hip as he moved. Of course. "I did not, though I should have realized it."

Footsteps sounded and then Richard and Ethaniel were beside them. Richard had a shovel in his hands and Ethaniel's fingertips danced with greenish energy. "What happened? My god," Richard panted out.

"The vault has defenses," Calix said, then shook his head as he realized that didn't explain it.

"Your mother entombed herself above her vault?" Ethaniel looked incredulous. "I thought you were merely retrieving some kind of key."

"It was the only wish of hers we could fulfill, besides keeping Rosehill with me and ensuring no one gained access to the vault unless they were in my presence. I think our other uninvited guest set off the wards," Calix said, gesturing to the satchel.

Silence

Then...

Aubrey choked out a laugh that bordered on hysterical. "The vault has magical turrets?"

Calix stifled a laugh. It wasn't funny. At all. It was clearly the exhaustion that made him stifle another, and then give up on muffling the sound. "My mother only told me I'd never have to worry about intruders with ill intent," he said, hiccuping every few words. "This is insane. This is insane! We should just burn the thing and be done."

Quick as a snake, Ethaniel held out his hand. "Let's find out."

And Calix let him have the bag before pushing to his hands and helping Aubrey to sit up. They sat on the ground, Richard looking as baffled as Calix felt desperate, and watched Ethaniel toss the bag into the middle of a path, about thirty feet from where they sat. "Let's find out," Ethaniel repeated, his voice now gravelly, almost growling. With his left hand, he pinched his thumb, index, and middle finger together at the tips, then drew a circle in the air around them with his right. Then he snapped his fingers and red magic flickered to life, which Ethaniel plucked up from his fingers and held in his right palm.

Ethaniel launched the magic at the bag like a wizard out of a fairy story. Flame roared through the air coalescing into a ball, which struck the bag directly. Fire engulfed the bag, crackling and popping and for a long moment, all they could see was fire..

Beside Aubrey, Richard screamed and fell to the ground in a heap.

Enough

Enough

You cannot destroy us…me…with flame

We are stronger than that

Richard kept screaming as blood began to trickle from his nose.

You have underestimated me, Oracle

But you've surprised me as well

A truce

Do not attempt that again

Take your valet back

I will hide my nature

I wish to see your trinkets

Truce

The last word felt like more of a question, and Calix latched onto that hope with both hands. It was all he could do while Richard screamed and Aubrey's hands shook as he tried to tend to the man.

"Fine!" Calix shouted. "You get what you want! No more! Ethaniel, put it out!"

The moment Ethaniel pulled back his power, the screaming stopped.

"He's alive," Aubrey said as he listened to Richard breathe. "Calix?"

Ethaniel rushed to grab the satchel while Calix hurried to Aubrey's side. "No, no, Richard, please," he said while Aubrey checked Richard over. "Please wake u p."

Richard's eyes fluttered and a moment later, he was staring up at them, confusion creasing his brow. "It's all right," Calix said softly. "We're going to get you inside."

Richard was able to get to his feet with some help, but Calix insisted he be the one to walk the man inside. Aubrey seemed to understand and stuck to hovering in their shadow with Ethaniel bringing up the rear. They pulled pillows and blankets from the second guest room, as Richard argued — albeit weakly — that he didn't want to be alone in a bed that wasn't his. They set him up on the long, wide sofa in the back parlor while they gathered around a small table to the side, eyeing the satchel warily.

Calix tried to explain what happened, but it only made sense after he told them about Convergence's threat. "If we can't get it into the vault, then what do we do?" Ethaniel asked. "This is pointless."

"I think Convergence means to hide its nature from the vault," Aubrey said after a long moment. "That's what I take from its fractured words to Calix, anyways." Aubrey's gaze went thoughtful. "Sentient objects almost always have a force of will, and we've seen that with this one. But there's something about the way it speaks that—" Aubrey suddenly sat up straight and pinned Calix with a stare. "It said *us*."

"It did. My god, it did." The frustration had been building in Calix's chest to this moment, making him want to chuck the book into the lake, or throw it into one of the many fireplaces in Rosehill. But that main voice had slipped up and said *us*.

Without thinking on it any longer, Calix pulled the book from the charred satchel, letting it thump onto the table. It looked no worse for wear from the fire. *Well, at least it was telling the truth there*, Calix thought with a snarl.

"Calix?" Ethaniel looked at him worriedly.

"I'm done panicking over this damn thing," Calix said. "I think we all are." He flipped the book open, letting it fall where it may. The pages were still blank, the paper thickly cut and still pristine. If it hadn't been for the voice in their heads, Calix would have thought it a beautiful specimen ripe for someone's diary.

"I want to talk to...whoever you are. The main voice. The one doing all this," Calix said, each word boosting his confidence. "You know a lot, but we don't know anything about you. That seems a tad unfair."

All three of them jumped back when a ghostly visage clawed its way from those very pages Calix had been admiring. A sound like thunder reverberated through Calix's ribs and he watched, transfixed, while the specter coalesced from gray-green mist into something resembling a face and two withered hands. The hands gripped the bottom edge of the book as though it clung to a cliff, while the specter worked its jaw, then stared at them with black pits for eyes.

"You may call me Convergence." The voice echoed around them and as it did, the magical sconces on the walls were snuffed out. The darkness of late day shadowed them all, its chill seeping into Calix's clothes and then deeper, like a coat of frost over his bones.

"So you do talk outside of our heads," Aubrey said, his expression a mixture of fascination and horror. Calix could see the museum curator snap into place and if he hadn't been as equally horrified by what they were seeing, he would have loved to watch Aubrey work. "You aren't like other sentient objects, are you? There's more to you than one voice."

The ghostly head turned to Aubrey. "I am the strongest," it rasped. "But there are others."

Aubrey muttered, "That's one way to answer my question, or not," pulling a pained noise from Ethaniel. Calix moved closer to him and Ethaniel shot him a grateful look. "How are there so many of...you in there?" Calix asked.

"I do not know."

Calix figured in light of that, he might as well be blunt. "What do you want?"

One of the clawed hands rose up to point at Calix. "Freedom, Oracle. Freedom. Do you not value freedom?"

Around them that word echoed. *Freedomfreedomfreedom.* A wave of it rolled over and through them until it rang in Calix's ears. The other voices chimed in to the cacophony and Calix's stomach turned.

"What the hell does that mean?" Ethaniel said as he stepped back. The man looked wan and was clutching his midsection as though he might be sick. Aubrey rushed to Ethaniel's side and Calix waved them back.

This book was his problem. He would deal with it, one way or the other.

Despite the chill over his body, despite his gorge rising, Calix pulled up a chair and sat directly in front of the book, as if he were pushing himself into its space. He heard the others' objections but remained true to his course.

"I want to make a deal," Calix said, as sure in his words as the steel in his voice. He was angry and tired and he wanted this to be *done*. "But it means some concessions on your end, Convergence. I won't pay the entire price. Do you understand me? Or so help me, I will throw you into the vault to never, ever see the light of day. And never taste your precious *freedom*. Are we clear?"

The room grew colder but Calix held his ground. Something prickled over his skin and the *zap* of electricity buzzed in his ears. He held firm.

"What do you propose?" Convergence asked finally.

Calix wouldn't let it see his relief, but his guard was still up. They couldn't trust this thing. And they didn't know enough about its history, its abilities, but the danger inherent in ignorance could be solved. Aubrey and Ethaniel were with him. He wasn't alone.

"What if we can separate you from the others, from the book?" Calix asked. Immediately, he heard Aubrey and Ethaniel protest. This had been the plan all along, but he understood why now they hesitated. "What if we can pull you away from them? It's not complete freedom, not yet. But it's a step forward. But you cannot, *will not*, harm anyone here again. Do you understand? We are willing to make a large sacrifice for you, but you cannot bite the hand that feeds. Or so help me, I will find a way to destroy you."

Calix paused, letting his words sink in. He felt jittery from the rush of adrenaline and fear, but he held. He had to.

After a few moments that lasted an eternity, Calix said, "Do we have an accord?"

Instead of out loud, Convergence spoke once again in his mind. "Agreed."

Twenty-Two

AUBREY
The next day

"This whole thing is madness," Calix said as they prepared themselves to tackle Convergence and the vault once again.

"At the bare minimum, I'd say," Aubrey murmured drolly while running his hand up and down Calix's back. They'd barely slept and were now huddled around the small cook's table in the kitchen while Martha, the cook, bustled about, tutting over how pale and skinny Calix appeared.

"I'd say what's madness is that none of you are feeding him properly," Martha sniffed. "Must I do everything around here?"

Calix let out a snort that was only half-laugh, then rested his head on his stacked forearms. "Martha, it's not their fault. And I'm grown, remember?"

"You won't stop me from fretting, Calix. You ought to know better by now." With ruthless efficiency, Martha plunked down a plate of warm, sliced bread and jam. The scent was so enticing it made Calix lift his head, and the moment he did, Martha pursed her lips in what looked like an aborted smile.

Aubrey liked this woman quite a lot, and it was clear she held a great deal of affection for Calix. But he had to laugh when she snapped her fingers at Ethaniel, who was busy drinking enough tea to fill a bathtub. "You. Ethaniel? Right, you come help me with this pot. It's too heavy for my old back and you look strong. I'd ask Richard, but Calix said the poor boy's not well today."

Ethaniel stared wide-eyed at Aubrey, and he made a shooing motion with his free hand. "Well, go on. Help the lovely lady."

Martha let out a snort. "Ain't been called 'lovely' since 1860." Then she shot Aubrey a small smile and said, "But I'll take it."

Ethaniel wandered off after her, so Aubrey claimed his still-warm tea cup and drained the rest. The black tea was strong enough to wake the dead and it sang on Aubrey's palette. Ethaniel would drink straight black tea all day long if he had the chance, but Aubrey knew the man was always far too busy running the shop and dealing with his uncle to indulge. He hoped they would all get the chance to linger over cups of tea and fresh bread and not have the threat of danger looming like a stormcloud.

"She's going to run Ethaniel ragged if possible," Calix murmured. They watched Martha direct Ethaniel to put the pot on the stove, then retrieve a bag of potatoes from the pantry. Ethaniel shot Aubrey a look that screamed *help me*, and with a sigh, Aubrey complied. "You stay," he ordered Calix. To his shock, Calix shifted further down in his seat and poured more tea. "Good."

When Martha was settled and happily whistling while peeling potatoes, Aubrey led the charge outside. Calix still carried the book, now wrapped in a scrap of fabric he'd swiped from Martha's sewing bin. The rain had cleared, leaving the gardens a soggy mess, and a low mist swirled about their ankles as they trudged forward to the mausoleum.

Aubrey's gaze lingered on the three large stone edifices. "They're a tad unsettling. I'm surprised the previous families never wanted to move the mausoleums."

Calix shrugged. "My mother always said it was their wish to let the dead rest where they'd been entombed, and that disrupting those wishes would be a grievous sin." Then he frowned and said, "Considering she wasn't a religious person, it always struck me as strange."

Aubrey nodded, sensing an old wound he didn't want to reopen. "We're certain...*it* will behave? I'd rather not dodge another magic bullet, so to speak."

Aubrey looked to Calix, who nodded, then to Ethaniel, whose tight frown and downcast eyes said so much. Ethaniel found eye contact difficult when his emotions ran high, and with the wind pulling at his queue of long brown hair, his coat fluttering behind him, he looked like a brooding hero ready for whatever lay ahead. But Aubrey didn't like the little furrow between Ethaniel's brows, or how tightly he'd stuffed his hands into his pockets. There was certainly more on Ethaniel's mind than the book.

Carefully, Calix unwrapped the book, then with a great sigh, he opened it. Power crackled through Aubrey's entire body as that gray-green mist rose from the pages once more, and the dread that lingered settled as much over his skin as it did in his belly. He *hated* this thing, but couldn't help his curiosity. Maybe one day he'd get to study it, push his power into those pages and discover what truly lay inside. One day, perhaps.

The face appeared once more, clawed hands clinging to the edges of the book as Calix held it as far away as his arms would allow. "Does our accord still stand?" Calix asked.

"It does." The voice writhed and wriggled under Aubrey's skin, as if it could find all his old wounds and bruises, a lifetime of small injuries, and reopen them. If it was a threat, it was an effective one. He tensed, waiting.

"Good. We're going inside. Don't anger my mother's tomb," Calix warned.

"We have an accord," Convergence said, as if Calix were a small child incapable of understanding.

Calix looked at him and Ethaniel. "Let's go."

Aubrey took the book from Calix while he undid the mausoleum's defenses. Aubrey saw all that magic dance across Calix's hands, zipping up his arms and across his neck and chest as he glowed golden and warm.

"It's like being next to a small sun," Ethaniel whispered in Aubrey's ear. "He's beautiful."

"He is."

Something *cracked* across the wind, and Calix's glow flickered, then faded, and the door to the mausoleum swung open. In his hands, Convergence's visage swirled, those unblinking black pits for eyes swinging around as if it could peer inside. It was an unnerving sight, and Aubrey didn't want to admit to how relieved he was when Calix took the book once more.

"Inside, Oracle," Convergence rasped.

The mausoleum's granite walls and floors were clear of debris, but spiderwebs and dust lingered in the corners. In the middle of a space roughly the size of a small parlor sat a single tomb, its sharp edges carved with elaborate filigree work and glinting with gold. At its base sat a small plaque that read:

LILY ADDINGTON

"WITH SIGHTLESS EYES AND FLIGHTLESS WINGS, SHE IS BORNE ALOFT"

No dates, no "devoted mother" or "will be missed by all" lines. It was the oddest memorial plaque Aubrey had ever seen, and from the way Ethaniel was staring, he felt something similar.

Calix handed Aubrey Convergence, then bent a knee before his mother's tomb and laid a reverent hand upon the cool stone.

"Hello, Mother," Calix whispered. "I'm sorry for the intrusion."

In Aubrey's hands, Convergence swirled, fathomless eyes staring forward. "You hide power below," it said, a note of glee in its voice. "I want to see it. You promised me freedom."

Calix snapped his head up, confusion marring his fine features. Aubrey felt that bit of dread in his belly bloom, a springtime flower unfurling for the first proper sunlight. "Everything in the vault is negated or dead."

"No," Convergence said, the glee building. It was almost giddy. "Take me. I wish to see."

Calix looked at them, his gaze pleading. "Can either of you sense anything? Ethaniel, with your patterns—"

Ethaniel nodded gravely. "Give me a moment. Aubrey, would you..."

Aubrey understood. Out of the three of them, Ethaniel was the most wary around Convergence. He stepped back as far as he could, his back now to the opposite wall. "What are you playing at?" Aubrey asked Convergence quietly. "Calix said the items in the vault are dead. Why lie?"

The head swiveled again and the eyes juttered, then settled. It tipped its chin up to meet Aubrey's gaze, then said, "I do not lie. I have never lied. Falsehoods are part of a game played by humans and demons alike, young magician. The vault contains magic. I can feel it. It tears through me like a wound, and yet I cannot resist its claws." Convergence's own claws gripped the edge of the book tighter. "I want to see."

"Patience," Aubrey hissed. "You will wait."

The visage's mouth snapped shut, but Aubrey doubted it would stay quiet for long. He was honestly surprised it even reacted.

Ethaniel stood roughly fifteen feet away now, eyes closed, hands held before him with fingers outstretched. He looked like a painter trying to frame up a scene for his next masterpiece. Aubrey could imagine Ethaniel paint-speckled and beautiful in the late afternoon light, his dark brown hair tied back, lips moving as he whispered to himself to make art from the world around him. No worries about magic and family and a book waiting with maw open. Just them. Together. When his gaze snagged on Calix, Ethaniel's power flared in the corner of Aubrey's eyes and they both turned to watch.

Ethaniel was effulgent. *Glorious.* The very air around him quivered with a color like the waters of the Mediterranean, unnameable and vibrant and so very *alive*. Ethaniel's eyes glowed softly, a match to the light building between his hands. Tiny threads of pure magic spread out, from fingertip to fingertip and back again, until Aubrey saw it coalesce into a web. But it had a squarish frame to it, and inside was something Aubrey couldn't even *comprehend*. It should have been neat and orderly and flat, exactly like a spiderweb. But this had depth; zigs where it should have zagged, curves and hills and valleys where it should have been all straight lines. And most shocking of all, it had *shape*. Ethaniel was building a bit of magic between his hands and it had dimension and weight.

It was art and architecture and Aubrey felt its power beating beneath his skin. At first he'd wished he had his monocle, so he might see the intricacies even better, but with the pulsing in his body, some kind of pain-pleasure level of ecstasy he couldn't fully understand, Aubrey had no need of it. He could feel Ethaniel's magic *inside of him*.

"There's a lot of magic inside that vault," Ethaniel finally said as the glow slowly faded. "*A lot.* But it's not like anything I've ever seen before. With many objects, I might be able to see bits and pieces of each pattern of their magic. But this feels like little pieces of one large tapestry, so to speak."

"What?" Calix croaked. Aubrey saw how pale he was and moved closer, lending Calix an arm on which to lean. Calix took it, wrapping his hands around Aubrey's bicep and squeezing. His hands shook.

Aubrey didn't know what to say. They were all likely thinking it — that Calix's mother, the woman he clearly adored, had lied to him. And quite a lot, it would seem. The betrayal, the pain Calix must feel. What could Aubrey say to help abate that? Calix's inherent ability to trust was simply who he was at his core, and he'd been taken advantage of yet again. With anyone else, Aubrey might have called them naive, and maybe Calix was to a degree. But trust was a tougher thing to swallow whole than cynicism. Aubrey worried this new betrayal might turn something in Calix that could never be righted.

Words might be difficult in such circumstances, but actions always lead to something. "Can you open the vault, Calix?" Aubrey asked after several silent moments.

"Yes," Convergence hissed. All of them startled, but Aubrey's instinct was to snarl at the thing in his hand. So he did. Convergence didn't seem bothered. "Open the vault, Oracle. So much power."

With a nasty glare at the book, Calix finally, even if haltingly, moved to the wall opposite the one Aubrey had been leaning on. Palms again flat to the cold stone, Calix breathed out and closed his eyes. Again, there was a golden glow, and again Aubrey was stunned at how beautiful they both had been when bathed in their magic. Calix his miniature sun, Ethaniel his endless ocean.

Beyond the wall, gears churned and clanked, and slowly the wall slid open to reveal a staircase. It was a very short, chilly descent into what turned out to be a natural cave. Aubrey heard water drip somewhere in the distance, and as they moved forward, torches on the wall flared to life.

"My mother's favorite place besides Rosehill," Calix said glumly as they walked into a space twice the size of the Collectio's workroom. On the natural shelves in the rock wall were dozens and dozens of strange objects. All of them silent.

Aubrey itched to explore, but Convergence said, "Yes. Yes. I can feel it here. A soul phylactery. I felt its stirrings before but here....the energy. Life. Blood."

Ethaniel eyed the book with disdain. "And if we can get you...transferred into this soul phylactery, then we've made good on our promise. Like we agreed."

"A deal," Convergence said, head swiveling as if to see Ethaniel better. "A deal, yes. We agreed."

The temptation to slam the book shut had Aubrey gritting his teeth, but when his attention snapped to Calix, the man had stepped before a short shelf just to their right. He was staring down at a handful of objects and, unable to resist the siren song of the strange and mystical any longer, Aubrey joined him. Ethaniel lent his support from the other side, putting a hand on Calix's shoulder.

"Do you think it's one of these?" Aubrey asked. "I don't feel anything. I don't usually need to touch something to know if it's dead or not and I feel...nothing."

"Nothing?" Calix echoed, disbelieving. There was a glassy look to his eyes that Aubrey didn't like. "At all?"

"No. But let's ask the expert." Aubrey set the book down on another shelf and waited for Convergence to reorient before asking, "Care to help us out, or are you content to simply ask for power and let us do all the work?"

Ethaniel let out a snort and even Calix cracked a smile at that. Aubrey supposed he probably looked a little silly, talking back to a book with some ghostly image rising from its pages. Perhaps the strain of the entire debacle was finally turning his brain to mush.

"A moment," the book said.

They gave Convergence a moment. While they did, Aubrey turned to the others and said, "Ethaniel, did you see any particular patterns that were stronger?"

Ethaniel shook his head. "It was just...power. A giant ball of it, all connected together." Then he paused. "Oh. Well, is that even possible?" He ran his hand through the air a mere inch above the objects.

Ethaniel had this habit that Aubrey always found adorable. When he was truly focused, the tiniest bit of his tongue would poke out, as if he wanted to bite his lip but knew it would hurt, so his tongue got in the way. Aubrey watched him do so now and realized, with a burst of joy, that Calix was staring at Ethaniel, too.

"Is what even possible?" Calix prodded.

Ethaniel turned to survey the cave and all its strange things. The book chained to a stalagmite with a padlock twice the size of Aubrey's hand. A small wooden statue of a woman carrying a basket over her arm, her eyes blazing with uncut sapphires. A rack of crystal bottles, stoppered with cork, in which varying levels and colors of liquid beckoned. A grandfather clock with no numbers or hands on the face. Objects Aubrey might have called death masks tied to sacks of flour, as if to give the viewer an idea of what they might look like with flesh underneath (or maybe it was his too-vivid imagination). And several bits and bobs of gold and silver and brass; medals and charms, cherry stones wrapped in cloth, even a fortune teller's crystal ball on a beautiful bronze stand.

"I think it's all being…well, covered, by one spell." Ethaniel waved his hand out over the cave. "Like a blanket. Lift the blanket, see the magic."

"Magical hide and seek," Aubrey mused. "It would be entirely clever."

"Very clever," Convergence rasped. "That is precisely what's happened."

And there was only one person who could have done that. Aubrey saw recognition on Calix and Ethaniel's faces, but Calix's expression was chased with sadness. *Another person who lied to him, used his trust*, Aubrey thought. Sympathy rushed through him anew.

"How do we lift it?" Calix asked, blinking away the shine in his eyes.

"Should we?" Ethaniel gestured to the shelf before them. "We don't know what any of these can do."

Aubrey had to agree. "It would be more than ill-advised," he said. "Ethaniel's right. Any one of these things might have enough power to warp our minds, for example. Overpower us. Possess us, even."

At that, Convergence hissed, the noise throaty, almost animalistic. "That was us," it said, head swiveling about as if to look at them all. "The book was a trap. A snare for those who dared to use it. Be warned, Oracle. Be wary."

Well, that was new information, Aubrey thought as he stared hard at the ghostly image. "Convenient to tell us that now," he snapped. Calix looked even more horrified, while Ethaniel took a step back from the book.

Aubrey had always been able to make strange leaps in logic, to connect dots that seemed to be of different lines entirely. Calix might be an Oracle, but Aubrey had instincts honed on blades forged in centuries of experience. Cunning Folk weren't called thus for a lark; *cunning* was an art and a science. And now all of that instinct told him to make the connections.

A magical trap.

Convergence in the lot of books he'd tried to win.

The book he'd sought had been that of a court mage of John Dee's order.

"I'll be damned," he said softly as realization struck true. "I think this is the very book I'd been trying to procure that day at auction. I've no proof, of course...except..."

With Calix and Ethaniel watching on in stunned silence, Aubrey leaned forward, toward the book, despite everything in his being demanding he back away. "Do you remember your name?" he asked, everything in him deeply suspicious. If this was who he thought, that changed *everything*.

Convergence swirled, the mist at its edges darkening to the color of tar. Those blank eyes looked up at Aubrey, claws gripping the edge of the book, and when it spoke, Aubrey felt it vibrate through him.

"Yes," it hissed. "Talbot."

Let this be one mystery solved, though if my wild hunch is correct, it's an entire Pandora's Box, he thought before saying, "Edward Talbot? Sir Edward Talbot? Assistant to John Dee, Queen Elizabeth I's court occultist?" The image's mouth opened, and Aubrey felt a surge of victory. "It is you. My god."

He straightened and backed away while Convergence sputtered and popped. The name seemed to have triggered something in its memory. The visage nodded and rasped, "That was my name. Yes. My name. I know it now."

Aubrey backed up, returning to the others. "Talbot was John Dee's primary assistant, and a competent scryer and alchemist. And a complete madman," he explained in a soft voice. "I knew the diary I sought had come from that same time period, and I'd hoped it would have some direct connection to Dee, but this is...extraordinary. And it makes complete sense why the Golden Order would want the book. Talbot's knowledge of magic was second only to Dee's, and no one has ever been able to figure out what they were actually up to when squirreled away in Dee's laboratory. And Dee's Book of Angels has been long lost. I shudder to think that might be their end goal, but it's all supposition at this point."

Calix and Ethaniel both looked so exhausted, so Aubrey hustled along his explanation. "Talbot should be able to find the soul phylactery for us, even in all of this mess, and without lifting whatever dampening spell or the like sits over the objects. I should be able to poke a hole in the defenses, which will let Ethaniel pull out the phylactery."

"Risky," Ethaniel said. "You're asking a lot."

"I am," Aubrey admitted. "But time is not on our side. We've no idea when, or if, the Golden Order strolls up to the front door and tries to—"

"Set us on fire again?" Calix said, all emotion gone from his voice. Aubrey could see the man shutting down, from the flat look in his brown eyes to the grim set of his mouth. This could be their only chance. "What should I do, then?"

"Go where Convergence — or Talbot, I suppose now — tells you to. I know none of us trust this thing, but we're between a rock and a hard place. We find the phylactery, pull Talbot into it, and keep the rest of those voices in the book, then hand it over to the Golden Order." Aubrey sighed and ran a hand over his short hair. "And after that...I don't know."

"Freedom," Convergence hissed. "You promised."

"And you'll have it," Calix said as he scooped up the book. "The phylactery will serve you fine."

Oddly, Convergence was silent. Aubrey highly doubted the phylactery would satisfy Talbot forever, but they had no other options. The book couldn't be destroyed, and it was clear Talbot had enough power to make them suffer if they didn't uphold their end of the bargain.

They would do what they could for now. After that, the future was only a question mark. But Aubrey knew his bond with Ethaniel and Calix was more than a fleeting thing; he would take comfort in it, hold it close, and know it would carry them through whatever obstacle was flung in their path.

"We begin," Convergence said as Calix held up the book.

Aubrey nodded to Ethaniel before pulling him close. He wanted them both near him, just in case. With everything that had gone wrong, he wasn't willing to risk more chances at this point.

"Everyone ready?" Ethaniel asked as his eyes began to glow.

Aubrey put a hand on their backs and breathed in deeply. "Onward we must."

TWENTY-THREE

CALIX

The last thing Calix wanted to do was hold Convergence, but there was no other choice. His powers of foresight were scattered at best, and he had no ability to break through magical incantations or patterns the way Aubrey and Ethaniel could. As he took the book from Aubrey, Calix realized his hands were cold. Though *cold* was not the proper word for it; perhaps *numb* was better. He didn't mind being numb right now. It provided a gray detachment that let him act, but also helped to push the traumatic realizations of the last few hours and days to the back of his mind. Without that detachment, he'd probably break down into a teary mess.

"Tell us where it is," he snapped, hoping there was enough steel left in his voice to make Convergence — or Talbot — comply.

"A moment," the book practically sang, the giddiness in its voice ratcheted up now that it was even closer to its goal. The dread pooling in Calix's stomach wasn't about to leave anytime soon, apparently, since the prospect of giving this...creature its truest wish was rather daunting.

Beside him, Aubrey and Ethaniel began to glow, their magic creating vast swaths of color and accompanying shadows along the cave walls. If this worked, they may have accomplished the extraordinary. Calix shook his head and refocused. Losing sight of the *now* would only get someone hurt.

"Remember," Aubrey said to them both as he formed tiny wisps of power at the ends of his fingertips, the strange third eye on his forehead opening sleepily. "Quick as a flash. No hesitating."

Ethaniel's own magic flared in response. "You're taking the biggest risk, Aubrey. Please…" He looked away for a moment, then straightened. "Be careful. Both of you."

Ethaniel's words were a lodestone. With a final look to them both, Calix moved forward while Convergence scanned the items. "Anything?"

"There," the book rasped, one clawed hand pointing to a small shelf on the left. "One of those. Closer, bring me closer, Oracle. I wish to *see*."

Calix moved toward the shelf and the others followed, left to eddy in his wake like a strange lunar tide. Convergence began to *hum* in his hands, a soft vibration that left Calix holding on, his knuckles turning white with the effort. The shelf held three objects: a dark green gem on a tarnished silver chain, the stone cut simply into a square; a flat disc of bronze carved with symbols Calix couldn't read; and a clear crystal bottle sealed with red wax.

Suddenly, the vibrations stopped and the ghostly face reared back as it pointed a trembling finger toward the bottle. "THERE!" it screamed and Calix nearly trod on Aubrey's foot in his panic. Behind him, Calix heard Ethaniel mutter, "For fuck's sake". The laughter that bubbled up inside him was tinged with hysteria.

"The bottle?" Calix asked once he got his heart rate under control. "You're certain?"

"YES!"

Aubrey licked his lips and nodded. "Then when we're all ready…"

"Do it, Aubrey," Ethaniel said, his hands flaring bright with ocean-blue power.

Calix's skin tingled in response to their magic and he waited, his breath coming almost too fast now.

"Preserve me," Aubrey whispered.

The flash of Aubrey's magic nearly blinded Calix and as his third eye opened wide, he thrust his hand forward. The very *air* in front of the shelf cracked, as if Aubrey's power were a stone against a windowpane. Aubrey pushed forward, gritting his teeth against the invisible spell meant to repel him, and that's when

Calix knew he was needed. Aubrey's forehead was beaded with sweat, his muscles straining against his shirt, and Calix didn't hesitate.

"Hold firm," he said as he put his hand on Aubrey's back and let Convergence fall to the floor.

Like the first time, Aubrey's power flooded through him the moment Calix let his mind open. It didn't feel like a stranger now, though; it was welcome, a warm touch to his cheek after a cold afternoon walk around the Village. The pop and crackle of a fire seeping into his bones. And beneath that, Aubrey's *passion* — for knowledge and magic, for the curious and antiquated, for a good book and a cup of tea. For him, and for *them*.

In his mind, Calix held doorways, tunnels and paths, and endless arrays of cobblestoned halls where he could envision and understand another. He'd always been so, so frightened of letting someone in, of not having total control of every single faculty of his mind. *You'll be taken advantage of* had been his mother's constant adage. But this was...an epiphany. Calix didn't just feel Aubrey's magic, he felt *Aubrey*. He could see what made up the man so willing to sacrifice himself for the greater good, and it spurred him forward.

The air before them *shattered*, the magic barrier clinking to the ground like broken glass.

Ethaniel was there, thrusting a hand forward and snatching up the bottle before slapping his palm over where the air sizzled, his magic weaving a pattern that echoed in Calix's bones. *Secure. Safe. Contained once more.*

Aubrey hauled them back as something snapped into place. Calix's foot caught on the book and he caught himself on his hands, the stone unforgiving, cutting into his palms.

"YES!" Convergence screeched, its voice echoing against the cave walls. "THE PHYLACTERY!"

As Calix fell, he saw Ethaniel stumble, twisting as he fell to the floor.

More glass shattered.

"NO!"

As Calix looked up, he saw a familiar shock of red-orange hair come into view, hazel eyes opened wide in shock at their macabre tableau. Something shot out of the remains of the bottle where Ethaniel had dropped it.

That energy, dark and swirling and reminding Calix so much of a whirlpool, hit Lawton square in the chest. He fell backwards in a heap.

Everything was sound and fury and the frenzied beating of Calix's heart. He heard Aubrey yell for him, felt Ethaniel as he tried to stop Calix's momentum with a hand, but nothing would hold him back.

Calix fell hard to his knees beside Lawton, a sob already building in his chest. The ache was exquisite. It would be his undoing if Lawton perished. He knew it. He would never be able to hide from that truth, as much as Lawton had betrayed him, had lied and cheated and crossed him and taken advantage—

"Calix?"

It was Lawton's voice, but the inflection was off. Softer on the tongue, slightly higher in tone. "Lawton," Calix managed to spit out as he fluttered his hands over Lawton's bandaged chest and bruised face. "Lawton, please."

"Darling." That tone again. Something shivered inside Calix.

It couldn't be.

Lawton sat up with preternatural grace and framed Calix's face in his hands. His touch was cool but almost foreign. Like a stranger, but not at the same time. "Lawton?"

Ethaniel and Aubrey came to his sides, their presence a much-needed comfort. "Careful," Aubrey said softly. "We don't know what was in that bottle."

"It was supposed to be empty," Ethaniel said. "We keep trusting the wrong...things."

"Not empty," Lawton said as he ran his fingertips over Calix's cheek.

Everything in Calix ground to a halt.

He knew that touch. That voice. The gentle, loving way Lawton blinked at him, then smiled.

Calix reached for her. He couldn't stop himself. "Mother?"

THE END

Book 2 coming soon

Author Thanks

My deepest thanks to:

- Željka Dobras, who created the astounding cover art

- Quinton Li, my fantastic editor and cheerleader

- Cayla Sander, my forever first reader

- Daze, who always helps me with whatever art questions I have

- Beta readers: Anna, Jenny Michelle, Kay, and Alex

- All the ARC readers who gave this book a chance before publication

- My HEX podcast family, because all that research we've done over the years made my life so much easier when tackling this book

- My OG D&D crew for teaching me that the fantastical and magical always have a place in our stories

- My dear friends, who keep me in check and always have my back

Sources and For Further Reading

Sources used directly in COUP DE COEUR:

- *The Madman's Library: The Strangest Books, Manuscripts and Other Literary Curiosities from History* by Edward Brooke-Hitching, 2020 by Chronicle Books

- *The Curse of the Marquis de Sade: A Notorious Scoundrel, a Mythical Manuscript, and the Biggest Scandal in Literary History* by Joel Warner, 2023 by Crown

- *Harlots, Whores & Hackabouts: A History of Sex for Sale* by Kate Lister, 2021 by Thames & Hudson

- *A History of Magic, Witchcraft & the Occult* by DK, 2020 by DK

- *Cabinets of Curiosities* by Patrick Mauries, 2011 by Thames & Hudson

- *Talking to the Dead: Kate and Maggie Fox and the Rise of Spiritualism* by Barbara Weisberg; 2004, Harper

- *The Dark Archives: A Librarian's Investigation Into the Science and History of Books Bound in Human Skin* by Megan Rosenbloom, 2020 by Picador

- *The Library of Esoterica: Astrology* by Andrea Miller, 2021 by Taschen

- *Cabinets of Curiosities* by Patrick Mauries, 2011 by Thames & Hudson

- Queer Oxford: https://queeroxford.info/selected-further-resources/

- Victorian Queer Archive: https://vqa.dickinson.edu/all-items

- Holywell Street: A Victorian Street for Friggers and Radicals: http://www.unofficialbritain.com/lost-london-a-victorian-street-for-friggers-and-radicals/

- The Secret History of Holywell Street: Home to Victorian London's Dirty Book Trade by Matthew Green: https://publicdomainreview.org/essay/the-secret-history-of-holywell-street-home-to-victorian-london-s-dirty-booktrade

- "The History of New York: 1855-1897": https://en.wikipedia.org/wiki/History_of_New_York_City_(1855%E2%80%931897)

- OldNYC: https://www.oldnyc.org/

- "Friday Night Fever: Haymarket": https://www.boweryboyshistory.com/2009/02/friday-night-fever-haymarket.html

- "Nightlife in the City" by Peter C. Baldwin, 2015, Oxford Research Encyclopedia: https://doi.org/10.1093/acrefore/9780199329175.013.178

- "The Rise and Fall of New York City's Private Social Clubs" by James Nevius, 2015: https://ny.curbed.com/2015/6/17/9950758/the-rise-and-fall-of-new-york-citys-private-social-clubs

- Gay Culture in 19th Century New York City: https://thegildedhour.com/gay-culture-in-19th-century-new-york-city/

- Connected: https://www.boweryboyshistory.com/2015/06/the-slide-19th-centurys-most-notorious-gay-bar.html

- New York Times Archives: https://archive.nytimes.com/www.nytimes.com/ref/membercenter/nytarchive.html

- NYC Fire Maps: https://www.nypl.org/collections/nypl-recommendations/guides/fire-topo-property-maps

For Further Reading

- *Selling Dead People's Things: Inexplicably True Tales, Vintage Fails & Objects of Objectionable Estates* by Duane Scott Cerny, 2018 by Thunderground Press

- *Disorderly Conduct: Visions of Gender in Victorian America* by Carroll Smith-Rosenberg, 1985 by Oxford Press

- *The Darkened Room: Women, Power, and Spiritualism in Late Victorian England* by Alex Owens, 2004 by University of Chicago Press

- *The Butchering Art* by Lindsey Fitzharris, 2017 by Scientific American

- *LGBT Victorians: Sexuality and Gender in the Nineteenth-Century Archives* by Simon Joyce

- The Whores of Yore: https://www.thewhoresofyore.com/about.html

- Wise-Women & Cunning Folk Healers - Witchcraft, Women & the

Healing Arts in the Early Modern Period - Research Guides at University of Alabama

- Cunning-folk in the medical market-place during the nineteenth century | Medical History | Cambridge Core

ALSO BY HALLI STARLING

Wilderwood

Twelfth Moon

Ask Me For Fire

A Brighter, Darker Art

When He Beckons

The Way We Wind

Always There For You

Book 2 of the Oracle, Tailor, Curator series is:

DEMIMONDE

2025

About the Author

Halli Starling is a queer librarian, reader, gamer, and author.

Halli has always been involved with books, and her love of the written word inspired her to get her MLIS and continue her book career outside of public libraries. When not writing, she co-hosts The Human Exception podcast, plays D&D, and spends time in the beautiful outdoors of Michigan. She is available for podcasts, interviews, panels, and book signings.

Website: hallistarlingbooks.com

Instagram: @hallistarling